07/01/01
LAS VEGAS
NEVADA

TO BARB
BEST WISHES
IN THE NEW MILLENNIUM

Charles R. Off

# WE AQUATUS

~~~~~~~~~~~~~

**Charles R. Clotfelter**

**Area 51 Publications**
**Las Vegas, Nevada**

# We Aquatus
## *by Charles R. Clotfelter*

Published by: Area 51 Publications
Post Office Box 44138
Las Vegas, Nevada 89116
Fax # (702) 641-6605

All rights reserved. No part of this book may be reproduced or transmitted in any form or by any means, electronic or mechanical, including photocopying, recording, or by any information storage and retrieval system without written permission from the author, except for inclusion or brief quotations in a review.

This is a work of fiction. All characters and events portrayed in this novel are either fictitious or are used fictitiously.

WE AQUATUS © 1999 by Charles R. Clotfelter
Edited by Patricia Frazer Lamb
Book Jacket Design by Melinda Vavra
Typesetting By Graphics Central

Library of Congress Cataloging-in-Publication Data
Clotfelter, Charles R.
We Aquatus / by Charles R. Clotfelter - 1st ed.
p. cm.
Preassigned LCCN: 98-71928
ISBN 1-892584-14-X (hdb.)

1. Human-alien encounters—Fiction. 2. Life on other planets—Fiction. 3. Camouflage (Biology)—Fiction. 4. Science fiction.

I. Title

PS3553.L588W4 1998

813'.54
QB198-980
98-71928
CIP

For My Wife
*Newt*

# INTRODUCTION

It happens.  Humankind has been found in the cosmos by Aliens with four times the mental endowment of the most intelligent of our species.  Although smaller in stature than ourselves they are fifteen thousand years our technological superiors.  What do they think about us?  What–if anything– do they want from us?  Do we *really* want to know?

**Chapter One**

The Estate was the dream that only two percent of the world's population could ever hope to acquire. Vincent Henry III had made his megabucks in the auto industry, having twelve dealerships in various key locations in California and Nevada. The fact that "The Old Man," Vincent Henry II, happened to have twenty million to throw into the deal may have had something to do with his son's successful entry into the business world. However, the businesses eventually made eighty times his original investment; therefore, young Vincent was able to pay Daddy back with interest before he died. What the hell, the kid ended up with the whole enchilada anyway.

The sixty-room mansion was graced by eight hundred and ninety acres of gloriously well kept, easy-rolling upstate New York landscape, majestically spread under the clear blue sky and warmed by the bright August sunlight. His heritage conveyed a sense of tranquillity, an unobstructed feeling that heaven might be a better place; but such a possibility never crossed the mind of anyone basking in its opulence.

The four retired marines in Mister Henry's employ were not by any stretch of the imagination nice guys. They had sent many of the politically incorrect enemies of Vietnam to heavenly domiciles. These were no-nonsense employees who knew their jobs well, never mixing business with pleasure. Knowing where their bread was buttered, they could earn in excess of $45,000 for their summer jobs at the Manor.

Two guards were on duty from six in the morning until six at night, and two guards from six p.m. until six a.m.; constant radio contact one with the other, heavily armed, ever watchful, diligent in their duties, yet obscure, they were a bad guy's worst nightmare.

The Lady of the manor, Mrs. Elizabeth Henry, was a well-maintained thirty-seven year old, green-eyed, ivory-skinned, strawberry blonde. She looked far younger than her years, but her appearance was less important than the intelligent, diligent and consistent way in which she delegated the responsibilities at the Manor.

The Henry's daughter Roxanne had just entered her twelfth year of life, and what a life it was. Lithe of frame, tossing locks of curly blonde hair, she moved through the Henry estate with the ease and flair of a goddess. Her every request might well have been granted by the domestics of the household, not out of fear of reprisal, but for the simple reason that it was difficult for anyone to look into those large aqua-blue eyes of this radiant child and say "no," except for her parents, who could say "no," and often did. "Which part of 'no' do you not understand, young lady? Is it the 'n' or the 'o'?"

Mom and Dad had studied psychology, and they would do all in their power to assure that no daughter of theirs would become spoiled and hedonistic. The best of private tutors gave weekly progress reports, and Mom and Dad were assured that her class work would be done; any grade less than a "B" was unacceptable.

The standing rule was, should there be any question whatsoever in the minds of the domestic help regarding activities in which Miss Roxanne should or should not engage, then one of her parents would have the final say.

Protected from the austerity of life by massive wealth, with diligent and caring parents, both with Harvard doctorate degrees, the girl had it all. All who saw her, as she moved gracefully through the Manor, could only say to themselves "and why not?"

Roxanne entered the main dining hall to request a favor of her mother, and even though Madam Henry was very busy, she was never too busy to consider an entreaty by her daughter. Elizabeth listened silently, admiring the lissome curly locks and blue eyes of the father found in the child. The young girl was asking about a patch of newly ripened blackberries, in the northeast corner of the estate. One of the landscaping crew had mentioned the berries and their location to the girl earlier that morning.

The child was an intelligent twelve-year-old, her mother reasoned, and by the girl's side, always ready for adventure, was her constant companion Pooche, a 160 pound Rottweiler, who could be totally rotten if he perceived the slightest threat to his beloved mistress.

Vincent Henry had been a bit disconcerted when the cute little Pooche had grown into a huge dog. He had even taken him to an endocrinologist to have his glands checked out, so very unusually large and well muscled a grown dog had the pup matured into. The tests had come back normal; the animal was simply a biological wonder, a most exceptionally large dog.

With permission granted, girl and dog happily set off to prepare for their blackberry quest.

Elizabeth remembered the day that she had found Roxanne and Pooche watching an X-rated movie on cable in the home entertainment studio. Not knowing quite how to handle the situation, she had gone to find Vincent, who was practicing his golf swing in the shade of a large oak tree near the stables. Vincent instructed the chauffeur, who had been giving him praise and encouragement, to gather up the balls and clubs.

He then set off in the direction of the studio to perform his parental duty.

The double doors swung open on their well-oiled hinges behind Roxanne and the dog. Had it not been for Pooche's keen hearing, the parents could have stood behind their daughter for the duration of the movie unnoticed, so absorbed was the child in the curious activity before her. Pooche, turning his massive head, gave warning with a small "woof" and the child turned, eyes wide as saucers, to meet the cold glare of her parents.

Vincent was as angry as his wife was bewildered, emotions that had not gone unnoticed by the ever-concerned Pooche. Vincent started toward his daughter with severe discipline in mind; flushed of face, cursing the Cable Company under his breath, he stopped short of the child when Pooche positioned himself between Roxanne and her father. Gurgling growls, lowered head, teeth on display-- nothing less than a shotgun was going to keep *this* dog from defending its most cherished mistress.

Elizabeth had never seen, nor would she ever forget, her husband's humble reaction to this event. Cautiously, Vincent had backed out of the studio, face now ashen, trembling with beads of nervous perspiration popping out on his forehead. Slowly he pulled the double doors closed, then at something between a fast walk and a run, set off to get Fred the chauffeur. Fred had raised and trained "that goddamn" dog when it was a puppy, and was the only person other than Roxanne who had rapport with the beast.

When he found the chauffeur, Mr. Henry instructed him to remove the dog from the room, either peaceably or not, and use extreme caution regarding the girl.

Actually the event worked out well enough in the end. Roxanne, with tears streaming down her face, was able to beg forgiveness from her father, thereby saving the dog's life.

Roxanne learned her lesson, and hardly ever got into trouble after that.

She was courteous and respectful thereafter, not only towards her parents, but to the domestic help as well. Both parents realized that, had they sent Pooche to doggie heaven, this probably would not have happened.

The child became totally committed to being good, and indeed would go to the extreme of chaining her dog before having a discussion with her parents on what she considered to be her juvenile "rights." It was for these reasons that the mother felt the dog would never again be a serious problem.

Madam Henry had just finished inspecting the silverware and accessories in the main dining hall, when she glanced up to see her daughter and the dog returning from their berry-gathering excursion.

Briskly the girl-dog-doll team neared the rear patio area and started toward the kitchen. Madam Henry, taking note of the time, decided to intercept the trio and instruct the cook on a quick lunch preparation. She would remark to a nearby maid, "That big old galoot of a dog is putty in the hands of that girl; she can do anything with Pooche."

Roxanne had apparently given one of her large dolls a ride on the dog as they set off to pick berries, and it was still riding high on the dog, like a jockey on an over-fed quarter horse.

En route to the kitchen Elizabeth stopped long enough to point out the dust on the cabinets in the entry area to the butler. Walking into the kitchen, she saw her daughter with Pooche, side by side at the rear of the kitchen with the large doll propped up against the dog, its arm over the dog's neck.

It was a large kitchen, but then every room in the Henry Mansion was well lighted, large and cheery. Elizabeth wondered where Vincent had bought the beautiful large doll with which her daughter now played, and why she had not seen it sooner.  It was unusual that neither husband nor daughter had brought such a lovely large doll immediately to her attention.

The mother walked briskly toward her daughter, wondering if she might perhaps have a touch of the flu, as she was beginning to feel a little queasy.  Smiling pleasantly however, Elizabeth continued in the direction of the trio, glancing about the bright spacious kitchen, wondering where in the world the cook had gone.

Her smile faded as she looked again at the trio awaiting her approach at the far end of the kitchen.  A tingling sensation began to develop in her lower abdominal regions, and she was beginning to feel an unusual dryness in her mouth.

Breathing more rapidly now, Elizabeth felt her bladder begin to develop a mind of its own.  Intuitively she knew that something was terribly wrong.  A sense of foreboding began to engulf her as now, more slowly and apprehensively, she drew nearer, coming to a stop seven feet away from them. She was praying to God, Christ, Mother Mary, and Saint Peter that the doll was only a small child dressed prematurely for a Halloween costume party.  (It stared back at her with large, luminous dark blue eyes and began to move easily about, now shifting its position, now petting the dog.)

Electrified, she realized that the doll-like "thing" confronting her was not a creation of some Asian animation wizard or a small costumed child, but something most obviously *supernatural*. Elizabeth, with bladder voiding, lost consciousness, joining the cook on the floor, who had gotten a previous close-up view of the bizarre creature through a window near the sink area.

**Chapter Two**

The butler, dusting the kitchen entry area cabinets as per Madam Henry's instructions, heard a thump followed by a surprised little shriek from Roxanne. Hurrying into the kitchen to investigate, he knew that something was terribly wrong when he saw the body on the floor.

Quickly turning on his heels, he ran towards the infirmary to find Bessie, the live-in registered nurse. Two of the maids, noticing the frenzied activity of the butler and nurse, set off to alert security. Within ten minutes of Madam Henry's fainting on the kitchen floor, eight maids, the butler and nurse, four security guards with weapons drawn, and the two assistant cooks, who had been on break, were gathered in the kitchen. With adrenaline pumping, the staff was unable to immediately assimilate or rectify the curious and perplexing situation taking place.

Most were dumbfounded, as they tried to bring Madam Henry and the Cook back to consciousness. When it became apparent that neither Madam Henry nor the cook was in imminent danger, the nurse then suggested they be assisted into available chairs. Madam Henry, the cook and all the others, now gazed apprehensively at the source of their anxiety.

The creature also, ever so slowly, smiling and graceful, eased itself into a nearby chair; there it ceased any movement other than vaguely perceptible breathing. Two .357 Magnum handguns were pointed at its head.

Out of fear or ignorance, humans, describing various familiar and unfamiliar life forms, often use the term's beast or creature. However, in the light of clear thinking, these words could in no way be applied to this unexpected guest that rode Pooche-back into Vincent Henry Manor on this unprecedented day. The only terminology that could adequately describe Roxanne's most unusual new playmate would need be a composite of "enchanting-splendid-dazzling," and even this could not take in the realm of what now sat before the Vincent Henry household.

The small living spectacle, approximately three feet tall when standing, was silver in color, not the metallic silver of a newly minted coin, but a bright living silver, as one might find on those beautifully vivid fish in and about a coral reef in a faraway tropical sea. It was slender, with what appeared to be budding breasts devoid of areola or nipple. The entity seemingly was wearing clothing, but no line of demarcation was apparent where fabric might reveal skin. The almond-shaped, hauntingly luminous eyes were larger than the largest human eyes, with no visible pupils or sclera.

Every now and then the eyelids would close slowly, in what appeared to be a moistening process over the deep, glistening, sapphire blue orbs; no other color could be perceived therein. These "mirrors of the soul" seemed to exude innocence, kindness, and good will. The constantly smiling, smallish, perfectly formed flower petal lips, along with the diminutive but precisely formed ears and flattish nose was nothing short of astounding. The amazing final descriptive of this corporeality, this living jewel, was what appeared to be well-groomed, medium-long, silver blonde hair. When all aspects of the being were assimilated, one was left with the impression that there, before him or her, was an exquisite young girl child, smaller in stature than need be, sprinkled with star-dust, intuitive, wizened and knowledgeable far beyond her years.

"Can she live with us? Can she, Mommy? Oh please, please, Mommy, can she?" ejected Roxanne.

The assembly paid no visible attention to Roxanne's pleas, but stared wide-eyed past her, silent, as if frozen in time and space, at the diminutive visage two feet behind her in the chair.

Vincent had just finished his "morning constitutional" upstairs in one of the more remote bathrooms of the Mansion. He often did this so as to be left alone while he quietly assimilated the morning newspaper. Paying close attention to his blue chip stocks in the business section, he finished off with the comic strip, a weakness he allowed himself. It seemed a fair enough exchange, physically getting rid of pre-digested food while mentally digesting the news.

Mr. Henry walked through the upper hallway and then down the winding staircase into the main dining hall; he remarked quietly under his breath, "Has this house ever been this peaceful?"

Peace and harmony were dear to Mr. Henry's heart. Little did he know what lay before him in the kitchen, as he eyed from the center of the staircase the gray skirt of the last maid to pass through its portal. Looking forward to a hearty lunch, having had only a slice of toast and a cup of coffee for breakfast, he entered the kitchen to find ninety percent of the household silently rooted in place, as if someone had stopped a motion picture projector on a single panoramic frame.

"What the hell is going on?" inquired the Lord of the Manor in a loud, demanding tone.

The throng then slowly began to give way, revealing the strange, apparently joyous creature, seated contentedly in a kitchen chair. Pooche now sat on the floor to its right and the girl stood perplexed, but hopeful, to its left.

Vincent Henry, his interest now piqued, moved deftly forward, with one eye on the dog and the other on the creature. Had he possessed a third eye it probably would have been upon his daughter.

Now exclaiming in a more pronounced voice he drew nearer to the cause of the disturbance: "I said what in the goddamned hell...?!" The words trailed off as he analyzed the situation confronting him.

Instinctively Vincent knew that this problem was going to be a tough nut to crack. He became fully cognitive of the fact that the apparition in the chair before him, gazing steadfastly in his direction, smiling sweetly, moistening its huge eyes as it slowly blinked, was not an animated joke in bad taste, It was *alive!*

"Oh, Daddy, can she stay with us? Please, oh please? She won't be any problem. I promise," pleaded Roxanne.

"Hush, child," softly replied her father, as he studied with intensity this mysterious, disconcerting spectacle before him.

"She is my best friend in all the world. She knows so much I..."

"Will you please *shut up,* Roxanne?!" replied her father, more sternly.

Madam Henry was once more to witness acute anxiety and dread on the countenance of her husband. The guards continued their vigilance, pistols pointing, waiting for the order from their summer employer, to put an end to what they could not, nor did they care to understand.

"Wait!" suddenly pleaded Mrs. Henry, "Wait just a minute, please!"

Moving cautiously out of her chair she slowly walked around to her daughter's side... the left side, the side furthest from that as yet unexplained object of her concern.

The girl was now totally despondent, tears streaming down her face, anxiety bordering on hysteria. The mother placed an arm about her daughter. Keeping a wary eye upon the mysterious being, she began to lightly tug her daughter away from the unknown danger she perceived.

"Of course you can't keep it, dear. We don't even know what 'It' is!"

"She's my very best friend in all the world!" replied the girl tearfully. "She knows a lot and she teaches me things!"

"We don't even know what the damned thing might eat!" replied her father, color beginning to return to his face, thankful that the marines were there.

"Any type of fish," replied a small voice.

The being had spoken.

"Any type of fish at all would be nice," It replied with an almost musical, clipped British accent.

The spectators gasped in astonishment, "It can speak!" They murmured one to another, "Wha-? It can *speak-?!*"

Vincent Henry was a well-educated man, never allowing impulse or rashness to take a part in his logical decision-making process. He needed answers, and answers he was going to get. He knew full well that any person or thing that can make its needs and wants known through conversation can answer questions, and the answering of questions is what leads to understanding.

Well thought-out decisions and careful consideration to particulars were kingpins to Vincent Henry's extensive success, and for these attributes he was well known in his corner of the business world.

Vincent motioned to the guards to holster their weapons, but they intuitively knew he did not wish them to leave the kitchen. Gwenia-San, one of the assistant cooks, stepped forward. Fish was his specialty at the Manor, and he knew all there was to know about its preparation. Fascination overcoming fear, the small Japanese cook, barely five feet tall himself, moved politely to the front of this newly arrived guest.

Hands together, he courteously bowed, then inquired, "How would Missy like her fish prepared?"

Roxanne was delighted with this turn of events and smiling now herself, she wiped away the tears.

The small being gazed upon the cook with obvious appreciation, but did not speak.

Gwenia-San, not to be deterred, inquired, "Would Missy like her fish steamed? Or perhaps broiled? Fried?"

Bending down a little further, so he could look directly into the luminous eyes, "Sushi?" he asked.

Upon mention of this, the cook knew he had hit the target. The smallish, but perfectly formed, perpetually smiling lips broadened further, revealing flawless sparkling white teeth.

The cook hurried off to one of the kitchen's large walk-in coolers, where he had laid up fresh fish that very morning. Yellowtail, tuna and cod, together with some very tasty roe (fish-eggs) which he had gotten at the fish market, along with the fishmonger's promise, "This fish was flown in at three this morning, on ice, never frozen."

The little cook was delighted with his discovery, as happily he set off to prepare the delicacy. He knew it would be a pleasing surprise for Mr. Henry as well.

Gwenia-San and Mr. Henry had found each other in a small sushi-bar in Japan, on one of Vincent's many trips to

"The Land of the Rising Sun," securing the best deals for several of his dealerships. Vincent had first started eating the raw fish out of courtesy to his Japanese hosts, but it didn't take him long to develop a genuine taste for the various uncooked fishy dishes. When Mr. Henry offered to bring not only Gwenia-San, but the cook's wife as well, back to the States, the cook agreed to the adventure, feeling it would be a cultural education for them both. The pay was exceptional as well; Mr. Henry seldom failed to get what he wanted.

# Chapter Three

Mrs. Henry was highly embarrassed about her anxiety attack, the fainting spell, and unintentional loss of her bodily function. Secure that her husband and security were now on the scene, she hurried off accompanied by one of the maids for a quick shower and change of clothing.

Off to the left, near the rear entry area of the kitchen, and next to a large picture window, were situated two large restaurant-type booths. They were each large enough to comfortably accommodate six people. The Manor household for informal meals, domestic help and the Henrys alike often used these booths.

Mr. Henry motioned to his most unconventional guest to be seated in one of the booths. Almost simultaneously the being slid gracefully out of its chair, walked dramatically over and effortlessly eased itself up and into the cushy leather seat.

No conversation was to ensue during the time that Gwenia-San was preparing the food. Sushi for the strange guest, Mr. Henry and Roxanne, a light crisp tuna salad for Mrs. Henry.

Roxanne was a chip off the old block when it came to eating sushi, having had it given to her by her dad in those formative years, prior to the knowledge of where her food came from, or from what it was made. If it tasted good to Roxanne, she ate it, enjoying the aquatic delicacy every bit as much as did her father.

Upon the rather quick return of Elizabeth Henry, she and Vincent sat on one side of a booth; the being and Roxanne sat facing them from the other. The girl sat straight and proper, as she had been taught in her etiquette classes, while the being sat up equally as nicely, but with legs folded beneath in a full lotus position.

Mr. Henry then instructed the assemblage, "None of the happenings on this day, or in the future, are to pass outside the Manor without my express permission."

He then dismissed them all to return to their household duties excepting Gwenia-San, and one of the guards. Some with relief, most with disappointment, curiosity unsatisfied, the domestic help gradually filtered out of the kitchen to tend to their numerous household chores.

The cook brought the food, under the scrutiny of the guard, and although this was an informal meal, Gwenia-San had outdone himself in its preparation. The small rice cakes were wrapped neatly around their sides with dark edible seaweed, and the thin and carefully sliced fresh fish had been laid neatly on top. The food was served on the finest china dishes, artfully decorated with parsley, sliced fresh ginger, hot green mustard and soy sauce on the side. A decorative and zesty tuna salad had been prepared for Madam Henry, complete with crisp iceberg lettuce and sliced garden-ripened tomatoes. For beverages there were four large glasses of freshly brewed iced tea in crystal tumblers, with sprigs of mint and lemon wedges.

The being gazed silently, smiling at Mr. Henry, who was disconcertingly wondering why the creature had not begun to eat. As his hand unconsciously moved toward the chopsticks the being did the same, and upon the first bite being taken by the Lord of the Manor, the feast began.

Roxanne and her strange friend each ate four pieces of sushi in rapid succession, so Gwenia-San hurried about the kitchen to prepare more. Mr. Henry soon caught up with the two. Mrs. Henry, still bewildered, wondering if this might be some kind of a dream or nightmare from which she would hopefully soon awake, took three bites of her salad.

More sushi was soon brought, and now the two friends and the father, eating more slowly, would glance at one another from time to time. All were smiling now, except for Elizabeth.

Vincent began to notice the delicate way in which the creature held its eating utensils in beautifully formed, smallish hands, with fingers that gracefully tapered off to slightly rounded tips. Startled once again, but certainly not for the last time, he noticed that the fingers were changing color! Glancing up to the creature's face, he was shocked to notice that the thing's entire physiology was changing color.

Out of a need to do something, anything, to release anxiety, for Vincent was definitely about to have an anxiety attack, he inquired of the being in a croaking voice, "Why are you changing color?"

Madam Henry sat petrified, riveted to her seat.

"Because I am no longer frightened," came the mellifluous reply.

Stunned, Vincent and his wife watched as the being before them turned golden! This was not the gold-plated color one would find on some cheap dime-store watch, but a deep, rich, beautifully lustrous, twenty-four carat gold, like the chains Asian peoples use to carry their sacred religious artifacts on and about their necks.

It seemed as if oxygen was scarce, as Mr. and Mrs. Henry found themselves transfixed, staring into the being's now deep glowing, amber eyes. Roxanne munched happily away at the meal before her, quietly pleased that her friend's hair was, once more, closely matching the golden blonde of her own.

When the guard, Danny Sarte, once more entered the kitchen, checking out the situation, much was weighing upon his mind. It was obvious from his slight frown, the lines creasing his forehead, and the intensity with which he regarded the now golden creature seated in the booth next to the girl.

Vincent Henry had regained his composure, and now that the formalities had been consummated, was preparing himself for a question-answer session that he hoped would get him to the bottom of this totally perplexing event.

"Sir?" ejected the approaching guard, diverting his glance from the being to Mr. Henry. "If it would not be a major inconvenience, sir, might I have a few words with you?"

Vincent had a great deal of respect for Danny, and he knew well his war record of action under enemy fire. Time and time again Danny had been commended for his cool, well thought-out decisions and bravery when confronted with the enemy. Vincent was well aware that the guard was not a man to be taken lightly. If Danny had something to say, it was best to listen.

The guard motioned Mr. Henry to accompany him to a distance he felt was out of earshot of the thing. He then began speaking in low tones he hoped would not be overheard.

"Mr. Henry, sir," began the guard, "when I was in Vietnam I was a very young man. I had lied about my age because I sincerely felt that my loved ones, my country, and religion, indeed the American way of life, might well soon be destroyed unless I was willing to risk my life to help prevent it. Of course I didn't remain this naive for the duration of my time in that country. I came to realize that the political leaders there, the same as here, were specialists in filling young and receptive heads with emotional bullshit. I killed young and old alike and have often wondered how many men, better than myself, would never again look into the eyes of their loved ones, or watch their children laugh, play and grow into adulthood."

The guard was now looking with great sadness into the eyes of his employer.

"Could we just cut to the chase here, Mr. Sarte?" asked Vincent. "If I'm ever to get to the bottom of this situation, I've got to get with the program."

"I apologize, sir, for getting you sidetracked here; it's just that under fire I knew who the enemy was," replied the guard, returning to his war-story, "but it was a young, beautiful, twenty year old girl that came the closest to costing me my life.

"My platoon had just entered a small village on a search and capture mission," persisted the guard. "The only residents there were old men and women, along with some children. I was surveying the perimeter of the village when I noticed this beautiful young girl trying to conceal herself along with her child in a dense brushy area. When she knew that I had found her out, she left the child behind in the brush, and came forward to meet me, smiling shyly, obviously friendly.

"I had a few dollars in my pocket, and as lonely and frightened as I was about what was going on around me, I would have given it up gladly, plus my next month's wages, for just one hour with this beauty. I'll never forget the gracefulness of that walk, that long dark hair, deep brown almond-shaped eyes, and flawlessly smooth skin.

"She took me by the hand, waving her small son to follow. After about a twenty-minute walk, we arrived at a nicely constructed bamboo hut by a little stream. She sent the boy to weed the garden, and we bathed in the small stream.

"Soon inside the hut we then made love twice in rapid succession; sex was another thing I was naive about in those days. The accumulated fatigue from hunting and being hunted, killing and fear of being killed, together with sex with the most beautiful girl I had ever seen, was too much for me. I lay there by that young girl's side relaxing; after about fifteen minutes I fell asleep.

"Two shots in rapid succession lifted me off the mat on the floor, like a gymnast off a trampoline. The girl fell to the floor where I once had been; where we had made love now lay my bleeding lover, my rifle still in her hands.

"I then turned to see my buddy, Frank, standing in the doorway, rifle pointing at the now still, crumpled form on the floor.

"'The bitch was gonna waste ya! Goddamn, Dan, what ya been doing?' anxiously asked Frank.

"Blood flowed down the left side of my face; a half inch more to the right, I would have been one dead puppy.

"The medics, along with the rest of the platoon, having heard the shots, were soon there. Patching me up was no problem; but with me always will be the memory of that dying girl's words, her son crying at her side. She told our translator how the 'Demon Americans' had bombed and killed her parents, then shot her husband as he tried to explain to them that he did not believe in war, and only wanted to tend his garden and care for his family."

"For God's sake, Danny!" ejected Vincent Henry, "I want to get to the bottom of this damn thing; I got the message!"

"Please, sir!" pleaded the guard, "anything with this kind of intelligence must have an agenda! For you and your family's sake, use maximum caution. I strongly recommend we call whatever government service handles these sorts of situations and let them take it from here on out."

As Mr. Henry turned from the advice of his concerned guard, he was well aware that the being had gotten into the

Manor by perhaps feigning innocence and good will, first with his daughter, then himself, a feat it probably could not have so easily accomplished by any other means. The being's obvious good manners, grace, beauty and intelligence were almost totally disarming.

Walking back towards the booth where sat this intrusive and curiously strange guest, Vincent began to lay out a plan. He must gain control of this most disquieting situation as quickly as possible. Mr. Henry well knew that situations beyond his control had often proven detrimental.

## Chapter Four

Vincent Henry had many acquaintances, and for obvious reason, he was rich. According to the latest tally of his wealth, there were close to three hundred million reasons to be friendly with Vincent Henry, but he also knew that he who has many "friends" in reality has no friends. He needed to contemplate his every move with care.

Foremost in his mind were two very good friends he had palled around with during his years at Harvard, both of whom he wished to hell were with him now. Bill, Dave and Vincent had been the best of buddies in college; had any of the faculty known of their escapades, not only would they have been thrown out of Harvard, but probably would have been thrown into jail as well. Like the time they had managed to remove a corpse from a local morgue, dress it up in typical Harvard attire, then left it, as though it was sleeping at the rear of Dr. Timothy Johnston's sociology class. Or the time they had gotten back at that sadist son-of-a-bitch Dr. Thomas "The Toad" Speelick for overloading them with so much busy work in his physics class that they had to struggle in their other classes to get marginally good grades.

This had been a classic repayment; they had hired a prostitute to show up at one of the faculty functions, and when she had gotten Dr. Speelick off to the side, she grabbed his hand, thrusting it into her generous bosom, just as Mrs.

Speelick had come looking for him with some of her distinguished lady friends. Dr. Thomas "The Toad" got to spend two weeks at one of the Fellowship Houses, healing from a black eye, a broken nose, and two badly bruised shins.

Fraternity brothers to the end, the trio's trust in one another was their bond; each of them could depend unquestionably upon the other. It was in those great old days that Vincent came to realize that there was never much need to explain himself; his friends didn't care, and his enemies would never believe him anyway. The bond with his two best friends was just as strong now as it had been fifteen years ago. This was one of the few times in Vincent Henry's life that money was certainly not going to be the answer; he was going to need his friends.

William Faraday had gotten his master's in business, and had somehow gotten hooked up with the State Department, while David Hauss had finished his education at the University of Hawaii, with a doctoral degree in zoology. Vincent always made sure that both Billy and Dave were invited to all the major social functions. Both were brilliant, both were at the top of their chosen professions, and Vincent always felt good when his friends were around.

Being politically motivated, Billy was happy to attend these functions. He appreciated the contacts he made, but David seldom showed, his excuse being that he was constantly busy all year long; he taught classes at the University at Lakeside. (The real reason he didn't show up for the majority of the functions was simply that he was overwhelmed with the grandeur of the events that transpired there. He was a modest man of modest means, even though he felt Vincent Henry to be his good friend.)

Mr. Henry gave instructions to the guard "Get in touch immediately with William Faraday and Dr. David Hauss, and then go after them and bring them back as quickly as possible.

Tell them nothing, and don't take no for an answer. Kidnap them if you must, charter a private plane, I want to see them within five hours."

Dismissing Danny Sarte who would do the job well, he walked quickly back towards the booth on the other side of the kitchen. The being, his wife and daughter were now standing. Mrs. Henry was nodding at the two before her, a slightly nervous smile now on her lips, the first that Vincent had seen since this unsettling episode had begun.

As Vincent approached the trio, his wife turned towards him, and with a bit of a nervous quiver in her voice, announced, "Vincent, dear, we are about to be entertained in the drawing room by...?" Turning back to the being she asked, "Do you have a name?"

With a truly golden smile, the being with its small and appealing voice replied, "Yes, you may call me 'Jay-see-ka.'"

Turning back towards her husband, Elizabeth explained, "Roxanne and Jayseeka are going to play a refrain on the piano."

The discussions with the being had begun, his wife having been the initiator. Of all the questions in Vincent's head, the being's name and its artistic talents were certainly somewhere near the bottom of the list. However, discretion is the better part of valor, he reasoned, and he wanted to move into the forthcoming question-answer session as smoothly as possible. Vincent nodded his approval, and the foursome, with guard close behind, moved off in the direction of the drawing room. In this room were situated many comfortable chairs and two Steinway concert grand pianos.

At the young age of twelve Roxanne was quite an accomplished pianist; her father had not heard her play for almost two years, having been busy with his many business concerns. Vincent enjoyed music, mostly classical; however, he regretted that he had not kept up with her musical education, leaving this aspect of her studies for his wife to oversee. Vincent was totally unaware that his daughter was such a prodigy.

Upon entering the drawing room, Roxanne seated herself at one piano while Jayseeka seated itself at the piano generally occupied by Roxanne's teacher. The two pianists entered into a production of "Blue Moon," each playing her own rendition, each in complete harmony with the other.

Engrossed in the musical activity before them, Vincent, his wife Elizabeth and the guard never thought to consider how Jayseeka, barely three feet tall, with small hands and fingers was managing the keyboard, not to mention the pedals near the floor.

The "girls" sang beautifully together, finishing up with strange melodious whistling sounds, somewhere between whale song and a silver flute, by Jayseeka.

Others of the household who had heard the music had filtered into the drawing room and all, including both Vincent and his wife, were amazed at the first performance. They found themselves absolutely flabbergasted as the two talented artists finished off with Mozart's Piano Concerto #21 in C Major.

Without an error, they had played gloriously and harmoniously together. Applause was naturally forthcoming. The audience was delighted, but no sooner had the spectators' clapping begun than it was cut short by Mr. Henry.

Rising quickly to his feet, he motioned for all once more to leave the room, except Jayseeka, Roxanne, Mrs. Henry and the guard. The Lord of the Manor wanted some questions answered. He would brook no further delays.

Approximately fifty minutes had elapsed from the time the guard, Danny Sarte, had gotten his orders from Mr. Henry.

Roxanne and Jayseeka were obviously pleased with the manner in which their recital had been received.

Seated comfortably around a small mahogany table in the drawing room, Vincent, his wife Elizabeth, the guard, Roxanne, and Jayseeka (who had been lifted up to a more comfortable height by three volumes of the Encyclopedia Britannica,) looked upon one another with searching eyes, waiting.

Roxanne knew well her father's disposition. There was a deep binding love and respect between them. Though the girl and her mother could not always understand his motives, they trusted his integrity. Sincerely they felt that the decisions he made, though not always corresponding with their wishes, were logically in the best interest of all concerned. Roxanne also knew that any explanation of her new friend Jayseeka was going to be a monumentally difficult endeavor. All waited for Mr. Henry to begin the discourse.

Vincent now looked intently into the eyes of his daughter. "Roxanne," he inquired, "how did you happen to meet Jayseeka?" He then waited with quiet expectation for the forthcoming explanation.

"Mother had given permission for Pooche and me to go blackberry picking over by the boat dock near the lake," began the girl. "I got a small bucket from Elvira, the cook, and then went upstairs and put on a tank-top, shorts and tennis shoes. After this we set off to find the berries where the groundskeeper said he had seen them early this morning. We got there quickly, running most of the way, and I began walking around the patch of blackberries, looking for the largest and blackest ones.

"As I neared the boathouse, I noticed Jaseeka sitting on the boat dock with her feet in the water. She was the prettiest thing I had ever seen. She is even a prettier golden color in sunlight than she is as you see her now. She looked at me and smiled, and then waved me towards her.

"At first I was a bit frightened." continued the girl. "But when Pooche just trotted right up to her, with his stumpy tail wriggling, and licked her on the side of the face, I wasn't afraid any more. She is so tiny and nice; I walked right up to her, and began to pet Pooche.

"I apologized for Pooche's rudeness, and she said that he was a very nice fellow and that it was okay if he wanted to kiss her. She said her name was Jayseeka and that she was happy to meet Pooche and me. We talked about different kinds of animals that lived about the pond and in the woods nearby; she taught me a song and we sang it twice together. I was very happy to have her for a friend.

"After a while, I asked her if she would come back to the Manor and meet you and Mother, and that I hoped she might be able to stay with us here and be my best friend. She said she would come back to the Manor with me and that she would always be my friend, but that she had many other things to do while she was here, and that we might be separated from time to time.

"She asked me not to be alarmed if she should happen to turn a different color soon, because the golden color happened only when she felt safe and secure, and that it was very dangerous for her to be around many people because some of them might injure or maybe even kill her out of fear and ignorance."

All eyes glanced at the beautifully formed, elfin being Jayseeka, whose only movement was a bit more of a smile.

"I promised her that Pooche and I would protect her," continued the girl, "and that my father and mother were both very good people and would see that no harm came to her."

Looking intently, first at her father, then her mother, the girl paused for a moment.

"You can see how tiny she is, so I just lifted her up, and sat her on Pooche's back. He didn't seem to care a bit, and we started back towards the house. I noticed she started to turn silver as we neared the patio area, and though I told her not to worry, she continued to change color and her eyes became blue. She explained to me that she sensed people were going to be very frightened when they first saw her, and that she hoped things would be all right.

"Would you and Mother like to hear the song she taught me?"

"No, not now, Roxanne," replied her father quietly, now turning his attention toward Jayseeka.

Vincent, realizing that Jayseeka was anything but human, inquired, "Are there any more such as yourself on or about the Manor grounds?"

"There is only myself at this time," responded Jayseeka, "and there will be no others for a while, if something should happen to me, or if my mission should not be successful."

*"Mission?"* replied Vincent, more than a bit disturbed at the thought that this being did admit to having an agenda.

"Yes, Vincent, I do have an agenda, but I can assure you that it is well intended."

"It read my *mind!*" exclaimed Vincent. Taking hold of the chair as if to rise out of it, he quickly reiterated, "You can read minds!"

The guard went for his gun, and in an instant Jayseeka had once more turned startling silver.

"Please, Daddy!" ejected Roxanne, eyes wide and frightened, more concerned with what the guard might do than the fact that Jayseeka could read minds.

The gun was four inches from the being's head. Slowly bowing forward, looking down at the table before it, even now a wisp of a smile still upon its lips. "I guess we were wrong," timidly came forth the sweet voice, evenly smooth. It then awaited its pending fate.

Now it was Elizabeth Henry who was on her feet, chair falling back behind her. "Stop this, Vincent! Please? You must stop this! We can't just *kill* what we don't understand!"

All was quiet in the room, Roxanne's eyes suddenly brimming with tears, while Elizabeth stood at the table trembling with emotion. Vincent had not intended for the guard to react as quickly and violently as he had. It was simply the gravity of the situation, coupled with the awareness that he could have no private thoughts with this mystical creature before him, which caused him to unravel. He had almost lost it.

Vincent Henry was somewhat of a mixed bag: equal parts control and caution, coupled with intelligence and education. Now he was confronted by a perplexing situation unlike any he had ever experienced before. To act stupidly or cruelly was not his nature. Here before him was a mystery intriguing him to the marrow, and he wanted more than anything to solve it; but at the same time he was considering the safety of his family, hell, just possibly the whole damned human race!

Vincent shot a disapproving look at the guard. "Put the gun away, Jackson!" he demanded.

"But Sir! I think..."

"Don't *think!* Put the goddamned gun away!" Vincent ordered more sternly.

He finished rising from his chair, motioning for the guard to follow. As he was being led away into the hallway, Vincent was talking as quietly as possible, while Johnny Jackson was protesting, in the most condescending tones.

"You almost killed that damned thing!" exclaimed Vincent.

"I was waiting for your order!" retorted the guard.

"Well, I have absolutely no intentions of giving such an order. Pulled your gun out and aimed at its head! We don't know anything about this thing. Where are the rest of its kind? What kind of defense mechanisms do the damned things have? What the hell were you trying to do, Johnny?"

"Well I was..."

"You were getting ready to blow the God-damn thing away! That's what you were getting ready to do," continued Vincent.

"No! I was..."

"Getting ready to blow it to *hell!*" emphatically stated his employer, "and the God-damned thing knew it. It could read your mind!"

Out in the hallway Vincent left the totally bewildered guard, with instructions to consider himself relieved for the day, and to call in one of the other guards for the swing shift. Johnny the guard needed a rest.

## Chapter Five

Look for constancy within.
Know constancy or know disaster.
Knowing constancy, the mind is open.
With the mind open, your actions are royal.
Open minded and open hearted,
The divine is within your grasp.

(Lao Tsu, 6th Century B.C.)

Returning to the drawing room, Vincent was rapidly analyzing mental data that he had so far collected, doing his best to make a determination on where to go from this point onward.  He knew the only path was to be as honest and straightforward with the being as was humanly possible.  It could read his mind!  Had he any other choice?

More than a trifle perplexed, Vincent saw his daughter now standing with her arm around Jayseeka. Her mother stood close by, speaking in soothing tones, as he walked briskly back towards the table.

Roxanne set her mother's chair upright, and Vincent once more sat down to the table.  When wife and daughter were once more seated, he looked again upon Jayseeka, mustering a genuine flick of a smile, and began once more the inquiry.

"Thank you, Mr. Henry," spoke Jayseeka when all were settled once more at the table.  "I apologize for upsetting the guard and you; it was not my intention to do so."

"Jayseeka," replied Vincent, "I am going to ask you for a personal favor." Though he knew it was no longer necessary to speak a word, as she knew what he was going to say anyway.

"I would like to place my hand on your hair and body; it's very important to me that I can verify, without a doubt, that which I am now experiencing is not a dream."

"A nightmare," replied Jayseeka.

"A *what?*" asked Vincent.

"A nightmare. You were thinking nightmare, Mr. Henry," replied Jayseeka. "Yes, it's quite all right if you touch me."

Vincent then slowly stood up, leaned across the table and put his hand upon the being's head. He felt the soft hair and, excepting for the unusual thickness of the strands, it felt much like human hair. He gave it a little tug; Jayseeka smiled, revealing her perfect teeth. She giggled when he touched her nose and left ear.

Vincent took his seat, nodding with the awareness that Jayseeka was indeed very real. This was not some grandly designed hoax; he had done the correct thing by sending Danny Sarte to get his two friends.

"It is okay that you sent for your friends, Mr. Henry," spoke Jayseeka, "and if you wish to speak, instead of just thinking your questions to me, that also is okay. It's good that you wish your wife and daughter to be able to easily follow our conversation."

"Where did you come from, Jayseeka?" asked Vincent calmly.

"Please believe my honorable intent when I say that I wish no harm to you, your family, or for that matter any living creature. When I explain my origin, I sincerely hope that you and your family will have open minds and try not to become unduly stressed with the knowledge."

"We will do our best," replied Vincent, glancing at Elizabeth and Roxanne.  Their heads nodded in agreement.

*"I am not from this world."* stated the being, giving the statement a full thirty seconds to sink in.

Vincent looked down at the table; he had guessed this earlier.  Elizabeth looked at her husband, and Roxanne quizzically looked at her new friend.

"Actually, our species has been coming to this world, off and on, over the last ten thousand of your Earth years," continued Jayseeka.  "However, up to this century, there was no need to make our presence known."

"And now it's time?" asked Vincent, looking into the once again deep glistening amber eyes of his guest.

"Oh, yes indeed, Vincent, it *is* time."

---

The more laws and restrictions,
The poorer are the people.
The more numerous men's weapons,
The more trouble in the realm.

*(Lao Tsu, 6th Century B.C.)*

---

The being had come to visit Vincent Henry Manor, and it was not intended as a casual visitation.  Jayseeka had come from a planet in a solar system many light years removed from Earth's star-sun and its surrounding planets.

She went on to explain, for Roxanne's benefit, "When on earth and looking up at the evening sky, the Milky Way which you see is our galaxy, consisting of multitudes of stars, oftentimes much larger than your Earth's sun.  Also many of those stars have planets about them similar to the planets Venus, Mars, Earth and Jupiter, et cetera, which orbit Earth's star which you call the Sun.  Earth is more fortunate than

Jupiter, because it has water and warmth, which can support life."

"You mean that our Earth is a part of the Milky Way, Jayseeka?" asked Roxanne.

"Yes, and now you are beginning to get some idea of the vastness of space," replied the alien.

"My home planet revolves about a star twenty kiloparsecs or approximately 57,000 light years from Earth's sun, on the other side of our galaxy's center, in the direction of the constellation Sagittarius.

"To travel the distance from Earth to my home would take a human, traveling the fastest speed known to your scientists, the speed of light, (at 6 trillion miles per year,) more than 57,000 years."

"Have you been traveling in space for this length of time to get here?" quickly asked the girl.

Her father, not liking the idea of his daughter taking the lead in the discussion, gave her a stern glance.

"No, not at all. With our method of transport, we can travel from our planet to yours in approximately one of your Earth years," came the answer.

"You may ask your questions," stated the being. It looked intently and directly at Vincent. "Or I can just answer your thoughts? A wise man of your planet once said, 'The most foolish of questions are the ones that are never asked.'"

Vincent was beginning to relax as the conversation continued; in fact, he was actually starting to like this small being with its beautiful characteristics, intelligence and melodious voice. It had not offered any resistance to the death threat from the guard, and seemed to enjoy the society of himself and his family.

"How were you able to build a spacecraft, so unique, for the travel over such vast distances? How are you able to travel faster than the speed of light, without risking disintegration? How did you find Earth? Why did you do it? Are there any more such as yourself in a spaceship nearby?"

These were five questions among many that Vincent would have liked to ask, but they would have to wait.

The butler came quickly into the drawing room, going straight to Mr. Henry. Bending over, he spoke quietly into his ear.

As the butler left the room, Vincent intently looked about the table. He then announced, "The police are here."

Henry called James, the previous guard's replacement, into the drawing room. "Listen carefully to what I am going to tell you, Jim," began Vincent. "Keep your weapon holstered. Do not, I repeat, do not make any threatening moves on the alien. Find a place for it to hide, and then stay nearby, doing everything possible to see that it is not found. It is of paramount importance that you follow my instructions *exactly!*" continued Vincent. "If you have any questions, or needs, we will discuss them later."

James Haggerty was both intelligent and faithful. He would do exactly as he was told; in fact he would willingly have risked his life, if need be, for the Henry family.

"I can handle it, sir," replied the guard. "You can count on me."

Vincent then started towards the front entry area of the Manor, motioning for his wife and daughter to follow.

No less than six police vehicles, two officers each, were in the spacious drive leading up to the front of the mansion. Sirens sounded, lights flashed, and police officers jumped out of their cars fully dressed in riot gear. It was obvious that the Vincent Henry abode was under siege and all its residents could be taken hostage.

Vincent wondered who was taking care of the bad guys in town. Indeed, if there were any, they were probably taking full advantage of the total police force absence to pillage, rape, and vandalize at will; even the police chief, Captain Pat Riely, had come.

Vincent had never known Captain Riely personally, but the Captain knew he didn't like the Henrys. First of all, he was offended that Vincent had hired his own security, which indicated that perhaps the local police were not up to the job of protecting the citizens, a definite affront to this burly, self-made man in his fifties. The pomp, and what he felt to be the arrogance of the Henrys, also had been sticking in his craw ever since he took over command of the local police department two years earlier.

Secretly, Captain Riely had always been a totalitarian type, and had always admired the government structure of the Union of Soviet Socialist Republics. Though he had never been there, he sincerely felt that people like himself would have done well in that country; he really liked to order people around. What he had heard of the Soviet Union was that "a few people had control of the country and they told everyone else what to do, and what worldly possessions they could have."

As the police chief began walking toward Vincent Henry, he was thinking how badly he wanted to humble this arrogant snob and relieve him of his worldly goods. Riely was a control freak in the extreme, and he never could understand why the political system in the USSR had failed.

It was a fluke that had got him his job as police chief; he never even suspected that his job had been "on the line" for the last three months.  His men hated him; his wife had left him long ago; even his cousin the mayor now resented the totalitarian and abusive way he treated people for even minor offenses.

Pat Riely honestly felt that all his social failures in life were due to the Vincent Henrys of the world.  Now he had his chance to project some of those pent-up hostilities on the Henrys, and he intended to take full advantage of the situation.

"Well, Mr. Henry," began Captain Riely, "it seems like you're having yourself quite a little *party* up here on the hill!"

Vincent knew immediately that things were going to get worse before they got better.  The police chief did not extend his hand, but stood glaring at the Henrys.  Vincent turned to his wife and daughter, asking them to see if there might be something good on cable, and that he could handle things from here on.

When Vincent turned back to the Captain, a warrant was rudely thrust into his hands.  Taking great pleasure in the power bequeathed to him by the warrant, Captain Riely ordered his men into the Manor.  The witch-hunt was on.

"Now, Mr. Henry, I don't really believe there are any little green men running around up here," began the Police Chief, as his eleven officers stormed the Manor.  Four positioned themselves in key locations outside, while seven others entered through the front.

"What I do think is that you have gone too far with some kind of a kinky, twisted sense of humor. Elvira, your cook, and Franceen, one of your maids, were so badly frightened when they came into the station that they are still under medication in the emergency room at Chapman Memorial. When my men come up with the evidence, I can assure you, Mr. Henry, that I will wholeheartedly testify on Elvira's and

Franceen's behalf in the lawsuit!"

Riely had started to walk arrogantly off, when something crossed his mind, and he turned back to Vincent. "Do you realize that each day that you exist as a decadent little rich boy, in a country that makes dog food for its pets, that there are people throughout the world who go to bed hungry, or die from starvation?"

"I realize this, Captain Riely," replied Vincent. "And it grieves me greatly that these poor and unfortunate souls do not, or cannot fight for the right to have a government such as our own, wherein they could also prosper, and even have pets and food to feed them with if they chose."

"Fucking smart ass!" thought Riely, "I don't give a flying fuck about poor people anyway," he muttered as he walked away in a huff. "Wait 'til I get that ass-hole in the courtroom!"

What Chief Riely had failed to comprehend was that the maid and cook never had any intentions of suing their employer. Vincent Henry had always paid and treated them well. When they had shown up at the police station they had been as much frightened for the Henrys and the rest of the household as they had been for themselves.

Pooche was on his chain at the back of the Manor. He didn't like the invasion of police officers, but this was not a stupid dog. He had tried before to break his chain, but after several tries he realized that steel was stronger than flesh. He lay there quietly upon the ground at the end of his chain, neither barking nor growling, but intently watching, hoping beyond hope, that one of the invaders would come close enough "so as he could *bite 'em!*"

## Chapter Six

---

Water,
Nothing is softer or more yielding,
And yet the solid and strong crumble before it.
Destroyer of mountains, upholder of life;
There is no equal.

*(Lao Tsu 6th Century B.C.)*

---

Vincent Henry soon tired of the snide remarks of Pat Riely, and concerned himself with the whereabouts of his wife, daughter, the alien and the guard.

In the entertainment studio, Elizabeth and Roxanne appeared to be totally engrossed in an old re-run of Roller Derby, though neither knew how to roller skate, nor did they like the violence that often broke out among the contestants. It was the first thing that had come up when they turned on the wide-screen TV, and whatever came on next was what they would also watch with equally apparent interest. They both waited patiently, hoping the police would give up the search without discovering Jayseeka and soon leave.

Vincent looked in on his wife and daughter, then left, without them even knowing he had done so. Vincent knew the Pat Riely vendetta would take a while.

James Haggerty, the guard, was sitting comfortably in a deck chair, approximately five feet from the side of the pool, when one of the search team came through the side door, which led into the drawing room. Jim had had sense enough to remove his weapon, and had stashed it in the drawing room gun safe. The boss had told him not to show it anyway, and he didn't want to go through the long hassle of explaining his permit to carry it.

The officer searched the shower room and dry sauna, then walked over to Jim, who was lounging in the deck chair, drink in hand, like a guest, rather than an employee. Pointing out the trash in the bottom deep end corner of the pool, the officer remarked that the pool cleaner was falling down on the job, and went on to investigate some other area of the large house.

Mr. Henry entered the pool area just as the officer was leaving. Walking over to Jim, absolutely amazed that he was not only sitting down, but also lounging on the job, remarked, "Where the hell is the alien, Jim?"

"In the pool, sir," came the response.

Vincent quickly scanned the pool, then redirected his focus on the guard. "Wha-where in the H...?"

Mr. Henry's question was cut short, as at that moment, a confounded Captain Riely strolled into the pool area as if he owned the place.

"I would like you to answer a few questions, Mr. Henry!" the officer stated acidly.

Mr. Henry suggested they go to the booth in the kitchen where they could get something to drink and sit comfortably across from each other. In reality, he wanted to get Riely far away from that area of the house where the being might be hidden.

Vincent left the pool area, thinking for all the world that the guard had lost his mind. He had seen nothing in the pool, except for the fact that it needed a good cleaning.

The investigation dragged on for six hours.  In the kitchen Captain Riely asked questions, and if Vincent felt his position could be compromised, he simply give Riely a blank, uncomprehending look and shrug.

Vincent Henry was not a man to abuse power, but enough was enough.  Just as he was about to make a personal call to the Attorney General's office in Washington (he had met this powerful man at several Washington functions, admired him, and had even contributed to his political aspirations), Danny Sarte strolled into the kitchen with Vincent's two good friends in tow.

A bit bedraggled from the impromptu trip, they both realized that their good friend was in some kind of trouble, and were happy that they had readily responded.  Smiling and patting each other on the back while shaking hands, it was a happy reunion.  As they turned to be introduced to Captain Riely, the officer simply turned his back and walked away.

"What kind of a shitty attitude is *that?*"  A sudden look of concern appeared in Bill Faraday's eyes.  "You didn't accidentally kill somebody, did ya Vincent?" he joked, partly serious.

"He thinks I'm harboring aliens," replied Vincent.

"What kind of bullshit is this?" responded Bill.  "I handled the immigration paperwork for Gwenia-San and his wife personally.  Everything was perfectly legal."

"Not that kind of alien," replied Vincent.

"Oh!  You mean," as he pointed upward, "*that* kind of alien?"

The two friends laughed loudly, Vincent smiled, and Bill took off after Captain Riely like a Sidewinder missile.

Faraday found Riely in the front area of the Manor, about to give further orders for his men to search the grounds.

"Pull 'em off *now!*" demanded Bill Faraday.

"Who the fuck are you?" responded Riely.

"Oh, pardon my rudeness. Let me introduce myself." replied Colonel Faraday, as he flipped open his identification wallet.

The color quickly drained from Pat Riely's face, as he fully comprehended the grave situation in which he now found himself.

"You can't just..." began the officer.

"I can and I am!" responded Colonel Faraday, lifting the cellular phone from his side. "Now as to you and your men, I don't want to see anything other than assholes and elbows! Furthermore, if you and your people are not off this property in ten minutes, I'm calling in the local National Guard unit, and they will throw you off! Do you get my drift, Officer Riely?" hissed Faraday.

He then gave Riely a look, which indicated far more than casual dislike. "Now, vacate these Manor grounds within ten minutes or I will personally see to it that you and every last one of your men are civilians before 10 tomorrow morning! Do I make myself clear, Officer Riely?"

The now nonplused Riely hurried away like a whipped dog, beating the proposed deadline by one minute and twenty seconds.

When Colonel Faraday returned to the kitchen, he noticed that Dr. Hauss was quizzically looking at his friend. As of yet Vincent had not let the cat out of the bag. He wanted them both together, not wanting to repeat himself concerning this most disquieting dilemma.

As Vincent Henry began to recapitulate the astounding events of the day, Bill and David were a bit chagrined. These were dedicated men with deadlines to meet, having little time for even well done pranks with dear old friends; college days were over.

When Roxanne and Elizabeth entered the kitchen with distinct wonderment on their faces and amazement in their voices, the two newly arrived guests began to believe that someone had dumped lysergic acid into the water supply of the Manor, and that the whole damned place had gone delusional.

By the time Vincent had gotten around to offering his two friends the opportunity to see for themselves (if the guard had not lost track of the thing) Colonel Faraday was rapidly becoming pissed. To think that some vindictive son-of-a-bitch would be brazen enough to drug the entire Vincent Henry household. Meanwhile, Professor Hauss was thinking that, just perhaps, he might be entering the Twilight Zone, somewhere over the rainbow.

As the fivesome walked through the drawing room, and out into the pool area, they found the guard, intently looking off into the swimming pool. He turned quickly about just as Vincent, family and friends, stepped through the doorway.

"Where is the alien, Mr. Haggerty?" asked Vincent."

"It's in the pool. But I think it's dead by now, sir. It never came up for air. I'm really sorry; I don't know what I could possible have done. It just dove into the pool and disappeared!" explained the guard, a hint of despair in his voice.

"Oh, brother," thought Bill Faraday. He was now becoming deeply concerned for the physical and emotional health of the Henry household. Reaching for his cellular to call in a medical team, his body stiffened, as up out of the clear blue water, with a splash and a splat, came the alien. Landing butt down on the side of the pool, feet in the water, It slowly turned its head to face the startled spectators.

The little alien gazed upon them, now with emerald green eyes; its body had become a shimmering aquamarine blue, and except for various internal organs and its eyes, was totally translucent.

"Hi!" It said, in a sweet small voice.

Colonel Faraday dropped his cell-phone; Professor Hauss had seen the signpost up ahead, and knew he was crossing over.

---

Good people are not aware of their goodness,
Therefore they are good.
Foolishly others try to be good,
And often become confused.

(Lao Tsu, 6th Century B.C.)

---

Humanity on planet earth,
The cruelest of animals,
This cruelty goes unrealized by most.

(Roxanne Henry 33 A.J.)

---

The small alien had gotten up from the side of the pool and now stood smiling, gazing slowly at each member of the spellbound audience.

Roxanne, stepping away from the group, walked quickly over to one of the poolside cabinets, and removing a large fluffy towel brought it to Jayseeka, putting it about her shoulders.

None of the adults moved or spoke.

"Thank you, Roxanne," came forth the small sweet alien voice.

Roxanne had been the only member of the group to become mobile. The creature's reappearance had riveted the adult audience in place, as they continued to stare, transfixed in awe and wonderment at the miniature strangeness before them. And then once more, amazement following amazement, this strangest of guests, within a minute, changed back to the rich gold color it seemed to find most favorable.

Vincent was either getting numbed, or accustomed, to the benign antics of his unconventional little guest. As he walked toward the drawing room he knew that all would follow. The alien certainly wasn't going anywhere; it was on a mission of which the Henry family was obviously a part.

Roxanne brought up the rear, towel-drying her small friend along the way, as the others funneled into the drawing room. All except Vincent would look back from time to time, still silently amazed.

Vincent selected a large oak table and Roxanne once more brought over the encyclopedias to give her friend a boost. Mr. Henry now looked at the alien through more accustomed eyes. His brain seemed to be taking a small, unintentional rest, as he noticed that the perfectly formed lips of his diminutive guest were a lighter rose gold, which fittingly contrasted with the deep gold color of the rest of her body.

All seated themselves about the table, except Jim the guard who took up his vigil just outside in the pool area.

"Jayseeka," began Vincent, "I would like to introduce you to Bill and David, two of my very best friends."

"I am most honored to meet Colonel Faraday and Professor Hauss," replied the alien.

Vincent realized that once more minds had been read; he had never used his two friends' titles except at social functions.

Both the Colonel and Professor found their voices simultaneously. Vincent was bombarded with tactical and biological questions for which he had no answers. Standing up, Vincent put his hands up, palms outward, in front of his chest, motioning for his friends to get control of their emotions.

As the commotion suddenly stopped, Bill and David's eyes became fixed on the alien.

"This is what I'm going to do," stated Vincent "I'm going to turn these questions over to Jayseeka. This is a most intelligent being who can fully explain them. I know little more than you guys do at this point."

"Please," continued Vincent, "let's be orderly. One of you may ask a question, and when it is answered, then the other may ask his question, and so on, until some plateau of understanding is reached."

Professor Hauss pulled a small tape-recorder out of his pocket only to find the batteries had gone dead. He quickly got up, following Vincent and the Colonel over to drawers wherein pencil and note pads were to be found; the three quickly returned to the table.

With as much dignity and reserve as possible, given the circumstances, each of the two friends motioned simultaneously for the other to begin; then both turned to the alien and began once more to speak at the same time.

This time it was the alien who motioned for silence. "I have a very good idea," said Jayseeka. "I will discourse for a while on items of importance concerning my visitation, how I got here and so on. I know all of you will have many other questions to ask me. Colonel Faraday and Professor Hauss will have technical questions according to their fields of expertise, and I will answer them in good time. I'm not going anywhere immediately; as most of you have rightfully assumed by now, I have come here with a purpose.

"Please accept my earnest apology for any and all disruption my presence here has caused. I believe you all will soon realize my Earthly objective is purely benevolent. It's getting late now; therefore, after I have finished my dissertation, it would most likely be best for all to eat the evening meal, and retire. We can begin again in the morning at an appropriate time; eventually all things concerning my presence here on Earth will be known."

The alien, in a kindly manner, had taken control, and though this was a little disturbing to Vincent, he was aware that "she" had all the answers. With mild concern, Vincent reasoned that Jayseeka's mind-reading capabilities left little other alternative anyway. If he was going to learn, he was going to have to sit quietly and listen, regardless of his emotional concerns.

The audience listened intently as this golden being from a distant world, with its sweet, near hypnotic voice, began to teach.

"My world," began Jayseeka, "is a watery world much like your own, located approximately 57,000 light years from your sun within this galaxy. Please realize that the words and labels I am using, and the English language I am now speaking, we use only in our studies of your world. I can speak fluently every language currently in use on your planet, and many others you call 'dead languages' which were discontinued eons ago.

"We call ourselves 'A-qua-tus' and strangely enough 'aqua' means 'water' on your planet. We Aquatus found this an irony because our species is more of the water than of the land. On earth, many of your life forms evolved from the water onto the land, and then for reasons speculative, advantage of greater body size, more abundant food, etc., they returned to the sea, but they could not regenerate gills. So they and their descendants remained air breathers, like the great whales, porpoises and other cetaceans.

"Apparently our ancestors evolved out of the water, but returned sooner than Earth's water-going mammals, to the watery abodes of our planet. We surmise this because only an eighth of our planet is landmass, with massive amounts of ice locked in our Polar Regions. Currently we live equally in the water and on the land; evolution has blessed us with both gills and lungs, for as you can well calculate, even the slightest warming trend on our planet, would find us totally in the water."

Jayseeka stopped her dissertation long enough to give all one of her prettiest smiles, and when all responded with a smile in return, she continued.

"We Aquatus have been visiting your planet for over ten thousand of your Earth years; we have had no reason until recently to make ourselves apparent. Immensely have we enjoyed your beautiful waters and small outcroppings of land in your tropical regions.

"There were even times when various of your whaling vessels found us by chance, sunbathing on the rocks and beaches. They called us 'mermaids,' for they could only observe us at great distances, as we immediately took to the water upon their arrival in our vicinity. We found it humorous how your companion-starved sailors often depicted us in their literature.

"We have visited Earth, much the same as you enjoy your visitations to other countries. Our interests lie mostly in the realm of the many amazing and diversified life forms and their evolution upon your planet."

Stopping once more, the alien flashed a knowing smile at Professor Hauss before continuing.

"These studies are our 'good times' and back on our planet the research is awaited with great anticipation by those who are physically unable to go through the preparation or spend the years of time to travel that hyper-space requires.

"Tomorrow I will explain how our species is able to travel in hyper-space to reach any number of solar systems. I will share ways in which we Aquatus can be of service to this planet, and also how we happened to choose this particular time and location to make ourselves known to you. Now the hour approaches 10 p.m., and though I'm well aware you wish to know much more, you will be refreshed in the morning and better able to assimilate what I will teach you. Therefore let us set a time, say 10 a.m.? For now I suggest we eat and retire."

Jayseeka politely looked for approval from Vincent Henry, who, with a nod of his head, gave his consent.

"Mr. Henry," said Jayseeka, now walking beside him on the way into the kitchen, "I know you wish to post a guard at my door for the evening, and that's okay; but would you please be kind enough to give the job to Mr. James Haggerty? I feel safest with him. Also, I perceive that you are doing this for my protection, and not because you feel I might escape."

Vincent had to smile sheepishly, for he realized that Jayseeka had become aware of his growing trust and admiration.

After a hastily prepared informal meal (Gwenia-San was now in charge)--quick steaks and salads for Vincent's wife, Vincent, his daughter and two friends, and more sushi for Jayseeka--all were ready to retire.

Vincent's friends were beside themselves with unanswered questions, but they were guests and they were very tired. In fact they were suddenly incredibly weary, which they attributed to their hasty journey, coupled with the emotional stress of dealing with a crowning mystery. Greatly fatigued, Colonel Faraday and Professor Hauss wanted to inquire, not retire; however, they were compelled to reason that when in Rome...

Jayseeka's closing words, delivered with beautiful smiles and melodic voice, were "I know you will all sleep well, and please do not concern yourselves with undue imaginings, as I have come to visit your planet with only the very best of intentions." Indeed the petite form and exquisite beauty of this star child conveyed nothing other than absolute amity.

The maids showed Jayseeka, the Colonel and the Professor to the guestrooms, and all retired for the evening, utterly exhausted from a most intriguing and eventful day.

## Chapter Seven

Approach the universe with insight,
And evil will have no power over you.
Although evil is powerful,
With insight you can direct its power away from others.

*(Lao Tsu, 6th Century B.C.)*

Professor Hauss, Colonel Faraday, and the Henrys, except for Roxanne, awoke curiously at approximately the same time, at or about eight the next morning. All were totally refreshed, each thinking that it was the best night's sleep they had ever had. As they bustled to complete their morning baths and preparations, each wondered if the events of the previous day had not perhaps been some grandiose dream.

The inquisitive looks on the faces of the men, as they greeted each other with a simple "Morning" in the hallway, confirmed the reality of yesterday. Each became fully cognizant that they were in for the intellectual and emotional ride of their lives.

As they hastened down the grand staircase, the smell of coffee and cooking food reached them. Upon entering the kitchen the three men looked quickly about, then at each other.

Gwenia-San turned from the stove, where preparation of the morning meal had begun, just as Elizabeth Henry walked up behind Vincent and his two friends.

"Roxanne and Jayseeka are in the pool for a morning swim," volunteered the little cook, which alleviated any major concern for the whereabouts and safety of two.

Elizabeth stayed in the kitchen to assist with the food preparation, as the three men, with as much dignity and control as they could muster, strode rapidly off to the pool area.

Seldom had Vincent seen his daughter in such high spirits, as she and her small friend frolicked happily in the pool. Upon seeing her father and his friends looking on with extreme interest and some amusement, Roxanne effortlessly backstroked to the shallow end of the pool. Jayseeka glided beside her, in perfect unison two feet beneath the surface. Upon reaching their destination, Jayseeka started off on another underwater lap.

Roxanne stood up, excitedly exclaiming, "Daddy, oh, Daddy! Look what Jayseeka has taught me!" whereupon she slipped beneath the water's surface. Kicking legs and feet in unison while undulating her body, arms at her sides, she amazed the three onlookers with a swimming ability that would have made a manatee proud.

Roxanne swam smoothly, with grace and speed, to the far end of the pool and back, without taking a breath, without breaking the surface. Jayseeka fell into rhythm with Roxanne in the last half of her lap, and the two aquanauts broke the water together at the shallow end of the pool. Teacher and student smiled their appreciation as the onlookers applauded.

There was fruit, bacon, breakfast steaks and eggs, sourdough toast, marmalade, coffee and milk, for the Henrys and their friends, sushi for Jayseeka. In the time it took for the brunch to be consumed, each of the domestics in the household stopped by the kitchen, at one time or another, to view the strange guest. Vincent was appreciative to all for their loyalty, assuring them individually that he sincerely felt that no one was in any danger.

Jayseeka smiled warmly as Vincent spoke, and each of the help returned her smile, some with slight apprehension. All seemed to feel safe enough; they believed in the sterling character of their employer.

It was now ten thirty; all knew there would be no more eating before dinner, and they had eaten a hearty meal. The hunger for knowledge now engulfed them as they moved out onto the patio. It was a beautiful and mild sunny day. The butler and a maid helped as they moved the comfortable furniture about so all could see each other well and hear the words of the small strange guest.

Roxanne ran to get a stack of towels with which to bring her miniature friend to the proper elevation.

"Jayseeka, I would like to start off this discussion by asking what you meant when you said, 'I guess we were wrong,' yesterday, when you felt your life was threatened by the guard," politely inquired Elizabeth Henry.

"This is not a question quickly answered," replied Jayseeka, "but if you will pay close attention to what I am going to tell all of you now, you will find the answer to that and other questions soon.

"As I explained before, we Aquatus have been visiting your planet for over ten thousand of your Earth years. I know that what I am about to say next will cause concern, especially to Colonel Faraday who is of a military mind. We have now, and have had for the last seventy-five hundred Earth years, orbital monitoring satellites observing your Earth. The observation of life-bearing planets, yours included, has been our education and entertainment for quite some time."

Colonel William Faraday was now sitting bolt upright in his chair. The color had left his face as he realized the strategic military importance of what the alien had just said.

Sensing Faraday's electrified concern, Jayseeka now spoke directly to the Colonel upon continuing. "Let me put all your minds at ease when I say that conquest has never been the Aquatus' desire in these latter times," continued Jayseeka. "We are a species that wishes only to observe and experience the wonders of various planets as they go through their natural evolutionary procedures common throughout the cosmos, much in the same manner as your naturalists and scientists observe the flora and fauna in your own various wilderness preservation areas. We are greatly saddened, as much as yourselves, when various animal species must meet the fate of extinction before their time."

Professor Hauss was definitely developing a growing liking and admiration for this pint-sized alien genius.

Jayseeka still focused her attention on Colonel Faraday, for she was well aware of his perplexity as she read his thoughts and observed his body language; he was still quite upset.

"Dear Colonel Faraday, would you not presume that if we Aquatus have been visiting your planet for over ten thousand of your Earth years, that we had the technological capability to conquer you long ago?

"What if you were to go back in history a mere two hundred years, with an arsenal of your current weaponry, could not you and a hundred men become rulers of your world? No question. No contest. Most likely, after several displays of superiority, fear alone would have brought the major powers of earth humbly to their knees.

"Still unsettled, Colonel Faraday? Yes, I perceive that you are," continued the alien. "You are wondering how we can have satellites observing you, when your current technology has not given any indication of their presence? I will ask you how ungainly and space-consuming were your computers and transmission-reception devices only 70 years ago? We have approximately eighty observatory satellites orbiting earth, many no larger than the tape-recorder Dr. Hauss has in his pocket. They are out from your planet beyond your lunar orbit, and can observe every square foot of your planet's surface, even to the deepest depths of your oceans."

The Colonel still didn't like what he was hearing, for if the alien was lying, it was obviously a bluff to simplify conquest. If it was telling the truth, Earth could be conquered on an Aquatus whim, for there could be little contest against such incredibly advanced technology.

"Please, Colonel Faraday," the alien's normally sweet melodious voice containing a note of sadness, "I hope you will come to trust me as much as I trust in the good judgment of all of you here today. I will inform you further so that all of you may realize that my own confidence in each of you is not impromptu."

It was a slow, lengthy, albeit magnificent process. The alien demonstrated its fantastic memory, and Aquatus technology, by giving a most intimately detailed history of the lives of its listeners. The group was further amazed when Jayseeka continued the historical narration to include fathers, mothers, and even grandparents of the Henrys, Faradays and Hausses. As all listened intently; Jayseeka, who amazingly knew of the most intimate details of their lives, took great care to protect the modesty of her audience. She highlighted only those historical events which she claimed were the reasons why the Aquatus had selected the Henrys and friends as the ones chosen to deliver their communiqué to planet Earth.

It had been a monumental chore on the part of the Aquatus. "You had fifty of your species to make a study of our families?" responded Dr. Hauss.

"Yes," replied Jayseeka. "However, the chore was a labor of devotion. We thrilled at the success of Grandfather Henry as he aided the poverty-stricken peoples in third world countries by providing them with the equipment, water pumps and seed to grow their own food. His motto was, 'give a family a bag of rice, and you feed them for a week; give them the tools and teach them to farm, you feed them for life.' He saw to the job himself, not trusting charitable institutions. We cried when on his deathbed he handed the chore over to your father, who in turn passed the gauntlet on to you, Vincent, and you have kept up the good work.

"We laughed at the college antics of you three boys, and cried with young David Hauss when he learned his Aunt Jan had been murdered in her cabin near Karisoke, in Rwanda, as she studied, and tried to protect, the last of the great Mountain Gorillas there.

"You, Colonel Faraday, with your intense desire to treat people as individuals, judging them according to their works, regardless of their race, creed, or national origin. You are steadfastly true to your country and its laws, for which you would make the ultimate sacrifice, should you be honorably called upon to do so.

"Elizabeth and Roxanne, how many small, injured and abandoned animals have you saved, on your own or through the shelter in town which you support?

"My arrival here on Earth was well planned," continued Jayseeka, "and had been in the works for decades. It was my responsibility to guide the study team and choose the proper time for my arrival here on planet Earth, here at Vincent Henry Manor."

"Therefore your statement, 'I guess we were wrong,' when at the brink of death yesterday," exclaimed Elizabeth Henry.

"Exactly," responded Jayseeka. "I felt perhaps that we had miscalculated the human emotional factor. Such an error was improbable, but possible.

"Also, I apologize for the predictability capabilities of my staff, as humans are generally offended to find that their future is often readily predictable due to their past activities. We were quite well assured beforehand, Vincent, that your lovely daughter Roxanne would invite me into your home for a visit, and that you would call in your friends, Colonel Faraday and Professor Hauss, prior to making any concrete decisions regarding my appearance in your home.

"I sense that all here, excepting Roxanne, have found it a bit disconcerting that we Aquatus have so accurately used the historical events of your lives to predict what would happen at humans' first contact with myself. However, opportunity can often be lost in the final hour; even when we thought the time was perfect, it still took Roxanne three weeks to visit the area of the lake.

"It would have been dangerous indeed should I have attempted contact with an agent of your government, in any other manner than I have been able to do with Colonel Faraday. Quite possibly I would have found myself dissected, and in various specimen jars under intense study, before I could have made the Aquatus intentions known. Then the whole blueprint would have come to naught. The same would have held true had fear overcome reason with the guard in the drawing room; and I most sincerely believe, my friends, that if we are not successful from this moment onward, grave is the horror and suffering that will transpire in the next hundred years. Not from us Aquatus, for conquest is not our way, but from Humankind's interaction with itself, and its environment." As Jayseeka spoke these prophetic words, the smile left her lips.

The humans contemplated deeply what they had heard. The patio session ended with its byproduct being even more unanswered questions, the main one being, just what was the Aquatus mission here on planet Earth?

Jayseeka seemed to want to take things in an orderly fashion, and in truth all she had to say so far had been of great interest to her admirers. Even the guard off to the corner of the patio within earshot of the group seemed spellbound by the body language, voice, personality, and beauty of little Jayseeka.

In spite of himself, Colonel Faraday also found himself liking the Alien; but he also loved his country, friends and family, and these things he would not jeopardize. Fear of the capabilities of such intelligence, and the magnitude of Aquatus technology, weighed far too heavily at the other end of the scale. The man of state knew that soon he must notify the intelligence community of the activities at Vincent Henry Manor.

Even though Vincent and friends felt that the patio session should have continued much longer, Jayseeka had assured them that all their questions would soon be answered. She then suggested it would be best to defer them until tomorrow, when all once more would be fresh and receptive.

As Vincent rose from his chair he asked that all meet in the main dining hall for the evening meal, and that afterwards he, David and Bill would confer in the study on information they had acquired so far. Vincent wanted to know more; in fact all were duly intoxicated with the idea of learning as much as humanly possible from the little alien, but it was beneath Vincent Henry's dignity to insist on further discussions, considering that it was now 8 p.m.

All their notebooks had been generously filled; stomachs were on empty, and bladders about to burst. All smiled at Jayseeka, and she smiled radiantly at each, as they adjourned from the patio.

Gwenia-San had once again prepared exotic foods from the Orient. His wife Trang had been waiting by the patio doors for the better part of an hour for the meeting to conclude. As family and friends arose from the table in the patio (Jayseeka had been accepted, and was now considered friendly by most), Trang hurried into the kitchen to begin the stir-fry of vegetables with chicken, beef, or pork, whichever each preferred. Sushi of yellowtail, tuna, sea cucumber and fish eggs had been prepared once more for Jayseeka. Trang had made a three-layer gelatin desert, and this was the only other type of food the little alien would eat. And eat she did - - three servings, with obvious relish, much to the delight of the cook's wife.

Trang enjoyed being of service to Jayseeka, and the alien seemed to take pleasure in her fussing about during the meal. Perhaps it was because of Trang's size. Shorter than her husband, she was an even four feet, six inches in height. Vincent picked up on this immediately and appointed Trang to look after Jayseeka's every need. Trang and the alien smiled at each other with delight.

All complimented the cook and his wife on the delightful meal as they adjourned. Trang took Jayseeka, Roxanne and Elizabeth Henry happily off into the drawing room, to teach them the fine art of tea service, Nippon style. Vincent, David and Bill retired to the Manor's study, where they would find the Encyclopedia Britannica and various other helpful reference books as they reviewed their notes from the patio session.

**********

"Are you trying to tell me that she's a goddamned *squid?*" intensely responded Vincent.

Professor Hauss was a bit taken aback at his friend's reaction to his observations, aware now that Vincent had developed a kindly bond with his small alien guest and would brook no demeaning comments.

"Makes sense to me," replied the Colonel. "Did ya see the way she got after that raw fish this evening?"

Drawing a heated glare from Vincent, Bill decided this was a wrong choice of words.

"I eat sushi," responded Vincent, "in fact I love the damn stuff! Does that make me a squid?"

"Now wait a minute, you guys," interjected the Professor, "let's try to be as rational as we can. Just take a look at what has gone down here so far. It admits coming from a world of mostly water. I say 'It' because we have not made a final determination as to whether it is male or female, or both male and female, which does occur in some of Earth's life forms, as difficult as you gentlemen may find this to believe. It also admits to having gills as well as lungs. Many of Earth's animals have gills in their early development, but lose the gills upon becoming an adult, for instance tadpoles and frogs. Then there is the proverbial mud-slapping lungfish down in..."

"Okay, okay!" responded Vincent, "let's cut to the chase here, David. I'm sure you have more substantial criteria developed by now."

"Well, it's a matter of fact, I do." came the professor's educated reply. "Now, I'm not proposing that the alien evolved from our earthly life forms; what I am saying is that perhaps the 'Aquatus' evolved from life forms analogous to our Phylum Mollusca, which encompasses squids and octopus. As you both well know, marine biology is my specialty; every day for me is a day of study. I have several large aquariums in my lab with a number of tropical and local marine animals in residence.

"I say, 'in residence,' because I care for them to the degree that when I am finished studying them, I make every effort to return them to their natural habitat. I almost flunked my first biology class because I couldn't bring myself to inject a live frog with dye. The intent was then to cut his stomach open so the class could view its circulatory system as it carried the dye into the various organs of its body..."

Colonel Faraday became agitated, almost spilling his brandy. "Please, David! Please get down to the nitty gritty on the now of things; time is most certainly of the essence," interjected Faraday. "I'm sure you are both aware that what we are dealing with here cannot remain this household's private secret for much longer. I am duty bound to notify the intelligence community and heads of state soon. It's a matter of national security. Hell, the whole of mankind could be poised for annihilation as we speak!"

Fixing the Colonel with a half-possible glint in his eye, the Professor continued with his dissertation.

"I have currently, in one of my aquariums, a female octopus which I have named 'Shela,' and I've been conducting experiments with this creature with the most fascinating results. One experiment in particular intrigues me. I withhold food until I am assured that she is hungry, and how do I know this? The darned animal turns from a mundane grayish-brown to a deep red!

"She becomes angry only at me, when I enter the lab, as she must know me as her captor and feeder. Possibly because I am the only one providing her with food. When I see the color red, I take a regular Mason jar, fill it with water, and place the food therein and screw on the cap. I am closely observed by this denizen of the deep during the procedure.

"She then swims to the area of the aquarium where she reaches upward, with three of her eight tentacles, as I open the small door which gives me access to her watery abode. Removing the jar from my hand, she takes it down under a rocky shelf I have provided for her, unscrews the jar lid, and gets her meal.

"Now let's keep in mind that Shela's brain is considerably smaller than a small marble, and she can most amazingly solve problems. Furthermore, if I am still in the lab after she finishes her meal, then I am observed with what I believe to be affection, as the creature stays closest to the side of the glass where I might be observed continuously, all the while I remain in the lab."

"Did you ever kiss the goddamn thing?" exclaimed the Colonel.

The Professor threw a wounded glance at Faraday.

"Now listen, Bill," replied Vincent, "let's not be demeaning to each other here. We wanted educated knowledge on the nature of the alien and that's exactly what we are getting. I for one am delighted that David is here. Remember this is certainly not our field of expertise."

Faraday was obliged to nod slowly in agreement.

"Can you give us an educated guess on how Jayseeka is able to produce those spectacular body colors, and why she does it, David?" asked Vincent.

"Well, as I was explaining before, my little guest back at the lab is not only quite intelligent, but quite adept at the changing of colors in an instant, depending on its moods or concerns. White is fear, red is anger, pale blue seems to be contentment, as this seems to be the hunger-appeased or affection mode. And as to other colors? This depends on the natural color of the rocks and sand that are contained in her aquarium. She has been able to assume any and all colors of protective covering by matching perfectly any color of sand or rock that I, from time to time, have placed in her aquarium.

"However, I'm absolutely intrigued by the fantastically vivid colors that Jayseeka exhibits. I can show you any number of bright fluorescent, beautiful colors found on the various tropical fishes of our southern coral reefs. But that aquamarine translucent blue we witnessed at pool-side yesterday seemed impossible, until I remembered a trip some associate professors and I took into the waters just off Grand Cayman Island in the Caribbean.

"Above was the boat where a lookout was doing shark patrol; my associates and I were below in the crystal clear waters, with our slurp guns, gathering specimens from the reef. It was the perfect day for this type of activity; the waters were calm, the sun was bright, and the white coral sand beneath us reflected the sun's rays into the crevices of the reef.

"As we were flippering about in this fluid paradise, I was suddenly overcome with the eeriest of feelings, as if I was being stalked. This, coupled with a pain in my ribs, as my partner poked me with his slurp gun startled me so much that I almost spit out the regulator to my air supply. Now believing that there were sharks in the water near us, I turned to look at my partner, seeing first his transparent plastic slurp-gun with a tiny gold and black fish prisoner therein. Then my partner's face swung into view; he looked at me and then away towards the surface in unblinking wide-eyed wonderment. The beauty of the reef, the clarity of the water, and now this.

"I felt as though I was in a dream world, for there near the surface, and approximately eight feet off to my right, I gazed upon a multitude of eyes! As they gazed upon me in return, each seemed perfectly spaced, about two feet each from the another, all seeming to have small dark bags in tow.

"As my fearless associate began to swim upward into the midst of this phenomenon, I gained courage and followed. Squid! There must have been hundreds of them, their translucent bodies blending perfectly with the surrounding waters. The only parts of them truly visible had been their eyes and digestive organs. The eyes because of being backed by the retina, and the various intestines due to the food which was therein."

Vincent smiled in admiration at his much-educated friend and biological detective. "So that explains how Jayseeka was able to hide in plain sight, in the pool yesterday. What I thought was trash in the corner of the pool was her visible internal organs!" exclaimed Vincent.

A few minutes of silence ensued as the men contemplated the biological wonders of the unearthly visitor. Then, finishing their brandies, each said "good night" and retired for the evening. The mental gymnastics of the day were now taking their toll, and all were extremely tired.

## Chapter Eight

Colonel Faraday awoke the next morning at eight o'clock sharp. No one had awakened him; he had set no alarm clock. He simply suddenly became wide-awake, feeling unusually well rested. Sitting straight up in bed, he had startled himself with the thought that perhaps last night's incredible fatigue, the sound night's sleep and punctual awakening might be more than coincidental. He knew himself well, and could not remember ever sleeping soundly in the middle of a crisis.

This alien at Vincent Henry Manor definitely posed a dilemma which could lead to a crisis of Earth-shaking proportions. As the man of state hastened through his bath, foremost in his mind was the question, "Am I being systematically drugged, and if so, why?"

The three men joined up simultaneously in the hall; none had been called, none had alarms clocks in their rooms. Words were few and unnecessary as each had independently come to the same conclusion: Mysteriously more than coincidence was at work in the Manor.

Sliced warm bagels with cream cheese, diced onions and lox, French toast covered with sliced fresh strawberries and lightly sprinkled with powdered sugar; ham and eggs, milk and coffee, was the breakfast fare; sushi for Jayseeka.

As the Colonel witnessed Trang slipping Jayseeka a gelatin dessert for breakfast ("On top of sushi?" he thought), he decided to ask the question which had been troubling him since he awoke.

"Jayseeka," inquired Faraday, gaining the little alien's attention, "Vincent, David and I have been sleeping very soundly and awakening timely the last two days and nights. We talked about this on the way to breakfast this morning. Can you shed any light on this strange coincidental phenomenon?"

"You need not disturb yourself with this, my dear Colonel. We all slept well, did we not?" As she glanced smilingly about the table, all nodded in the affirmative. "Some of us Aquatus have the gift of being able to telepathically put the mind at ease and we give this gift, as a small favor, when we are guests in the homes of our friends and families on my home world. Have I done something in bad taste?"

Colonel Faraday was very concerned about the fantastic abilities possessed by the little alien. He tried to avoid showing his discomfort and anxiety at being intellectually and emotionally manipulated. Faraday went directly on to say, "I suppose that you are aware that I am duty bound to contact our Heads of State, as well as the intelligence community, concerning yourself and the occurrences here at the Manor?"

"Absolutely," replied the little alien, apparently not the least bit concerned by Faraday's statement, "and we will discuss the ramifications concerning your obligation soon."

They wrapped up breakfast after an hour, and once more adjourned to the patio. There, with notebooks ready, they prepared to be further amazed by this ever-gracious, coyly smiling other-worldly guest.

"Hydraulics!" exclaimed Dr. Hauss, having watched Jayseeka's fingers elongate as she picked up the glass of iced tea the butler had brought.

"That is very astute of you, Professor," replied the alien.

"Hydraulics?" asked Faraday.

"When we Aquatus first evolved onto the land, the ability to raise ourselves upright was of tremendous evolutionary advantage," began Jayseeka. "The fossil record of the Australopithecines, Humankind's ancestors, indicates that they also did very well from the upright position. How very grateful you should be to those creatures at the dawn of Humanity, and their ancestors as well, who descended from their aerial abode in the trees. Fantastic survival became their birthright. Being able to stand upright gives a species the ability to manipulate tools and objects with the free appendages, a definite evolutionary plus. Neither your species nor ours could have developed our technology without this ability.

"The Aquatus ancestry was derived without bones to support our frames, but we did have an internal hydraulic propulsion system that aided us greatly in the water. Gradually we evolved, over the eons of time, to where we could close off this internal system, originally used for propulsion, and channel it so as to support our bodies in the upright position."

Jayseeka then looked at her young friend Roxanne and smilingly explained, "Hydraulics is the principle of positive and negative fluid pressures that the Human species currently uses to mechanically move its heavy battleship guns about, as well as many other uses, such as being able to touch a small brake pedal on a car with the foot, hence stopping that heavy machine with a minimal amount of effort."

Professor Hauss was intrigued with this discovery, writing the information diligently in his notebook.

"What is the technology used to get from your planet to other solar systems and their planets thousands of light years away?" asked Faraday.

"All of your television programs are received by us within a year of your viewing them here," explained Jayseeka, "via our earth orbital satellites which I described yesterday. We were amazed that many of your science fiction movies revolved around an ability to fold time or space. I suppose that, for lack of better terminology, I can use unfolding to describe the process that we use for interstellar travel. We also use a mild but similar process, to transmit information back from many planets to our own for investigative purposes.

"We are always most interested in your science fiction programs, as here on Earth," continued Jayseeka. "It is the same as on our planet; yesterday's fiction often becomes tomorrow's reality.

"It is possible, through your most modern electron microscope technology, to view the components of certain types of matter, which you call molecules. If you were to have greater technology, you would be able to clearly see the atoms that make up the molecules. Further breakdown would allow you to observe the electrons, protons and neutrons that make up the atoms. Finally, the last step would make you aware of the pure energy strands that wrap about themselves, to form the infinitesimally small particles of which the electrons, protons, neutrons, quarks and various subatomic particles are composed.

"Now, then! If you were to take this pure energy, unravel it, projecting it out the back of a interstellar craft, you would gain a degree of thrust which could propel your craft at a speed very close to that of light, approximately six trillion miles per Earth year. Taking into consideration the foregoing explanation we now come to the final analysis; this pure energy I have discussed, when unwrapped, is not simply elongated strands, but wavelike or, if you choose, folded.

"For example, if you were able to take a length of this pure energy, enhance its diameter to the size of a pencil, it would easily stretch from Richmond, Virginia, to San Francisco, California, in most cases.  However, its sideways wavy motions would then be spaced approximately only six inches apart, and its sideways wavy motion would extend to the north into Canada and to the south into Mexico.

"Now!  What do you suppose would happen to the speed of your interstellar craft if its thrust was not only the pure energy that could move you along at light speed, but unfolded or straightened energy at your discretion?  The obvious effect is a craft that can move through the void at speeds limited only by the integrity of its structure."

"By unfolding energy, rather than by folding space or time!" exclaimed the Professor.  He was enthralled by this magnificent and brilliant concept.  "However," continued the Professor, "it has been speculated, among our scientists, that objects approaching the speed of light become that wave-like energy of which you spoke."

"Very good, Professor," replied Jayseeka, once more taking over the discussion.  "That would be exactly so, except that time is an important aspect of any object's integrity, and time very nearly comes to a standstill at the speed of light and beyond.  I might add that time, rather than being a dimension that penetrates the totality of our spacecrafts at light speeds, is barely able to penetrate the hull of our crafts. We have made great strides in the science of metallurgy and the integrity of our interstellar ships hulls will only allow for time penetration of approximately one picometer for each light speed achieved.

"Actually, the result of the 'fourth dimensional' penetration of our crafts' hulls has a strengthening rather than weakening aspect.  For example water in liquid form has zero rigidity; however, if you reduce its outermost temperature to below zero centigrade you can create a blade of ice, still liquid at its center, which can easily punch through a sheet of snow. This 'rigidity' aspect of our ships' hulls, upon reaching light speed and beyond, allows us to pass through most interstellar debris at high speeds with ease, should we encounter it in our journeys between the stars."

After a long drink of her iced tea, Jayseeka continued with her technical narration. "The sophistication of our on-board equipment allows us to detect any object, of substantial size, which could possibly intersect our path. Of course, interstellar journeys at these incredible speeds must meet but few hindrances; but I can assure you all, that emptiness is in abundance throughout the cosmos. Space travelers, using the methods I have described, have ample time to avoid, slow down, or stop, if needed.

"You may go to the rest room now if you choose, Colonel," spoke the alien.

"It knew! *Damn*, it knows my every thought!" Aware of his vulnerability, Colonel Faraday headed off to the rest room. The last bit of information had been emotionally stirring and created anxiety within him, having an effect on his lower intestines.

Sitting on the toilet, voiding himself of the now fluid contents of his bowels, Colonel Faraday decided that his limit of frustration had been reached. Reaching down, he retrieved his pocket cell-phone. The battery had gone dead, which he thought strange, as he had charged it just yesterday and had not used it since.

Cursing under his breath, he reconsidered notifying his fellow colleagues in the State Department until after the patio session. It seemed that he was suddenly overcome with the realization that the alien was certainly communicating freely, and that he was learning things which could be of tremendous military significance in the future. He did not want to spoil his chance to learn more.

Returning to the patio, Faraday found that Vincent had put the discussions on hold pending his return.

Courteously, Professor Hauss waited until Bill had once more taken his seat; then he asked Jayseeka if she would be kind enough to explain the mechanics used to generate the "unfolding of energy" which allowed the Aquatus interstellar propulsion and communication.

"Now this could be of tremendous significance," thought Faraday.

Jayseeka looked upon him with a slight smile.

"Approximately fifteen thousand of your earth years ago, we Aquatus developed the ability to travel to moons, planets, and asteroids within our solar system. We were never short of basic raw materials on our planet, as our world is half again larger than Earth, and our populations have never exceeded more than eight hundred million.

"It was rare elements we were after, which would allow us to build our increasingly more sophisticated technology. Our most prevalent mining activities were upon nearby asteroids. Upon excavating these special elements, we would then form them into sheets, with a cold weld process we had developed, attach propulsion devices to them and literally float them off these various asteroids. We would then send them to our home planet, floating them down into our atmosphere for a soft landing in shallow water areas.

"We had been doing this for approximately a thousand of your earth years, when we discovered a smallish, extremely heavy asteroid in the outer rim of our system, about one half the size of your moon. Upon exploration, we decided to mine the asteroid, as it was laden with elements tremendously important to us.

"A mere two hundred years later several of our miners were injured severely by what they claimed to be invisible objects; parts of their appendages had been severed. With brighter lighting, and upon closer investigation, we discovered strange crystals embedded in the walls of the mine. These crystals were so pure and condensed that in the original dimness of the mine they refracted only minimal amounts of light, and were almost invisible to us. With brighter lighting we were astounded to find that they would throw a cascade of brilliant and colorful hues throughout the mineshaft.

"Where the crystals were fragmented, the edges were so sharp that one could lean up against them unknowingly, and the flesh could be cut clear through the protective clothing of the workers, without any immediate awareness of damage or pain.

We located forty-eight of these crystals with our detection equipment; however, after blasting them out of the cavern's walls, we then had to dig them out of the mine-shaft floor. Even the smaller ones, approximately only six by eighteen centimeters in size, weighed over one and a quarter metric tons each. And with their very sharp edges, they had embedded themselves almost two meters into the floor of the mine before coming to rest.

"At the beginning of our experiments with these crystals, we surmised that they had come from the interior of a 'dwarf star' which had the power to compress matter to an almost unimaginable density. We also surmised that this dwarf star had been struck by a huge asteroid, or exploded because of some inner nuclear force, flinging these fragments into space; which finally came to rest within the asteroid we were then mining.

"After a thousand years of off-and-on-again experimentation, we discovered the energy unfolding aspects of these crystals. It then took another four hundred years to devise a means to crush a portion of the crystals. Using only infinitesimal bits we set up our communications network; the larger shards we used to drive our interstellar craft. Hence, shortly after this, we were able to begin our voyages to the planets of other nearby stars, and then to planets orbiting more distant stars within the galaxy."

Colonel Faraday had now become eighty percent convinced that confrontation with the Aquatus, should it occur, would be a disaster, but he was only one man privy to information that was clearly beyond his ability to understand fully. He needed a team of intellects to decide on a course of action; and if those intellects made the wrong choices, it could mean slavery, or the annihilation of humanity.

He suddenly became aware that all was quiet, and the conversation had stopped. Faraday looked about the table and all eyes were upon him. He had drifted off into his own realm of thought and had been there for more than eight minutes. He quickly realized why he had now become the center of attention. Looking directly into the glistening amber depths of the alien's eyes, now regarding him intently, he knew that 'It' knew what he had been thinking; his every thought had been an open book.

"Colonel Faraday," spoke Jayseeka, "I know how difficult this must be for you. A creature from another world is suddenly in your midst, with a technology which humans cannot even begin to fathom in their current state of development. You have no earthly idea what can be done, indeed if anything can be, should this meeting of our two worlds lead to direct military confrontation. Please do not take my pleadings with you as a sign of weakness. Had we decided on conquest, humanity would not have come to an end with a bang, but rather with a whimper, leaving all other life forms intact.

"Let me ask you this, Colonel." Jayseeka was now, with the utmost intensity, staring into the bottom-most part of the Colonel's soul; the radiant little smile had left her lips. Her small features now portrayed a sadness that could have broken the heart of a stone Buddha. "Is it the intent of your own species to annihilate your beautiful great whales, or the remainder of the majestic lions and Mountain Gorillas in Africa? How about the deer and fish in your wildlife preserves? No, of course you wouldn't; the general attitude of most humans is to give these creatures a break, protect them if possible for the future enjoyment of their children, and children's children.

"We Aquatus have enjoyed watching your evolution for thousands of years; we wish for it to continue, and we desire also to continue to visit Earth from time to time as our studies here bring us much pleasure. Indeed, my good Colonel, we have no intention of enslaving or harming your species in anyway whatsoever. We are neither cruel, nor are we violent without cause; we have come in peace. It is humanity which must be saved from itself. Humankind has reached a point in its evolution where it has inadvertently set in motion forces which, if left unchecked, could abolish 75 percent of all life on the planet within eighty years; or perhaps destroy Earth's ability to support life altogether. It is beyond doubt that you cannot save yourselves or this planet without our help.

"Even if you were to kill me now, there would be no retaliation by the Aquatus. I would have failed in my mission just as Jan Dossy, upon this planet, failed in hers, and you would only have succeeded in killing the only chance you had to save yourselves, and your planet."

The little Aquatian stopped speaking, reached out with one of her perfectly formed hands and touched the large pitcher of iced tea that had recently been brought to the table. "There is enough energy contained in this beverage before me to destroy all life immediately within an eight hundred mile radius, and, in the process, heave a cloud of micro-dust into the atmosphere. This in turn could block the Sun from warming the Earth for as long as 15 years; few indeed would be the species to survive it.

"We Aquatus learned long ago that the greatest of lies are those that we tell ourselves, and this same wisdom holds true for Humanity as well.  As I speak, there are those hostile elements in various parts of this world who are negotiating with angry intent for, or already have in their possession, nuclear and biological weapons of catastrophic capabilities. You can only speculate on the numbers and locations; we, on the other hand, know the numbers and locations, and I can assure you all that it is not a pretty sight.

"Wars, and rumors of wars, have not ended on your planet, but only in your dreams.  Is what I have said not true, Colonel Faraday?"  The alien was once more looking into the very marrow of his bones.

The Colonel was one of the more informed members in the intelligence community, and well he knew that the nukes and bugs were still out there, and not all in friendly hands. As to total numbers and locations?  He could only speculate; gazing back into the intensity of Jayseeka's vision, he knew that she knew that his bluff had been called.

Vincent didn't like the idea of being compared with a Mountain Gorilla as a species worthy of being saved, but then who could fathom the IQ of this alien?  She had made her point.

Professor Hauss would have sold his soul for the biological information the little alien possessed.  He identified with her eighty-five percent, convinced that hers was a compassionate species with genuinely benevolent intentions of helping Humankind solve environmental problems--problems that, if left unchecked, would be disastrous not only to Mankind, but most other life forms on Earth as well.

Unanimously, all agreed that it would be a good idea to allow Jayseeka another day to lay out the groundwork of her mission. Even Colonel Faraday was beginning to feel that all was not as bad as he had originally supposed; after all, hadn't Mankind historically been its own worst enemy? Most certainly, there had been Dark Ages when it came to the exploration of the world, literature and the mind, but from the use of a club, to the development of atomic bombs, had there ever been a dark age for weapons?

It was almost 8 p.m. when the day's patio meeting came to an end; twilight was gathering, as they departed for the dining hall. Time had passed quickly in the company of this golden child from beyond the stars. Her actions and intellect had been well schooled; the formulation of her mission had begun on August 12th, 1946, exactly one year and six days, Earth time, after the first of two atomic bombs had fallen upon Japan.

*********

The brain of ex-Police Chief Pat Riely was squirming with hatred and malice like a can of worms, as he glanced through the telescopic lens of his camera. He goddamned well knew that something was going on at the Manor which was not within the normal routine. "That goddamned son-of-a-bitch cousin of mine!" he internally fumed, "I would cut the goddamned little prick's throat and dump him into the Long Island Sound so the crabs could eat him, if I could just get alone with him one more fucking time!" he muttered to himself.

Riely's cousin the Mayor had fired him in front of every member of the force in a frenzy of emotion, and Pat Riely was never going to forgive or forget the taste of shit in his mouth on that day. "Oh, hell no!" he thought. "As soon as I get these photos into the proper hands, I'm going to make that asshole Mayor eat shit, just like he did to me. I'm going to have his job and he'll be out of town on a rail; wait, just wait and fucking see!" he snarled.

Animosity was not a recent aspect of Pat Riely's miserable life. When he was in high school, no one spoke to him much, no one hung out with him, and no one ever invited him to a party. His youth would have been totally void of social contacts had it not been for Bobbie Cox. This was his only friend, and Bobbie was a pitifully cruel coward of a boy.

Humanity has tried, down through eons of time, to understand why cruelty becomes so prevalent in some, and all but totally absent in others. Is it instinct gone mad? Is it the result of bad family life, environment, or the devil? There are those who are kind and caring in their youth, turning to evil later in life, and sometimes a rotten little brat of a kid will convert to goodness, becoming a man of the cloth.

There would be no saving grace for Pat Riely and Bobbie Cox. While others of their age were flying kites and teasing the girls, Bobbie and Pat were capturing small animals, tying them to trees and using them for slingshot practice.

It was the local veterinarian who suspected evil afoot, as he viewed the poor, pitifully mangled bodies of the local town folks' small dogs and cats. Most of the small creatures brought to him in pathetic tortured conditions he simply put to sleep; they were beyond repair.

One day after school, two older boys were on their way out to a nearby lake with their girlfriends, when they heard the most pitiful animal screams coming from behind an old barn nearby. Upon investigation they found Riely and Cox, one cat tied to a stake doused with gasoline and set on fire, and two others tied up nearby ready for the same. The older boys had tried to catch the two, but Riely and Cox knew the wooded area behind the barn all too well, and they escaped into the thickets.  Upon burying the one cat that had died its painful death by fire, the two older boys brought the other animals back to town, turning them loose to find their ways back home.  They then went to the town's sheriff and told him what they had witnessed.

Animal rights wasn't much of a deal back in those days, but theft of other people's property was. The town was up in arms!  Their animals were their private property.

Pat Riely and Bobbie Cox thought they had struck quite a good deal with the sheriff.  They wouldn't have to go to jail if they would show where they had buried their victims' bodies. The condition of the dead animals was so pathetic that it turned the stomach of all but Riely and Cox, who were smiling as they described the various tortures they had used on each, eighty-five in all, not counting the ones that had escaped.

Both boys were institutionalized; society had wronged them and made them cruel, so after all it wasn't their fault. They had been toilet-trained too early, or perhaps heard sounds from their parents' bedroom, as Mom and Dad made love. The doctors determined them to be abused children, much to the horror of their parents, who had always given them each the best they could afford, treated them as well as most parents would, and saw to it that they said their prayers each night before going to sleep.

Pat and Bobbie were released from Ivy Oaks Asylum three years later, with hate in their hearts and vengeance towards law enforcement and family on their minds.  Oh, how they had plotted their retribution during their confinement at Ivy Oaks.  They would probably have carried out many of their plans, except that Cox blew himself up in his attempt to build a bomb for his "Dear ol' Mom and Dad."

The sheriff tried his best to make it look like Pat Riely had killed Cox out of malice, but try as he might; he couldn't establish guilt beyond a reasonable doubt. Riely walked on all of the charges, but knew he would be under tight surveillance for as long as he remained in town.

Riely may have been unbelievably cruel, but he was certainly not stupid, and he swore to himself that he was not going to do any more time. In fact, he even admired the power that law enforcement could wield over others. He finished high school, went to college and studied criminology. He was drafted during the Vietnam War before he could find a job in law enforcement, went to O.C.S., got his commission and ended up in Vietnam. There he was in his height of glory (or perhaps gory would be a more suitable choice of word).

Many were the innocents who lost appendages, sanity or their lives in that war of carnage, civilian and soldier alike, but Pat Riely was in a place he had always dreamed of, and never lost the opportunity to inflict pain and mayhem whenever possible.

Lieutenant Riely didn't give a damn about safeguarding the world against communism; in fact he rather liked the power its debased form could exert on its masses. Furthermore he just loved putting bullets into living things, and now he could do it to people with impunity. He enjoyed watching them writhe in agony, and never stopped watching until the body stopped moving.

He would often fantasize that his victims were his mother or father, or the doctors in the institution in which he had been incarcerated, or the sheriff who had tricked him and Bobbie those many years ago. Riely often bragged about his ability to get information out of the enemy; he reveled in the gore of torture; his dreams were wet with the remembrance of the sorry souls he had mutilated.

Just as in high school, and college, Riely had no friends in the army, and they who were privy to his thoughts and activities went to great lengths to avoid him. He never got a promotion in the three years he was in Nam. Towards the end of the war Riely got separated from his platoon, largely because the enemy numbers were nearly the same as his own men; and not liking the odds he ordered his men up front, lagged behind, and ran for it when he got the chance. Eventually he had stumbled from fatigue and fallen into a trench wherein a young Vietnamese mother and her two small girls were hiding.

Riely tied up the mother and her two children with their own clothing, brutally tortured and raped all three, then shot them, thinking he had killed them all. The youngest girl, only nine years old, was found shortly after Riely had left her for dead by an American reinforcement unit, and miraculously lived to tell of her family's horrible ordeal. It fell on deaf ears; the badly injured child died two days later. The war was at an end and the evacuation of the troops took precedent over all.

# Chapter Nine

> This teaching is eternal:
> "Violent men die violent deaths."
>
> *(Lao Tsu, 6th Century B.C.)*

Lieutenant Pat Riely was heralded as a hero upon his return from Vietnam, and got a job as a police officer with the 8th precinct in New York City. He was on the Mob's payroll one week after completing the academy.

Discreetly evil for thirty years in the city, Riely got into trouble seldom; but when he did, he bought his way out with the graft money he had saved specifically for this purpose.

Riely married three times, the first marriage lasting a week, the second a month, and the third, to an Italian girl named Angela lasted long enough for this terribly abused wretch of a girl to get pregnant.

Riely was not aware, nor did he even stop to consider, who Angela's relatives might be. The only types of relations that got his attention were sexual, anal intercourse being his most abusive favorite. As it would fortunately turn out, Riely never got to see his daughter; the mother had caught him trying to fondle the neighbor's little boy early on in her pregnancy, and this had been the final straw.

Angela went to see her Uncle Antonio, a mob kingpin of the era. After hearing of the vile abuse his niece had suffered, the uncle considered filling her husband so full of bullets that cement shoes would have been unnecessary to sink his body to the bottom of Long Island Sound.

"Don't kill him, just get him out of town," pleaded the mother, "for the baby's sake!"

Riely was beat to a pulp, and dumped outside the city limits with the warning that if he ever returned he'd be put, piece by piece, down a garbage disposal.

Escaping the city with his life, Riely went to the one person in his family who knew him the least, his aunt Mildred up in Little Falls. After filling her full of the most incredible bullshit stories about his heroic ventures in Vietnam, followed by "Mr. Nice Guy Cop," who was beat up and run out of town by the Mob because he wouldn't take a bribe, Aunt Mildred insisted that the current police chief, a really good and honorable man, be fired and Pat Riely put into the position.

Now Aunt Mildred could make this type of power move because she was quite well off, and it was her money and influence that had gotten her son elected mayor of Little Falls.

Reluctantly Mayor Fisher gave in to the demands of his mother; he was campaigning for state senator, and planned to use Mom's money and influence as the bumper.

Pat Riely was made Police Chief of Little Falls, and he was going to "Kick Some Ass!"

Abusive of his power as police chief, hated by his staff as well as the mayor; Riely's KGB-type assault on Vincent Henry Manor had given his cousin just the excuse he had been looking for.

Mayor Fisher had listened first hand to what Vincent Henry's maid and cook had to say, and had become convinced that they were on some type of drugs. Who could possible believe such a cockamamie story? The mayor let Riely have the rope, leaving all decisions regarding the incident in his hands; and, just as the Mayor had planned, Chief Riely hung himself.

Upon hearing about the sad treatment of "that pillar of the community," Vincent Henry III, even aunt Mildred was to say to her son Fish (her pet name for him), "Fire that idiot Riely!"

Fire him he did, in the most humiliating and embarrassing way he could think of, in hopes that Riely would leave town, never to return.

Pat Riely was not to be easily thrown out; he had gotten his investigative gear together and returned to Vincent Henry Manor. He parked his car in the vicinity of the ninety-acre lake and hiked over to an area of ample trees and shrubbery, which would conceal his clandestine activity, less than a hundred and twenty yards from the Manor.

Riely could now view the Manor with impunity. He smirked, thinking how clever he was. He had tried unsuccessfully to get some full frontal pictures of a strange little female dressed in golden tights for the better part of two days. He realized that the small person must be female, although diminutive for her age, because she had turned a bit, from time to time, and he had photographed a portion of a budding breast. He also ascertained that it was this small gold-clothed person who was instrumental in the alien hoax now being perpetuated by the Henrys, which had so badly frightened the cook and maid.

Riely was taking careful notes on all that transpired, taking pictures at opportune times and noticing that eighty percent of the attention in the patio discussions was directed toward the small pixie-like girl. This was the second day that the

Henrys and friends had gathered on the patio, and from the amazed expressions on the faces of Colonel Faraday and Professor Hauss, which he was able to film, Pat Riely knew something very strange was definitely going on.

It was 8 p.m. when the second patio meeting began breaking up. As the last of the group left the patio area, Riely cursed, "Why the fuck is it I can get a frontal shot on every individual coming and going from that patio, except that strange little one dressed in gold tights? I'll be a Goddamned son of a bitch!" he fumed, as he began to pack up the camera tripod and equipment, little aware that his curses concerning dogs were to have a ring of truth.

Planning his return the next day, Riely hid his equipment in some old wooden crates he happened to find in the boathouse near the lake. Before stepping back out onto the pier that ran along its side, he scanned the area to see if he might have been observed. Determining the coast to be clear, he stepped out onto the pier and started for his car.

Riely was about to leave the pier when he heard a splash behind him, which sounded like the biggest fish he had ever heard breaking water. Out of curiosity he turned about, and froze. There was someone sitting near the end of the pier just past the boathouse!

Dusk was gathering fast, as Riely once more scanned the area to see if others might have found him out. He saw no one, as he pulled out his hunting knife and held it behind him as he walked towards his unwanted witness.

As Riely drew nearer, he could better determine that it was a young girl, a black one at that, and she had been skinny-dipping in the lake. The water still dripped from her jet-black hair and ran in rivulets down her back and over her budding right breast. She was gazing to her left and out into the lake away from Riely.

The pier squeaked from time to time as Riely crept towards her. He began to notice the smallness of the girl as he approached, but his mind was concentrating on stealth above all, for fear that he might scare her off the pier and back into the water; obviously she was a pretty good swimmer.

"The little black bitch must be deaf!" thought Riely, as he closed in on his target. Stopping about fifteen feet from his mark, and speaking in the friendliest tone he could fabricate, he called out softly to his would-be victim, "Oh, little girl, do your mommy and daddy know where you are?"

"No," came back the cloying little reply.

In an instant the darkest of malignant desires stormed Riely's evil brain. "The boathouse," he quickly calculated, "I'll drag her into the boathouse and later," he thought, "when I'm finished, I'll..."

But Riely was never to finish his calculations to dispose of his intended victim's body. The alien slowly turned its face towards him, gazing now upon him with huge glistening obsidian eyes. Riely froze in horror, knowing in the depth of his heinous soul that Karma had finally caught up with him.

The four paws of the huge dog landed in the middle of Riely's back, knocking him face first, flat onto the pier, where he slid on chest and face to within two feet of the alien, 160 pounds of canine brute riding upon his back. The knife flew from his hand out into the lake. Death came instantaneously, far more than Riely deserved, as the dog's cavernous jaws clamped down, crushing the base of his skull and three inches of spine as if they were a crisp apple.

The alien spoke soothingly to the dog in fluent English, leading him off the pier and into shallow water where she washed the blood from his mouth and fur.

After this she assured him, "It's okay, everything will be okay." Then, stroking his fur, she telepathically commanded him to return home, and pointed him in the direction of the Manor. Pooche dutifully disappeared into the gathering darkness.

Returning to the body on the pier and with unusual strength for one so small, she hefted it off into the water. Finding a bucket in the boathouse, she collected it along with the photography equipment. Using the bucket to wash down the pier of all visible traces of blood, she then threw the photography equipment and bucket off the end of the pier. She then dropped into the water beside Riely's floating carcass. Small fish were already nibbling at the shredded flesh of Riely's neck. Catching hold of one arm of the corpse, she and the late Chief Riely, sank quickly into the deep waters of the lake. For all practical purposes, Pat Riely had ceased to exist.

It was the fourth day since the Aquatian's arrival at the Manor, and breakfast was finishing up. "It is difficult to imagine," thought Vincent, "that this being, so small yet appealing, so very intelligent and well-schooled in the social graces of Earth, had come from a planet in some far-flung part of the Milky Way bent on conquest."

A summer storm had blown into the area at about 3:30 that morning, yet all slept soundly until 6 a.m., when it was time for the domestic help to arise and begin their daily chores. Henrys and friends would sleep soundly, undisturbed until 8 a.m. Then wakening again in a timely manner, they looked forward to another day of unprecedented intellectual adventure with the Aquatian.

Once more, comfortably seated in the drawing room, the Henrys and friends prepared themselves as best they could for the knowledge pertaining to the Aquatus aspirations regarding planet Earth.

"As I previously indicated, we Aquatus eventually get all of Earth's television programs. It takes them almost a full year to reach us from the time they are beamed from our orbital satellites surrounding your planet," began Jayseeka. "We view these programs, every one, with purposeful interest. We also have a school on our planet which admits three hundred of our finest students, and its only purpose is to observe and record all that they see and hear concerning the evolution of Earth's flora and fauna.

"As I explained earlier, it is your science fiction movies, and such, which we most carefully observe, for this gives us an enhanced ability to form predictable outcomes regarding Earth's future. Unfortunately, most of your fiction regarding aliens is fanciful to the point of absurdity, and this is why we had to calculate so carefully our every move concerning our eventual contact with your species.

"One of your motion pictures in particular depicts an alien species so hardy it can survive the harshest, most food-less environment imaginable. This is compounded with incredible speed, dexterity, and the exoskeleton equivalency of a Sherman tank. Now all the above is combined with an unbelievable appetite for any living thing! The biological law, which shoots the entire concept down, is that there is a very good reason why earth's largest insect is about the same size as your smaller mammals.

"As an insect increases in size, the weight of its exoskeleton becomes a weighty suit to carry about. If you consider Earth's ever-so-slow and tired Goliath Beetle, which can weigh in at little more than a kilogram, it could hardly move at all at a kilo and a half."

Professor Hauss was nodding in agreement.

"So you see," continued Jayseeka, "a more believable creature, of mayhem and horror, is one that has already come and gone on planet earth, Tyrannosaurus Rex, with bones inside much like yourselves; now that was a real meanie, but nothing man and his technology couldn't have subdued today.

"The point which I'm making is that motion pictures, though fanciful and entertaining in the extreme, have left a wound in the human subconscious, a wound that could probably lead to dire consequences, should we Aquatus simply pop into a United Nations meeting and announce our intentions, no matter how peaceful and benign. On the other hand, any technological show of force would most probably have triggered a latent territorial instinct in your species. An instinct so strong, that whatever minor nuclear damage it may have inflicted upon us, it would almost certainly have been suicidal to yourselves and 85 percent detrimental to the rest of the flora and fauna of your planet.

"It was with years of careful planning and observation that we chose Vincent Henry Manor, the altruistic personalities herein, and this time of this year, to make our peaceful entreaty to planet Earth."

It was admirable how amazingly well young Roxanne listened and took notes together with the adults. She never acted as if she was bored, nor did she ever leave the side of her most intriguing little friend Jayseeka. Therefore nobody quieted or ignored her when she asked questions outside the current topic of conversation. After all it was Roxanne who had been selected by the Aquatian as the first human contact.

"How old are you, Jayseeka?" inquired Roxanne.

"In four more earth days, Roxanne, I will be exactly two hundred and eighty of your Earth years old."

"I was just about to say that you didn't look a day over a hundred and fifty," humorously interjected the Professor.

The light laughter about the table broke up the intensity of the mood that had developed from the more or less one-sided conversation.

"Were the Aquatus visiting Earth at the time they were building the great pyramids? If so, how did they move those massive stone blocks?" once more inquired Roxanne.

"Teams of elephants," replied Jayseeka. She then went on to say, "The huge pachyderms were highly esteemed by the ancient Egyptians, and were fed on the various grains and grasses that grew abundantly in the Nile River Valley.

"It may interest you to know also that many of the treasures placed within the tombs in that long ago time are still there. The Pharaohs spent much time contemplating how they were to preserve their treasures, along with their bodies; and they certainly fooled many. Even today many of the secrets are well kept."

Jayseeka and Roxanne smiled at each other, whereupon the little alien once more returned to her topic.

"Our species has evolved to a longevity of approximately six hundred and twenty of your earth years," continued Jayseeka. "So you see, on my planet Roxanne, I am often viewed as a young person much like yourself. I was chosen especially for this mission because Earth has been my life-long study. This, combined with my exceptional abilities as a linguist, made our leaders feel that I would have some advantage in soothing any hostilities that could develop. As I mentioned before, I am fluent in all current languages now spoken on Earth.

"I know all of you here would like to have known up front exactly why we Aquatus have now chosen to interact with Earth and its inhabitants."

The seriousness of the information soon to be imparted hung in the air like a storm about to break.

"Oh boy, here it comes," thought Colonel Faraday.

"It was determined that a small select segment of your species, yourselves specifically, be contacted and educated as tactfully as possible concerning crucial problems on your planet, problems which could develop, if unchecked, into global disaster.

"I believe we have gotten to know each other well enough at this point so that I can now effectively, in a manner of speaking, get to the bottom line. I previously mentioned the situation of nuclear armaments and biological weapons, currently in the hands of those with incredible animosity clouding their judgment; and they are planning a blackmail type of policy, as we speak, that may well lead to a third world war.

"From this type of disaster the Earth could probably begin to recuperate in eight to twelve hundred years; however, your species and the vast majority of the rest of Earth's current flora and fauna would not. You see," continued the alien, "egotistic pride, a product of evolution which served humankind well in the days of primitive warfare, has become, in these current days of technology, its own worst enemy. There are those of your species who are currently in control of nuclear and biological armaments. They would use their entire arsenal before suffering the humiliation of defeat, not even thinking of the environmental consequences of their actions. These ambitious ones are politicians, and most unfortunately they lack much scientific knowledge.

"There are also the greenhouse gases in the atmosphere and various chemicals being dumped into your rivers, lakes and oceans. Millions of tons of human waste are also being hauled out to sea in barges on a daily basis and unconcernedly dumped. It has been our observation, on our own planet as well as others down through time, that there is only a certain amount of pollution any ecological system will tolerate before its ability to cleanse itself becomes devastated. The end product is nerve damage, birth defects, and cancers, hence a painfully shorter and poorer quality of life for all.

"Last, but certainly not least, are the heavy human populations which are crowding other animal species throughout your world. Now it's not just the crowding of humans, at the expense of all others, about which we need be concerned. It is quite well established, by your own naturalists and scientists, that animals (and trust me, you are animals, the same as I) seldom populate to the point of depleting their food supplies. Often, a virus or microorganism will enter into the densely populated group and devastate its numbers. For example, as man encroaches on earth's tropical rain forests, there are deadly viruses patiently waiting in ancient places to make their move.

"We Aquatus have feared for the survival of man for the last fifty years. We have been amazed that a 'hot virus,' such as the ones which brings on Lassa Fever or Ebola/Zaire, has not arrived in New York City, Hong Kong, or Mexico City, to wipe out eighty percent of their populations. Currently there are 23 such 'hot viruses' which have been identified by your men and women in microbiology and the medical professions, but I can assure you that there are many more.

"So there you have it," spoke the alien. "We Aquatus have taken it upon ourselves to attempt a rescue of your planet. Except for a few, such as yourselves, it is obvious that human technology has out-paced human morality."

Having laid out the problems waiting in the wings to devastate humanity, the alien had won over Professor Hauss 100 per cent. He was well informed and knowledgeable; the little alien had spoken the truth.

"And just how do the Aquatus plan to effect this rescue, and save us from ourselves?" asked Colonel Faraday, a glint of suspicion in his eyes, a hint of acid in his voice.

"We will begin by placing a clinic right here at Vincent Henry Manor, and we will invite all those who are terminally ill to come to this clinic for free treatment," replied the alien.

Jaws slacked, mouths dropped open; twenty seconds of amazed silence ensued.

"Let me see if I fully understand what may be going on here." Vincent Henry was the first to speak after the lull. "What you are saying is that you have come thousands of light years' distance, bravely risking your life on a planet that may shortly be obliterated by nuclear holocaust or viral devastation, for the purpose of building a clinic at my place?"

"Yes," replied the alien.

"And how will the building of a clinic further the cause of saving Earth from the evils now poised to plague it?" asked Professor Hauss, a note of incredulity in his voice.

"This clinic will not be a run-of-the-mill, ordinary Earth type of clinic," replied Jayseeka. "This first of many clinics will be equipped with the most sophisticated of Aquatus medical science. Not only will we treat the hopeless and forgotten, but we will make them whole once more, revitalizing their overall physiology, which in turn, will greatly increase their life expectancy."

"Are you saying that any human treated in this proposed clinic, for any type of physical or emotional ailment whatsoever, inclusive of lost organs and appendages, will be made completely whole?" demanded Faraday.

"Not only will they be made completely whole, my dear Colonel, but their total physiology will be rebuilt and revitalized," answered Jayseeka. "No, we cannot raise the dead, in answer to your next question. We must have living DNA from which to rebuild." She had known his thoughts.

"Brilliant!" thought Professor Hauss.

"Go ahead with your analogy, Dr. Hauss," requested Jayseeka, now pleasantly smiling in his direction.

"By using your fantastic medical technology, and making whole the hopeless, hence giving them once more meaningful lives, you will have gained your end in proving your amiable intent regarding Earth. Those whom you heal will be a living testimony to your benevolence," explained Professor Hauss.

"Undoubtedly the Aquatus are well aware of the health of Earth's leaders," added Vincent "and if they are not sick, then obviously many of their family and friends could use the services that are provided for free?"

"Absolutely free!" added Jayseeka, now smiling as widely as her small beautifully formed lips would allow.

Dr. Hauss made a mental note of her perfectly formed, ivory-white teeth.

"All world leaders would then be quite intrigued concerning other technological gifts that may be bestowed upon them. They would be wide open to suggestions to help clean up pollution, conserve natural resources, and put an end to aggression in trade for these gifts," responded Faraday.

"Bravo to you as well, Colonel!" replied the alien.

The cat was out of the bag! Vincent Henry had suddenly gotten very uncomfortable.

"I have often believed that 'enough is the same as a feast,'" began the Lord of the Manor, "and I believe I can speak freely for my family on the matter which you have proposed, Jayseeka.

"We would be honored to help in this most benevolent of all undertakings, even if it would mean retiring to a more modest standard of living. However, Jayseeka, our personal wealth, although substantial, is limited. We would have no problem in building and equipping quite a large clinic or hospital, if need be, here at the Manor. But let me point out that by liquidating all our major assets, we would probably have only enough money to build and furnish perhaps twenty smaller clinics throughout the world. However, this would hardly be enough for a medical undertaking of the magnitude you have suggested."

The little alien then looked smilingly upon Roxanne who, returning her smile, reached to the floor and lifted her small handbag to the table top, dumping out eighty or so of the most magnificent gemstones the spectators had ever seen. As these magnificent condensations of wealth bounced and rolled to a stop on the surface of the table, all seemed hypnotized, excepting Roxanne. She reached down and lifted a gloriously glittering 19-carat emerald, for all to admire.

"Is there no end to the wonders we are witnessing?" thought Elizabeth Henry, as she reached to pick up a brilliant white 30-carat bauble that had rattled and rolled to within three inches of her hand at the end of the table. It was a perfectly cut, flawless diamond, and as its facets refracted the light, it sprayed the ceiling with a rainbow of colors, Undoubtedly it was the most exquisite gem she had ever seen, and being a lady of means, she had seen the best.

There was virtually a Pharaoh's ransom on the table before them, and no one would inquire if they were real; the answer was apparent. As the assembly excitedly conversed among themselves and with Jayseeka, none realized that Roxanne had left the room, until she returned lugging a three gallon bucket, nearly full of even more spectacular gems. The girl would have dumped these also upon the tabletop, had she not stumbled in her excitement, spilling them out instead upon the floor.

"There is much more of the same where these stones came from," Jayseeka assured the group, as the precious glittering tide rattled towards them on the polished hardwood floor, bumping up against their shoes.

Vincent, his family and friends were all now completely aware that money, or indeed the lack thereof, would be no hindrance to the benevolent objectives of the Aquatus.

## Chapter Ten

*Power:*
*Opium of the Ego,*
*Quest of the Ages.*

Even Colonel Faraday had been won over in the end. Under pressure from his friends and just plain common sense, he had agreed to gradually, and tactfully, make solid contacts among his colleagues in the intelligence community. In various think-tanks he would suggest, "What if this, and suppose it was that," and with the factual information gained from the Aquatus orbital satellites he would amaze them all with the armament status of hostile elements throughout the world.

As part of the agreement to withhold information concerning the Aquatus and their intentions until the appropriate time, Jayseeka had given Colonel Faraday numerous CDs, videos and informative photographs of dirty political and powerful criminal mainsprings throughout the world.

Faraday was overwhelmed with the power the alien had placed in his hands. Fully cognizant of the capabilities of Earth's own spy satellites, able to get photos of auto license plates and persons 89 percent discernible under good atmospheric conditions, he would be absolutely astounded by what the Aquatus could produce.

"Why not?" postulated Faraday. "Look at our own electronic technology not even a hundred years old. Give us fifteen thousand years, and see what we can do."

However, Faraday continued to be amazed as he ever so slowly doled out the sensitive information to a trusted handful of his even more amazed colleagues. They would not know, nor would they soon, where it had come from. Faraday was to become a star of the intelligence community.

The holographic videos and CDs had the image clarity of multimillion-dollar film productions, complete with zoom shots of clocks, calendars, fingerprints on glassware, even retinal eye scans. Sound so crystal clear that even one's breath could be made audible with minimal effort. Except that this was not theatrics, this was real life, with real bad guys. The photos and videos which Jayseeka had provided for the Colonel were spectacular, to say the least. World leaders who feigned acid hostilities towards one another in public could be clearly seen, hobnobbing with each other in private in the most amiable manner.

There were embarrassing photos of United States congressmen on vacation in various countries, living in opulence in the palatial estates of the wealthy, enjoying the finest of food, wine, and female consorts. It became all too apparent that the powerful and wealthy foreigners had used their diplomats like pawns. These in turn were clearly seen and heard bribing various United States government legislators to help negotiate huge loans from U.S. banks, moneys which had supposedly been for the purpose of subsidizing various agricultural, hydroelectric, and medical programs, etc.

"To help bring their poor huddled masses out of poverty."

"Oh, worry not, Mr. Banker. These loans will be guaranteed with the best collateral in the world," mewed the corrupt politicians. "The Government of the United States of America!"

Of course they were correct. Those patsies known commonly as the U.S. taxpayers inevitably picked up the tab. Only a small portion of the funds, and often none at all, went towards the programs for which they were intended. Free money into the pockets of the corruptly wealthy, with no intention of ever being repaid.

Oh yes; suspicions confirmed. Presidents and collaborators of those "non-profit societies" were getting richer by the day. Using those sad, big-eyed little boys and girls living in the most squalid of habitats? Less than five percent of the take went to the children, the rest into Swiss and other offshore bank accounts.

Faraday's trusted compatriots often believed him to be on the edge of a nervous breakdown, so intensely and diligently was he involved in his work. Within two short years he would rise swiftly through the ranks at the State Department.

Professor Hauss, turning over his classes at Lakeside University, took a sabbatical which he used to make and remake acquaintance with various intellectuals in the science community, "eggheads" whom he felt to be not only genuinely gifted, but genuinely good persons as well. Showing up at various universities, Dr. Hauss would make a phone call and then proceed to solve a sticky problem of science, claiming that "many heads were better than one." He feigned conversations with other university colleagues, while actually speaking to Jayseeka.

The Aquatian had also bequeathed Dr. Hauss a small bag of miracles, with which to astound his colleagues: cures for the common cold, diabetes, and vaginal warts, among other previously "incurable" diseases. Institutions of learning and scientific research throughout the world would eventually grow to love him. In a short time David Hauss would become internationally famous and very well published. Even in the most obscure centers of learning throughout the world, he would help his colleagues solve their problems, taking them out to lunch and dinner whenever possible. His quick wit made them laugh; he won their love on an individual basis.

Vincent Henry began construction on the hospital by purchasing an additional two hundred adjoining acres, which would be most suitable for the project. He then hired the very best of general contractors. Always on the job-site, Mr. Henry took a personal interest in even the smallest of details. Time was of the essence, and to expedite construction Vincent gave subcontractors all the overtime they could work, at double union wages; a new prosperity had come to Little Falls.

Elizabeth Henry had been a student of gemstones and, though she did not overly indulge herself, she had quite a nice collection of her own, having acquired them as gifts from friends, family and husband. Elizabeth well knew the value of the condensed wealth bequeathed on behalf of the Aquatus, and she knew the contacts whereby she could get the very best prices. Discreetly, and with great caution, she conducted the sales of the gems, staggering the senses of those skilled in the art from Bogota to Zurich.

When it came time to dismiss the summer domestic help, all got bonuses hefty enough to close the mouth of a cave. In addition they received the good news that the Henrys would stay on through the winter of that year and into the next, for as long as it took to complete the hospital. The overjoyed employees looked forward to preparing the Manor for winter habitation, and the festive holidays to come.

Construction of the new hospital had been in progress for three months, and fall was about to become winter, when Jayseeka announced, "I have other objectives to see to on my home planet, and I must leave soon; however, I will be back upon completion of the hospital." She then fixed the date at two years four months in the future.

Roxanne was beside herself with grief, as she tearfully inquired when her little friend would be leaving.

"Soon," answered Jayseeka affectionately, putting her arm about the despondent girl and giving her a squeeze. "Very soon."

All would miss the little alien, but none as much as Roxanne. They had been inseparable from the first day of the Aquatian's arrival at the Manor. Jayseeka, Roxanne and Pooche, always happy in their companionship, swam, hiked, and played tennis; but most of the time they spent composing music or studying birds, squirrels, and various other flora and fauna in and about the Henrys' estate. The music Roxanne and Jayseeka had composed together would later become quite popular, and the girl was happy that much of it had been due to her own creativity.

It was October, and the nights were becoming quite cool. A storm front was moving rapidly into the Little Falls area and it arrived at the Manor just after midnight. All were sleeping soundly despite the lightning, thunder, and torrents of rain that inundated the estate. The little alien arose from her sleep and retrieved a small water-resistant backpack, which she had previously placed beneath the bed for the purpose it was soon to serve. Then walking into the bath she removed one of the large fluffy towels from the clean towel storage area and, folding it neatly slid it into her backpack.

The task was accomplished quietly in the dark, as Jayseeka's night vision was excellent. No longer brilliantly gold in color with eyes of amber, she was now as black as the storm raging outside the Manor, with eyes of lustrous obsidian. Stepping through the balcony doors, closing them cautiously behind her, the alien grasped the rain gutter and, like an acrobat in a circus, slid effortlessly to the ground where waited that large canine friend, Pooche.

Swinging herself up and onto the dog's back as the rain poured down upon them; the alien directed the dog towards the lake, arriving there at a run in about thirty minutes. The alien spoke soothingly to the dog, as she thoroughly wiped him down with the large towel in the boathouse, all the time suggesting to him strongly via telepathy that he remain within the shelter until the storm cleared in the morning.

The Aquatian stepped out onto the pier. Leaving nothing to chance, she closely surveyed the area with her superior night vision. The dog had sensed her departure and whined his sadness and disapproval. Smiling and gazing once more at the despondent Pooche, she confirmed her previous telepathic command; then, turning about, she walked to the end of the pier, diving deftly off into the rough dark water.

The huge, dark, disc-shaped craft lifted slowly from the eighty-foot depths of the lake, whipping its waters into a frenzy of turbulence. As the massive starship slowly cleared the surface, the ninety-acre lake temporarily lost three feet of its overall depth. The hum and whine of the ship's powerful anti-gravity drives were inaudible above the fury of the raging storm. Rising vertically, and quickly gathering speed, the magnificent interstellar craft cleared Earth's atmosphere in less than ten minutes, beginning its incredibly long journey home.

The storm was dumping tons of water on the surrounding hillside of the Henry estate, and Jayseeka was satisfied that the lake would be brimming once more before the night ended. Turning to her shipmate, no longer in need of words, she inquired if there had been any difficulty in the preparation and preservation of the "Long Pig" which had attacked her three earth-months earlier.

She was informed that all had gone well.

The two Aquatians prepared to enter the chambers of deep sleep where they would dream away most of the long journey back home, awakening every tenth of the way so as to recondition their body processes. Jayseeka, by now quite put off by the constant fish and gelatin meals at the Manor, was happy that "Phase #I of Earth" had gone so very well. She was also pleased that the "Long Pig" had cured out so nicely--there would be plenty to snack on during the long trip home.

---

What is time, but the imaginings of the mind?

---

Two years, four months, and twelve days had passed since Jayseeka had struck out for her home world. Professor Hauss and the new "Director" Faraday of the State Department had been calling the Manor on a daily basis since the first of the month.

Vincent Henry Hospital had finally reached completion.

The staff of thirty doctors, ninety nurses, and forty medical technicians was moved into the Little Falls area, and had been contracted for at excellent pay scales. Excepting for a small cleanup crew, and several fussy equipment installation technicians, this monolith of health, equipped with the most sophisticated of medical equipment and personnel, awaited its first patient.

Director Faraday, for survival purposes, had built a near impregnable barrier about himself. He had accomplished this by gathering about him only the most honorable and dedicated employees; they believed in him with a binding respect bordering on a religion. He would need every bit of their loyalty when the whole truth concerning the Aquatus became apparent.

The dynamic Faraday had made some powerful enemies, many of them wealthy, and many of them not only wealthy, but currently in federal prison where he had helped to put them. He had pushed very hard.

Professor Hauss was continuing to receive abundant correspondence from his friends in intellectual communities throughout the world, friendships often frowned upon by many and various bureaucrats, stateside and abroad. Nevertheless the Professor answered each letter at length, calling upon various translators as needed.

Elizabeth Henry had negotiated the sale of all but a handful of the glorious gemstones and had built up enough capital to more than cover the expense of the hospital's construction. The charitable endeavor had caught the attention of others of the benevolent wealthy, who wanted to contribute to the project. Even more wealth began to accumulate for the purpose of eventually building, equipping and staffing numerous free clinics in depressed areas of the United States, and abroad.

Roxanne, two years older, was at that awkward lanky stage approaching maturity. She had been offered several very attractive contracts as a composer, and could have done quite a good job of it had she agreed. However, the girl always seemed to have an older head on her shoulders and had decided it best to finish her schooling. Although two grades ahead of most girls her age, she still had at least seven years of college to finish.

With the greatest of expectations and ever-building joy, the young girl patiently awaited the return of her "forever best friend" Jayseeka. When making a journey over thousands of light years of distance, one could be forgiven for being a few days late in reaching her destination.

Spring was just around the corner and the occasional warmth had brought some green to the countryside. The last major winter storm was to make its pass in the Little Falls area. It was about one o'clock in the morning when the storm swept with gusto towards the Manor. Starting out as heavy snow it would become a rain-snow mixture upon reaching the lower levels of warmer air.

As the star-ship neared Jupiter it began to change from bright silver, to dull grayish black, reaching Earth thereafter in little less than two hours at greatly reduced speed. A person would have had to be at the edge of the lake to hear the low hum of the ship's anti-gravity drives. The Aquatus were assured that no humans would hear or see the event, as they had done a precautionary scan of the entire area prior to descent. They also suspected that all humans at Vincent Henry Manor and vicinity were soundly asleep, excepting two of the Manor's security guards, and they could not have known what was going down in the area of the lake.

The massive craft descended through the turbulent cover of the storm. Lightning crackled with fantastic voltage over the hull of the colossal craft, only to be deflected back into the atmosphere where it would continue its original earthward journey, followed shortly thereafter by the monumental starship. Water displacement and fish churned up and over the concrete spillways, as destiny settled once more into the womb of the lake.

At 4:15 on the morning of the starship's return, Roxanne was awakened from a deep sleep and was mysteriously compelled to descend the spiral staircase into the main entry area of the Manor. Standing near the large carved oaken doors, a bit bewildered and confused, she was trying to remember what had inspired her to make the sleepy odyssey when she heard a resounding "woof" outside the Manor.

"Pooche?" exclaimed the girl, as she opened one of the huge doors, setting off security alarms throughout the hallways. Within three minutes the guards were in the front entry area; within eight minutes two thirds of the household was present, including Mr. and Mrs. Henry.

Jayseeka had returned! She had been lifted up and was being carried about by a joyous Roxanne, while Pooche, standing in a puddle of water, happily looked on, trying as best he could to wave his little stump of a tail.

One of the maids had gone for towels, and when Jayseeka, Roxanne and Pooche were thoroughly dried off, Vincent and Elizabeth escorted all three into the drawing room.

The butler wasted no time in stoking up a rosy crackling fire in the large marble fireplace, and the rest of the morning was spent on small talk, as sleep was out of the question. After brunch the Henrys and Jayseeka took a nap.

The storm had subsided just after eleven that morning; Director Faraday and Dr. Hauss were to arrive at one thirty that same afternoon, arousing the little alien and the Henrys from their naps.

A bit of a chill still in their bones from the trip, David and Bill had made themselves comfortable in two sofa chairs before the large fireplace in the drawing room. Gratefully accepting the "three fingers" of brandy, which had been poured for them into sparkling crystal snifters, they began to compose their thoughts.

Jayseeka was delighted at the progress that Bill Faraday had made in the State Department and assured him that whatever information he needed in the future would be readily available to him for the asking.

The little alien had gazed out of the west windows of the

Manor, at the beautiful structure which was Vincent Henry Memorial Hospital, for a long, satisfying period of time. She then eloquently complimented Vincent and Elizabeth on their industry and good taste. The little alien was most delighted, as well, to hear about the other financial contributors to the project. Jayseeka was assured that the free clinic network throughout other parts of the world would go more smoothly than what had been originally planned.

The time would eventually come when the world would need to know of its participation in Operation Clean Sweep, Planet Earth. Upon reading the massive intellectual correspondence from scientists around the world, Jayseeka glowingly complimented Dr. Hauss on his broad-minded and openhearted success. She then assured them all that no industry would be taken away without being replaced by a better and cleaner industry in return. There would be no loss of jobs or vested finances.

The opening date of the hospital was scheduled for two weeks hence, and Jayseeka informed them that the Aquatus medical equipment would arrive within the next few days and also that it would be easy to install and use. No one, not even Director Faraday, had thought to ask how this equipment was to be delivered.

Jayseeka was not only telepathic, but she was adept at instilling powerfully suggestive thoughts and selective amnesia in the minds of others, and none would be the wiser.

After discussing some of the finer points of progress made by the Henrys and their friends, it was 9 p.m. and a late supper was laid out in the main dining hall. Sushi had been prepared once more for Jayseeka, but after some encouragement, the little alien tried a bit of the standing rib roast. Much to the delight of all, including herself, she found it quite delectable. Faraday was pleased to see that his golden friend liked something other than raw fish.  It sort of spoiled his appetite for others to be eating raw meat when he could see it.  Little did he know...

## Chapter Eleven

Jimboy and Sally had told their parents that they were going to a movie over in Herkimer. Instead they had driven out near Vincent Henry Manor where they could park, and do those things that young people do, mostly in a confused sort of way.

Sally was willing but not easy, putting off Jimboy's ardent advances until almost 11:30. She wanted her reputation to be "good when had" but definitely not "had easily."

Finally, in the back seat of his mother's compact car, juicy Jimboy had gotten Sally out of her panties and bra, and was trying, with as much cool as possible under the close circumstances, to install the condom. The latex device, upon removal from his wallet, had left its rounded imprint in the wallet's thin leather; most likely in protest of having been sat upon, gassed, crushed and tortured for the last eight months.

With pants down around his ankles, and Sally's dress up about her neck, Jimboy was ready for the big moment, because that was about how long it was going to take.

"What's that?" asked Sally in a harsh whisper, reaching up and pulling the dress out of her face.

"What's what?" responded Jimboy, more than a little agitated at being interrupted prior to the grand moment of conquest.

"That humming sound!" retorted the girl, a bit irritated herself at her would-be lover's thoughtless and inconsiderate attitude.

Jimboy held his breath for a few short seconds, then, repositioning himself, tried to view the outside through the little car's steamed up windows, his right hand inadvertently coming to rest upon one of Sally's ample breasts. In an instant Jimboy decided that he was more interested in what was throbbing in his groin, rather than what was humming outside the car, and began his final approach to the tunnel of love.

Sally sat bolt upright, and reaching painfully through Jimboy's legs with her right hand, she opened the car door, and with her left hand gave him a push.

The rejected "Romeo" found himself flat on the ground, pants around his ankles, looking up at the stars. The humming sound was louder outside of the car, and as the dejected lad lay on his back trying to regain his breath, there was no mistaking the sound, size and shape of the large disc-shaped craft that passed overhead blocking out the stars.

With his ardent weapon of desire now reduced to the consistency of an over-cooked noodle, and testicles trying to climb into his belly for a place to hide, the totally terrified boy bounded up off the ground like a live rubber ball. Simultaneously pulling up his pants, he nearly pulled the door handle off the little car in his haste to enter the vehicle and get the hell outa there.

From the back seat the frenzied girl screamed, protested and threatened all the way back to town, with Jimboy doing speeds in excess of ninety.

The parents had gone to bed long before their son arrived home in a panic, and perhaps it was best, for if they had witnessed his pale and sickly complexion, and listened to his babbling about flying saucers, they probably would have had him hospitalized within an hour.

The house was dark and Jimboy was having a great deal of difficulty convincing himself that what he had seen near the Vincent Henry Estate was just a hallucination. Sally and he had gagged their way through a "joint" earlier in the evening; maybe it was true what his parents had said about the devil weed.

He spent the rest of the night under his bed, instead of under the covers. It would be more than a week before Jimboy would tell his story to several close friends. Although Sally would never date Jimboy again, eventually she would corroborate his story, leaving out the romantic details, of course.

It was twelve midnight and the full moon would soon be out to light up the night sky. With moonlight for certain, and no cloud cover available for the next eight days, it was decided to move the medical equipment to the new hospital right away, as all was in readiness and time was of the essence.

The shuttlecraft, laden with supplies, was loosed from its locks within the mothership and floated out of the cargo bay doors, slowly rising to the surface of the lake. Though considerably smaller than the mothership, the shuttle was not necessarily a minicraft, and could have carried all the needed supplies for five hospitals in a single trip. The shuttle's only navigator had known of the nearby auto and its occupants long before leaving the mothership. She had watched and recorded the mating ritual with fascination for several hours, but the threshold of maximum concealment was fading fast and the onboard Aquatian was obligated to recalculate the plan and get on with her chores.

As the shuttle lifted off the surface of the lake, the intent of its navigator was to skirt the vicinity of the nearby auto and its impassioned occupants. With minimal gravilift operational, the craft came about to seek a northwest trajectory when one of the equipment containers loosened from its magnetic moorings and began to slide dangerously. The navigator was obligated to instantly go to computer-pilot, which simply selected the shortest distance between the lake and the new hospital. This happened to be directly over the top of the little car and its hard-breathing occupants.

An honest mistake had been made. If man survives another millennium, he also will most probably make a major goof now and again. The sensitive equipment was delivered on schedule.

At breakfast the next morning Professor Hauss asked, "When will the Aquatus medical equipment arrive?" He was as excited as a small boy wondering what his birthday gifts would be like.

"It already has," replied Jayseeka. She then asked how soon it would be before she could be taken to the new hospital.

"As soon as we finish breakfast," came Vincent's proud reply.

Gillie had arrived from Thailand ten years earlier, and had been married to a U.S. Air Force Major for only three years, before he lost his life on a training mission in the Middle East. It took the young lady several years to get over her loss, and having no immediate family living in Thailand, she was invited to live with her deceased husband's sister in Little Falls, New York.

Industrious by nature and having been quite a good dress designer in Thailand, the girl had taken a summer job at Vincent Henry Manor as a maid. She hoped to save enough money to open a small shop in Little Falls, where she could make clothes, do alterations, and try as best she could to restart her life.

Vincent had been a little too optimistic about taking Jayseeka to see the new hospital immediately after breakfast.

Gillie was asked to alter some of Roxanne's old but tasteful clothing, while Roxanne and Elizabeth went into town to get some large wrap-around sunglasses, gloves of different colors, full-length stretch-stockings, and make up.

After three hours of alterations and two hours of makeup, and a fashion debate between Elizabeth and Roxanne, the end result was a new Jayseeka. She had been transformed into a very human looking child of movie star quality, ready for her first debut.

It was 2:30 p.m. before the Henrys and friends arrived at the new hospital. The hospital's security staff had been bribed early on by the local newspaper and television studio to notify them immediately when the Henrys came as a family to inspect the structure. This would indicate that the grand opening time was near, and a date could be fixed.

Less than thirty minutes after the Henrys and friends had stepped from the stretch limousine, three reporters and the Channel 5 TV studio's well-equipped van were at the hospital's main entry begging for interviews.

Neland Nester had taken the freight elevator and caught up with the Henrys and friends just prior to their stepping out onto the spacious hospital roof, most of which had been enclosed with glass framing. Vincent was about to show off the swimming pool, gym, and lunchroom that he had built for the hospital's soon-to-arrive staff.

Off to the left, outside the sizable glass canopy housing the existing staff perks, was a vacant area almost half again as large, where Vincent had thought to eventually put in a skating rink for winter recreation. This space currently stood host to six large square silver containers each approximately fifteen by ten feet in size.

Vincent was a bit irritated when Neland informed him of the local newspaper and television stations' surprise arrival. He had not planned on going public until everything was in complete order. True it was that the human medical equipment had been completely installed, but what about the Aquatus and their equipment? Where was it and how long would it take for it to become operational?

Mr. Henry was about to dismiss Neland the guard with the message of "no interviews today," when Jayseeka, tugging on his coat sleeve, indicated she had something to say.

"It's okay." She spoke quietly into Vincent's ear as he bent down to listen. "Two days are all I need to have our equipment operational."

So Vincent then informed his security that he would allow an interview at the hospital's main entry area in twenty minutes. Later in the week he would schedule the Mayor and all other dignitaries and investors for a detailed tour of the "up and running, fully-staffed facility."

As the guard went to deliver the message, the tight little group stepped out onto the roof through the entry doors, and Vincent began to elaborate on what had been done for the employees in that area. Turning to his left, Mr. Henry was about to point out the lunchroom steam tables and kitchen area. Suddenly in unison, as if drawn by some mysterious magnetic field, all heads turned to look outside the glass-enclosed canopy at the large silver containers occupying the proposed ice rink area. The Aquatus medical equipment had most certainly arrived.

The twenty-minute interview at the hospital's entry area was to go more smoothly than Vincent had previously thought, excepting for a bit of journalistic overkill with regard to Jayseeka.

The news media soothsayers, disappointed at not getting a fixed date for the hospital's grand opening, began to scrounge about for endearing news tidbits; the camera quickly picked up on Roxanne's unusual little friend Jayseeka.

"What a darling little girl you are!" exclaimed the Channel 5 newswoman, thrusting the microphone within three inches of Jayseeka's petite nose. "What is your name?"

"Jayseeka," came the quick response, clearly audible.

"What do you think about this big, big, new hospital?" baby-talked the newswoman.

"I think Mr. Vincent Henry did an exemplary job!" replied Jayseeka, much to the amazement of the now disconcerted newswoman. "And," continued the alien, in her clearly audible and melodiously beautiful voice, "I sincerely hope that all who see and hear this broadcast will admire him and his family for this most benevolent and unselfish gift to those less fortunate than themselves."

"Uh, yes, uh, yes, of course," replied the now astounded news commentator.

One of the newspaper reporters quickly jumped in with, "Where are you from, Miss Jayseeka?" but was quickly brushed aside by security, as Vincent hastily explained.

"I sincerely apologize that we simply have no more time as we are all late for a very important appointment!" Then with his left arm about his daughter and his right hand gently nudging the back of Jayseeka's golden locks, he ushered friends and family into the waiting limo.

Hospital security officer Neland Nester was a bit put off when he received a call from the Manor the following day. It was Vincent Henry, informing him that he knew who had tipped off the news media and that if it happened again, he would fire the entire hospital security staff. Also that he would be coming over soon, and wanted Nester and his men to take the day off with pay, and that the Manor security would cover until 11:30 that night.

Only Nester had remained on the premises when Vincent Henry, Dr. Hauss, Director Faraday, Jayseeka, and three of the Manor's security personnel arrived at the hospital. Roxanne had wanted to come, but realized that she would be more in the way than of any service. She wanted to finish the lyrics to a new song she had written, anyway.

Neland Nester was more than a little concerned about his job. "How the hell did Mr. Henry know about his deal with the news media?" he thought, as Henrys and friends exited the limousine. Then, spotting Jayseeka, "Why in the hell would they leave their daughter at home and drag that little pixie girl around with 'em? What about those big silver containers up on the roof?"

When he had phoned in the strange occurrence to Manor security chief Dan Sarte, he was simply told, "Don't worry about it." Neither he nor any of his men could remember that delivery; it would have taken a crane or at least a goddamned helicopter to lift them frigging things to the hospital roof.

Neland's stream of consciousness seemed to be almost out of control. "The night watch swore, and be damned, that the things just seemed to appear sometime after 12 p.m. and before one a.m. None of my four guards on duty saw or heard a thing, except a low humming sound, which came and went in a matter of a few minutes. Another thing: how the hell are they going to get those damned things open anyway?"

He and one of his men had tried to find an opening. The unusual containers were as smooth and cool to the touch as glass, but tough and resilient as well, with no visible place into which a crowbar could be wedged. "And now they want me and my men to take the day off?"

The bewildered Nester's thoughts had understandably become a bit radical as he got into his car and drove off into town; but then he was not the only person to think that strange and unusual things might be happening in and about Vincent Henry Manor.

Vincent had one of the Manor guards cover the elevators and emergency stairway area, and the other two at the hospital's main entries front and back.  Vincent, Jayseeka, and friends stepped out upon the roof of the huge complex, whereupon Jayseeka simply walked up and put her small hand on the side of the nearest container.  It immediately slid open with a hiss.  The container's five by five-foot doorway revealed numerous shelving areas, and a small wheel-less truck-type vehicle directly in the opening.

On each floor of the sixteen story hospital was a large empty room, having been specifically built as per Jayseeka's instructions, to house the Aquatus medical equipment.  It took little less than four hours to unload and deliver the equipment to its designated areas.  Jayseeka did most of the work, zipping about on the little anti-gravity transport eight inches off the floor, loading and unloading with astonishing speed, aided by robotic magnetic cranes within the self-lighted containers.

The diagnostic-medical devices, when touched in a certain area by human or alien, unfolded themselves with no further assistance, appearing to be little more than four and a half foot squares.  Light in weight, the three segments for each instrument could be easily placed end to end, which in turn formed a tunnel four and a half feet wide by the same in height, and thirteen and a half feet in length.

Vincent, Dr. Hauss and Faraday had easily assembled them in each of the rooms designated.  Each of the three sections, which formed a complete unit, locked together as if by some inherent magnetic force.  Once in place, numerous highly visible, brightly colored liquid crystal displays lit up the side panels within the membrane of the walls. It seemed that almost every color of the spectrum had been utilized. The displays were for informative purposes only; the equipment would need little interaction on behalf of the human beneficiaries who would use them. The multicolored digital displays of the assembled equipment would reveal the total physiology of its patient before and after treatment.

Dr. Hauss viewed with fascination the glowing digital read-outs on the panels of the other-worldly equipment. Several of the diagnostics he understood, such as body temperature, pulse, respiration, electrolytes, body potential, etc., but there were also many other displays and he was going to need many explanations.

Jayseeka noticed the good doctor's bewilderment. "Don't worry, Professor," she had said, pulling up beside him on the anti-grav. tractor, "it will all be explained in due time." Then giving him one of her now famous smiles, she continued with the tasks at hand.

When the alien equipment had been dispatched to and assembled in the designated areas, Jayseeka briefly explained how it was to be used. "As the patient passes through the equipment, tugged gently along by an inclusive interior tractor-beam, the equipment will automatically diagnose, prescribe, and administer the cure. The instrumentation will then give digital readout information as to what the illness or illnesses had been; this will be for the recording benefit of the hospital staff.

"We thoughtfully designed the equipment to be user-friendly," continued the alien. "Little will need to be done by the staff, who simply start the patients at one end, and receive them out the other, recording the medical information displayed at each end of the units."

Each completed unit glowed softly from its own integral power source. "Simply activate the equipment," explained

Jayseeka, being a bit redundant, "touching it here, and the automated device will roll the patient through the unit, in one side and out the other, thirty seconds per patient."

All were incredulous at the beauty and sophistication of these marvels of alien technology. Professor Hauss anticipated with joy the medical mysteries unfolding before him. A sum total of six hours and twenty minutes from start to finish, and the otherworldly equipment was ready for its first patient.

Jayseeka drove the anti-grav vehicle into one of the now empty containers, then sealed them all with the touch of her hand. They would be picked up by the shuttlecraft and returned to the mothership before ten that same evening; a dense fog was rolling in.

Henrys and friends left for the Manor, leaving two of the Manor's guards to stand watch until the regular hospital security team returned at 11:30 that night. On the short trip back to the manor, Jayseeka assured them all that the Aquatus medical equipment was thoroughly in readiness, whereupon Vincent requested the use of Bill's cellular phone, and called the Diamond Employment Agency.

The agency's director, Dustin Beancroft, was delighted when Mr. Henry instructed him, "Call in the staff, and get the hospital up and running A.S.A.P."

Beancroft estimated that a week would be needed before the first patient could be admitted. He had followed Vincent's instructions, sparing no expense in searching out the best medical personnel available within an eight-state area, and was aware of the staff's well-paid potential. With Beancroft calling the shots, the agency had done an outstanding job, and he had been rewarded handsomely for his timely effort. Dustin was unaware that the hospital's first patient was in the making, and would be on premises by ten thirty the next morning.

# Chapter Twelve

Immortal were we in our days of youth,
Thirty years was all we wanted.
Torturing tissues with social fads,
We pushed through life undaunted.
All too soon, now old and sick,
We turned to look behind,
To realize with but one more chance
A Heaven we could find;
Too late in life do we realize,
Our youth had been so kind.

Thommie Fratalga had arrived at his eighty-seventh birthday with more things wrong than most dead people. He had diabetes, only one lung (and still smoked two packs a day), heart problems, advanced prostate cancer, glioma, glaucoma, A.I.D.S. and several other severe medical problems which to date had not yet been diagnosed. About the only thing Thommie knew for sure that he didn't have was money.

Puffing and wheezing about his very small studio apartment on the previous day, he had dreaded the visit he was compelled to make to the Internal Revenue Service on the morrow. In his anxiety he had felt those all too familiar pains in his chest. After eating a handful of aspirins he had lain down on his musty second-hand couch at about four o'clock that afternoon, and losing consciousness, did not awake until seven the next morning.

The pains were still in his chest, though not as severe as they had been yesterday.  He went about finding something to eat and preparing himself for his 9:00 o'clock visit with Ginger at the new IRS building downtown.

Five years earlier Thommie had hit it big at a casino in Las Vegas and had checked out with the intention of never paying a dime's worth of taxes on the money he had won.  The mistakes that Thommie had made were registering at the casino using his easy-to-trace credit card and not wanting to carry around thirty thousand dollars in cash.  He had given his correct name to be put on the check the casino had issued for his winnings.  Thommie had knowingly conspired to defraud.

About as joyous as a really sick man can be, Thommie had taken his (and the government's money) home to his small studio apartment in Little Falls, stashing it in a shoebox in the closet.  One night, four years after his big win in Las Vegas, Thommie would invite a younger gay "friend" over for a bit of wine and gayness, more or less a final attempt for this sick old wreck of a human.

He lost consciousness from the effort of it all, and awakening six hours later discovered that his "friend," the small remainder of his casino winnings, his only credit card and most of his clothes were gone. The "friend," skipping town was never to be seen or heard from again.

Pitifully sick, and once again pitifully poor, Thommie's problems were compounded when the IRS caught up with him a mere two weeks later, and good ol' Thommie found himself on the hook for back taxes, penalties and interest. Considering doing himself in, the despairing Thommie had called the local suicide hot-line--they put him on hold.  Still he could not find the courage to end it all.

His problem with the IRS was not a real problem, as sick as Thommie was and on the government dole anyway, except that he could do jail time for the willful fraud. Ginger (the IRS agent) had miserable ol' Thommie believing he would be wheezing the rest of his life away in a dank and dingy jail cell if he didn't come up with some of the long green. Naturally they did not believe his story about the money being stolen; they had heard that one before.

Fate had determined from the beginning that Thommie would never be a rocket scientist. In fact he would never complete the ninth grade, but instead ran away with a gay older man, who ditched him after showing him the wonders of the big city. Those were formative years, and young Thommie Fratalga would eventually go to work selling the only thing he had, which was himself.

Most probably the young Thommie had been one of the first male exotic dancers in New York City and did not begin to show his age, at least not in the dark, until well into his forties. He had to choose another profession after that. Thommie had lived hand to mouth those years as a dancer, one party after another, never learning a trade; but he learned quite quickly that a Thommie without cash was a Thommie without friends.

Alone, dejected and broke, he returned to the only real home that he had ever known in Little Falls, New York. Thommie's father had died years before, and his mother died two years after his return. Working as a security guard in a department store downtown, he was forced into retirement at age fifty-nine for medical reasons, ending up on Social Security.

Ginger, the IRS agent with whom he had been consulting, knew his life story from his previous visits. The friendly Thommie, never too bright, always told people more than they needed to know.

There are many who believe sadism to be a prerequisite for a job with the IRS. Ginger didn't really believe that she could get this wheezing, sick, old wreck of a man behind bars. She was going to let him off anyway, but wanted to get something, if only a little revenge, for the stupid paperwork he had put her through. She and several of her cronies, who either consciously or unconsciously hated men, had conspired to get ol' Thommie to attend one of their private parties, and dance nude for their sick amusement.

Thommie regretfully accepted the "one more show for old time's sake" if Ginger would promise to do everything possible to keep him out of the slammer. The instant the deal was struck, the agent began gleefully surveying her calendar. As she was deciding on the best date, she would giggle from time to time, mentally visualizing this sick, ultra-skinny old fart of a has-been, gyrating, wheezing and pumping away in front of an audience of her half-drunk buddies as they pelted him with snide verbal abuse.

Upon hearing a weak plea for help, Ginger's joy was cut short as she looked up to see a now paler than ever, forlorn and bewildered Thommie, clutching his chest. He slipped out of the chair before her and onto the floor.

"Now if that's not damned fucking inconsiderate!" thought Ginger, as she dialed 911.

At 9:40 a.m. Thommie was in an ambulance, life signs ebbing fast, on his way to Chapman Memorial. The hospital had been established for quite some time in the community and was well known for, often as not, being understaffed.

When the ambulance with its wretched cargo arrived at Chapman Memorial, the drivers were informed that the only doctor who could be of service to Thommie was already in surgery. He would not be free for at least another hour, in which case Thommie would be dead. The ambulance drivers, either out of dedication or the desire to run up a larger delivery bill, hit upon the idea to rush their more-dead-than-alive consignment up to Vincent Henry Memorial.

The newly employed surgeon, Doctor Karl Justin, just happened to be inspecting the emergency entry area, when the ambulance pulled into the drive. He made a quick phone call to the Manor, prior to diagnosing Thommie, for permission to admit the patent. The conscientious Dr. Justin had been the first to arrive at the new hospital.

Vincent Henry had always been a hands-on sort of fellow, and picked up the call immediately from Dan Sarte. "Are we set up to handle this situation?" asked Vincent.

The patient had been rolled directly up to Dr. Justin, who was now calling to a nearby nurse to help locate various drugs that could hopefully be used to stabilize the patient.

"If this guy was a potato, I wouldn't even have to stick a fork in him. He's done!" responded Justin. "His pulse is so weak it barely gets a reading on the instrumentation here in the emergency room. We're losing him! Stand back," commanded Dr. Justin as he hit Thommie with an electrical charge.

"Got to move fast, is it yea or nay?" demanded the Doctor.

"Well, hell yes, Justin. Do what you can!" said Vincent, handing the portable phone back to Danny Sarte.

"Let's go," said the little voice, as Vincent was gathering his thoughts. Turning around and looking down, there was Jayseeka, who didn't have to be told what was going on.

"Use the equipment?" asked Vincent.

Her silence and movement toward the front entry was his answer. The little alien carried a small bag with her; from it she pulled a petite dress, lengthy gloves, stockings, makeup, and her sunglasses. She was dressed in the short time it took to drive from the Manor to the hospital.

Twenty minutes after the doctor's call to the Manor, Vincent and Jayseeka walked into the emergency operating room. The now despondent Dr. Justin was shaking his head.

"I guess it doesn't matter if you two aren't sterile. We lost the old codger five minutes ago anyway. I couldn't even stabilize him, let alone cut him open!"

"Not meaning to be rude, sir," continued Dr. Justin, "but why would you bring that little girl in to see something like this?" As he looked at Jayseeka, he thought for a moment that he had seen something strange behind her large wraparound sunglasses.

"Would you and the nurses move the patient off the operating table and back onto the gurney, please?" asked Vincent.

Thinking it strange that Vincent was there to begin with, and now giving orders, the doctor nodded to his assistants, who rolled the gurney over and lifted the patient onto it.

"Bring him this way," motioned Vincent as he started through the double doors into the hallway.

"Now wait just a damned minute!" protested Dr. Justin. "Where are you going with that corpse?"

Vincent ignored the now irate healer as he and Jayseeka headed off down the hallway, dutifully followed by the two nurses, one of them pushing Thommie along on the gurney. They knew all too well who would be signing their paychecks.

As Vincent, Jayseeka, Thommie, and the two nurses approached the secured room containing the Aquatus medical equipment, Vincent instructed the nurses to remain outside as he stood before the lens activating the retinal scan. The large door slid open, then quickly closed behind, as Vincent pushed Thommie into the room, followed by Jayseeka.

Once in the room, Jayseeka activated the alien equipment by touch at the topmost front end of the unit. The brightly-colored digital displays immediately lit up the side panels, as eight legs slowly lifted the entire apparatus three additional feet off the floor, as if by hydraulics. Out of the front end of the equipment, which now took on a bluish-green glow in its interior, emerged a transparent panel, flat side parallel to the floor. The panel was approximately a single inch thick, four feet wide, and eight feet long, with no visible means of support except where it was attached to the interior of the apparatus.

As Vincent began to move the totally nude Thommie from the gurney to the panel, the room's entry door once more slid open, admitting Dr. Hauss, who began to help with the activity. The Professor was to be the designated supervisor of the equipment's use, and was pleased that things had finally gotten under way.

Vincent started Thommie into the front end of the equipment, which now began to glow with greater intensity. Dr. Hauss began to record the information from the brightly-lit digital displays onto a nearby computer. The apparatus now pulsed vividly with activity, as the patient was gently tugged along on his journey through its belly.

"According to these readings," began Dr. Hauss, "you put a corpse in one end, and half a minute later got a living man out the other!"

Vincent looked down at Jayseeka, who smiled knowingly.

Dr. Hauss, who thought he was going to get used to the impossible, could not quite fathom what he had just witnessed. "Didn't you say you couldn't bring back the dead?" he exclaimed, looking down at Jayseeka.

"The DNA was still fresh and vital," she responded, "and please see to it that when the patient regains consciousness, which should be in about four hours, that he gets all the food and fluids he desires, be it at regular meal times or in between."

"I'd better get out in the hall and try to smooth Dr. Justin's ruffled feathers," volunteered the Professor, regaining his composure. "He was pretty hot with those nurses when I passed them in the hallway. Damn! You must have really knocked his dingus in the dirt!"

"If he's still out there, bring him and the nurses in. I want to talk to them," requested Vincent.

**********

"The man was *dead!*" exclaimed Dr. Justin. "He had absolutely no vital signs whatsoever. I tried everything I could possibly think of and..."

"Well, now he's alive," calmly explained Vincent, as Dr. Justin examined Thommie Fratalga.

"He damned sure is, the man is definitely uh-a-alive!" stammered the physician, as he realized that he had given up for dead a man who could be saved.

The two nurses stood ready to assist, pale and quietly frightened by what they had witnessed. The dismay and concern on Dr. Justin's face was enough to let Vincent know that the good doctor had tried his best, and was suffering a guilt complex unparalleled in his career as a heart surgeon.

"How did you...what did you...?" began Dr. Justin, as Vincent put his hand on his shoulder.

"I have an MD, as well as an MBA, but I don't practice medicine as most of my time has been spent running my business operations. I couldn't give that up. It wasn't really anything I did anyway; it was this equipment you see before you that did the job."

The doctor's eyes fell on the equipment, with its glowing interior, and brightly-lit multicolored displays.

"I will explain it all to you and your colleagues soon," continued Vincent, "but for the time being I want you to keep in close touch with me regarding this patient's recovery. I want to know everything that happens from the time he opens his eyes until he's finally discharged. Dr. Hauss will provide you with the particulars regarding the patient's care."

Then informing his friend Dr. Hauss that dinner would be at six, Vincent took Jayseeka by the hand and left the room.

Dr. Hauss talked with Dr. Justin for another hour or so, then left the hospital, knowing its first patient would be in capable hands.

As the nurses performed the patient care duties, placing Thommie in a suite and hooking up the monitor wiring, Dr. Justin lay down on the other bed in the same room for an hour before regaining his equanimity.

"Just when you think you've seen it all..." he mumbled, glancing at the patient now and again, but he was soon to see much more.

After checking out his patient's vital signs, Dr. Justin noted the unusually good color of the man's complexion. "For one who had sustained the trauma of heart failure, this is really amazing!" he thought.

Then leaving the room, relieved and surprised that all was going so well, he met one of the nurses in the hallway, and apologized for his earlier short-tempered remarks. He asked her, "Please draw blood from the patient and get it to the lab A.S.A.P., and also send a courier to pick up all, if any, of Mr. Fratalga's medical files at Chapman Memorial."

Every half hour or so the doctor stopped by to check on Thommie; each time he left the patient's room he became more baffled at the improvement taking place in such a short period of time. "Amazing," he would say, "amazing!" But the real fun would begin when Thommie awoke at four fifteen that afternoon with the hunger of a half-starved hippopotamus.

The two nurses and Dr. Justin had ordered two medium pizzas earlier for lunch, but in all the excitement regarding the hospital's first patient, they had simply forgotten to eat them. They lost their appetites later for the cold and hardened fare.

While the nurses conferred on the probability of ordering in other food, Thommie awoke in his suite down the hall, drank all the water at the side of his bed, got up and went into the adjoining rest-room to get more water, urinate, and take a "dump."

The patient had pulled loose the monitoring wires hooking him into the observation units at the nurses' station. Inadvertently he had set off the alarms, which brought the nurses on the run, thinking Thommie had fallen out of bed.

As the two nurses rushed into the room, their worry turned to panic when they could find no patient. Neither on, beside, nor under the bed.

"What ya got to eat around this place?" asked the hungry man from his perch on the bathroom's toilet.

The two nurses spun around, rushed into the bathroom and grabbed the startled Thommie under each arm and began to haul him back towards the bed.

"Whoa! Just one fucking minute here! I'm not finished yet!" ejected the disconcerted patient. "Gimmie a chance to pinch off a loaf here--for shit-sakes!"

The two nurses stopped their reflex actions and set Thommie back once more upon the throne. These were not the remarks of a sickly heart patient; in fact this patient not only looked really good, but also younger.

The two nurses stood looking wonderingly at Thommie on the stool for about twenty seconds, and he looked back at them, confused about their forwardness.

"Uh, would you two mind? I'll be through here in a minute or so; if you really want to help me I'd appreciate some food. I'm so goddamned hungry I could eat the asshole out of a skunk."

The nurses waited for Thommie to leave the toilet then escorted him back to the bed, totally mystified by his agility as he climbed unassisted between the sheets. After being wired once more to the monitors, the nurses scolded their patient thoroughly, one threatening to "slap him upside the head" if he didn't do what he was told.

"Okay! Okay!" agreed Thommie. "I'll do anything you ask, but please, can you find me some food?"

Leaving Thommie's room, one of the nurses went to find Dr. Justin, while the other set off to the kitchen area to try and locate something with which to abate the patient's hunger.

Doctor Justin was in his office, where he had been for the last thirty minutes, poring over the file on Thommie Fratalga that the courier had recently delivered. The doctor was shaking his head and talking to himself under his breath when the nurse found him.

"Sir, the patient is awake, and seems to be doing just fine, in fact he got out of bed and went to the rest-room unassisted, shaking loose his monitor wires and..."

The information stopped as she found herself now looking into confused eyes, more those of a frightened little boy, than of a forty-nine year-old doctor of medicine.

"That patient is not Thommie Fratalga!" responded the doctor. "I've got the file on Thommie Fratalga, and the man in this file could not possibly be..." His voice trailed off, then started up again. "I just got the lab tests back, and there is no way the patient we have and Thommie Fratalga could be one and the same person!"

"But Doctor, according to his wallet and the identification we found...?"

"Yes, well, he must have stolen the wallet," responded Dr. Justin as he picked up the file and started in the direction of his patient's room.

Thommie greeted Justin with "How ya doing, Doc? You people really know your stuff around this place; I haven't felt so damn good in years." Then shifting his glance from doctor to nurse, "Did ya find me something to eat? Damn, I'd sell my soul for a hamburger."

The doctor found a stool and rolled it up beside Thommie's bed, laying the patient's file on a small table nearby. Then looking intently into Thommie's eyes, he asked, "You're not Thomas Fratalga, are you?"

"Yeah, of course I am," responded Thommie. "What are ya trying to do, find an excuse not to feed me?" asked the now disconcerted patient.

"Why, hell no!" countered the doctor. "This is a charitable institution. Anyway, it doesn't cost you a dime to be treated here, and we do feed our patients. I just want to know where you got the wallet you were carrying when they rolled you in."

"Alrightie then," Thommie's eyes brightened. "You get me something to eat, and don't be stingy, and I'll tell ya where I got the wallet."

Dr. Justin had promised himself that he was not going to lose his cool, but he wanted sensible answers, so as to make a sensible diagnosis, and he didn't feel he was getting any cooperation.

The doctor looked up from his patient and into the eyes of the remaining nurse. "Will someone get this man something to eat, for Christ's sake!"

"The kitchen is not set up yet," replied the second nurse, walking through the door carrying their uneaten lunch, two stone cold pizzas.

"Pizza!" exclaimed Thommie, sitting bolt upright in bed.

"Now, wait a minute," protested the doctor, "I don't think his guts can handle that crap!"

"Gimme," pleaded the now salivating patient, stretching his arms out to the nurse, "and I'll tell ya where I got the wallet."

"Oh hell, give it to him." ejected the doctor, who then had to sit patiently and watch Thommie wolf down four repulsive cold pieces in rapid succession.

"Where did you get the wallet?" once more tried Dr. Justin.

"Stacy's," came the muffled answer, as Thommie started on piece number five.

"Stacy's?" exclaimed the doctor.

"That's right; on special for two bucks eight years ago."

"Then you are Thommie Fratalga?" quietly reiterated Dr. Justin.

"I already told ya I was, yes. YES!" replied Thommie. "Now I've got better things to do with my mouth than talk, so if you have any further questions, please wait until I'm finished eating. Oh nurse, could I have some more water, please?" Thommie then dug into the rest of the pizza like a concentration camp escapee.

The nurses stood by with silly grins on their faces. When Thommie was halfway through the second pizza, with no sign of slowing down, the nurse that had brought the pies decided to go back down to the kitchen and try to find a can opener. She had spotted some canned goods in the pantry on her previous trip.

Dr. Justin waited with conservative wonderment as Thommie finished devouring his pizzas. He further marveled as the tiniest bits that had fallen to the side were diligently pinched up and consumed by his apparently now fully recovered patient.

**********

"What I'm reporting to you now, sir, you probably won't believe," began Dr. Justin, once he had Vincent Henry on the phone.

It was 6:30 p.m. that same day, and Vincent Henry Memorial's first patient was striding his way to a rapid recovery.

"If this patient we have here is who he says he is, then God himself must have come down and breathed a new and healthy life into his body," continued Justin. "I see absolutely no reason to operate. According to his electrocardiograph and all other aspects of his physiology, the man's just fine, in fact he appears to be getting younger. The illnesses that plagued Thommie Fratalga are either gone or in rapid remission."

After a short pause, and then speaking in a most serious lower voice, Dr. Justin continued, "What I'm now most concerned about is, how did you, with the use of that unusual equipment, not only diagnose, but effect a cure for absolutely every medical problem the man had. When only hours ago he was either, or almost dead?"

"Continue to keep an accurate record of all that you observe regarding this patient, and I will Have Dr. Hauss get with you tomorrow. You are in on the ground floor of a new medical technology," explained Vincent, "and we must keep it highly classified until the appropriate time."

"Rest assured, Dr. Henry, that you can confide in me," came the response. "I plan to remain in the building throughout the night, and one of my nurses has agreed to pull overtime as well. I will most certainly be looking forward to discussing these sensational findings with you and Dr. Hauss tomorrow."

As Dr. Justin hung up the phone, he realized that fascination and wonderment were not substitutes for food. The nurses and he had missed lunch. Thommie had indicated that he was still very hungry, and the hospital's kitchen staff wouldn't even begin to arrive to set up for their new jobs until tomorrow afternoon. "Road Waiters" were about to get very busy.

# Chapter Thirteen

"At first I thought that his stroke had destroyed that portion of the brain's nervous tissue that turns off hunger. However, upon closer observation I noticed other unusual things starting to take place. Exterior skin tissues seemed to--no, hell, not seemed to--were stretching tight over new and growing muscle tissue groups beneath the surface.

"His body seems to have gone into a renewal of body tissues overdrive, fueled by the enormous quantities of food he was eating. He definitely is not growing fat; he, plain and simple, is going through some type of a, uh, oh hell...*rejuvenation* process."

Dr. Justin, obviously quite confounded by his observations, paused in his one-sided conversation with Dr. Hauss to take a drink of water at a nearby fountain. Then reshuffling his copious notes together with numerous blood and tissue tests, he fixed Dr. Hauss once more with the bright and questioning eyes of one who had witnessed things far beyond commonplace, and began once more his report.

"The patient only slept about four hours last night. I know, because that's all the time I got to sleep as well. I was diligent in taking blood and skin tissue samples from time to time. The nurse kept bringing the food; skin and blood samples continued to improve, until all of them taken recently are vigorously healthy. I called in the lab technicians early this morning and they have been busy ever since.

"In checking out his vision I discovered he now has 20/20 and no longer needs glasses. I even took dental x-rays and found tooth buds starting to form in the eight areas where teeth had been pulled years ago. Hell, I've stuck my finger up his butt and checked his once tumorous prostate so many times that he's beginning to think I'm gay! What do I find? A prostate, which was supposedly so tumorous and cancerous as to be inoperable two months ago, now as benign as a mother's love.

"The guy is who he says he is because I sent all his fingerprints over to City Hall and they sent back a match. The guy is Thomas Fratalga, nicknamed Thommie."

It had been 10:30 in the morning when the disappointed Dr. Hauss was able to join up with Dr. Justin concerning the new hospital's first patient. He had not wanted to miss anything concerning the progress of this patient, who had literally been brought back from the dead by the spectacular equipment from another world. Unfortunately he had some pressing over-the-telephone obligations to solidify with several colleagues offshore. He hurried over to the hospital as soon as he could; his mild disappointment would not last long.

As Vincent had instructed, Dr. Justin was delivering his astounding report to the Professor. The Professor himself was also clearly astonished, but he didn't feel that allowing himself the luxury of showing his amazement to the confounded Dr. Justin would be of any benefit to either Justin or himself.

"Dr. Justin, please take me to see the patient," requested the Professor, putting his arm across Justin's shoulders in hopes it might settle him down a bit.

On their way down the hall, Dr. Justin continued to inform the Professor, as best he could, about all that had gone on concerning Thommie Fratalga.

"When we admitted that frail old man yesterday, he was so close to death that his only real luck was no luck at all. According to his file from Chapman Memorial he was a victim of diabetes, inoperable prostate cancer, glaucoma, progressive glioma, was HIV positive, had a bad heart, and only one lung. No telling what else could have been wrong; Chapman Memorial just stopped looking, prescribed some heavy duty drugs, in an attempt to kill pain, which Thommie used almost immediately, then proceeded to hound the doctor's and pharmacist for more.

"None of the illnesses I found in his file are apparent at this time. By taking periodic x-rays I was able to watch him grow a new lung." Dr. Justin stopped short, catching the sleeve of the Professor's sports jacket just outside Thommie's room.

"Have you been listening to me, Dr. Hauss? I said the man *grew a new lung!*"

As Dr. Hauss turned to look at the harried Dr. Justin, Justin could tell by the beads of perspiration on the Professor's forehead and upper lip that he had indeed heard. It was always an even seventy degrees inside the hospital, and Dr. Hauss was only wearing a lightweight sports jacket.

"You saw him yesterday, wait until you see him now!" exclaimed Justin, as he pushed open the door and entered the patient's room.

Thommie had heard the footsteps and voices just outside his room and pulled the sheet up over his head as the two doctors entered. "No more x-rays, no more blood, no more tissue samples, and no more sticking your finger up my butt. I don't think I want to play 'doctor' any more!" punned the now healthy and feeling-good patient.

"Come on out, Thommie or I'll cut off your food supply," good-naturedly countered Dr. Justin. "I have someone here I would like you to meet."

The sheet snapped down immediately.

"What's for lunch?" inquired the patient.

Professor Hauss couldn't hide his amazement at the physiology of the now robustly healthy patient. There could be absolutely no comparison between the pathetically sick eighty-seven year-old Thomas Fratalga that had arrived in emergency yesterday and this beamingly healthy patient now confronting him in the bed; and yet they were indeed one and the same man.

Dr. Hauss got out his tape recorder and rolled a small-wheeled stool up to the side of the bed.

"Wait a minute," requested Thommie, "I got to take another dump. That will be the third time this morning," he volunteered. "I know it's a shitty suggestion, but you might wanna put that in your notes," he smirked, hopping briskly out of bed and striding into the rest room.

The Vincent Henry Memorial Hospital opened for business the following week, and in the first two days treated eight hundred and two forlorn souls that the rest of the medical world had given up on. All services were absolutely free, and donations were accepted only if volunteered by patients, friends or family.

When the rest of the hospital's staff began arriving to set up for business in their new habitat, Thommie Fratalga was still in residence for observation and investigative purposes. Gossip spread quickly among the staff concerning Thommie, and they, not yet aware of where the hospital's fantastic medical equipment had come from, dubbed them "The Lazarus Machines."

This would be the strangest hospital any of the staff had ever worked in. Patients would be brought in and immediately taken into the rooms on each floor wherein resided the strange and unusual Lazarus Machines. They would be given documents of agreement to sign, and if they couldn't, their families would sign for them.

Then, stripped of their clothing, they would be passed through the interior of the fantastic apparatuses. Seemingly fast asleep when taken out the other end, the patients would then be gurneyed off to their assigned rooms. Upon awakening, they would be fed all they could eat of whatever the kitchen had available.

The kitchen staff was soon to increase tenfold, and rooms that had been designated for now obsolete equipment, would be used for food storage, once the equipment was removed. Most of the staff's activity revolved around detailed documentation and feeding the ever-hungry patients.

Patients could have been released earlier in the beginning, but there was a certain amount of education needed to prepare them and their families for what was taking place concerning the patients' physiology, and their unusual needs for vast quantities of food.

The amazing Aquatus apparatuses would literally cure each and every functional or organic illness, rejuvenate any and all appendages, organs, nervous tissues, connective tissues, bones, cure addictions, and also increase the IQ of the patients by up to thirty percent. The Aquatus had not only kept their promise; they would be seen as saviors who had embarked humanity upon a new era of fulfillment and accomplishment.

The only benefit not yet discovered from the use of the apparatuses (it later would be) was that all those who traveled through the belly of the alien apparatuses could look forward to a longevity, from birth to death, of between one hundred and fifteen to one hundred and twenty-five years of excellent health, if not meeting with an unnatural death. The Grim Reaper, when he finally did make his cold approach, would be compelled to do so quickly, with absolutely no pain or suffering.

It would be two weeks and three thousand patients later that Government personnel of every manner and description would descend upon Vincent Henry Memorial. The cat was out of the bag, and it was going to be impossible to catch.

Secretary of State William Faraday was able to seize control of the situation quickly; he had seen the domestic concern and conflict coming early on. He was really surprised that the incredible healing and rejuvenation of the first several hundred patients hadn't gotten any more attention than it did.

He had placed a conference call to the President and Secretary of Defense only minutes after the local National Guard began to arrive and set up barriers around the hospital. Faraday was prepared to give his all for what he had come to believe was in the better interest of his country and the world.

**********

"It seems we have an 'extra-terrestrial' scare going on up here, Mr. President. I have inside information concerning the situation, but I'm going to need your permission to declare martial law if needed, until I can get it cleaned up and ready for presentation," informed Faraday.

"Now look here, Bill," began the President. "I have some pretty hot documents here on my desk in which you are personally implicated. I need to know what's happening there in Little Falls. What's this bullshit about aliens? What in the Sam Hill is going on, Bill?"

"Mr. President, give me permission to institute martial

law," requested Faraday, "and I will clean up the situation, package it and make a presentation within five days."

"Okay, Bill, you have five days, but Christ! We're starting to get coast-to-coast news media on this incident. If it's aliens we're supposedly dealing with, well, that would fall within the realm of the State Department. I'm dispatching copies of the documentation I have before me; you should get them within the hour, along with my consent to use martial law if needed. Keep in close contact with me Bill; let me know what you need. Aliens, for Christ's sake!" muttered the President, hanging up the phone.

"Who gave you permission to call in the National Guard, Mayor Fisher, and why?" began Faraday, immediately putting the young Mayor on the defensive.

"A little more than two-and-a-half years ago," began the Mayor, a bit apprehensive at first, "a maid and a cook working for the Henry household reported having seen an alien at the Manor. They apparently were terrified to such a degree that they had to be sedated and hospitalized for several days. The police chief at the time was a Pat Riely, a fellow I never liked very much anyway. He had gone up to the Manor, and after a rude, obnoxious, but extensive search of the estate, was told to leave by yourself. Sir, I'm sure you remember?"

Faraday nodded his head.

"Well, I fired Riely for having harassed the Henrys; the truth is, I had been looking for a good excuse anyway. Later I was informed that Riely might have gone back to the Henry estate, as one of the officers saw him loading his telescopic investigative equipment into his car, and presumed that he had not yet given up on the case, even though he had been fired.

"Later, Riely's landlord noticed that he had not returned home for several days and called the station, learning then that Riely had been fired. After several more days the landlord thought it strange that his renter would leave and not take any of his personal effects. He called the station, reporting this also. Riely's car was later found in the area of the Henry estate, but Pat Riely and his investigative equipment were never seen again."

The young and visibly uncomfortable Mayor Fisher then coughed, shook his head while clearing his throat, and began once more his explanations. "The cook and maid, Elvira Mergess and Franceen Haprowe, later took lie-detector, uh, polygraph tests, and the results indicated that they had been telling the truth."

"Most of us continued to believe that the two had gotten onto some kind of hallucinogenic drug and simply believed their own preposterous stories. Both Elvira Mergess and Franceen Haprowe left town soon after that. Only a very few ever believed their stories; I suppose they were too upset and embarrassed to stay.

"Then, less than three weeks ago, two kids got the crap scared out of them by what they believed to be a flying saucer near the Henry estate. Now there is this fantastic medical equipment at that new hospital that the staff and even the patients claim can raise the dead! Now you tell me, sir, what the hell would you have done, at that point, had you been me?" exclaimed the disconcerted young Mayor, with a bit of testiness in his voice.

"The President has allowed me to declare martial law, if need be, until we can get a grip on this thing," stated Faraday, turning to the new police chief and the FBI agent standing nearby.

"We're not going to challenge you, Sir," spoke up Alex Maston from the FBI, "but I would certainly like to stick around and help out if need be. I'm really concerned with what's going on here."

Faraday nodded his consent.

"I'd like to stick around also, Sir," announced police chief Jack Webster, "but I just got word over my cellular that all the patients that have been treated and released from the new hospital to date, are getting together with friends and relatives. They are planning to march from town to the hospital tomorrow to stand behind the Vincent Henry Memorial Hospital's staff, and the Henrys themselves if need be. I don't really see how things can get ugly, most of them upstanding citizens and all, but one can never tell for sure."

"I appreciate your concern, Jack," responded Faraday. "Let's exchange cellular numbers, and I'm going to ask that you be diligent in keeping me informed."

"Absolutely," replied the police chief, firmly shaking Faraday's hand, then starting for the door.

Leaving the Mayor's office and driving up to the hospital, Faraday was surprised that the National Guard unit in Little Falls had so many troops, but then this was good. Things could possibly get a little out of hand.

During the ride from town, Faraday got a call from Vincent, who was a little upset with the obnoxious news media trying to interview at the Manor.

Faraday stopped first at the hospital to inform the ranking guard officer there that he was assuming command of the local unit and that there would be no further news media allowed on the premises until a time he would designate.

Then driving up to the Manor, he informed the disappointed television and newspaper reporters from all over the country, "For the safety of the citizens and all concerned, it will take a while to get this situation under control." He promised them a news conference tomorrow afternoon; he would set the time and all would be invited. He then instructed them to leave the Manor grounds until that time.

While the nation, indeed the world, waited for the news, Faraday entered Vincent Henry Manor being greeted by Professor Hauss, Jayseeka, and the Henrys; it was definitely conference time.

## Chapter Fourteen

There were several questions to which Secretary Faraday had wanted answers, but whatever they were, they had refused to enter his conscious mind during last night's strategy meeting with Jayseeka, Dr. Hauss and the Henrys.

The meeting had lasted about four hours and upon its conclusion, all participants, including Faraday, were convinced that there was a higher morality to be ordained for the human condition than the United States Constitution or Bill of Rights. Each of them was destined to act as an instrument, with an almost religious commitment, to set humanity free from the evils of ignorance, starvation, pollution and disease. Under no duress they had drawn logical conclusions. By witness and association of the Aquatus and their wonders, each would become a willing participant in a new dawning of Mankind.

Day One

At 8 o'clock the following morning Secretary Faraday arrived on the steps of Vincent Henry Memorial Hospital. There he informed the news media that the hospital's staff would be available to explain and substantiate the testimony of the patients who to date had been treated and released.

"The ground rules are quite simple," explained Faraday. "Ten doctors from each of the three eight hour shifts, each ending at 9 a.m., 5 p.m. and one a.m. respectively, will be available before and after each of their shifts. They will stand with any of the hundred or so patients they have treated, answering any questions the legitimate news media might ask.

"There will be absolutely no admittance to the interior of the hospital by the news media, or other persons, unless they are immediate friends or relatives of the patients within. However, at a time yet to be designated, four or five days from now, the media will be taken to view the so-called Lazarus Machines in small and orderly groups."

"And what happens to those that enter the hospital without the gracious consent of your Majesty?" sarcastically asked a surly young reporter. He was a representative for one of those "predatory rags" one often sees mutilating the truth.

"From now until it is lifted, I am declaring martial law to protect those within the hospital: patients, relatives and staff alike," responded Faraday. "There are temporary facilities currently being constructed, and others already available in town, for the purpose of accommodating those who do not obey the law. The only thing I can promise those foolish enough to be taken into custody is that the food will be palatable for the duration of their incarceration."

"And what time will the news conference be held this afternoon?" inquired an out-of-state newsperson holding up her microphone.

"It has been decided that the conference will be best if re-scheduled to a time after we have taken you all to view the Lazarus Machines and after the doctor/patient interviews. By that time most of you will, in all probability, have most of your questions answered. After this we will be better able to focus on the remaining, more meaningful questions."

"Hey! How about the aliens?" asked one of the newspaper reporters.

"Yeah! Tell us about the little mean greenies!" shouted another.

The audience laughed.

Faraday smiled, then looked upward and lifted his hands toward the sky; the audience laughed again.

"We will discuss that also at the conference several days from now," finished Faraday.

Leaving the steps of the hospital and heading for his now designated sedan and driver, he would be under maximum protection from that time onward. There was a minority of persons in the audience who had not laughed at the ruse concerning aliens. They had seen and heard things. After the first few hours of patient-doctor interviews, laughter would be a rare commodity in and about Vincent Henry Memorial Hospital, across the nation, and around the world.

Day Two

The patient was eloquent in his description of the machines that had cured him, and his doctor verified all that he said.

A religious news reporter, with fire in his voice, had suggested, "Machines that can heal in the manner described by you and your doctor could possibly be the work of Satan!"

"I don't care if the Devil himself made the machine that cured me! If it could be proven, and I'm sure it can't, that Satan did indeed make those machines, then most obviously we have been worshipping the wrong Deity!" responded the affronted patient.

Most of the crowd listening in on the interviews didn't give much credence to the patient's indignant statement, but there were others of a more religious conviction who did. When it came over the airwaves and out of their televisions, they quickly began to marshal their organizations. They wanted to know the origin of the miracles occurring at the new hospital in Little Falls, New York.

"What the hell are you doing, Bill?" exclaimed the President when he got Secretary Faraday on the phone. "I keep looking for a method to your madness, but it has now become quite obvious that instead of media disinformation, containment and the shutting down of that situation in Little Falls, I'll be goddamned to hell if we don't have around-the-world news coverage on the goddamned thing! Now Bill, I think that perhaps under stress, you may have gone off the deep end, and I want you to come on home now and take a rest. I'm going to send someone else down and see if we can't get a handle on this goddamned thing. I'll expect you in my office by ten o'clock this evening, and I strongly caution you not to be late."

"Mr. President, what area of the mansion is your current location?" coolly asked Faraday.

"I'm in the goddamned kitchen eating a sandwich. What the hell has that got to do with...?!"

"Mr. President would you go to the Oval Office, and look in the back of the bottom-most left hand drawer of your desk? Review what you find there, then call me back."

"Now wait just one frigging minute here, Faraday. Are you starting for home now or--? "

"It would be in your better interest to do as I ask, sir," insisted Faraday.

"Don't hang up!" ejected the President. "I'm going to get to the bottom of this right now! I'll pick you up in the Oval Office."

Two of the White House security officers had tuned in to the anxiety of their perplexed boss; the President handed the phone to one of them.

"Put this S.O.B. on hold!" he instructed. Then dropping his sandwich, he stormed off toward the Oval Office with the other guard close at his heels. Once in the room the President ordered the guard to look into the drawer designated by Faraday, he standing a good distance away on the other side of the desk.

"Well, what is it?" asked the President as the guard held up a small plastic container.

"It's a video, sir," replied the guard, with a relieved grin on his face. "Just a video." he repeated, holding it up to the light.

"Give it to me," instructed his boss.

Realization was beginning to dawn as the President picked up the phone re-connecting him with his Secretary of State. "Is this what I think it is, Faraday?" asked a now subdued President.

"You're a star, sir," came back the reply on the other end of the phone.

Motioning for the guard to leave, the president walked over to the video machine and slipped in the cassette. His blood turned to ice water as he viewed himself at a younger age; the Governor who would be President, buck-naked on a large sheet of polyethylene with two nude large-breasted girls. They were well smeared with vegetable oil and squirming together like freshly dug earthworms. There were close-up shots of easily defined faces, contorted with lustful passion, together with guttural moans and grunts a pig would envy.

The B skit would finish off with the three sitting in the same area after gratification, still well oiled, smoking several joints of marijuana. Smirking, they made loud sucking sounds, giggling, then laughing loudly at a stupid joke that wouldn't be funny to any straight onlooker.

"Ears to you," said the nation's future, trying as best he could to hold in his lungs a large hit off the glowing joint as he passed it on to one of the giggling girls.

As the President stood transfixed by what he was witnessing, the voice at the other end of the line would snap him back to reality with the question, "Well, did you inhale, Mr. President?"

"I'll review your report here in my office the day after tomorrow, Bill," replied the president.

"I'll need three more days," replied Faraday.

His bewildered Boss simply hung up the phone.

Sensing a conspiracy in the making, his first thought was to call in the Joint Chiefs of Staff. "God, I hate that fucking word 'joint,'" he said under his breath, as he thought about setting up the meeting. Well he knew the brilliance and thoroughness of his Secretary of State. Well aware he was that if anything should happen to Faraday, intentionally or by accident, every single television station in the country would have a copy of that goddamned video!

Day Three

It was 10:30 p.m. and the nurses were making their periodic rounds, checking up on the well being of the patients. Two of the younger nurses were seen in the hall by one of the on-duty doctors, and the girls were doing all in their power to stifle the giggles which were shaking them from their noses to their toes.

More than a bit agitated by the unprofessional activity of the nurses, the doctor asked cynically if he might share in the joke. One of the nurses took him by the hand down the dimly lit corridor where he could glance into one of the rooms and its "very senior occupants." Two of the beds in the four-bed suite were empty, and the other two beds shared active double body occupancy.

The stunned doctor made his report the following day, and from that night forward, separation of even the most elderly of patients, of the opposite sexes, would be carefully observed.

Leaving the meeting after his report, the young doctor was heard to say, "I know that one old codger personally-- one of my patients--first time in my life I ever witnessed or even heard of such a thing. That old codger is 92 years old and according to the on-duty nurse, he kept it up until 3 a.m. this morning. His partner was 86!"

Day Four

"I have been given a new life," stated the beamingly healthy patient standing before the ever-swelling crowds of the concerned and curious. "How old do you think I am?" he asked the crowd.

"Thirty-five."

"Forty-two."

"Thirty-nine," came back the shouts from the crowd, as the interviews began to take on a carnival-like atmosphere.

"I'm 82 years old, and up until last week I was dying from irreversible emphysema. During the day I suffered from incredible pain and fear. When I could sleep, my nights were filled with nightmares that none but those afflicted as I could know. Countless were the times I had asked God to speedily take me, or, if by some remote reason of grace He decided to make me whole once more, I would serve him and the truth the remainder of my few years.

"Well, I was indeed made whole at this hospital, but more than this, I have been given back my youth. I can see without glasses, missing teeth are growing back, even my hair has grown back. My God, people, look at me!" he held his arms up and turned around.

"Dr. Hannal," asked the newswomen, "your patient, one among many testimonies we have heard and witnessed with our own eyes, has claimed that the Lazarus Machines not only cure sickness, but seems to have a restorative of youth effect as well?"

"Absolutely." responded the Doctor, "and not only that, but we have given numerous Intelligence Quotient tests, commonly known as IQ tests, to those we have treated. All we have tested to date have shown enhanced IQs boosting most below average persons up past normal, and normal persons to the realm of near genius!"

"So," continued the newsperson, "what you are saying is that anyone using the Lazarus Machines in sickness or in health, would not only retrieve their lost youth, but also experience an incredible increase in their mental acuity."

"Now, hold on there, young lady. I know what you're getting at here, and many of our staff have shared this same idea; but we have the very sick and terminally ill to treat first. And more are arriving from across the nation every day. You may rest assured that we will treat them first, before experimenting with the healthy."

People across the country and the wealthy from other parts of the world, were beginning to plot as to how they could regain their youth and increase their intelligence. Many hypochondriacs and calculating persons had already passed through the Aquatus apparatuses by using falsified medical documents. The physicians in every case knew exactly who they were.

These types of individuals were not pulled out of the machines, as it only took a thirty seconds to pass them on through. The bright digital displays told all, and as the frauds awoke they were immediately discharged from the hospital. They would have to fend for themselves concerning the food they would need to complete the rejuvenation process, although in the long run it was a cheap price to pay.

Most curiously though, in almost every case, when the frauds were informed of their demeaning morality, by taking the place of persons genuinely in need of immediate medical assistance, they were despondent upon leaving the hospital. Most promised to make amends for the now fully realized cruelty of their deed.

Day Five

Mail concerning the happenings in Little Falls began to arrive at the White House by the truckload and was escalating daily. There was no conceivable way that the mail crew could sort through that much mail, even though they had called in as many security-cleared personnel as they had room for.

The White House phone crew had been super busy answering and screening calls twenty-four hours a day after the first group of fifty or so patient-doctor miraculous testimonies had gone News International. The President would speak with ranking dignitaries of other countries only if threatened. His entire Staff speculated, argued, and planned their agendas around the pending report concerning Little Falls from the Secretary of State.

Faraday had kept his word, and took the national and international news media, complete with translators, to see the spectacular equipment within the hospital. All were amazed as they watched the patients rolled in, passed through the interior of the glowing apparatuses, and rolled off to the now crowded rooms. They interviewed patients upon awakening in their assigned rooms, where the food never stopped coming, and the toilets never stopped flushing.

Before and after, the media viewed the patients, as did the world.

When confronted once more on the hospital steps prior to his departure, by a now awed and solemn news media, Faraday would be asked, "Is the fantastic medical equipment from another world?"

The Secretary of State in turn would ask a question that was destined to go into every future history book and be written and repeated in every language in the world. "Well, if this wonderful equipment is from another world, should we tell them to take it back?" inquired Faraday.

"God bless them!"

"No!"

"Please don't!"

"Tell them we love them!" and many other emotional endearments would arise from the throats of the hundreds of cured, clear-thinking ex-patients, their families and friends.

On the following day, the traffic at the Little Falls Airport was so congested that even Faraday couldn't get his chartered flight safely off the runway. A storm was blowing into the area as well, and it pretty much torpedoed any attempt to drive into the District of Columbia for his meeting with the President.

Faraday knew who was in the driver's seat when the somber presidential voice on the other end of the line explained that he would keep his guests overnight. "They would be ready to meet with him any time after one p.m. the next day," purported his boss.

It was two o'clock in the afternoon when Secretary of State Faraday arrived at the White House to present his case before the President and his Cabinet. The President's security personnel did not question the admission to the mansion of Professor Hauss (who was carrying a small, specially made chair, obviously for the smallest of the group), Mr. Vincent Henry, his wife Elizabeth, their daughter Roxanne and the daughter's unusual little elf-like friend wearing her exaggerated sunglasses. All were admitted without fanfare; they had arrived as a group with Secretary Faraday.

Leaving his friends in one of the spacious reception areas of the White House, Faraday entered the conference room, whereupon all conversation stopped and silence prevailed as he lay down a thick folder and seated himself at the long table.

"I am greatly distressed, Mr. Secretary, that you failed to keep us better informed on the Little Falls activity," said the President, directing his gaze at Faraday."

"It was not my intention to be rude or blatantly evasive, Mr. President," replied the Secretary. "However, in the better interest of discretion, I was obligated to make a determination, as an individual, of when would be the most appropriate time for the release of this most sensitive information," replied Faraday. He then cast his eyes on the thick folder that lay before him on the table.

Silence endured for fifteen or so seconds before the President spoke again.

"Will this body of duly elected and appointed representatives of the government of the United States be privy to this information now?" acidly asked the Chief Executive. There was no mistaking the disdain in which he now held his Secretary of State. "Are there *aliens* in Little Falls, New York, working magical cures at Vincent Henry Hospital?!"

"Not exactly, sir," responded Faraday.

The President's entire cabinet had watched the Little Falls testimonials, and not exactly was much too close to yes to be of comfort to any of them. The color drained from most of their faces. Beads of perspiration began to appear on many a forehead, upper lip, and in the palms of hands. They anxiously anticipated what was coming next.

"Then please, Mr. Secretary, tell us exactly what is going on in Little Falls?" The acid had gone out of the President's voice, being replaced with a tone of grave concern bordering on fear.

"Aliens are involved; however, humans are conducting the cures through the use of their medical apparatuses, which are the aliens' gifts to Humankind," replied Faraday.

Two of the staff quickly got up from the table and were now standing behind their chairs, with dread on their faces.

"Are we, or any of our citizens in danger at this time?" asked the Secretary of Defense.

"Absolutely not." answered Faraday. "The medical equipment currently in use at the Little Falls hospital is from another world, but there is only one alien to date that we have had contact with. There may be several more, but many... at this time I find it doubtful."

"Mr. President," responded the still standing Secretary of the Interior, "might I suggest that perhaps Secretary Faraday has suffered emotional trauma due to the stress--?"

"Mr. Secretary," replied the President to his still standing officer, "have you read your briefs? Have you even been watching television? Do you have a better explanation as to what has been going on in Little Falls? Please take your seat, sir; this is going to be a long meeting."

"What do these aliens call themselves? When do we meet them, and what is the price humanity must pay for their benevolence?" asked the President, redirecting his gaze to his Secretary of State.

"They call themselves 'Aquatus' and wish nothing other than our consent to visit earth from time to time, in small groups, with the intent of studying the flora and fauna of our planet. They have shown no interest in leaguing themselves with any individual nation, wishing only to help humanity as a whole rid itself of sickness, ignorance, and pollution. They do not wish to harm the political or financial structure of any country.

"As for when you will meet them, I can have a representative of the Aquatus meet with you at your discretion, any time you choose," finished the Secretary of State.

"Today! What about today, Mr. Secretary?" asked the President.

"What about right now, sir?" responded Faraday to the now stunned heads of state; all nodded, or held up their hands in agreement.

As Faraday got up from the table, the Secretary of Defense got up as well, "If you don't mind, Bill, I would like to ride along with you. I have several things I would like to discuss with you during the trip."

"As you wish," responded Faraday, "but I can assure you it will be a short trip," he added, with a hint of humor in his voice.

Ten minutes later, Vincent Henry, Mrs. Henry, Dr. Hauss (still carrying the small chair), Roxanne and her small friend entered the room. The Heads of State had not even had a chance to speculate on what they had heard so far.

"Now, Mr. Secretary, I don't believe that this is the time and place for friends and family," protested the President, as the group entered the room.

"These friends and family are material witnesses to what I have been explaining, sir," responded Faraday. "Please listen to what they have to say."

"Sir! We would be better served by speaking to the Aquatus as soon as possible," volunteered the Attorney General, eyeing curiously his now visibly disturbed friend, the Secretary of Defense, who was nervously seating himself.

Professor Hauss walked to an unoccupied space at the table, and placed the specially designed chair into the larger chair in that space, then reaching down, he picked up the smallest of the group and set her into the adaptation.

The little alien removed her oversized wraparound sunglasses, gazing at the President with huge glistening eyes. The audience froze in wonderment and apprehension, sitting immobile more then fifteen seconds, as if turned to stone.

"Mr. President, members of the Cabinet," spoke Faraday, breaking the ice, "I would like you all to meet the Aquatian, 'Jayseeka.'"

"Mr. President, members of the Cabinet, I am honored to make your acquaintance," spoke the Aquatian in a clearly audible and melodious voice. "As Ambassador to Earth from the planet Trepleon within our Galaxy you call the Milky Way, I bid you greetings. You may inquire of me at your discretion."

The President was greatly displeased with his premonition. "God, how I hate it when I'm always right," he thought. It was going to be a very lengthy meeting.

# Chapter Fifteen

"Jacta est alea."
Caesar brooded no more at the Rubicon.
"The die has been cast."

The formal introduction of the gracious, beautiful, and amazingly intelligent extraterrestrial life form Jayseeka, Ambassador of the Aquatus, to the officials of the United States government, was to be the first official contact between other-world intelligent life and planet Earth.

Having witnessed the beneficent medical wonders of the Aquatus technology, the charm of its petite Ambassador, the salesmanship of the Henrys, Dr. Hauss, and Secretary Faraday, even the most skeptical of the President's Cabinet decided it would be best to follow the lead of the Attorney General, Secretary Faraday and the President. The suggestion had been that other world governments would be informed in due time, but not immediately. The cold war had been won, and no one wished to fan a spark that could lead once again to military buildup in other parts of the world.

It was generally felt by the assembly that others of the world's leaders could perhaps become fearful of an American-Aquatus alliance that might attempt to impose its will upon them, leading to undue paranoia and disruption of trade. The alien aspect of the medical wonders in Little Falls would be played down by using humor, ridicule, and media disinformation. Later, it was decided to make all the information concerning the unearthly technology public at a more appropriate time.

Even though the far-reaching benefits of the marvelous Aquatus technology was meant for the benefit of mankind as a whole, a unique plan was devised that would be one of the best-kept secrets the world had ever known. The new hospital in Little Falls would continue its work; however, a certain number of special executive requests for treatment from other countries would be honored, but only if recommended by a high-ranking official.

The plan was brilliant simplicity in action, the result of which would be the immediate treatment of the world's leaders, their families and friends first. The most obvious result being that once treated and released, looking years younger and completely sound in body and mind, those so treated would become staunch allies of those by whom they had been treated.

It was estimated that after a six-month utilization of this plan, it would be safe for Ambassador Jayseeka to go before an assembly of the United Nations and officially offer the wondrous Trepleonian gifts of technology to all of humanity.

It made sense to the majority of the world's leaders: those that had would get. They came, the fraudulently sick and the honestly sick, were cured, and returned home by the thousands during the allotted six-month time frame. Most of the first patients to arrive from other countries came for treatment as a last resort; no one else could cure their illnesses--they were the terminal ones.

Later came the wealthy and spoiled elite, to be cured, for the sake of expediency, of anything that might be a problem from hemorrhoids to baldness.    Lastly came those recommended by even minor officials.

Strangely enough, all (non-American patients and others treated regardless of their wealth, power, or family background) emerged from the Lazarus Machines humanitarians in an almost religious sense of the word. It would be acknowledged later that more then 60 percent of the world's major dignitaries had been treated using aliases and falsified medical documentation. For whatever reasons--real illness or imagined, wanting to gain or retain intellectual superiority over others, or perhaps just the vanity of wanting to regain their youth--they somehow realized that the machines could give them an advantage over their peers, and this was certainly correct.

The plan had worked beyond everyone's expectations, everyone except the Aquatian Jayseeka who had been diligent in telepathically planting the secretive ideas in the mind of the President during that first contact with him. When the Chief Executive expounded upon ideas he thought to be original, the Aquatian then conveniently planted and enhanced them telepathically in the minds of the others as they listened intently. Such was the total mind control ability of the alien during that first White House conference, and none would be the wiser.

During its initial six months, Vincent Henry Memorial Hospital in Little Falls would take in nearly two million patients, curing every one. First tents, then trailers and recreation vehicles--later 24-hour construction crews would build structures to house numerous patients who only needed medical supervision for a limited time.

Many and varied were the benevolent associations that aided in the care and feeding of the patients.

The Lazarus Machines would prove 100 percent effective for every malady known and even some unknown to man.

When the curious inquired as to the nature of the curing mechanisms within the extraordinary medical devices, they were informed that it was done through genetic revitalization. The inventors were to remain out of the public eye for safety reasons and the protection of their work.

Numerous recipients of the Aquatus medical marvels had already formed highly intellectual organizations with an international intent: to rid mankind of its maladies. Many donated their fortunes, abilities and lives toward this most noble cause.

Vincent Henry Memorial would receive daily calls inquiring about where the fantastic instrumentation know as the Lazarus Machines could be purchased, and at what cost. Little did these benevolent associations know that the apparatuses would soon enough be not only free but numerous. The moneys and personnel they had amassed would eventually go for the purpose of making available the large amounts of food the rejuvenation process required after treatment. In areas where food was in short supply this did not mean a lack of healing or rejuvenation; the process simply took longer-- months instead of days.

The nature of the United Nations call to assembly was delivered by personal envoy six months later after the introduction of the Lazarus machines; no sovereign nation was neglected. It read, "It is our honorable duty to inform all nations of the world that we have had verifiable contact with intelligent alien beings. Please do not construe this notification as dangerous, or to mean that we have been, or will be invaded. Quite the contrary, it has been made absolutely clear, through their most gracious Ambassador and by their deeds, that their only desire is to aid Mankind in the elimination of the afflictions plaguing our planet, such as sickness, ignorance, starvation, and pollution.

"These other-worldly beings call themselves Aquatus, and so sensitive are they, that they have sent but a single representative to our planet to convey their wishes. They feared that we might construe numbers as possible intimidation on their behalf.

"It has also been well determined that these other-worldly visitors have no intent of exacting benefits from us in any form, excepting for our permission to return to Earth from time to time, in groups of a hundred or so individuals, for the purpose of studying the flora and fauna of our planet. Much in the same way that we ourselves enjoy the study and preservation of the indigenous inhabitants of our great nature preserves and parks throughout the world.

"We look forward to your representation at this most historic occasion of the United Nations."

All nations of Earth were indeed represented on that unprecedented day that would live throughout the eons in the minds and literature of Humankind. Eighty-five percent of all Earth's inhabitants were to be given representation through their primary leaders, with lesser dignitaries in attendance.

The Ambassador from the planet Trepleon, the Aquatian Jayseeka, beyond question charmed each and every Nation's representative on that memorable day, and did so using each country's own language. Boldly in the open, no longer behind a disguise of human makeup and young girl's dresses, Jayseeka stood before the vast audience of the United Nations. The entire world would witness the graciousness of her words, her beautiful features, the golden glory of her petite physique, and the intense, deep glistening amber of her luminous eyes.

When ask by the president of Chile, "Why did not the Aquatus come immediately to the United Nations to present to the world their intentions?" Ambassador Jayseeka explained that such an action might possibly have been construed as a veiled act of aggression.

She went on to say, "By first proving our world's honorable intent, by allowing Earth the use of the Aquatus medical equipment in Little Falls, New York, for its sick and maimed, the intentions of my people cannot be disputed."

The Chilean President was flattered when Jayseeka answered his question in perfect Spanish, with a Chilean accent and inflection. He bought the alien logic along with the rest, lock, stock, and barrel. But there was a flaw in the logic apparent to very few; those who had sent Jayseeka were not "people"; they were Aquatus.

When asked when other nations would receive the medical devices such as the ones now located in Little Falls, Jayseeka informed them that transport was currently in progress, and upon arrival each country would be notified of a location where their sick and injured could be immediately treated.

The only expense involved would be transportation to the location, and sufficient food to complete the healing process induced by the medical equipment. If means of transportation and food were scarce in any area, there were various charitable societies currently active, and others being formed, that would provide these necessities.

Once again there was a fly in the ointment, for only the Aquatus were aware that the equipment had arrived months ago on planet Earth. It could be placed in the areas previously designated by Professor David Hauss, as quickly as any moonless or cloudy night occurred.

It was an historic day at the United Nations, and the Aquatus promised many things. As time went by there would be fewer and fewer skeptics. The Aquatus would deliver a cornucopia of technological wonders to improve the human condition on planet Earth. Soon all, excepting a very few, would acknowledge that a true Golden Age for humanity had been born.

Within three years time of Earth's first official notification that the Aquatus had arrived, all the world's human inhabitants would experience, directly or indirectly, the wonders of a new and advanced technology, great strides that most probably would have taken humanity 200 or so more years to perfect.

Highly simplified techniques for parting the bond holding the hydrogen and oxygen atoms of water together gave man clean-burning hydrogen in various adaptive forms. This would replace gasoline, diesel, and coal. Anywhere there was water, there was pollution-free energy; fossil fuels quickly became a thing of the past.

The ownership and distribution of this new power source became the property of those who had originally produced fossil fuels and they were distributed fairly throughout the world. Hydrogen fuels became cheaper for the consumer; those who owned the technology made more money than they had previously done from fossil fuels. The owners of the new fuels were happy, their bankers were happy, and even consumers throughout the world were happy. There was a small stipulation of course; in order to obtain the technology to produce the hydrogen fuels, countries could no longer use nuclear power.

But then this just made good common sense, for was not the driving purpose of Mankind and Aquatus alike to end pollution? Nobody could ever figure out a safe way to deal with nuclear waste anyway. It only stood to reason that the next great boon would be the neutralization of atomic wastes throughout the world. Specialized apparatuses were carried throughout Europe, Asia, and the Americas, quickly and effectively turning all nuclear waste into simple lead anywhere within a thousand miles of the instrumentation.

Of course no nation at the time realized that all uranium ore, at less than a nine hundred-foot depth on planet Earth, would also be turned into lead, or that all nuclear arsenals throughout the world had been neutralized in the process.

Agriculture was to receive its benefits as well; genetically engineered hybrid plants could generate three times more produce than their ancestors had. All were almost completely resistant to the insects that had previously compelled mankind to poison the pests, his environment, and inadvertently himself. In remote areas, where insects were especially pestilent, a cheap, environmentally safe insecticide was developed. The bugs would never develop immunity to it, because they simply refused to eat the plants that were sprayed with it; they hated the taste of the stuff.

Garbage and trash in all industrialized countries would go to specialized locations that had been efficiently constructed with amazing swiftness through use of military personnel. The military now had little else to do around the world, as planet Earth hovered on the brink of a new prosperity. The refuse was hauled to the front end of the complexes and dumped into receptacles unsorted, and out the other end came extrusions of many dimensions which would replace wood products. These were as biologically degradable as natural wood. Also recaptured were copious quantities of glass and metals.

Sewers would drain into special locations, and the end product, from the rear ends of humans, would become high-grade, environmentally safe fertilizers. Eventually this would accumulate to be far more than the industrialized countries could use. The surplus was shipped to third world countries, replacing foreign-aid hard currency which, often as not, didn't go where it had been intended anyway.

The cities and towns would reap the benefits from the sale of these reclaimed products and fertilizers, and would eventually vie for the purchase of debris from across the country and around the world, as the nation's landfills eventually emptied.

The huge lumber concerns, which previously had been rapidly eating up most of the great forests throughout the world, would inherit the technology to make the new wood-like materials, called strood. These new products were more to the builders' liking anyway, as they were totally free of defects, and cheaper and easier to work with. The strood could also be converted with simplicity into an excellent quality of paper and its products.

All liquid discharge from various manufacturing and mining projects would pass through diversified and amazingly effective filtering devices. These, when compacted, were also hauled off to the refuse complexes, dumped in, and cheaply processed back into their original forms to be used over again.

Eventually, virtually 75 percent of all products used by humans would be the product of these grand refuse complexes. Needless to say these vast complexes were fueled with the cheap, pollution-free and abundant hydrogen fuels now readily available.

It then became apparent that the Aquatus could make the Lazarus Machines and deliver the ten thousand or so devices throughout the world, as easily as humans could make and distribute cars. The strange thing was that the reclusive Aquatus were never seen making the deliveries. The apparatuses simply showed up in various predetermined locations and were activated for the peoples in those areas.

The explanation given by the Aquatus Ambassador was simply that her people did not seek fame or praise for their beneficent deeds. They did not wish to be caught up in the admiration and pageantry of the grateful crowds that would turn out, had they made their exact times of delivery known. They wanted only to help, not be glorified. Therefore, at the various delivery locations, all humans were asked to stay away until after delivery, or delivery would not be made. Humanity complied.

It took less than one year for all the sick and maimed people of Earth to be treated by the otherworldly apparatuses, assisted by highly ethical and intelligently run charitable associations.

Once an individual obtained the benefits of the Aquatus medical apparatuses, a second trip through the machines would do no good. Once the DNA had become genetically revitalized it could not be enhanced a second time. Everybody got a fair and impartial chance at good health, increased intelligence, and long life.

The following three years would be spent in ridding the earth of harmful microbes and viruses in the thalamus, livers, kidneys, and various other organs and body areas of the healthy, young and old alike. Even pregnant mothers, who had not yet received the benefits of passing through the Lazarus Machines, got their chance, baby included.

Except for a very few, all Earth's healthy human inhabitants would be overjoyed, for now it was their turn. They and their children would benefit from a long life of excellent health, accelerated intelligence, and the assurance that all the hazards of deadly microorganisms would be cleansed from their bodies and the Earth. Henceforth the knowledge of the horror the little nasties had created would be found only in history books.

Many healthy individuals who had not been treated in the fantastic medical devices found themselves at a decided disadvantage in their businesses and in the work place. There was difficulty in competing with the higher intelligence that the Aquatus medical equipment had bestowed upon the once sickly and aged. Beamingly healthy persons, with the knowledge and wisdom obtained throughout many years, coupled with elevated IQs, proved to be very stiff competition.

All were encouraged to participate as soon as possible by the Aquatus. There were other worlds, throughout the galaxy, which were also in grave need of the medical apparatuses. So Jayseeka, Ambassador from Trepleon to Humanity, informed them on planet Earth.

Not totally in keeping with the Aquatus promise to "do no harm to industry," there were several that would suffer because of the revitalizing effect of the medical devices, but nobody said much about it. Those that had once made them available could broach few arguments in their defense. These would be legalized drugs and their illegal counterparts.

Once a person passed through the belly of the Lazarus Machines they found that their addictions to tobacco, alcohol and various prescription and illegal drugs had been cured. Increased intelligence and remembrance, of the point to which the drugs had degraded them, steered them away from repeating the same mistake twice. Destruction of one's body through the use of poisonous substances no longer seemed "cool" to those who had been given a second chance.

Of course some hallucinogenic drugs continued to be ingested, along with alcohol in moderation, but the days of profiteering in hard drugs, such as cocaine and heroine products was simply no longer worth the effort. Addictive-prone individuals who had previously used various drugs as escape mechanisms were now endowed with higher intelligence and they found the reality of life and good health to be the true joys. There soon followed a flourishing of gymnastics and the arts.

With the knowledge that the use and access to the Lazarus Machines would not last indefinitely, the biological cleansing and rejuvenation of all incarcerated persons also began. The results were amazing.  All but the most hardened criminals would eventually get parole.  Having easily learned new skills and trades in prison, the parolees found that they could do quite well in the business world, without the need to resort to dangerous criminal activity to earn a livelihood.

Prior to a study of the results, most considered it naive to think that most criminals would cherish lawful pursuits in place of their previous unlawful activities.  However, once they had been treated, this became the rule rather than the exception.  Many citizens feared that the treatment would release on the world a more intelligent criminal and therefore a worse scourge on society, but then the real truth was that the hard way just looked easy.

Therefore with increased mental abilities, society's original misfits realized that before, they had only thought they were smart, and that real intelligence was something altogether different. However, and unfortunately, there were still those few who continued criminal lives.  But since law enforcement had received an intelligence boost as well, they would be countered.

Entering the fourth year since the introduction of the miraculous Aquatus technology to planet Earth, the vast majority of Humankind throughout the world now thankfully acknowledged that Life Was Good; and so it was...(?)

## Chapter Sixteen

All things real or imaginary,
Are only One.
As the One moves,
Therein moves the truth.

Vincent Henry Manor had become the Trepleonian Embassy for the little Aquatian Jayseeka. Only rulers de facto and duly elected top-ranking officials would be allowed conferences with the Ambassador from Trepleon. They were politely advised to be on their best behavior, at least giving the appearance that it was their people and not themselves for whom they sought the alien technology.

All the leaders of Earth well knew the importance of the fantastic technology, which would bring the cheap energy, luxury and wealth flowing into their countries. All who came to honor the Aquatus would leave in the best of spirits, having been wined and dined in the opulence of the Manor. They were addressed, humored and flattered in their own language by the charming and gracious Ambassador Jayseeka.

Four and a half years would come and go, and the Henrys enjoyed the status of being hosts to the top echelons of international culture. They would never tire of the knowledge they gained, or the magnificent gifts of art and other tokens of appreciation bestowed upon them for opening their house in such a regal manner.  Jayseeka insisted that the Henrys keep all the cumshaw.

It was a rainy Sunday in mid-March, and Jayseeka put interplanetary politics on hold.  She placed a personal call to her friend Professor Hauss and requested that he take her to the zoological department at the University of Hawaii.

The little Aquatian had desired for quite some time to bestow upon the earth's life sciences a window into the true nature of animal intelligence.  This would give researchers an understanding of that which had heretofore gone unnoticed, due to human inability to communicate directly.  Jayseeka had indicated that someday she would need to return to her home world for an extended stay.  She had expressed a desire to bring humans and others of Earth's animal species to a better understanding with one another, believing it to be of the utmost importance to posterity.

Dr. Hauss was excited and wasted no time in visiting the Manor to escort his little friend Jayseeka.

Roxanne was now 18 years old and on spring break from college.  Having been filled with wonder at an early age, she had opted for the life sciences, selecting Zoology as her major.  She begged to be allowed to accompany her friends to the island research center.

Once more dressed in the clothing of a stylish young girl, and wearing her extra large sunglasses, Jayseeka, unbeknownst to any but the Henrys and household, left the Manor incognito with Roxanne and Dr. Hauss.  Within an hour they were airborne in the Henrys' recently acquired private jet, on their way to San Francisco, the first fueling stop prior to making the hop to Oahu, Hawaii.

It was 10:15 p.m. when the trio arrived in San Francisco, and Jayseeka asked that they stay over for two days, as she had something to do concerning the pending research.  The

Aquatian also wished to mingle with the citizens of Chinatown to obtain first-hand entertainment for those Earth buffs on her home world.

The next day was bright and sunny, and the slight chill in the air was invigorating as the trio left their hotel and set off in the direction of Chinatown. The market place was busy as usual with the buying and selling of every type of food, furniture, and nostrum known in the Orient.

They found a restaurant whose bill of fare specialized in fishy dishes, and all ate heartily and were in the best of spirits as they set off to see the rest of the bustling market place.

Roxanne and Dr. Hauss were discussing the biological aspects of flying fish when they found themselves a half-block from the restaurant and no Jayseeka in sight. Rushing back to where they had eaten, they found the little Aquatian standing before a large glass case wherein was displayed various uncooked fish delicacies for sale.

The Chinese fishmonger was very concerned about the little person observing his wares and had just finished asking Jayseeka in his native language, as he knew no other, "Are you lost? Small person, if you tell me your telephone number, I will attempt to call your family, if you like?"

Dr. Hauss and Roxanne were about to step forward and claim her, but another minute passed while Jayseeka gazed into the glass case without speaking.

Dr. Hauss and Roxanne, focusing on the objects of her attention, noticed the neatly laid out rows of octopus and squid before them on the crushed ice. There was a certain sadness in her voice, and the seemingly perpetual smile was no longer on her lips as she thanked the kindly fishmonger for his concern about her welfare (much to his amazement), in perfect Mandarin dialect.

The three left the restaurant.

Roxanne asked her little friend, "Are you tired? Perhaps you want to return to the hotel?"

"Absolutely not." came the reply, as happiness returned to her voice and lips. "We are going to do the town!"

All laughed as they set off to partake of the sights, sounds and smells of the bustling borough.

The next day would be of the utmost concern to her two friends as Jayseeka requested to be taken to a remote area up the Pacific Coast Highway early that morning. She then informed them that she would be ready to be picked up at 5 p.m. that same day.

"Please don't worry about me," she said.

It was difficult for Dr. Hauss and Roxanne to realize that their diminutive friend was really not the little girl her stature suggested, but an adult individual with an intelligence quotient quite possibly two times that of theirs combined.

Jayseeka knew exactly what she was doing at all times and had admonished her two friends good-naturedly, as she handed her sunglasses to Roxanne. Wiggling out of her clothing with the comment "See you at five," she walked out on a rocky outcropping and tumbled off into the surf.

The two friends sat down upon the sand, and Dr. Hauss explained to a tearful Roxanne that her friend Jayseeka was quite possibly more at home in the water than on land.

"Consider if you will," began Dr. Hauss, "her amazing telepathic abilities. I'm convinced that this ability can also be extended to other life forms, and I'm also equally sure that Jayseeka knows what other life forms may be thinking, simultaneously with them as the thoughts are formed. I don't believe she has a worry in the world about being attacked by some denizen of the deep. She is a strong swimmer, capable of amazing protective color adaptation, which is the best camouflage."

"I know that I'm acting a little immature," responded Roxanne, "but what is she doing out there? Just swimming around?"

"Now, I know it's unusual to our manner of thinking," answered Dr. Hauss, "to just jump into the ocean by oneself, and go paddling out to sea, but we are not Aquatus. Certainly she has some purpose in mind, and we shouldn't be unduly concerned about her behavior, anymore than I should be concerned if you decided to go shopping by yourself in a mall back home."

"It has always amazed me that Jayseeka, with her obviously smaller brain size could be so very intelligent...and the telepathy? Can you explain these curiosities to me, David?" asked Roxanne. She was beginning to accept the idea that her little friend was most probably doing just fine somewhere out at sea.

"It has become quite clear to scientists that brain size is a crude indicator of intelligence," began the Professor. "What is intelligence anyway, but the intellectual way in which an animal deals with its environment in order to most comfortably survive?

"You may not consider your cat Fluffy back home to be a prodigy, but within him lie many biological attributes, which, when intellectually enhanced, could give him a survival capacity greater than your own.

"Imagine, for instance, that your cat and yourself found each other in a wilderness area without society, tools, warm clothing or matches. A nighttime drop in temperature would be detrimental to you, while Fluffy could simply curl up in a ball and go to sleep. When the pangs of hunger set in, Fluff could reach into a mouse hole and snag a meal, or quietly sneak up and catch a bird, while you would be hard-pressed to find enough insect protein to nourish your much larger body.

"If danger were to present itself, ol' Fluff could quickly climb any type of tree, as well he knows, and he has sharp claws as well with which to defend himself and enhance his escape. Excellent nighttime vision and a more acute sense of smell and hearing than yours also give him a decided advantage. You could run, but chances are you would not be fast enough to outrun an old hungry mountain lion or grizzly bear.

"If I were a gambling man, I would put my money on Fluffy to survive the wilderness longer than you under those circumstances; but then does this indicate that your cat is your intellectual superior? Not at all, as with just a tiny bit of current technology--matches, warm waterproof clothing, and a rifle--you become undisputed Queen of the jungle.

"But still we know little of the way animals think. In times gone by we convinced ourselves that animals didn't think. I suppose by indulging in that obvious naiveté, Humanity didn't have to deal with the guilt of eating a creature that may well have experienced love, joy, fear, and all the other emotions that we ourselves experience.

"Or perhaps looking upon animals as living computers, i.e., purely instinctive, removes most people's guilt about the burdens we oppress them with, or the beatings we may inflict upon them with impunity. By simply presuming that animals' only purpose on Earth is to serve or be eaten by us, ordained by God so to speak, we thereby escape guilt and retain the illusion that we are kind and benevolent.

"Recent scientific research indicates that animals do reason, and indeed 'think.' Consider if you will a laboratory rat with a brain no larger then a bean. Every scientist that ever created a maze to run them through was surprised at how quickly they learned, secretly thankful that he himself did not need to compete against the creatures of his experiment for his own meal.

"No, Roxanne, bigger is not necessarily better when it comes to a brain in any creature; in fact it has been postulated that bigger could be worse, as distance may impede rapid communication between neurons within the brain. Furthermore it is estimated that the Human animal uses but a mere 20 percent of his brain capacity anyway. But then the more intelligent of Earth's creatures, such as elephants, dolphins, chimpanzees, and whales, do have larger brains.

"It still appears to be a running debate, and perhaps we will have more information on the subject soon, as this appears to be the intent of our small friend from Trepleon. The one thing we currently know for certain is that Jayseeka, with a brain one third smaller than our own, is quite obviously our intellectual senior.

"Concerning telepathy," continued the Professor, "This is an even more mysterious aspect of animal consciousness. How many times have you picked up the telephone and the person you were thinking to call was already on the line in an attempt to call you? Probably not many times, but the several hundred thousand to one odds pretty much rule out coincidence for it to happen even once, and it has probably happened to just about everyone at one time or the other."

Roxanne was nodding her head in agreement.

"We have observed what we believe to be telepathic abilities in such creatures as fish and birds, as it seems that the turning and weaving in perfect uniformity, whenever a predator is acknowledged nearby, leaves little room for any other speculation. Strangely enough and often as not, it's the hapless little creature, be he sick, old or foolish, who fails to turn, dodge or weave in perfect unison with the rest of the school or flock, that ends up being the predator's meal.

"Once more we can only speculate about these telepathic abilities in others of Earth's creatures. Perhaps we used such ability in our evolutionary past and somehow lost it along the way. Perhaps we use it now when we have our personality clashes with people we don't even know, somehow sensing that they are a danger, perhaps unkind, cruel or evil."

It was about 11 a.m. when Dr. Hauss and Roxanne rose from the sands of the desolate beach. They still had six hours to go before they would see their small half-aquatic friend again and had decided to get out of the sun and go to find a hamburger somewhere, exploring a little until time to return.

Brushing the sand from her clothing as they hiked back towards the small rental car, Roxanne thought what a wonderful thing it was to have such a kind and knowledgeable friend as Dr. David Hauss. She somehow knew she could always trust and confide in him.

It was five minutes to five, according to the Professor's watch, and it was an expensive model he always kept set according to Greenwich Mean Time. Glancing at his watch, then out to sea several times, he said, "Oh well, Jayseeka doesn't even have a watch; if she's late by even an hour, it would be a pretty good estimation on her behalf."

But the Professor and Roxanne were a little disconcerted that they hadn't yet seen their little friend. When Dr. Hauss glanced at his watch once more, the second hand was sweeping along past forty seconds to five.

Roxanne jumped up, and pointing out to sea exclaimed, "I see something! There she is now!"

They both hastened towards the edge of the surf, getting their shoes wet in their excitement.

Jayseeka caught a large wave, body-surfing it to within five feet of where the two were standing, her body quickly turning from translucent green to a vivid, deep rose gold, as she gained her footing on the sand and stood up. Roxanne walked into the water and threw a large fluffy towel about her friend.

Jayseeka thanked her saying, "I'm not in as good a shape as I should be. I should swim at least every other day from now on."

The little Aquatian had clearly outdone herself and after dressing once more in her pleasing young girl disguise and taking a long drink of fresh water given her by Roxanne, she fell fast asleep in the car on the way back to the hotel. She had to be carried to their room and put into bed without food or shower by Roxanne.

The trio of friends would be in Hawaii the next day. Both Roxanne and Dr. Hauss would be amazed at the quantities of food the little Aquatian would consume to replace the tissue due to energy breakdown spent on the previous day's marathon swim.

## Chapter Seventeen

Learning, fear, and the unknown.
Is your hunger for knowledge greater than your fear?

It was the second day after the Aquatian, Professor Hauss and Roxanne arrived in Hawaii.  All were well rested, had eaten breakfast, and were huddled together over nautical maps.  Jayseeka was pinpointing the area of latitude, longitude and minutes, where she wished to be taken that afternoon.

The university's department of zoology had been notified of the alien visitor to their island and the intent of the research to be conducted, although as yet none had been given specifics.  The schools of Anthropology, Psychology, and Zoology were recessed for two weeks and the head of each department was invited to attend and participate in the research.

Permission to allow a press conference was given; but all would respect the wishes of Jayseeka that it would take place after a week of scientific information had been gathered from the investigations.  No human knew quite what to expect, except Dr. Hauss and Roxanne, and they didn't know everything.  They had gotten into the habit of never telling anyone, outside their small inner circle, anything they didn't need to know.

It was 3 o'clock in the afternoon when the pilot would carefully observe his location instrumentation. He was preparing to set the pontoon aircraft down at 158 degrees longitude, one mile south of the Tropic of Cancer and northeast of the island of Kauai, the most northern in the Hawaiian island chain. Dr. Hauss, Dr. Zimmerman, and Roxanne would need to assure the pilot from time to time during the trip that they were sure of what they were doing and not to worry. However Dr. Zimmerman was not absolutely sure himself what they were flying out to the middle of nowhere to do.

The flanges on each side of the pilot's compartment would block his view, and as the plane neared its destination the pilot could not see what he believed to be a very young little girl hand her extra-large sunglasses to Roxanne, step out of her quaint little pleated dress and kick off her smallish loafers, in front of a very concerned Professor Zimmerman.

When Jayseeka had wiped the makeup from her face and hands with a dampened towel, she gave the appearance of an angelic pixy, dressed in golden, silky, thin tights, ready to do a motion picture part for Fantasy Studios.

"Did you hear about the lady who was married to a ventriloquist?" asked Jayseeka of Dr. Zimmerman.

"No," came the response.

"Well, when he talked in his sleep his wife had to go into the closet to hear what he was saying."

It was a lighthearted jest that could be told in mixed company, and it brought giggles and chuckles to take the edge off things; things were just now a little bit edgy. Nobody except the alien really knew what they were doing in a small aircraft miles from anywhere, which would eventually perch above more than a mile's depth of crystal blue water in the immense vastness of the Pacific Ocean.

The pilot touched down and taxied the plane easily into the wind, where it rose and fell gently on the smooth mild swells.

Jayseeka reached into a bag she had carried with her on the trip, removing two cylinders, each approximately an inch in diameter, and four inches in length. These she would attach just above the ankle of each foot with small straps. This was the first time that Dr. Hauss would notice that Jayseeka's small perfectly shaped feet, the proper length and width for her diminutive size, had no toes.

Her instructions were simple: "Look for a red flare, then florescent dye on the ocean surface; I will be at this location at 8:30 this evening."

The Aquatian then stood up, walked down the aisle to the side entry of the plane, opened the door and tumbled out into the blue depths of the ocean.

A pale and exasperated Professor Zimmerman, stammered anxiously, "A-a-are you all nuts?" He hastily began to remove his shoes, his intent being to retrieve the small creature that had fascinated him with charm and wit from the perils of the watery depths.

Both Roxanne and Professor Hauss were hard pressed to restrain the desperate Doctor from diving in after Jayseeka.

"Hold on, Hercule!" pleaded Dr. Hauss. "She has gills; you do not!"

As realization began to dawn, Dr. Zimmerman sat back down in his seat, "What in the living hell does she expect to do out here anyway, I'd like to know?"

"What ever it is, she will let us know in due time; this I can assure you," was the answer from his friend David.

Nevertheless, beset with conflicting emotions, it would be ten minutes before the good doctor would put his shoes back on. "But it will be Goddamned dark at 8:30!" he protested.

"She has a flare, and she has florescent dye," explained Roxanne, "and unless I miss my guess, sir, they are not ordinary location devices by any stretch of the imagination."

In the time Jayseeka took to complete her quest, Dr. Hauss gave his friend Professor Zimmerman, and the equally astonished pilot, an extensive course on the wonders from the planet Trepleon.

Dr. Zimmerman had been correct; it was dark at 8:30. As the plane returned, circling the area, they saw the bright red flare as it lit up the sky approximately three miles from their location. It couldn't have been missed had they been thirty miles off the target area. The plane headed due north as the flare settled slowly into the ocean.

At a mile or more distance they saw the bright green florescent dye. Bright did not adequately describe the brilliant spectacle, which appeared as if lighted from beneath by floodlights, The more than ample marker had rapidly spread to cover a hundred-foot area, but thereafter held that circular pattern as if glued to the surface of the sea.

The amphibious aircraft put down just outside the brightly-lighted area, then taxied to its center. The door was opened and a net ladder dropped down into the water now teeming with numerous small creatures attracted by the light. The plane stayed as close to the center of the florescence as possible, but it was another fifteen minutes before they would see the Aquatian.

Suddenly, up from the depths she came with an agility that would have shamed a dolphin. Bypassing the ladder and into the doorway, with a splash and a thump, arrived Jayseeka, knocking Dr. Zimmerman off his feet where he stood watching.

"Oops! I apologize, sir," exclaimed Jayseeka to the startled Zimmerman, who found himself seated on the floor and literally looking at, and through, the translucent aquamarine blue body of the alien's protective coloration.

As Jayseeka began her color change, returning to a deep, almost rose gold, Professor Zimmerman began to regain his composure.

"I apologize for getting you wet and upset, Doctor. The smaller creatures in the water, attracted by the brightness of the marker, had tantalized in turn much larger fish that were hungrily appreciative of the opportunity to feed. So as not to be on the menu, I was obligated to wait beneath the lighted area and make my exit when the way was clear."

"That's quite all right, absolutely not a problem at all," replied Dr. Zimmerman, now smiling. He was delighted to see the small golden enchantress unharmed and safely back aboard the aircraft. The island Professor had never been so fascinated by or intrigued with anything as wonderful as the little alien in his life; the next evening he was to be astounded.

**********

Jayseeka and company were to temporarily take over the University's bio-lab the following day. They watched with fascination as the little alien rapidly disassembled the state-of-the-art electroencephalograph. She then proceeded to install various electronic chips and materials into its circuitry.

Having reassembled the electronic equipment to her fastidious satisfaction, Jayseeka proceeded to wire this maze into very sophisticated electromagnetic equipment. This had also been brought up to speed with various electronic software data she had written and burned into the memory chips she had carried with her from New York

Ralph, the little chimpanzee in a nearby cage, watched

Jayseeka's electronic wizardry with keen interest, as it broke up the boredom of his captivity. Ralph had no other chimps to socialize with, and none of his human captors had even bothered to leave him a toy with which to amuse himself. In fact it was such a pathetic situation that if something didn't come up from time to time, he wouldn't have had a thing to play with all day long. Little did the hapless creature realize that he would soon get an opportunity to voice his pent-up opinion to his captors.

"Finished." At last the word all wanted to hear after four hours of non-stop, disassembling, assembling, wiring, and soldering.

Jayseeka took a long drink from the iced tea that good Dr. Zimmerman had brought her, then looked directly and deeply into the instantly frightened eyes of Ralph the chimp.

In another instant little Ralph felt a concern and compassion emanate from Jayseeka unlike anything he could ever remember. He had been taken away from his mother at a very young age, and she had died shortly thereafter in an experiment gone wrong.

The little chimp reached for Jayseeka as soon as they removed him from the cage and hugged her tightly, putting his face next to her neck. Ralph did not protest, much to the amazement of Dr. Zimmerman, as the wires from the newly assembled apparatus would be lightly attached beneath the hair of his head.

Ralph was so enthralled by the affection he felt toward Jayseeka that he began to get an erection but his enamored fantasies were quickly ended. Jayseeka, lightly touching the tip of his penis, delivered it a snapping shock that sent the sensitive member looking for a place to hide, its owner painfully protesting with, "Eeek! Eee, eee! Sheee!"

In this experimental test Ralph was to quickly learn that love was not the answer. The little chimp caused no more problems, for it had become perfectly clear that just because someone really liked him, it didn't necessarily mean that they were going to indulge him in his sexual aspirations.

Ralph was on his best behavior as the crew, with broad grins on their faces, reattached the sensors to his head.

"Still stings!  Oooah, hurt Ralphie." responded the equipment's speakers in stereophonic sound.

As the mental process of the chimp passed through the equipment, it paralleled the voice of a young boy five or six years of age.  The scientists in the lab were astonished, not having known quite what to expect.  Their greatest expectation had not stretched to include the human-like thinking of a chimpanzee, in stereophonic English.

The next amazement would be to Ralph himself, for as his thoughts that had become words simultaneously reentering his mind as thought with sound from the speakers, he realized that he could *talk*.

"Tell us what you are feeling, Ralphie, now that you can talk," requested Jayseeka.  As Jayseeka spoke into a microphone, the words were converted into thought, which the chimp could clearly understand as it passed through the extraordinary apparatus back into and melded with his mind.

"I want to go outside and sit in the sun.  I want to eat some ripe bananas and sit in the sun.  Please take me outside. I want to play and eat bananas."

The observers were amazed at parallelism between the animal's thoughts and those of humans.

"We will go outside soon and find you some ripe bananas," responded Dr. Zimmerman, thinking that just perhaps he might be the butt end of some elaborate joke.

"Also some meat, please. I like meat; the only time I get meat is when Pete gives me bites from his food. He never gives me much."

"Who is Pete, sir?" asked Roxanne of Dr. Zimmerman.

Zimmerman simply stood there staring at the little chimp for another full minute before answering. "Uh, he's the janitor, and we have repeatedly told him not to feed the lab animals," responded the Professor. His mind churned with the possibilities of the amazing technology within his grasp.

"Please be nice to Pete," pleaded the now tuned-in chimp, "or he will not give me any more meat."

Professor Zimmerman's countenance had taken on a bit of a grayish tone as he began to realize the tremendous scientific importance of what he was now witnessing. He was carrying on a dialogue with a thinking, rational being. He was observing intelligence criteria he had previously presumed to be lacking in the worlds less-than-human life forms.

"Excuse me," replied Dr. Zimmerman, "but I simply must visit the bath-room for a bit and also find my tape recorder; I simply must..."

The visibly troubled Professor was mumbling as he left the room. The other observers' emotions ranged from awed fascination to delight.

The little chimpanzee requested more meat, a larger cage with more material to make a softer "nest," ripe bananas, guavas, mangos and bread every day, as well as a friend to take him outside into the sunlight for play time.

Ralph's wish list probably would have been more extensive had his audience more time; however, these were the wishes Dr. Zimmerman felt he could easily oblige the little chimp with.  Now, with a more enlightened mentality, the good doctor promised the chimp that he would definitely see to the feeding and habitat upgrades the very next day.

He had not made it obvious, but Zimmerman had felt a bit foolish as he carried on the conversation with his laboratory animal Ralph.

Jayseeka reminded the investigative team that they were to be at the zoological observation center, to the windward side of Oahu in Kaneohe Bay, and on location at 9 o'clock that evening.  It was already 5 p.m. and they were advised to allow time to eat in the schedule.

Each of the team took the time to wish the best to Ralph the chimp, each smiling and giving him a hug of affection. They assured him that everything would be okay and that they were happy that his requests were soon to be granted.

The little fellow was despondent as the group left the room, but he would have the most pleasant dreams of expectation that night, when sleep finally close his eyes.

The skiffs were ready and loaded with the heavy lighting and camera equipment when the investigative team arrived on the small island at the center of Kaneohe Bay.  The team consisted of Jayseeka, Dr. David Hauss, Roxanne Henry, Dr. Charlene Gwinnett, Professor of Anthropology, Dr. James Nicholas, Professor of Psychology, and Dr. Hercule Zimmerman, noted head of the zoology department, and the most widely published ichthyologist in his field.

Each of the department heads was allowed to bring two of their most promising students, to help with the equipment as needed.  The students had responded diligently, arriving first on the island to load the three six-by-eighteen foot skiffs, in preparation for an investigation into the animal intelligence of fish...(?)

Kaneohe Bay was quite shallow to begin with, and stars would have lighted the night alone, had the small crafts not been able to light their own way with their floodlights. The tide was out, and the waters of the bay were at their shallowest.

For quite a way out from the little island research center, a person could easily have waded along the coral reefs in the two to three feet of crystal clear water that covered them. The three skiffs gingerly picked their way through the shallows in search of the deeper channels toward the mouth of the bay.

The expedition was lead by Jayseeka, who directed the lead skiff to where the reefs suddenly dropped off into an inlet of crystal water thirty feet deep and sixty feet wide. Anchoring the skiffs securely to the surrounding coral reef all pitched in to set up the equipment of the mobile laboratory, as per the little Aquatian's instructions.

The traffic of marine life passing in and out of the bay through the clear waters of the channel was nothing short of spectacular, and could easily be viewed. The floodlights lit up the area with daylight brightness.

Jayseeka, for reasons soon to be discovered, sent a bright red flare into the night sky, which slowly parachuted itself down approximately five hundred feet from the skiffs, in the obviously deeper waters outside the bay.

Another thirty minutes of wonderment would pass, as the team watched the creatures of the bay passing through the lighted area of the channel, entering and leaving for reasons known only to themselves.

Taking notes and absorbed in the procession of strange sea creatures winging and finning their way through the channel, the team watched entranced. Suddenly there was no more creature transit into the bay, and those leaving were noticed to turn rapidly about, heading back in the direction from which they had came. Immediately, as if a large invisible hand had swept all moving faunas from the water, no motion of a living thing could be seen in the channel.

The unsettling mystery continued for approximately five minutes, when out of the inky darkness of the waters beyond the lights, and into the horrified vision of its human spectators, with power and astonishing fluidity, materialized a fantastically huge, nightmarish creature. The audience observed the frightful phenomenon instinctively motionless for approximately ten seconds; icicles of mindless fear pierced them to the quick.

Before the full impact of the occurrence registered on the group, the full body of the horrid specter, which had flowed into the channel, became motionless. "It" lay on the white coral sand just beneath the three skiffs and their startled occupants.

"Sweet Jesus!" shouted one of student helpers, as he leaped out of his boat and onto the reef, with the intent of making his way back to the safety of the island as quickly as he could wade.

Just about everybody in the skiffs thought the terrified student might have a pretty good idea, when they realized what "It" was that now occupied the channel's limelight. Exclamations of terror and the smell of urine filled the balmy night air as the monster lay on its side staring up at its now nearly deranged observers with one of its huge, baleful, tire-size eyes.

It was a giant squid of the most disturbing proportions; its body was at least fifteen feet in diameter, and its thick tentacles reached far back into the black waters of the ocean that had spawned it. Most of the spectators were frozen with fear as they viewed the specter beneath them, when suddenly Dr. Gwinnett jumped toward the back of her skiff to loose the anchor in hopes of escape.

"Wait! Please stop and listen!" It was Jayseeka speaking, and for an unknown reason, uncommon to human nature, they did so; suddenly and strangely things did not seem to be as bad as they had first appeared.

"I knew she would be here; I asked her to come." explained Jayseeka to her stunned audience.

Dr. Zimmerman had just gotten the answer to his question of yesterday, about what they were doing in the middle of nowhere in a plane, and joy was far removed from anything he was feeling.

In a voice mingling fear and anger, Dr. Nicholas, in low forceful, but whispered tones, informed the Aquatian, "It might have been a real goddamned good idea if you had explained your objectives more clearly. I for one would have reconsidered my invitation!"

"That monster can eat each and every one of us like peas out of a goddamned pod, and there wouldn't be a frigging, goddamned thing any of us could do to prevent it!" responded Dr. Gwinnett. Her surprisingly forceful words failed to encompass the scope of her emotions. The knuckles of her hands were white with effort as she tightly gripped the rope leading to its solidly embedded anchor.

The rapid splashing sounds of the runaway student suddenly stopped somewhere in the dark shallows beyond the lighted area.

"Are you all right, Bruce?" called out Dr. Zimmerman into the darkness.

"Yeah, Jeeze! I'm all right. Are you guys okay over there?" came back the anxious reply.

"I believe we will be okay." responded the doctor, eyeing Jayseeka with a mixture of suspicion, betrayal and apprehension.

In the quiet of the night, all could hear clearly as Jayseeka voiced her apology for the failure to properly inform the team of what they would be up against. (The truth was that she had known from the very beginning the reaction her aquatic friend was going to have on the human investigators. She had known their minds, and most of them would not have undertaken the excursion had they known what lay before them, at least not unarmed, as had been the request of her gargantuan guest.)

"If is not too late to regain your trust, there are scientific investigative materials here that will assure each and every one of you a place in history. I cannot do it alone, and I beg your indulgence."

All were aware of the past accomplishments of the little alien, and for some reason rationalized that if she was not afraid, then perhaps they should do their best to overcome their emotions. As a group they would decide to get on with the spectacular scientific opportunity that lay before them-- or beneath them, as was now the case.

The cameras were now rolling, above and beneath the water's surface. Jayseeka dropped over the side of the boat, sinking to the vicinity of the creature's huge dour eye that stared unblinkingly upward at the information gathering, intrigued, albeit disconcerted investigators.

Tape recorders were storing individual perceptions of the event, while Jayseeka appeared to be stroking and communicating with the massive mound of flesh, laying immobile on its side, its upper body surface a mere fifteen feet beneath the skiffs.

After about twenty minutes Jayseeka rose to the surface, reached into the lead boat, pulling the extensive cables with their suction attachment devices off into the water. As the fascinated investigators looked on, she descended once more to attach them to the apparently complacent creature beneath.

Again arising and climbing into the boat, the Aquatian carefully checked to see that the conduits were firmly and properly attached to the apparatus she had built and used on little Ralphie the chimp. Then sinking once more to the area of the huge sensitive eye, she deftly but gently covered it with a weighty plastic-type of material she had taken down with her.

Upon Jayseeka's final return to the surface, she quickly toweled herself dry, clicked on the communication equipment, and hooked the apparatus into the same power packs charging the floodlights.

All was in readiness as humankind, for the first time in the history of the world, prepared to exchange thoughts with an aquatic alien mollusk from their own planet.

## Chapter Eighteen

Life exists upon the Earth,
As this is meant to be.
Minds of Great Beasts have thought great thoughts,
Unknown by you and me.

The faint sound of the topside whirling cameras and the light slap of water against the side of the boats were all that could be heard. The investigators waited with bated breath in their plume of light, within the shroud of darkness.

"GREETINGS, CREATURES OF THE ETHER WORLD!" boomed the speakers, fraying the nerves once more of the audience.

"It's okay. Easy now, please remain calm!" encouraged Jayseeka to her human counterparts. She quickly reached for the controls to turn down the volume of the communication apparatus.

When the sound monitor had been adjusted downward to one fourth of its original intensity, Jayseeka handed the cordless microphone to Dr. Gwinnett.

The Professor was a bit taken back by the implications of the gesture, but all eyes were upon her now as she cleared her voice, and spoke into the device which would convey the message to the giant creature beneath her. "And greetings to you as well, great water-dweller of the deep!"

"I sense a certain apprehension in your voice," responded the Denizen. "You need not fear me; I wish you no harm. This adventure is as mysterious to me as it is to you. I had wished for the opportunity to extend my appreciation for the two human offerings you sent me in the past."

The team looked at one another with a mixture of puzzlement and concern.

"Could you refresh our memories, kind sir," requested the anthropologist, "as to these gifts?"

"Has Jayseeka not informed you that I am female, taking the name of Xenophonzia?"

"Oh! I do apologize, Madam. Yes, she did, but in my excitement with this encounter I failed to make a mental note of it."

Each of the human crew then introduced themselves to their massive guest.

"I am deeply honored to meet all of you, and also to be a part of this most noble enterprise of knowledge and understanding. The gifts to which I was referring," continued Xenophonzia, "were the two of your dead you sent down to me with rocklike weights around their lower appendages, 22,360 high tides ago. The gesture was a kind one, but after a small taste, I was compelled to leave the remainder for whatever creature that might find them, as they were not to my liking. They seemed to have had poisons in their bodies that tasted very bad to me, or did you mean to intentionally poison me?"

"Not in the least were our intentions dishonorable," quickly countered Dr. Gwinnett with a mixture of fright and concern. "However the two dead humans may have indulged themselves in the euphoria of various toxic drugs, prior to their demise and descent into your world. We are sincerely saddened to realize that the gifts were not well received."

All of the crew were grateful to and admiring of Dr. Gwinnett, who had given a quick and pacifying explanation to Xenophonzia.

Human imaginations had instantly gone wild in speculation as to what discontent could produce in the mind and body of the powerful and intelligent beast that lay beneath them.

Dr. James Nicholas was quick to inquire as to how the huge mollusk could keep an accurate record of the ocean's tides, whereupon Xenophonzia explained that she was able to do this by using various sized rocks which she had laid out in areas of her underwater territory.

The unspoken realization of the humans was that murder had been done, and it crossed more than one human mind that perhaps it might have been an explanation to the Hoffa mystery.

Jayseeka encouraged the team to make the most of their time, as there was only about an hour of energy left in the battery packs; therefore their conversation with the aquatic behemoth beneath them would have to be limited.

The scientists learned that her great size was largely due to the huge job that was required of her, as she explained where many of the larger forms of marine life went at their death. Numerous whales, dolphins and sea lions actually sought her out with the intent of putting an end to the sufferings of old age. Her age was 110 years, and she believed she would know life for at least another 50 years.

Her primary enemy was not considered to be humankind, but that fierce menace, the sperm whale, against whom she was constantly on guard while rearing her young, its favorite food. She was greatly disappointed when humans began to ease up on the hunting of this archrival.

As it turned out through the research, the giant mollusk had an intelligence equal to that of humans. Many times, on the darkest of nights, she had lain alongside, and often even attached herself to, large pleasure craft at rest in various bays throughout the Hawaiian Islands. Covertly she had listened to the conversations, radios and televisions therein. She had done quite a good job of keeping up on current events around the world, and had been doing so for more than 70 years.

Human words she could never speak, without the aid of the communication device built by Jayseeka, but human desires and the understanding of English words she knew well. She had made a hobby of studying the human condition.

As the floodlights began to lose their intensity, Jayseeka dropped back off into the channel to retrieve the equipment contacts from the body of Xenophonzia, as well as the covering she had placed over the sensitive eye.

In a stunning display of agility, the mother squid had raised one of her giant tentacles out of the water, and deposited three of her golf-ball size eggs at the feet of a startled Dr. Zimmerman, with the explanation, "Only a very small number of my young will ever survive the perils of the sea to become adults. I bequeath these living pearls to Dr. Zimmerman, if he will care for them properly, not cause them undue suffering while in captivity, and return them to the sea when they have hatched and grown to at least ten kilos in weight."

The Professor sincerely promised his honorable intent; grateful for the additional knowledge he would gain from the offspring of Xenophonzia. The others of the team were secretly grateful when the huge tentacle withdrew back into the water.

A certain sadness gripped the investigators as the magnificent and intelligent beast known as Xenophonzia withdrew her massive body from the channel, returning once more to the depths of her world.

Another scientific milestone had been reached, and more were to follow within two days.

**********

It had been a monumental full day's work to get the two large barges cleaned up, properly rigged, and spaced for the task they were soon to perform when pulled out to sea on the following day.

A wealthy hotel owner living on the island of Hawaii volunteered his sizable pleasure yacht for the purpose of hauling the makeshift rest area out into the deep blue. The next round of insight into animal intelligence was about to begin.

The barges were to anchor in a hundred feet of smooth water two miles northeast of the Big Island. All the previous crew and necessary equipment would be aboard the barges as they put out to sea. Jayseeka, Roxanne, and Dr. Hauss would catch up later via the pontoon aircraft.

Circling an area about ten miles in diameter, fifteen miles from the two anchored barges, Roxanne would be the first to spot the whale's spout as it surfaced for air. She was about to ask Jayseeka how she knew that this particular whale was going to be at this location, when she remembered the lone beach north of San Francisco and Jayseeka's watery trip. She did grasp the opportunity to inquire as to the navigational knowledge and timing awareness of the sizable mammal.

"Actually humans could learn a lot from the navigational abilities of whales," explained Jayseeka. "These marvelous creatures had been roaming the oceans long before mankind was to utter its first word. As for timing, they are quite adept at calculating their arrival at any area in the ocean, thousands of miles away, and to the hour. This is no modest mathematical feat, when one takes into consideration tides, winds and currents. The sensitive environmental clock of a whale is an extraordinary evolutionary accomplishment of their species."

The plane's pilot was asked to calculate as closely as possible the path of the whale and drop down in front of it at about 300 yards distance, stopping the plane's engines.

As Jayseeka got ready for her rendezvous with the multi-ton monstrosity, she explained to Dr. Hauss and Roxanne that she would meet with them aboard the barges in less than an hour. "Please prepare the investigative team for our arrival."

She then neatly dove from the exit of the plane, cutting the water with hardly a ripple, disappearing into the crystal blue of the sea.

It was a Pacific Right Whale that soon surfaced to the west of the waiting barges. The small object on its back, just below the spout, turned out to be the Aquatian. In about another twenty minutes, after its sighting from the barges, the rare monstrosity slid easily between them. The long, wide nylon straps took up the slack, holding him from beneath at just enough depth, so his blowhole could easily obtain the large quantities of air his massive body required.

Once guided into place by Jayseeka, the creature rested still and apparently complacent between the two barges.

When all necessary preparations had been performed according to Jayseeka's instructions, the Aquatian, with more of her most surprising agility, jumped to the spacing plank six feet above her head. Swinging herself to the top, she walked across it to the barge on which was located the necessary communication equipment.

The science team applauded.

Jayseeka returned by walking the same plank to its center, dropping back onto the sixty-foot multi-ton mammal. She then went about attaching the cables with the light suction devices at their ends.  This having been completed, she returned once more to the barge in the same manner as before, and whistled sharply into the microphone of the communication equipment.

The speakers sounded forth with a bright clear note, an octave below Jayseeka's original flute-like tone.  The process of communication with the whale had begun.

As the whale had not the understanding of American English language as had the giant Squid or even the little Chimpanzee, Jayseeka was obligated to remain on the back of the great whale, establishing a telepathic bond between them.  She translated the information; as best she could, via a small cordless transponder, which she had hung about her neck.

Thoughts and sounds from the whale, and words from humans and Aquatian, all fed into the deciphering apparatus on the barge.  These were translated and sent accordingly through the equipment, the result being a close approximation of what whale and scientists intended.  All activity was documented through state-of-the-art camera and recording equipment.

The thought patterns of the whale were more like those of poetry and music than the syntax of spoken language. Jayseeka was literally obligated to say or sing the words into the microphone, as best as she could determine the emotional telepathic meanings of the whale.  There were times when Penzantee the whale felt that Jayseeka had not translated his true meaning.  Not understanding the questions of the humans, all his exquisite fluting, humming, drumming, and clicking would stop.  When the humans could convey a clearer understanding, then the musical stories would once more continue.

Penzantee sang sad songs of past memories, from when he was very young.  He had lost first his father when he was less than one year old, and then his mother a month later to the whaling ships who hunted his species relentlessly until the tribe's numbers had been reduced from 63 to only 6 in number.

He described the massive scarlet plumes of blood that had spewed forth from his father and mother as the whalers shot their exploding harpoons into their flesh. He remembered the taste of their blood in his mouth, when he helplessly followed them as they were hauled towards the ships for the live butchering. He had wanted to save them, to help in any way he could, but there was nothing he could do.

At the death of his mother, he would have died as well, had his aunt not given him love and milk, which he shared with his cousin Sevelyn. With the death of his mother, all that remained of the tribe were his aunt, his baby female cousin, two six year old females, a young male scarcely three years of age, and himself. Leadership of the tribe had fallen to his aunt Hindilah who led them into the Polar Regions of the Pacific. The waters were bitterly cold, but they could safely navigate amongst the ice floes, where the great whaling ships would not venture.

The sadness of the whale song, as Penzantee recounted his early life, had brought the human audience to the cold realization of what humans had wrought upon the intelligent and sensitive creature that lay before them, and his tribe.

Jayseeka had difficulty at times with the translations, as she was so caught up in the emotional trauma of the magnificent creature. While performing the requiems for his loving parents, the strains of musical sadness were so hauntingly and beautifully pure that there was not a dry eye to be found among the grieving and despondent listeners.

The whale-song and telepathic dialogue continued for about four hours, with musical composition that would have enthralled Mozart or Beethoven.

Penzantee sang of huge caves of ice, which he and the remainder of his tribe had found in the safe arctic regions. Vents of warm water would churn up from thermal fissures in the ocean floor, beneath the overlying sheets of ice, forming vast miles of caverns. In many places the caves were a mere ten to twenty feet below the surface of the ice. In the perpetual daylight of the Arctic summer months the surface snows would melt, allowing the sun's rays to readily find their way through the clean ice into these huge caverns, lighting them up with glorious crystalline hues of aquamarine blues and emerald greens.

The warm waters harbored bountiful krill that fed upon the massive nutrients, which rose with these warm waters from the ocean floor. This in turn attracted a magnitude of fish and large crustaceans. Daily, Penzantee and his tribe would feed upon the harvest beneath the ice; when full they would lie within the perfect acoustical formations of the caves. Floating near the surface of the warm waters, they sang songs together, thankful for the love of family, which bound them and thanking the Majestic Great Creator for her mercy and kindness in leading them to the safety and bounty of the caverns.

But paradise was not to be perpetual, as the endless day would eventually be replaced by a long winter night. The small tribe would be forced out of the caves and into the perilous journey south into the nutrient-rich waters off Mexico and Chile where waited those Dark Angels of Death, the whalers. Penzantee sang in praise of Hindilah, his aunt, and her brilliant leadership in always leading the small tribe in the underwater direction opposite to that which the whalers could anticipate, into beds of kelp and rocky bays where the Evil Ones could not safely venture.

The tribe had now grown to twelve in number, and Penzantee was proud that another of his children would soon be born from one of the now older females that had escaped with him and the others to the safety of the Arctic ice.

In his numerous yearly trips into tropical regions, the glistening black and white denizen of the sea also sang of things above the water, such as islands, cliffs and mountains that he viewed when surfacing for air. He recounted what he saw below the waters as well, such as sharks and fish of unusual size, deep channels, islands that had sunk but still retained strange structures he presumed had been built by humans, ancient shipwrecks, and rich feeding areas of abundant krill and small fish.

When the scientists explained as best they could that there were growing numbers of influential humans throughout the world that were appalled at the hunting of his kind, Penzantee was delighted, but saddened that he had nothing to give to those who had been so kind. When asked by the investigators if he could somehow give the locations of the various sunken islands and shipwrecks, the great mammal trembled with delight to find that he indeed did have something to give.

When it was explained that artifacts of ancient human societies were of great value to human historians, the great locator sang and fluted in higher octaves of delight. Giving the distances from shore by the lengths of his body, which was sixty-one and a half feet long according to the scientists' measurements. He also gave amazing descriptions of the seashore and underwater terrain in detail.

As it would turn out, the aquatic mathematician was able to give locations down to the smallest detail, his organic sonar proving to be incredibly useful and accurate. When informed that the treasures that might be gained from his knowledge would go to charitable foundations for the preservation of his kind, his joy was boundless. He composed a grateful song of joy on the spot, donating it to the scientific team.

In the time allotted Penzantee, the tired humans had witnessed and documented seventy-one different and original whale-song lyrics and musical compositions from the huge, gentle creature.

A strange, sad joy encompassed the investigators as the rare and magnificent survivor departed from them. He set his course towards that speck in the vastness of the Pacific where he would be greeted warmly by his tribe. All would be thankful that he had returned to them safely and anxious with anticipation to hear his profound musical description of the solitary adventure.

A king's ransom in Mayan and Aztec gold and silver artifacts would be uncovered within the year from some of the many Spanish galleons that had sunk during the quasi-religious plunder of the ancient South American cultures, most of them in international waters.

The same scientific team that had been the first to communicate intelligently with Penzantee would also lead and supervise the recovery of the numerous ancient, priceless relics. Their rewards would eventually allow each of them a most comfortable life, but their greatest reward would be the knowledge that ninety percent of the proceeds had gone to a well intentioned "Save the Whales Society" with themselves as primary board members.

The newly created well-funded society would have the documentation and the ability to finally bring Humanity to the realization that morality should pertain to others with whom they shared the planet.

The acknowledgment that Penzantee the whale and others of his kind were astoundingly intelligent, and in some aspects more so than the land mammals known as humans, would give the phrase "save the whales" a momentous reality throughout the world. All would know the truth.

# Chapter Nineteen

Purge the evil from your own heart,
Regardless of what others may teach.
Search within, Oh Aspirant of Noble Quest;
Hence to realize, **The Truth was always with you.**

*(Roxanne Henry 33 A.J.)*

Imprisoned Asian and African elephants in zoos and circuses around the world had been the victims of massive suffering at the hands of their human captors. With amazing compassion and understanding, the huge pachyderms had borne the ignorance of "humanity," in many cases growing quite fond of their caretakers. While bearing humans no ill will, they had yearned daily with almost unbearable sorrow for their family tribes and the freedom to roam once more the green jungles and golden savannas of their ever-shrinking wilderness homelands.

Jayseeka would no longer participate in the investigations of the researchers, as they now had the understanding, funding and instrumentation needed to proceed quite well on their own. Many would soon join them in their quests around the world. Humanity began to understand what the Aquatus had known long ago regarding the true nature of animal intelligence, be it human-animal or other animal species.

**********

They came in dark clothing, with little rings of white about their necks; they came in robes of black, red and white, most closely-shaven, some with beards and hats.  They came one by one, two by two, and in small groups.  Some came on foot, some came in beautifully polished luxury cars, and some came with horse and surrey.  Some came not at all, out of fear of what they might hear.

There had been pressure for years from religious communities around the world.  They wanted to inquire as to the religious nature of the inhabitants of the planet Trepleon.  They wanted confirmation of their beliefs, each of them believing that their particular deity or messenger must surely have visited and preached to the Aquatus at some time in the past.

All these men and women of the cloth were well informed about the visitations of the Aquatus to Earth over the last 10,000 years.  They were sure that the pious and miraculous claims of their various and sundry historical books and their faithful interpretations of these texts would be at last indubitably vindicated.

There was also an ever-deepening concern regarding attendance in the various houses of worship, which had seen a steady and predictable decline over the last three years.  Vindication would most certainly bring back the flocks.

It was with misgivings that Jayseeka, Ambassador from the planet Trepleon, finally agreed to the conference, but only if a full representation of all the many religions, and their various sects, could be expected.

Much indignation, jealousy and downright hostility ensued, and had to be overcome, before the "conference of the holy" could be consummated.  Having finally been agreed upon and scheduled after two years of bickering and brooding, this was felt by most to be a modern day miracle.

Except for very few, all in attendance at this religious meetings of the minds knew that his own chosen, pious path was the one closest to God. Down through the centuries many of the ancestral adherents to these various beliefs had slaughtered one another, each in the name of God in a violent attempt to prove it.

Often as not, "This is God's Will" had been the excuse for the plunder, rape, and slaughter of the innocent. Strangely enough, in the last three years parts of Europe, Africa, and the Middle East, where war had been nearly perpetual for thousands of years, the hostilities were dramatically beginning to dwindle.

There were three hundred and seven religious leaders and their translators present at the assembly; all gave each other the courtesy and kindness due to visiting guests, but these were outward appearances only. Smiling and shaking hands, most wished secretly that the others and their heretical doctrines would be burned from the face of the earth.

The little Aquatian, Jayseeka, Ambassador from Trepleon, took the podium, which had been especially adapted for her. A sudden hush fell over the audience, as she stood clearly before them in all her golden splendor, smiling graciously, which was her way. Projectors cast her appealing visage, many times enlarged, upon screens above and to the back of the podium.

The news media were also in full attendance, raising the total number of persons present to over 800.

Smiling with apparent warmth and compassion the Aquatian began to teach.

"Would those among you who have been chosen by God to preach the true religious doctrine please stand?" requested Jayseeka.

The entire assembly, except the news media, rose quickly to its feet.

After motioning for all to take their seats again, she asked, "Will all those among you who have been chosen by God to preach the false religious doctrine please stand?" Chuckles and spontaneous muffled laughter filled the room.

She stood silently on the podium before them for five minutes so that all would have a chance to realize what had just happened.

"Those of you who believe that the others present here today are deluded by false religious doctrine please stand."

Once again the entire assembly was on its feet. This time there was no snide humor within the group, as each began to verbalize his emotions.

"A hundred foot tall Jesus came to me in a dream!"

"Mohammed spoke to me in a cave while I was meditating!"

"Moses appeared in the flames of my fireplace!"

"The Buddha manifested himself in the air above me!"

"A statue of the Virgin Mary spoke to me!"

The assembly was beginning to fragment as delusions and downright fabrications began to be professed as truths.

Jayseeka motioned for the sound technician to enhance the equipment, then fluted with amazing shrillness and clarity into the microphones before her. All quarreling ceased abruptly, and Jayseeka once more motioned for the assembly to be seated.

"In our observations of Earth down through the centuries, I am reminded of the little boy named LeeRay, whom we had the opportunity to observe. LeeRay wrote a letter to 'God' in which he asked, 'Dear God--it's okay that you made different religions, but don't you get mixed up sometimes?'

"Hopefully we can rise above LeeRay's young naiveté, as LeeRay himself did in later years. Hopefully we can realize that although there is but a single omnipresent 'God' or 'Ultimate Principle' or whatever we perceive the origin of all things to be, that it is indeed the 'human elements' on planet Earth that created the sundry 'religions.'

"In this inquiry let us attempt to rise above myth and indoctrination. In an orderly fashion I will answer your questions, but please be kind enough to realize that time is not unlimited. Therefore, please ask only those questions each of you considers most pertinent concerning your beliefs, and I will answer according to that which is most acceptable on Trepleon.

"I would like to impress upon all of you that in Trepleon's past we Aquatus also had many religious confrontations as to who held the 'true doctrine.' However, as the obvious became more elucidated, through our better understanding of the universe, we were obliged to gradually abandon those aspects of our beliefs which we deemed to be founded in arrogance rather than reality.

"I would also like to make it perfectly clear from the beginning that if we believed that God had made us in his image as you believe, then it is more plausible that we would be the 'chosen ones' rather than yourselves, even though we retain gills and have not a single bone in our smaller bodies. We are a more ancient species than you are and much further technologically advanced.

"On planet Trepleon we had our eras of conflict, in which each of our many religions was thought to be the 'One True Religion.' Our ancestral adherents to those sundry religions each believed that they were 'the chosen people' and all those of a different belief inferior, hence justifying the extermination of them if possible.

"We also believed that God was all good, and that there was another entity, 'Devil' if you will, that was all evil, and that the 'Good' eclipsed the 'Evil.' So as you ask your questions, please remember that our historical beliefs did indeed parallel your own."

**********

It was now more than five years since the first patient had passed through the bowels of the Lazarus Machines. All but a very few of the Earth's more than six billion human inhabitants had benefited from the mental and physical enhancement therein, including those attending at the long-awaited "religious conference."

Many of the religious personages had previously, and quietly, read numerous scientific journals that, prior to their treatments in the Aquatus medical apparatuses, they would have considered heresy. They had begun to notice the quixotic imperfections in the logic of their religious literature. Openly, they would profess their commitment to the age-old beliefs, while secretly they searched for better explanations.

**********

Jayseeka started from left to right as she selected individuals in the congregation to ask their questions, but later would simply lapse into Aquatus theology in the hope that all their questions would find an answer at some point during the discourse.

The grand old patriarch, in his flowing white silk robe, rose slowly to his feet, conscientiously grasping the religious artifact that hung about his neck. He had been well pleased to be treated in the Lazarus Machine. It had cured his prostate cancer, clarified his vision and intellect, as well as adding forty healthy years to his life.

He was a kindly person, sincere in his service to others,

and felt he was putting the little Aquatian on the spot when he asked, "Well then, if the image of God is neither human nor Aquatus, what pray tell does God look like?"

"I will explain what we Aquatus believe, but it is with the mutual understanding that you are in no way obligated to believe as we do. You may accept what I have to say, as being closer to the truth, or reject it; I will not be offended.

"We believe the Image of God to be a Human image, but we also believe it to be Aquatus, as well as fish, fowl, snake, mouse and every other life form on this planet, or whatever life forms exist on our own planet, and every other inhabited planet throughout the cosmos. We are monotheistic the same as yourselves; however we see God or, in our understanding, 'The Ultimate Principle,' as the total composition of all that exists, animate or inanimate, and fail to see how "It" could be anything other than the totality of all things."

"If this be the case then how do you explain the existence of God's Laws that have been handed down to us through the centuries which encouraged us not to lie, cheat, steal, bear false witness, to love our neighbors as we do ourselves?" The patriarch went on, "Surely evil activities do not come from God. Why, we would be nothing short of barbarous without His laws!"

"My dear man, you were barbarous even with these laws to govern you, for you took them lightly, and considered only those professing your own religious beliefs to be your neighbors, and, in most cases, all others unworthy of any consideration. Morality is simply the product of society. If individuals are to benefit from a group effort, there are certain rules that must be followed. If these rules of which you speak are 'God-given,' well then, there are many animal societies which share a goodly portion of these attributes, be they wolf pack, elephant herd, lion pride, chimpanzee societies, and others too numerous to mention. Plain and simple, the more of these moral attributes any given society could accommodate, the more it enhanced their means of survival, and survive you did. Rather well, I might add."

"What of good and evil?" asked a concerned Rabbi. "Do the Aquatus disclaim its existence?"

"Two sides of the same coin," responded Jayseeka.

"Are we to believe then that God is both good and evil?" exclaimed the now confounded teacher of his faith.

"I understand that it is your belief that God is all good, and that he only destroys evil; but then how do you explain your portion of the scriptures wherein 'God' is the all-knowing creator of all things? Surely if God is all-knowing, then he must have known that evil was going to be a problem when he created it; or do you suppose he created evil, or the predisposition for evil in man, so he could have the pleasure of destroying it, or indeed casting humans into hell for the pleasure of watching them suffer?

"Then if you should say, 'It is man who chooses good over evil because he has freedom of choice,' this also misses the point, because God in his infinite wisdom, according to your scriptures, already knows beforehand what the choice is going to be, as 'he knows all things.'

"We Aquatus do not deny the existence of good and evil, nor do we deny them to be very powerful entities throughout the cosmos. Evil is most obviously the cruel giver of pain and anguish, in effect the eternal destroyer, while Good is the eternal builder and giver of joy and happiness. However, we believe both to be derived from the same source, a source we have designated as the Ultimate Principle. Even though words or thought cannot take in the scope of the Unblemished Truth, I will attempt to simplify this concept with a parable.

"Somewhere on planet Earth is a small grassy field. In

and upon this field live a number of field mice, which happily and industriously go about their lives, sleeping, waking, digging, eating and procreating. The mice are totally unaware that any other world exists, and the grassy field encompasses the totality of their existence.

"They see the Sun as their supreme God, as it warms the earth, drives away the snow and ice, causes the grasses to grow from whence come the seeds which is their food. The Rain is their second good deity, as it also aids in the growth of the grass, and gives them additional moisture for their small bodies and cools the earth at times during the hot summer.

"The Hawk is their Devil, as she daily observes the mousy field in hopes of, often times successfully, snatching one of the unwary rodents in her bloody talons, carrying it away to her nest, there to be mutilated and devoured by her young. Only the healthiest and most clever of the mice in the field survive, and if the Hawk does not constantly improve her hunting skills, she and her offspring will soon come to an end as well.

"Without the Hawk, the mice would soon breed themselves into annihilation, as all their offspring would survive, both the sick and the simple. This would soon deplete their food supply to the point at which they could not store up enough to maintain them through the long cold winter, if disease did not first deplete the dense population.

"So you see, from the field mouse's point of view, the Hawk is evil; however from the Hawk's point of view, the mice would be evil if she could not catch them from time to time, as she and her family would soon starve to death.

"The true reality of the parable is that without the Hawk the field-mice could not survive, and without the mice the Hawk could not survive, and that it was none other than God or the Ultimate Principle acting as initiator, hence bringing them both into existence to begin with."

"You are teaching that God is the architect of Evil?" blurted out one of the red-faced clergy.

"You must consider more closely what I have explained to you. I will attempt to take the example a bit further. The constructive forces of Good and the destructive forces of Evil work hand in hand to bring about change. These changes that started eons ago on your planet and others throughout the cosmos are what has given rise to the often gloriously beautiful and intelligent life forms that populate this and other worlds."

"So then, according to your beliefs, there is no final retribution for evil deeds?" ejected another of the stunned listeners.

"Oh, please, do not construe what I have said to mean that a cruel person's 'numen' gains the same favor as that of a good person; remember that evil is debasing while good is benevolent to living things.

"Now then, we must always keep in mind what is truly evil and what is truly good. Evil is not simply the belief or non-belief in a certain scripture or dogma because a vast number of persons believe it to be the truth. However, evil can be defined by the needless pain and suffering it inflicts upon the innocent, whatever that innocent life form might be.

"For example, if one animal hunts another for food which it must have for its survival, or kills another animal in self-defense, in order to preserve itself or family, then this is mildly evil but acceptable out of necessity. The evil effect upon the 'numen' is minimal and can be completely neutralized, as long as that animal did the killing for a good reason, i.e., food or protection for itself or family.

"On the other hand, should killing be done not out of necessity, and the animal which is doing the killing derives pleasure, or worse yet, prolongs unnecessarily the death and suffering of its victim, this will have a dreadful effect upon the 'numen' of this evil one. His or her life form quintessence will be compelled to undergo an equal cruelty (neither more nor less) in its current life form, or some future life or lives.

"Minor evils such as greed, envy, lust, sloth, wanton deception, mental cruelty, etc., will also leave stains on the 'numen' which must eventually be compensated for by the enactment of benevolent endeavors."

"You have insinuated several times that we are animals, but I can assure you, Ambassador, we are humans," egocentrically asserted another agitated man of the cloth.

The little Aquatian, from her modified pulpit, fixed the indoctrinated human with a steady gaze, the smile yet to leave her lips as she spoke. "Well do I know what species you are; however, in this world, as well as all other inhabited ones in the cosmos, there are four basic discernible substances from which all things derive: animal, vegetable, mineral or gas. Which of these are you, sir?"

Refusing to hear more, several of the audience left the meeting.

"Many of the once faithful of our congregations no longer attend our worship services. Is it because of something your healing apparatuses did to them when they took advantage of your gifts?"

"Perhaps yes, and perhaps no," continued Jayseeka. "Upon passage through our medical devices, which all of you did, in order to gain the advantages of a longer and healthier life, all gained enhanced mental potential as well. Perhaps many of your original following found they could no longer accept the various religious dogmas of your teachings.

"Many of your previous flocks may have decided to increase their knowledge of the world by returning to school where they perhaps came into contact with various scientific works. Many may have come to the realization that biologists, anthropologists, archeologists, naturalists, and others did not do their extensive research and publish their enlightened findings for the purpose of contradicting religious canon. On the contrary, it was because they wished to enlighten others, as they themselves had been enlightened.

"So you see it might very well be that many of your previous flocks (a term not in keeping with the idea that you are 'human' and somehow not animals) have put away their fear of death and the unknown and have gotten on with the building of better lives for their families and themselves."

"Are you proposing that the Scriptures, the Words of God are false?"

"Your scriptures are not totally false, nor are they totally true, but they are undoubtedly the words of men who felt they were inspired by their God," replied Jayseeka.

"Remember, we were visiting your planet when the history of which you speak was unfolding. It was only a short time ago--several hundred years--in the history of European religions that persons could be put to death and sometimes were for suggesting that the Earth traveled in orbit about the sun. For the belief was then, supposedly supported by religious text, that the sun traveled around the Earth or that the Earth was flat, for heaven's sake.

"Those who may have professed beliefs contrary to the beliefs held then--perhaps those who may have believed in theology held over from the ancient Greek and Roman Empires--were tortured until they confessed to some absurd religious crime, then burned at the stake as witches.

"A most glaring example of this was Giordano Bruno, a bright Italian philosopher, who had been a champion of the Copernican theories of astronomy. He was burned at the stake, as recently as 1600 A.D., by the Inquisition. He had the audacity to suggest that perhaps there might be other worlds throughout the cosmos.

"Often presumptions can be cast into the category of half-truths, which can be very dangerous, by the way, as they are easier to accept than out-and-out lies, by those who have a need to believe literally what they read and hear.

"I would like to cite an example from a religious text which I hope will not be construed by those who believe in that particular faith as an attack upon them, or the several other religions which have their roots within that older religion.

"According to the Exodus story, wherein the children of Israel left Egypt to migrate across the Sinai desert to the Promised Land some 200 miles distant, the journey was to take 40 years, according to their documentation. With the supposition that the Israelites knew where their leader was taking them from the beginning, they would average approximately 3 yards per hour, allowing for night stops, 24 yards per day, until finally reaching their destination 40 years later.

"The world's speediest land snail can travel at 55 yards per hour. An incredible speed when compared with the progress of the Israelites as they headed for their Promised Land. The truth of the matter is that, as nomads are wont to do, they wandered about in the desert (there was more water and grass for their flocks in those days), toughening themselves, studying the arts of warfare, and increasing their numbers to the point that they could take a more fertile land for themselves. By no means was it a gift; it was a fight, and the spoils went to the vanquishers.

"If their leaders could convince them that God was on their side, as leaders are often wont to do, and that somehow they were God's Chosen People, then this positive reinforcement would only serve to psychologically strengthen them in pursuit of their conquest. In other words if one was killed in battle, he went to heaven.

"I will give a very simplified sketch of what we Aquatus have come to believe over the eons of time on our world. I will ask God to give us a sign or exterminate me now if the statements I'm going to make do not closely parallel the spiritual reality of the cosmos."

Silence prevailed in the great hall for five minutes.

"Well, I suppose that makes it quite clear. Had there been an anthropomorphic God observing this assembly, I'm sure I would have been burnt to a crisp if what I'm about to say is not at least somewhere within the realm of truth. After all, we are on worldwide television hookup.

"It is the Aquatus belief that there are no chosen peoples. There are absolutely no peoples on this planet who are any more spiritually special than any others; nor are there any other life forms throughout the cosmos who have a direct two-way conversational link with God or the Ultimate Principle.

"It is the Aquatus belief that the 'numen' of all living creatures is enhanced or defiled according to the intensity of the good or evil deeds they manifest towards other living things, and the environment which surrounds them.

"The good that a living organism accomplishes motivates the 'numen' to transmigrate, not only on this world, but across space and time to other worlds throughout the cosmos, continuously being born into increasingly happier life forms, until it finally enters that joyous state that humans describe as Heaven or Nirvana. However, an 'evil numen' continuously manifests itself in the suffering of life throughout the cosmos. An evil numen may be plagued with disease, or in constant fear of starvation or being eaten. However, evil and suffering will eventually act as a learning/teaching mechanism, wherein one will come to realize that which is truly good and that which is truly evil. Eventually a numen will suffer for and repay its evil debt with goodness. However the debt that must be repaid will be neither more nor less than the pain or sorrow it caused others to suffer, through deed or action, in previous life forms.

"I would also like to make it perfectly clear that we Aquatus believe that evil activity must be counterbalanced with good activity, indeed paid in full before one's spiritual quintessence can enter Heaven or Nirvana. Furthermore, we consider it highly unlikely that any other spiritual persona either embodied or without a body, will intercede upon behalf of an evil one, as all things in the end will be perfectly balanced; an evil debt must be paid by the quintessence by which it was incurred.

"What about prayer and the miraculous healing and comfort it has brought about? This is well documented, I might add," inquired a solemn, bearded man in black, as he politely removed his large-brimmed black hat.

"There is no doubt that a prayer can be answered, but most of you here today should be aware that it not dependent upon a particular religious doctrine. It has undoubtedly either happened to, or been witnessed by, just about every religious personage of each religion represented here today. However, it is most probable that each of you failed to realize what really took place, as you believed it to be a confirmation of your particular religious beliefs.

"From time to time we Aquatus have experienced this same phenomenon. There have been those of our species who contracted various illnesses, on planets other than our own, that stumped our most brilliant medical minds. But in that individual's darkest hour, with life signs ebbing fast, there was a sudden and amazing recovery, which, we were assured, was not the natural outcome of the illness.

"Upon the total recovery of these individuals, they had the most amazing stories to tell us concerning their dreams and happenings during their unconscious state. We Aquatus attribute the fruits of meditation or, as you humans might say, the answering of a prayer, to a profoundly deep spiritual movement within the individual who has prayed or meditated in utmost sincerity. In so doing, he or she gave himself or herself completely and humbly over to that spiritual essence that dwells within us all.

"Hence the elimination of many dark spiritual scars upon the numen, or, put in the vernacular, the removal of sin. It seemed that those miraculously healed, for reasons inexplicable, became aware of how they could be of benefit to others, as well as themselves, further enhancing their benevolence as opposed to evil. It appears that death was stayed so that these individuals could act upon their new convictions in their current life forms.

"Perhaps there are those of you who may feel that it was the loved ones offering up prayers for the sick who brought about the healing, but we Aquatus believe it to have been an activity within the sick individual that brought about the cure. In our experience the healing occurred even when others, for one reason or the other, did not pray for the individual.

"It is not altogether unlikely that we can take upon our spiritual essence the sins of others, but most assuredly we must compensate for this acceptance of evil upon our numens at some time in the future. Perhaps the individual whose evil we accepted may once more, in some way, take it back upon himself in some distant future, yet-to-be-determined lifetime.

"Many have been those who believed their benefactor to be a Mohammed, Moses, Jesus, or some image or entity they perceived to be a Saint. The reality of the occurrence, we Aquatus believe, stemmed from the spiritual essence within themselves rather than a deity from without.

"We believe this because it seems most ludicrous to presume that the answer to a prayer occurs because of a particular religion, due to the diversity of the beliefs. In truth, the only common ground that most Earthly religions share is Monotheism, with lesser Saints in assistance, and the basic moral principles that bind human social groups.

"Further, it is the Aquatus belief (and I do not mean to infer that, if you choose not to believe what I say, you will necessarily suffer because of your non-beliefs), that a good life form is good, regardless of its beliefs, as long as those beliefs do not maliciously harm the innocent. An evil life form is evil regardless of its beliefs, when its beliefs and activity maliciously do harm to the innocent. Most life forms throughout the cosmos harbor both good and evil in varying degrees.

"We Aquatus believe that there are degrees of good and evil, such as the evil necessity of harming creatures which mean you no harm, to obtain food. This is deemed acceptable as long as it is accomplished swiftly, with pleasureless empathy, or sorrow. However, to sadistically kill, or cause suffering for evil gratification, will result in the evil one performing these acts to be at the receiving end of pain and cruelty at some future date in its current or a future life form.

"Furthermore, there is current research being done which will settle once and for all the questions, 'Are all creatures on Earth, other than human, simply mindless living computers? Do they evolve here on this planet simply as food for humans, or do they share with humans the same or similar emotions, having as well a spiritual quintessence?'

"We Aquatus believe that there is a spiritual essence housed within in all living creatures throughout the cosmos. These will eventually find their multiple ways to paradise, and none will be denied. For all of you here today, indeed all life essences throughout the cosmos, were then and are now,

Loved From The Beginning, and will not be denied by their originator. Great and wondrous is that mystery of all causation, the magnitude of which we can only tacitly begin to realize.

"We Aquatus encourage all who hear my voice to cease thinking that evil is greater in others because of race, religion, or country of origin. This is utter nonsense and will continuously lead to evil cruelty, war and bloodshed.

"The historical Moses outlined a moral code for his followers, and worked the various ideas which he called 'laws' into the religion of the Israelites as they journeyed in the Sinai wilderness. He believed God had given these laws to him and his people. I will reconstruct these beliefs from modern day scriptures, and then give an Aquatus analytical view, as to the manner in which we see their reality and intent.

"Moses said that God said, 'Thou shalt have no other gods before me.'

"This statement we Aquatus would view as an impossibility, as there is only a single Ultimate Principle and no matter how many other deities one might believe in, it is little more than a waste of time and energy.

"'Thou shalt not make for thyself a carved image, nor bow down to serve them, for I thy Lord God am a jealous God.'

"Even though there are many such relics in homes, temples and churches around the world, these inanimate images do living creatures little good, except perhaps for remembrance purposes. However, we Aquatus believe that you need not concern yourselves one way or the other as to whether it is good or evil to worship them. If bowing down to an inanimate object causes one to intensify his inner goodness, then perhaps this is acceptable.

"We believe, however, that beings should be reflective more on the Essence of the Ultimate Principle residing profoundly within themselves. One of your own great spiritual philosophers, Lao Tsu, maintained that 'knowing the good and evil in others requires wisdom, while knowing the good and evil residing within oneself is enlightenment.' So then we Aquatus suggest that to look within for spirituality is more practical than searching for spirituality in an inanimate object.

"As for God or the Ultimate Principle being jealous? Why would It be concerned with such trifles? There simply is no possible greater beauty or power.

"'Thou shalt not take the name of God in vain.'

"Names are only handles we attempt to place on objects. It is ludicrous to think that we can order about, at our discretion, the power and magnitude of the Ultimate Principle, the sum totality of all things. So then what would we Aquatus say? Totality damn it? To what avail?

"'On the seventh day thou shalt do no work, for in six days the Lord God made the heavens and the earth, and on the seventh day he rested.'

"It's good to take at least one day in the week off, especially on Trepleon. Our planet is nearly twice the size of your Earth and orbits its sun on nearly twice the elliptical path as that of Earth. It also takes Trepleon approximately 47 earth hours to revolve 360 degrees. Therefore one of our days or weeks is approximately double that of yours. We Aquatus enjoy our family and friends and we do spend daylight time with them. However, it is no crushing evil, or much evil at all from our point of view, if one chooses to put in longer hours at work, but one should be conscientious that the family does not unduly suffer because of it.

"I can tell you most assuredly that it took longer than 144 hours to create the heavens and earth. You have but to look through the lenses of your powerful Hubble telescope to see huge clouds of gas and debris, millions of light years in breadth and length, which will eventually give rise to other suns, planets and galaxies. The heavens are currently, and will quite probably be forever under construction.

"'Honor thy father and thy mother that your days may be long upon the land which the Lord God has given you.'

"The honor of elders in the family and tribe stretches far back into history long before the written word, on your planet and ours, as well as on all planets which harbor social life forms. The strengthening of family bonds allows the family unit to function more effectively, and hence the society as a whole is strengthened. As for God giving away land? Well, we Aquatus suppose it was something that needed to be said at the time.

"'Thou shalt not kill.'

"We Aquatus found it strange that such an ideal would appear within the moral ideology of human society, as it seems that the human species as a whole didn't have a problem with it. Humans are carniverous creatures and you certainly need to eat. Bloodshed was definitely necessary if the Israelites were to have their Promised Land or the Christian Europeans were to usurp the American continent from its native inhabitants but a few hundred years ago.

"The phrase, 'thou shalt not kill,' most of humanity construed to be wrong within one's own tight-knit society, in which mostly all shared the same beliefs. We Aquatus see any killing as evil, be it performed for any reasons other than self-defense, defense of the innocent, or to obtain necessary food.

"'Thou shalt not commit adultery.'

"This phrase has been construed by humanity to pertain to sexual activity with individuals other than the one contracted for as wife or husband. We Aquatus do not view the sexual process as evil in itself, as all sexual life forms must do it in order to continue life; however, it can lead to complications.

"Humans have discovered down through the eons of time that if they were to place a control mechanism on the biological need to procreate, that the family unit would remain intact, thereby allowing for a more wholesome environment for mate, children and self. In other words, by utilizing this social control mechanism, more emphasis would be placed on the gathering of food, creating stability on the home front, and raising and teaching the children, hence enhancing survival, instead of devoting valuable time and energy to various promiscuous sexual activities.

"Also, the transmission of the various and sundry venereal diseases were held in check at a time when there were no cures. This was and is a very good idea on behalf of the human species, but I will point out that pair bonding is not unique in the cosmos. Indeed there are any number of fish, fowl, and mammals on your own planet, and various life forms on ours, that form a family bond, and mate for life. Most often they do this more effectively than humans have been able to do.

"'Thou shalt not steal.'

"It is extremely difficult to hold together any advanced society, whose members steal from one another with impunity. We Aquatus simply believe it is evil to wrongfully deprive others of what they have earned through their mental or physical initiative. We also extend this ideal to include other species that we encounter, regardless of society, race, creed, religion, nation or world of origin.

"'Thou shalt not bear false witness against thy neighbor.'

"No society on Earth, Trepleon, or any other world

throughout the galaxy would have been able to elevate itself to any meaningful level of accomplishment, had there not been a sense of honor, or fairness, to bind them from within. We Aquatus extend this ideal to all societies and individuals as well.

"'Thou shalt not covet thy neighbor's house, wife, servant, nor any of thy neighbor's possessions.'

"It is really quite small-minded to envy others for what they possess. When we encounter this within the framework of Aquatus society, we strongly suggest that these small-minded ones get out and earn these desirable attributes for themselves if they can, or forget about them if they can't. This hopeless yearning of those pathetic ones is more a waste of time than it is an evil.

"It may be of interest to most of you to realize that in our observations of Earth approximately two thousand years ago, a fellow who had been named Jesus was honored in his youth by those who believed him to be a messenger from God.

"Setting off into the Orient, at a young age, Jesus went in search of those who had so honored him. He had a burning desire to learn more from them, and then return to his people in an attempt to bring them into nobler state of grace.

"In the course of his travels he accepted reincarnation, among other beliefs, and worked it into his teachings: Thou shalt be born again. This he taught to his followers. This belief was later construed by future teachers of Christianity to mean 'in the spirit' rather than in another life form. But I can assure you that Jesus meant another life form; hence came his saying, 'I shall return' prior to his death, which he most probably did. Not, however, in the mysterious manner as depicted in current biblical scriptures (Luke 24-39). Most assuredly, we Aquatus would have been aware if his dead corpse had come back to life.

"Though this person, who later became known as The Christ, could indeed read and write, as he was educated in the Hebrew manner of the times, his writings were either lost or intentionally destroyed after his death. As his deeds and teachings were told and retold, much of what he had said would later be exaggerated, enhanced and manipulated by others, finally being written down many years after his death.

"We Aquatus have experienced the same as yourselves, religious leaders who felt they had somehow fallen heir to a universal truth. Leaders who somehow felt that it was okay to enlarge upon their belief, thinking that the result, i.e., saving souls, would be the ends that justified the means.

"What evolved years later, to be changed even more with many additional copies of these 'scriptures' over the hundreds of years after his death, was a theosophical doctrine open to all people who wished to partake of it. This would prove to be beneficial to many, as the teaching was not a 'closed religion' open only to a certain society or culture. His teachings later became construed into a doctrine that could be, and was, forced upon others, often with the choice between 'If you don't believe this, you are probably a witch' (a crime punishable by death), and 'If you don't believe this, you are my enemy' (a reason to be executed), or, 'You will go to Hell upon your death!' Clearly this was not in keeping with what Jesus originally taught.

"Many were those who loved him, for he was apt at teaching in parables and just about everybody loves a good story. Many of his teachings such as the widow's mite and to treat your neighbor as you yourself would wish to be treated and his expounding on the religious teachings of Moses did manage to survive through the centuries.

"However, the idea that if a person didn't believe what Christ had taught meant that he or she would go to Hell upon their death was definitely not any teaching of his. One can find where it has slipped through in the translations and many copies, by reading (Matthew 9:13), 'For I am not come to call the righteous, but sinners to repentance.' His meaning was that, in his opinion, there were good people in the world, regardless of their religious beliefs at the time. Those beliefs, he was convinced, were not bringing malicious harm to others.

"But he did hope that all would listen to his teachings, as he felt he could guide them towards perfection, or a guarantee of heaven. Also he was well aware of all human shortcomings, within himself as well as others. He believed God and the predisposition to good or evil to be within himself, as he believed God to be within all people, and in the heavens as well; you may read this for yourselves (John 14:10, 11, 20).

"He became upset when asked, 'Good Master, what shall I do that I may inherit eternal life?' to which Jesus replied, 'Why callest thou me good? There is none good but one, that is God.' This you may find in your Bibles (Mark 10:18).

"Needless to say, Christianity became a widespread religion; however, the Jesus we Aquatus witnessed would have been utterly appalled at the butchery and cruelty that ensued in his name after his death, especially to the Israelites. He and his followers derived their lineage from them, and though he felt many of them had gone astray from the laws laid down by Moses, it was mainly the Jews whom the Rabbi Jesus went to teach.

"Unfortunately, we did not document the activities of Jesus during his life, as well as we should have; we didn't necessarily think that he would become such a star to later generations. His real teachings, though good and beautiful, were not so unusually brilliant but more or less an enhancement of the existing Hebrew teachings of the time.

"We Aquatus found it strange that the later Christian

religions would set about persecuting the Jews, thinking that it was they who had been responsible for his death.

"Christ was a dynamic individual when it came to professing his beliefs, and this greatly concerned the Romans, who ruled Israel at the time. The young Rabbi Jesus was creating a following among his Jewish audiences, and this concerned the Romans, who thought that he might usurp power and lead the Jews once more into war against them. It was Rome that wanted him dead. This should be most obvious, as Israel had always been a rebellious province.

The Jews were a freedom-loving people and wanted self-rule, and had been so from the time that they left Egypt. They hated it when their freedoms were restricted. But they were under the heavy hand of Rome during the life of Christ, and the primary objective of Pontius Pilate was to preserve peace, as he saw it. All of Rome was delighted when the Emperor Vespasian finally crushed Judea 45 years after the death of Jesus.

"Oh, there were some less popular up-and-coming Rabbis who didn't like Jesus very much. A few may even have been glad when he was crucified, but this was a small minority. Most of the Jews he came in contact with thought he was an acceptable person, a little fanatical perhaps. But there were others who loved him, especially the poor for whom he grieved and to whom he sought to minister.

"In as little time as 65 years after his death, Christians would grow dramatically in numbers, as this was an open religion, originally with the best of ethics, and its adherents were of a missionary persuasion. It might be of interest to those of the Hebrew religion here today that the Emperor Nero, looking for scapegoats for the problems of his empire, blamed the Christians, a small minority in Rome at the time.

"The Romans for three centuries thereafter never tired of

arresting Christians, clothing them in animal skins so that dogs and lions, deranged with hunger, would tear them to pieces in the arenas, amusing the crowds wild with blood lust. Later during your World War II, atrocities would occur by Christians toward Jews, albeit in greater numbers. The Jews were supposedly the problem in Europe at the time. Something humanity should keep in mind is that your cruelty towards one another, throughout your history, increased proportionately to the increase in your populations.

"I hope I am not being redundant when I say that we Aquatus had religions in ancient times very similar to those professed by your Moses, Jesus, and Mohammed, but our age of prophets occurred long before your theologians ever appeared on Earth, even before your species reverted from 'hunter-gatherers' to agricultural societies.

"The adherents to one religion in particular were able to control large numbers of our ancestors. They professed the belief that the Great God Pyetathus who lived in a crystal bright heaven somewhere in the depths of our oceans, had sent an individual named Reenish to teach the true path. As it turned out, down through the ages, those who maintained and kept rigidly to the laws and morality of that religion were pretty good individuals, within their society and realm, and they did prosper. However, they were pitilessly cruel and bloodthirsty in their treatment of outsiders.

"The Reenishes later became disillusioned when our technological advances in underwater craft gave us the ability to search the deepest crevices of our oceans. They felt much the same way humans felt when you arose above the clouds in your aircraft and found no heavenly abode wherein your traditional God was thought to dwell; and no, we have seen no anthropomorphic God in our distant journeys throughout the galaxy either.

"We Aquatus have come to believe, down through the eons, that the magnitude of the Ultimate Principle or God is far beyond the ability of any living creature to truly know. For knowing is a thought process occurring within the minds of living creatures, a process of life if you will, and very elusive. For example, should any living creature, including yourselves, attempt to think of an end to space, they would find it impossible to imagine.

"Let us suppose that one of you here today could gain access to a spaceship which would take you the end of space, far out beyond all galaxies. There, upon your arrival, you stopped that spacecraft, stepped outside, and shot an arrow straight in front of yourself, and it struck something and stuck there; then what could possibly be on the other side of that barrier? If the arrow were to continue straight-away its trajectory, with no solid object to obstruct it, then this would certainly mean that you, our long distance traveler, had not yet reached your objective - the end of space.

"We can postulate that space curves, and soon, if you continued to travel in your amazing spacecraft, you would once again return to where you had originally started. However, this appears to our minds to be just about as nonsensical as postulating an end to space, when one considers a right angle at some point of the trajectory.

"Just as we Aquatus, like yourselves, cannot truly conceive of an end to space, we do not pretend to have a total understanding of the Ultimate Principle. However, we do believe that through very deep contemplation and meditation a certain realization can take place, beyond the process of thought, and therefore closer to the true nature of the Ultimate.

"Does it not seem plausible to you that all things indeed existed in one form or the other before the advent of organic thought? Suppose you were in a terrible accident wherein two-thirds of your brain and its ability to function were destroyed. Does the thinking process, contained within the two-thirds that was destroyed, go to Heaven and await the eventual demise of the remaining one-third? This is indeed a preposterous assumption, but not totally unlike other religious concepts we have encountered in our own archaic beliefs, and others throughout the cosmos.

"Therefore we Aquatus believe that beyond organic thought, there is an even greater awareness wherein dwells the answer to all mystery. Furthermore, it is the Aquatus belief that this Infinite Awareness is beyond the power of any organic mind to fully realize. However a subtle awareness of It can be accomplished by any good and sincere seeker, one who explores the depths of his or her spiritual nature to the astounding degree that he or she has somehow managed to form a 'concept' totally unsupported by thought. Hence he or she opens the mind to the deepest spiritual realm, wherein resides the most spectacular of vehicles, which, when obtained, will speed that aspirant along in his or her divine transmigration toward Heaven or Nirvana and felicitous union once more with the Ultimate.

"For the remainder of its current lifetime that Being which has realized itself in the Ultimate will be as one knowingly awake within a dream. For this singularity of realization, this unique individual will view the physical nature of the world about her or him, and indeed the universe, in its truest concept.

"We Aquatus also believe that this profound realization has occurred many times with certain unique individuals on your planet, as it has occurred on ours and other planets which support life throughout the cosmos. Once more I will emphasize that it was the sincerity of these Aspirants that brought about this spiritual insight or momentous

'Enlightenment' if you will, an insight so profound that it was, and is, beyond the capacity of mere words to describe.

"Make not the mistake of believing that it requires a highly enhanced intelligence to realize the profundity of the 'Ultimate.' On the contrary it can be accomplished by life forms wherein merely lay the intellectual capacity with which to pursue it. This would currently be inclusive of all within this assembly and most others who are currently within the hearing of my voice around the world, as well as other life forms currently dwelling upon this very planet and on others throughout the cosmos.

"Of those who would opt to take this profound journey of the spirit, only those who follow the path of benevolence will complete the journey in a single lifetime, eventually rising above the duality concept of 'good' and 'evil.' If it be possible for them to complete this journey beyond the 'Ego,' it will have been regardless of race, creed, species, nation or world of origin.

"Think not that we Aquatus believe this Ultimate awareness, this profound realization, to be easily gained. It requires the giving over of one's physical and mental totality, through extensive inward reflection and meditation. It is within yourselves, and ourselves wherein dwells the Most Divine, The Most Blessed and Sacred--this do we Aquatus believe.

"It is with deep sincerity, and humility that we Aquatus view God or to us The Ultimate to be esoteric, profound beyond thought, and yet inclusive of it. For how could it possibly be that the Ultimate Principle, profoundly beyond organic thought, could be of lesser awareness than the myriad of organic life forms to which it has given rise? Integral within each and every creature, great or small, throughout the cosmos, resides this esoteric principle.

"So profound do we believe this Ultimate of which I speak to be, that all the myriad life forms throughout all the galaxies, their varied intelligence, dreams, ambitions, and accomplishments, are as but flecks of foam upon the great and mighty oceans of worlds throughout the cosmos.

"Vast indeed are these multitudes of life forms which must travel long and troubled paths before they can possibly begin to fathom the spiritual depths upon which they float, and yet none is forgotten. From worldly kings to the mouse in the wall, all are loved with compassion beyond the ability of an organic mind to conceive.

"All things are of this Absolute Totality and are known to It down to the smallest particle of their composition. This most profound esoteric principle resides within all living things, which are in a constant state of change and spiritual transmigration, and will eventually return to the source from which they sprang. Unstained, without blemish, without end, beyond the concept of good and evil which is the driving force of living things.

"The Ultimate Principle is none other than Omnipotently Pure, Undefiled Truth.

"For those of you who may ask, 'If this Ultimate of which you speak is not flesh and blood, and has not a mind such as ourselves, how then can it know compassion?' I would ask in return, do you naively think that all the things of which living creatures are comprised--organic, inorganic, emotional and spiritual were not here in one form or the other from beginningless time?

"Without threat of hell fire or eternal damnation do we offer this theology of the Aquatus unto you, for our desire is to speed you along in your spiritual travels throughout the cosmos. We are convinced that the transmigratory spiritual persona of all living things will eventually find their ways back into the bosom of the Ultimate.

"Our sincere hope is that perhaps you will understand, early on in your journeys, that the nature of true evil is to bind you time and time again to a physical existence of suffering. Goodness eventually leads you back to your spiritual home wherein the words and feelings of joy, happiness and bliss can not begin to take in what you will find there.

"Circumvent evil, no matter how enticing it may appear; for in this way only can you rise above it. You may be assured that the beguiling nature of evil makes its destructive path look easy, and that the constructive nature of good appears difficult to pursue, but these are appearances only; do not be deceived.

"For those of you who are of a deep religious conviction, we encourage you to look deep within yourselves through contemplation and meditation for the answers. It is possible in your current lifetime to realize the deep and profound nature of the Ultimate. Indeed the act of proper meditation alone will convey unto you numerous methods with which to destroy numerous sins of both this and past lifetimes. However, do not be so deluded as to think you can destroy sins with the evil intent of enacting new ones at your discretion. If you do so, you will soon find yourself on a retrograde path most unfortunate.

"Although meditation can raise you above good and evil, at this point will you realize that you must time and time again descend into the realms of suffering and despair in an attempt to rescue others. In this way, and in this way only, can you eventually repay, through benevolence, the total debt of evil, which you incurred during numerous lifetimes. It will be a labor of love. Strangely enough you may suffer the harshest of existences to repay your debt; but you will suffer willingly. Upon the realization of that which resides within, you will at once become totally aware of your destination and your eventual joyous reunion with the Ultimate, even though you may need to endure numerous more lifetimes. Once aware of the profundity of the Ultimate, in each of your remaining lifetimes will you come to realize this truth.

"If you are able to achieve this spiritual realization you will find that, just as one may digress on love and compose numerous analogies as to what its truest meaning might be, one cannot truly understand its meaning until it is realized from within. Upon this realization, all the poetry of the ages cannot capture the true emotional depth and yearning of the lover for his or her beloved. Only in its realization lies the truest understanding.

"As the lover responds to the beloved, so it will be with you upon realization of the immense profundity of this Principle of which I speak, albeit with far greater depth. Furthermore, though it will be extremely difficult to convey this most profound realization to others, you will go unto them anyway. Your very presence among them, and what little they can understand, will serve to greatly shorten their transmigrations throughout the cosmos. Indeed, we are all spiritual travelers in the realms of space and time.

"Be constantly on guard that you allow not your ego to interfere with your progress, for the worlds of common creatures stand upon the ego--hence the making of titles and riches for themselves. On the contrary, be humble, like those sages of old who put little store in riches, but were as professional guests, teaching others for their bread and board.

"Very soon will you come to realize that those very characteristics of good and evil are within those to whom you would minister; indeed you will find devils and angels among them. For those benevolently oriented, you will help to straighten their paths. For those predisposed towards evil, you will endeavor to turn them about. Both will you attempt to guide towards the light. With the profoundest of insight you will not hesitate to help them all.

"Your efforts will cause you suffering, indeed. Perhaps from time to time your efforts will cost you your very life. Your reward in the end will be incredibly great, beyond anything imagined in these physical worlds. This is not simply a promise to you for doing good, but what you yourselves will have realized upon making that journey deep within, beyond thought, beyond the tactile senses, beyond the fear of falling into the void, never to return. There in the deepest seat of your consciousness will you experience a turning about, so pristine, so very profound. All at once you will understand your original true nature, that which you were and are now. Indeed, that which you were before you entered the womb of that very first life form, countless eons ago on some far-flung planet of the cosmos.

"Think not that the profound Ultimate Principle can be found in magnificent temples or churches wherein dwell those who would manipulate you through golden images of supposed deities, politics, and threats of hell and damnation. Should they say, 'you must believe as others have believed!' I can assure you that a statement such as this is but pure nonsense. Most certainly it is an attempt to bend you towards their will, so that they can manipulate and use you towards their ends. Such is the delusion of those who would attempt to make the world in their own image.

"Be good and decent creatures, for innately you know mostly what is good and what is evil, and much of your sojourn here in your current lifetime is to learn more completely the nature of these two driving aspects of life. Evil is the malicious harming of the innocent (the destructive force), and Goodness is the helping of those who are in need of your guidance, love and attention (the constructive force).

"Beware that the laws of state often corrupt the true morality.

"I know that there are many here today who will not, or cannot, understand the meaning of my words; however, for those of you who have, my advice to you is to be contemplative in your understanding and cautious should you choose to teach it to others.

"Construe not my words to cause others to believe that I was on a mission from some anthropomorphous or aquatomorphous God, nor attempt to read between the lines that I, Jayseeka, Ambassador from Trepleon, was somehow angelic. Worse yet, should they begin to make images of me and bow down to worship these images, thinking I can intervene so as to save them from their fate, tell them to put these notions aside and look within themselves for their own salvation.

"Within us all, indeed within all living entities, resides the Ultimate Principle, and I have said no other than this. Should any contrive to teach, saying I said other than what I have spoken (perhaps as a mechanism with which to control others, or deprive them of their substance), I caution you that no matter how pristine they may appear, no matter how numerous may be those who believe them, no matter how sublime may be those teachings, they will be misconstructions of my words, and thereby false."

With the words "Be diligent," the Aquatian Jayseeka, Ambassador from Trepleon, left the podium.

So ended the "convention of the pious." As the assembly dispersed, they were mentally stumbling over the strange and confusing aspects of the Aquatus beliefs. Many were astounded, some were frightened, while others joyously believed they had found the answers for which they had searched throughout their lives.

# Chapter Twenty

Death hovers near all life,
It was in the bargain from the beginning.
The wise are aware of its eventuality,
The foolish haven't a clue.
Wisdom is a goodly mixture
Of kindness and understanding;
With open mind and open heart,
The true beauty of Heaven and Earth are open to the wise.
The foolish seek power, wealth and titles
At any spiritual cost;
Consumed in the fires of the ego,
They feel not the cool breath of death against their necks.

*(Roxanne Henry 41 A.J.)*

It was a small country in South America, governed by a handful of wealthy landholders. The duly paid for and corrupt President of the little republic professed to be a man of the people, an actor who would not have done well on the stage, or in the political structure of any other country. Though he was sure that all, except his bosses, believed the pretense, the majority of his subjects knew him for the counterfeit that he was.

Flamboyantly self-impressive in his heated orations, both public and televised, Martin Alonzo Piolet harangued the people of his small country, promising, but never to deliver, land, hospitals, and schools.  A corrupt puppet dictator of a pathetically corrupt republic, wherein the vast majority of families could save a lifetime for a car, and never get one, he had found his glorious calling.  Coddled by the rich, hated by the poor, the magnificent El Presidente Martin Alonzo Piolet was truly a legend in his own mind.

Every average man or woman will find out at least once in his or her lifetime that wealth does not necessarily preclude those who have it from grasping for a few dollars more.  Indeed, greed is a powerful driving force, and legion are those who have used, and are currently using, their lofty positions to fuck over any available patsy for just a few more bucks.  Most unfortunately they are there, within the framework of societies throughout the world, and Piolet was living in his finest hour.

He had wanted to charge the impoverished peasantry of his country for the use of the Aquatus medical apparatus, a device intended as a free gift and blessing to the numerous sick and malnourished suffering daily in their crushing poverty beneath his boot.  However, his employers had informed him, in no uncertain terms, that if he tried such a maneuver, "You will most quickly disappear without a trace!" a remark which heated his contempt towards those "pinche maricons" who were his owners.

The landholders had seen from the beginning the benefits of a healthier peasantry to work their fields, and had no intention of letting their pompous ass of a Presidente screw it up.  The land barons had insisted that each and every man woman and child pass through the belly of the loaned Lazarus Machines, before they were to be returned.  Piolet "was to see that this was accomplished by any means possible, or soon there would be another in his place."

Upon receiving this information from those to whom he was indentured, the arrogant puppet began to plot his freedom.

At the risk of his life, it would be a well thought-out plan; however, this was only his thinking.

Presidente Piolet had instructed the Ambassador from his small country to deliver his letters to the Ambassador from Trepleon and to "speak as little as possible" about the political situation in his country. He had an ace in his boot, as the tiny South American country was one of the few places where Professor David Hauss had not previously set up a holding area for the Aquatus medical equipment. He had left it up to the discretion of the ruling powers there to make the determination.

Although the Aquatus could watch closely anyone they chose, they simply didn't watch everyone, even though Piolet was one whom they should have. He had earlier made his trip to Little Falls, New York, and had passed through the Aquatus apparatus there, using a false name and falsified medical documents. He returned to his small dominion, beaming with good health, enhanced intelligence, and unfortunately an even more sinister evil nature than before.

Unrealized as yet by human doctors of the mind, evil would prove to be an elusive phenomenon, often harbored in the deepest crevices of the psyche, beyond the ability of even the amazing Aquatus medical equipment to ferret out and correct. Regretfully, true evil is often far more than just a mental illness. Such was the case with El Presidente Piolet.

Though no recipients of the Aquatus medical equipment would ever know exactly when it was to be delivered or retrieved (it was the desire of the Aquatus), the Lazarus Machines had been delivered. They performed well their incredible task, leaving the delighted inhabitants of the small country, wealthy and poor alike, beamingly healthy, except for very few.

Juan Niccolo Blanco and his wife Gemma, who was seven months pregnant, had been kidnapped by Piolet's personal bodyguards and taken to that forbidding and hapless cave of horror known only to Piolet and his four so-called "trusted dogs."

The reason the guards were faithful to their employer wasn't necessarily because they liked him, as creatures such as these, with less morality than any dog would possess, did not even like themselves.

Piolet's trusted dogs enjoyed their work, and performed it diligently and in detail, following all their leader's instructions; but the shrewd Piolet would leave nothing to chance. In the course of their internship, Piolet had numerous photographs of them taken while they worked. The graphic photos and recordings had been clandestinely made by a now dead photographer (Piolet didn't need him anymore) during the recruitment period.

His henchmen had tortured and murdered their way into his favor. These pathetically cruel devisors of misery always delighted in assisting their president in wringing information from the peasantry. They were often called upon when he had only the faintest suspicion that a revolt might be stirring.

They had been specifically selected by Piolet, these decadent misfits of society, a very good reason why the tyrant had defied his bosses and not allowed his four guards access to the Lazarus Machines; he liked them just the way they were. Often would he remind them, in no uncertain terms, that "should anything happen to him, the sordid information which he possessed of them would certainly fall into the hands of the families from whom their unfortunate victims had been taken."

Piolet had found the well-hidden cave quite by accident, when a peasant he had captured for some minor crime had attempted to buy his freedom with the information of its location. The desperate man had claimed there were some ancient artifacts therein, perhaps some of gold. Upon investigation, Piolet found that the cave led deep into a secluded hill, and although it had been used by some ancient Indian culture in the past, and there were artifacts aplenty therein, that there was no gold would cruelly cost the poor peasant his life.

Upon a slab within the cave (a sacred relic once used at some time in the dark distant past for human sacrifice), the blood of innocents once more was spilled. Piolet and his men laughed at the irony, as the wretched man insane with pain and fear, pleaded for his life, but to no avail. His executioners had found there, in that ominous cave of antiquity, a razor-sharp, ornately chiseled, cultic flint dagger, which they used to slowly dismember their pitiable victim. They thought that perhaps he had told others who might know the whereabouts of the gold that had been in the cave. He knew nothing.

When the pain had become so unbearable that it necessitated buckets of cold water to bring their lamentable victim back to consciousness, they then forced that ornate dagger of human butchery slowly through his chest and into his heart. The screams from the atrocious acts had given Piolet and his men great pleasure.

The obscure location of the cave and the nature of the hill that housed it would unfortunately prove to be an excellent concealment for heinous activities the Marquis de Sade would have envied. Piolet had wasted no time in constructing a rather large building on the site, supposedly "for storage of surplus military equipment," directly on the nearly flat part of the hilltop just over the cave's large chamber.

From the storage structure on top of the hill he had his men tunnel into the cave below, and it was here that they would conduct their cruel interrogations of their wretched victims, killing them in the end. Within the cave, just beneath that chamber of doom, ran a large underground river that carried the mutilated bodies away, deep into the dark bowels of the earth. Only Piolet and his men knew the location of this most sinister pit of despair.

Senor Don Segudo Jemes, the wealthiest of the country's landholders and the principle political instrument used to catapult his cousin Piolet to the presidency, had heard of the numerous disappearances of the peasantry. Until his passage through the Lazarus Machine he had believed his cousin had simply been keeping various malcontents from causing trouble.

Don Jemes had presumed that Piolet would take these trouble-prone individuals outside the country, there to threaten them with their lives if ever they returned. Don Jemes was wiser now, and one of the Lazarus Machines that had been on loan to them had disappeared. The disappearance of malcontents was one thing, but the disappearance of some very sophisticated instrumentation which could cause reprisals from some otherworldly, highly technical race of creatures was more than he was willing to deal with. He suspected his cousin Piolet.

Contacting the Central Intelligence Agency of the United States, the deeply concerned Don Jemes told them of his unfortunate dilemma.

Just ahead of a hurricane, which was stirring up the Gulf of Mexico, three men stepped off a chartered flight in the small banana republic. They gave appearances that suggested three good ol' boys who had run away from home for a week of sun and fun in paradise. In truth Director Faraday had hand-picked them from the best of his agents.

After two days of getting a feel for the assignment and a feel of the giggling cocktail waitresses from time to time in one of the local bars, they soon had Piolet under surveillance.

The Agents were tailing their mark, as he and two of his guards drove a military jeep down the narrow coast highway, then inland on a secluded road to the cave.

Therein, later to be discovered, would be Piolet's two captives, Juan Blanco and his wife Gemma, the other two of Piolet's guards, as well as the sought-after Lazarus Machine.

The first large drops of rain were beginning to fall, as Hurricane Clara was beginning to make her move inland and up the coast. Piolet and his men knew they would be safe from the storm within the confines of the cave.

Shortly after the dictator and his men disappeared into the lower, well-hidden cave entry, the tailing CIA agents stealthily approached the area. They had prepared well, dressed in water-repellent clothing and in possession of the latest technology in lightweight, night-vision equipment, should their mission stretch on into the night. Well armed with state of the art automatic silencer weaponry, well they knew their job, and it wouldn't be long before they knew what was going on within the interior of the caverns.

## Chapter Twenty-One

To govern wisely is like cooking a small fish,
Care and caution must be used.
They of great understanding know,
Those who govern least, govern best.

(Lao Tsu 6th Century B.C.)

With the consent of her host Vincent Henry, Jayseeka, Ambassador from Trepleon, allowed a press conference to be held at Vincent Henry Manor. The main purpose was to answer news media questions and the numerous letters she had received regarding the nature of government on her planet.

Were there as many types of governments as on Earth? Were there kingdoms? or queendoms? or a single Trepleon government? What were the laws utilized by the Aquatus to govern themselves? What was the severity of penalties if laws were broken?

It had often been speculated that perhaps the Aquatus didn't need laws to govern themselves, as they most probably had risen intellectually above the necessity.

Journalists from newspaper and television media from around the world had arrived by special invitation, 146 in all. The Manor would be busy, but not for long.

The conference began at 9:00 a.m. There would be a very nicely prepared buffet from 11:00 a.m. to noon, followed by two more hours of informative discourse, ending at 2:00 p.m., allowing a meager four hours of actual discussion.

The shortened time for the long-awaited conference seemed a bit unusual to Vincent Henry, especially since his daughter Roxanne mentioned that she and Jayseeka had plans to gather blackberries up by the lake that afternoon, as soon as the conference was finished--definitely not a very pressing engagement.

From her special podium the golden enchantress looked out upon her audience, which fell silent in anticipation.

"I will describe to you the government of Trepleon, and when I have finished, any of you whose questions were not answered during this dissertation will be free to ask them in an orderly fashion, and I will hopefully answer them to the satisfaction of all."

So did the bestower of extraordinary, otherworldly gifts inform Earth's international news media. Once more she stood before them at her special podium, radiant of form, endearing of voice, impeccably gracious, appearing to all as innocently pure as crystal spring water.

"I will give brief analogies of methods used by various governments that we have seen come and go on your planet, as well as our own, over the last four thousand or so years, and draw current parallels between our system and your own. However, I wish to make it perfectly clear at the outset that I am not being critical of your governments when I point out the differences between ours and yours, but merely analytical for better understanding.

"We Aquatus have been a territorial and aggressive species down through the ages of time, much like yourselves. We fought numerous battles for property, wealth, and dominance over others, often using differences in religions, physical characteristics, or even language as superficial reasons to dehumanize, or in our case 'deaquatanize' our victims or enemies. By so doing we could slaughter and usurp with a guiltless conscience. We had ignorantly convinced ourselves that others were, by our own definition, lower life forms then ourselves, obligated to us, while we owed them nothing in return. Some of our most popular demeaning names for others, of a different religion or race, were 'zeds,' 'huglets,' 'sukes,' etc., while on this planet terms like 'goys,' 'gooks,' 'heathens,' etc., were coined.

"Evidence throughout the history of our world, and yours, indicates that there have been dark ages for learning, but absolutely no dark age for weaponry. More and better weapons were continuously being built and improved upon until a point is finally reached when it must either stop or total destruction of all becomes imminent.

"Earth has had cruel kings, queens, and dictators as well as benevolent. However, in Earth's historical records, as well as in our own, benevolence and morality were always something the victors had, while the vanquished deserved their fate, or 'got what was coming to them.' Often they were the innocent, young or old, and others who were simply the victims of aggression, not in sympathy with the war-involved actions of their governments.

"In almost every case, those who lost a war went down in history as the evil ones.

"We on Trepleon had watched the actions of Earth's despots and dictators from afar, often amazed at the butchery and depraved cruelty that passed before us a year after the fact, as our Earth observation equipment projected the horror over the vast distance between our worlds.

"No, we didn't interfere, and why not? Because we had grown wise enough by that time to see that the same evil was within ourselves. We had inflicted these very same cruelties upon ourselves in our own bloody wars down through the ages. To interfere and force your species into our image of what humans should do, think or feel, would clearly have been a step backwards in our own morality, perhaps once more awakening the dark impulse to subjugate others, establishing dominion over them. Hence in the process of deciding who would own which worlds, we would have taken the grave risk that the demons of warfare might once more rear their ugly heads among us. This was and is a risk which we are unwilling to take. For in such a conflict, with our available technology, all we Aquatus would have been the losers.

"It has been observed in fiercely territorial species, such as humans and Aquatus, that whatever the arsenal may be, no matter the devastation of its use, it will be used in lieu of subjugation by others.

"On our planet, as on your own, there has never been a weapon made that had not been used, either as a threat, or as a destructive force. The time eventually came when it became apparent that we must either put an end to our warlike passions or tread the dark path of extinction. Therefore we were obliged to put aside petty grievances and establish the fairest and least oppressive form of government possible. A government wherein all Aquatus could live in peaceful harmony and the ugly demon of tyranny could not raise its defeatist head to suppress free thought, creativity, or the pursuit of happiness.

"We have been successful in ending warfare among ourselves for over twelve thousand of your earth years.

"I was not yet born when the first colonies established themselves on the northern portion of this continent called America, but I was certainly looking on, with absorbed amazement, at what was happening in this small area of your world by the time, by our standards, I was a teenager.

"There were then thirteen colonies on the North American continent, and they were in the process of throwing off the governing shackles of a kingdom known as England.

"Actually, we were amazed that an attempt was even being made to do so, as England was far distant from America, and English taxes were not nearly as prohibitive in the colonies as they were to other English subjects around the world. Nevertheless an attempt by England to enforce the Stamp Act, which would have placed a paltry tax of 1 percent on tea, was amazingly more than the colonies were willing to accept. In 1773 AD, in protest against this tax, revolutionaries dumped large quantities of English tea into the Boston Harbor of Massachusetts.

"Had there been a gypsy about at the time, with the spectacular ability to read harbors, as well as teacups, she would have seen that brazen act as the first major step on the path leading to eventual self-government by the colonies.

"By 1783 the United States of America had won its war for independence, and the founding fathers of the fledgling government were well aware that survival depended upon the creation of laws whereby all governed would feel an overriding sense of fairness, with minimal corruption.

"It was Lord John Acton, a brilliant British historian and educator, who coined the phrase, 'power tends to corrupt and absolute power corrupts absolutely.' Though he lived after your Great War of independence, perhaps he arrived at this conclusion after studying the U.S. constitution, which your founding fathers developed after their great struggle. Or perhaps from being in a position of power himself and viewing history through the ages, he reached this conclusion. But that it was intuitively contemplated early on by several of your founding fathers, we considered pure genius.

"There are many facts of history that are not apparent on the surface of your current historical literature, but I can honestly inform you, as we have it filed away in our archives, that George Washington had in mind for himself a kingship rather than a Presidency. Had it not been for Samuel Adams of Massachusetts that may have been exactly what would have happened.

"Samuel boycotted the Constitutional Convention. It seems that he would not sign on to the deal, viewing it as too centralized and more in the interest of government, than of people. Sam was most sincerely a man of the people and would settle for nothing less than Government by and for the People; hence was created The Bill of Rights. These additional amendments to the Constitution, guaranteed the citizens of the new nation that they would be governed in their best interest, not by those who would usurp the power from them, concentrating it into the hands of the few, returning them once more to the whim and fancy of kings or dictators.

"To date the inhabitants of the United States of America enjoy a sense of freedom unknown in most other parts of the world, where the only 'bills of rights' are the monetary bills one may have in his pocket. With the advent of Samuel Adams, who came to you in one of your finest hours, I became a devoted history student of planet Earth, and have observed you very closely to date.

"Oh, I know that the experiment of by-the-people government had been utilized by the Greek city-states early on in Earth's history. With your founding fathers drawing upon this, and the wisdom of Samuel Adams, I knew the government of the United States of America would hold together and prosper, as its governing laws were so similar to our own.

"We had hoped that others of Earth's nations would see this prosperity and soon follow. Indeed, many have, though not in detail.

"Yes! Amazingly enough, planet Earth had formed an honorable government similar to our own. The improbability of such a happening, many of our philosophers speculated, might just be the eventual evolutionary result of all surviving intelligent social species, as we have noted many similarities on other worlds we have visited throughout the galaxy. How might such amazing evolutionary similarities occur?

"As an example of comparative evolution, birds and bats both began as wingless creatures on your planet. Later in time, they ended up with the ability to fly. We need not belabor the fact that the attribute of flight is a very successful means of survival, as is evident by the number of winged species on your planet. However, it was a bit of an embarrassment to our historians to watch an independent quest for government, by and for its citizens, absolutely uninfluenced by any interaction on our behalf, become formative in a primitive society such as you were, less than three hundred years ago. We Aquatus observed spellbound, as the North American Colonies developed their free and equitable government. We were amazed that it would happen at all, and astonished that it had happened at a much earlier date in human evolution than it did in the separate evolution of we Aquatus."

Other governments, Earthly and Trepleoneon, were then referred to, and parallels given.

At 11:00 a.m. all adjourned for the luncheon, which was thoroughly enjoyed and complimented by all. At 12:00 noon all were back in their places; the final two hours had begun.

"We Aquatus have been united as a two world government for well over six thousand of your earth years. I say 'two world' because there is a planet in our own solar system which is as near to Trepleon as the planet Mars of your own system is to you. However, and fortunately for us, Spargus is blessed with abundant water and ample atmosphere. We were able to colonize Spargus 14,800 of your earth years ago. Still it is an adventurous place and only those of us who love the challenge choose to live there. They and their families are amply rewarded for their heroic efforts with the majestic beauty of Spargus, much like the few of your species that have chosen that grand state of Alaska as their home.

"Instead of comparing the many ways in which the United States government is similar to that of Trepleon (and Spargus) I will focus on the ways in which they are different, and all of you can thereby more easily see the difference in a shorter period of time.

"There are 38 countries on Trepleon and six on Spargus, which are fully represented by 'Statisticians'; these types of emissaries on your world are called 'Senators.' Our Statisticians are of three political parties, which are: 1. Pro-Environmental, 2. Pro-Educational, and 3. Pro-Commerce. One individual is selected from each of these three persuasions per each twenty million individuals, or fraction thereof, within each country. There is no House of Representatives, therefore far less confusion, as a Statistician represents the people in the same way a Representative or Senator would represent the people.

"There is one of your United States governments, Nebraska, which in 1934 by a vote of its people, set up its state government on this same principle. It is a one-house type of government, and repeated attempts to change it have been resisted by a large majority of its populace. The people of Nebraska seem to feel that the simplicity of this type of government decreases corruption, and from our observations this is truly the case.

"Our president is called Grand Elder and is selected by the populations at large. We have no Electoral College, so it is simply a majority vote of the people whereby he or she is elected.

"In every case, down through the ages, the person who has generated the most love and trust of our citizens was the one to be elected to the esteemed office of Grand Elder. The Grand Elder's cabinet is selected from the retiring Statisticians who have completed their terms in office. They may be asked to serve, but are not obligated to do so.

"We Aquatus salute the wisdom of your philosophers who believed that that 'All power tends to corrupt' and that 'The highest reach of the unjust man is to appear just'; we, through cruel experience, have also learned these truths. Therefore we obligated our legislators to follow the strictest rules we could envision:

"1. Although a Grand Elder can be duly elected by the citizens from the ranks of the Statisticians, he or she can serve no longer than a seven year term, whereupon comes the obligation to retire permanently from all aspects of government for the remainder of their lives.

"2. A Statistician, duly elected by the citizens, can serve no more than two terms in office, five years and three years respectively, whereupon they are obligated to retire permanently from all government activities for the remainder of their lives, unless elected to the office of Grand Elder or selected as a member of her or his cabinet, after which that individual may serve an additional seven years.

"May it be understood that when I say 'years' that I am using earth time, as our years are nearly twice the length of yours. Therefore two years earth time is only approximately one of our years.

"The reason for enacting these strict term limits was that we felt that if the political objectives of a Statistician, having been sent to our Congress by the citizenry with several goals in mind, could not bring the citizens' goals to fruition within an eight year time frame, then it was time for another good citizen to give it a try.

"The other reason, and not by any means the least reason, was that when we tried the government of Professional Politicians, such as many of Earth's legislators currently enjoy, we found that, often as not, these long term Statisticians would form bonds of collusion amongst themselves. New Statisticians, who often had excellent objectives, could not get their legislation passed unless they 'played ball' with the entrenched professionals.

"With great sadness we discovered that many of these entrenched legislators were for sale to the highest bidder, and their votes would often, and most regrettably, enhance the power of small special interest groups, thus giving them unfair advantage over the citizens at large.

"As you are all aware, we Aquatus are gifted with the ability of telepathy, and once each year our legislators must go before the Council of the Readers wherein each legislator will be asked questions regarding the office and his or her integrity in fulfilling the obligations thereof. Should a legislator be found wanting during this examination, it will be recommended to the citizenry from which they were elected that they be dismissed from office. Should it be found that a legislator used his or her office as an instrument of personal gain, receiving bribes, kickbacks, etc., then that legislator will be tried for treason. If found guilty, by a jury of their peers, (who have never held a political office), they have but a single year to prove their innocence, or be put to death."

Noticing that many of her audience had been taken aback

by the extremity of the penalty for government corruption, Jayseeka explained the logic of the Aquatus.

"The survival of our species was dependent on fair and honorable government; we knew our only escape from extinction was to elect leaders who would truly work in the better interest of those who had elected them, their primary tools being honesty and fairness.

"Yes. On our world we do believe in fairness, and as has been proven down through the ages, the truth has made us free. Though we do not believe in nearly as harsh a judgment for our citizens at large, who have been less than honorable or truthful in their business and personal dealings, we Aquatus find government corruption most repugnant. For a citizen, who has earned the trust and faith of those who elected them to the noble office of Statistician, to turn around and use his esteemed position for personal gain, be it power or wealth, we believe to be the severest of crimes. Our governing entities were elected to their exalted offices for the purpose of better government. To use this trust for any other purpose is a magnified crime against those by whom they have been elected.

"We Aquatus see the end product of corrupt government officials as the eventual deterioration of that very same government they swore to uphold and defend. Such a deterioration we well know leads slowly, but inexorably, to the loss of cherished freedoms, renewal of slavery, and/or warfare.

"As a species, we Aquatus are wise enough to realize the imperfections within ourselves. Some do foolish things when they are young and learn from their mistakes. Some of our citizens live pure and clean lives in younger years only to regress in later years into miserly or obnoxious lifestyles.

"We have noticed among humans that you expect perfection in the citizens you elect to office, thinking that the zebra cannot change its stripes, so to speak. Although it would be nigh impossible for a zebra to change its stripes, the premise that humans and Aquatus alike cannot learn from past mistakes is utterly false.

"Unfortunately for the United States of America, you have often elected to power those whom you believed to be honorable, but, as the evidence indicates, they were only those with the greatest ability to deceive. For many are those ambitious ones who will claim any virtue and disavow every weakness in order to gain power over others, or to amass the wealth from illicit activities which are their real objectives. Hence your joke, 'How can one tell when a politician is lying?' the answer of course being, 'When his or her lips are moving.'

"Should one of our citizens aspire to the office of Statistician, we know that perfection is a myth, but those elected must perform in the office to which they were elected with only the most honorable of actions, or risk suffering the extreme finality.

"We Aquatus realize that it would be foolish to elect to any office one who has had greed and deception as her or his life-long companion. What I am attempting to communicate to you now is that the mistakes we make in our lives, often as not, are not as important as the lessons we can learn from them.

"There are three other crimes that bring the death penalty on Trepleon: child molestation, the intentional killing of an innocent in the commission of a crime, and the torture of one individual by another to the point of damaging them beyond the possibility of emotional or physical repair. In every case, should such individuals be proven guilty in our courts of law, they have but a single year to live, unless they and their attorneys can produce evidence to prove their innocence.

"Oh, yes. The death penalty is a deterrent to crime, if the population as a whole is aware that there is no doubt as to the outcome, should they be rightfully apprehended and found guilty for the commission of one, or several of the four major crimes. Also, the knowledge that the penalty is sure and swift is a positive reinforcement in the minds of these types of evil or would-be criminals.

"I might add at this time, although your species does not have the telepathic abilities which we Aquatus enjoy, that you do have the technological ability to create infallible instrumentation. Instrumentation that, if operated by a qualified psychiatric expert, could be used to distinguish truth from lies in even the most psychotic of individuals.

"However, it would indeed be a difficult task on your part to get legislation passed requiring its use on your elected officials. Though not all who would resist you are dishonorable, when it comes to the performance of their elected jobs, they would be against you simply because each of them wishes to retain, as far as possible, the egocentric facade of perfection in the eyes of their constituents.

"There is also other instrumentation, a gift from us Aquatus unto yourselves, which is currently being used by various biological and psychiatric experts throughout the world, to study thought patterns of other creatures on your planet. These could also be greatly effective as enhanced polygraph instrumentation.

"However, those of you who wish to tread the path of greater honor amongst your judges and legislators should be aware that the reason a polygraph test is not considered a valuable tool in the courtroom is not because they don't work, but because your elected officials themselves fear they may fall under the scrutiny of its use.

"Upon total realization of the most obvious fact that we Aquatus were, and are, an instinctively territorial species, laws were passed to guarantee the possession of personal property to all who would inherit it or earn the right to possess it. Hence we derived our nearly sacred rights to private property. We have no inheritance taxes, as the property's owners throughout most of their lives pay minimal taxes. For government to penalize those who would inherit it, we find immoral.

"All owners of property pay taxes up to senior citizen age, which is equivalent to 50 human years, whereupon they are exempt from this type of tax for the remainder of their lives. Those who buy or inherit the property from the seniors must begin once more to pay its taxes. There is also a limit of one house and 100 acres of land, and/or adjoining water, which falls within the tax-free benefits of the seniors.

"No government entity or private citizen may trespass upon the property of another, unless it is suspected that unlawful activity by its owner is taking place therein, but then only with a warrant from a judge allowing access. If a warrant is granted, and no incriminating criminal evidence is produced, then the invasion of private property is duly noted about who did it and when it took place. The government agency and individuals who took part in this invasion of privacy are not only severely reprimanded, but all property of those wrongfully invaded must be replaced exactly as it previously was and monetary damages paid to its owner or owners.

"In your state of California, more money is spent on the prison system than is spent on its universities. This would lead some to believe that the judicial system is somehow faulty. We do not see it this way, but rather that the incarcerated are not obligated to realize that they can survive by means other than criminal activity.

"On Spargus we have a penal colony which allows each inmate ten acres of fertile land and a comfortable cabin with a wood-burning stove and fireplace. Please don't think that this is some form of easy retirement for those incarcerated, for as I mentioned earlier Spargus is a pretty rough place to live. Should those incarcerated attempt to escape, which is nearly impossible, this will serve only to lengthen their detainment.

"There are some basic necessities provided, the equivalent of your tea, salt, sugar, flour, and vitamins. The remainder of the necessary food, for the inmate's survival must be grown on his or her parcel of land, and they must care for the environment as well by recycling nutrients back into the soil, etc.

"The prisoners are not allowed television or movies; their only source of entertainment is the trading of home-grown food items and any literature they choose to read. Needless to say, they read many books concerning agriculture and animal husbandry.

"Those who rebel against this system serve an extended term, while those who prove they can provide for themselves serve a reduced term. We have strict laws governing prisoners, and remember, we know who the malcontents are in every case. Any violent or aggressive activity by any inmate, or group of inmates, is dealt with harshly, but not in a cruel or unusual manner, and the length of stay is extended for these types of individuals.

"It is only the most hostile of individuals who are locked away, and rare is the individual who would wish to serve out his or her sentence in a cage. If an individual is too old or sickly to support himself, then allowances are made for this, and medical attention is freely given to all inmates who are in need.

"When parole is finally earned by an inmate, they will be released as relatively free persons. However the once-incarcerated are expected to make every effort to pay, if possible, a reasonable monetary reward, to those whom he or she had injured in the commission of the unlawful activity for which they were incarcerated.  Failure to do so over a reasonable period of time may well bring about re-incarceration of that individual.

"We spend very little money on the incarceration of criminals, and their rehabilitation and reentry into society is excellent.  Many elect to stay on Spargus, not as prisoners, but gainfully employed.  There are numerous mining enterprises there and the pay is exceptionally good.

"We Aquatus know conclusively that all humans are not created equal as your Founding Fathers so believed; a truth also among us Aquatus.  We are not even sure your Founding Fathers believed literally such a statement as 'All men are created equal.'  That all should be equal before the law, regardless of wealth, status, creed or race, was a given for fair and equitable government, and that all are of the same potential spiritual equality is also an obvious truth.  We Aquatus suppose that the statement 'All men are created equal' was one that needed to be said at the time.  Those leaders of the fledgling government of America must certainly have wanted its people to know that they were 'equal' to the task of throwing off the oppression of a colonial government, which indeed you were.  However, if taken and believed literally, such a belief can lead down the tyrannical road to collectivism, a proven failure leading to unrest and suppression amongst those who have attempted it in its purest form.

"I will take the above analysis a bit further for those egalitarians that may be among you.  A single healthy productive human male is capable of producing enough sperm to father as many children as there are humans currently alive on your planet, and each would be a distinct individual.  Each individual would have different fingerprints, different retinal eye scans, and different DNA fingerprints. Each would vary in their interaction within their environment and society-- some slightly, some dramatically, and some in between. All would have varying capacities with which to pursue various goals. Even identical twins, which may well appear identical to an untrained eye will exhibit these varying characteristics and would not be the same.

"That all deserve the same benefits and comforts, regardless of personal initiative or exceptional abilities, has never been a positive constructive force within any civilization which we have observed down through the ages. The more any civilization indulged in collective practices, the more rapidly it brought about its eventual decay from within.

"In our observations of numerous civilizations, down through the eons of time, it has become apparent to us that the very nature of government is to oppress. In some cases this oppression has been for the good of the greater number of its people; but in the case of abject socialism, communism if you will, this oppression rapidly takes on the form of tyranny. It seems that the most benevolent of governments are those wherein the majority of the people elect their leaders by a majority vote. Unfortunately even these types of governments can slowly began to enter upon devious paths, should their citizens fail to question the actions of their elected leaders.

"We believe that for any government to levy a tax for what it deems to be a benevolent purpose is wrong. Our citizens' welfare help is handled 100 percent by religious groups, as the helping of the needy rightfully falls within the realm of religious morality and initiative. Charity is wholly funded by those who wish to be generous and kind, and not forced upon those who do not.

"The creation of a proper educational system, within any society, is not a benevolent action on behalf of a government.

On the contrary it is a necessity. All citizens should be allowed the opportunity to gain the tools with which to productively enter the work place. And those of lesser potential should be allowed additional tutoring and materials with which to learn. However when the gifted are neglected in favor of the less fortunate, it is a grave mistake on behalf of that society, for it is robbed of its greater potential. We Aquatus are completely aware that the future survival of any species rests upon the education of its young, and to this end a third of our legislators are devoted and committed. With extreme caution do we tread any socialistic path beyond the education of our youth.

"It is difficult indeed to legislate morality, as the morality of various individuals may be construed from different perspectives. For these reasons our religious donations are tax deductible, as are various religious retreats and properties, within reason of course. Our religious groups do not own businesses, which are established strictly for profit, but may own businesses that are dependent upon donations for their revenues.

"We have no personal income tax on wages, as most taxes fall into five categories only: property tax, sales tax, transportation tax, imports and exports, with property tax being the most lenient.

"We Aquatus believe that government's primary responsibility is to provide a safe and fair environment for its citizens. In this environment any that so choose may pursue his or her happiness and security in any fair and reasonable manner, as long as it does not take the form of harmful predation upon one's neighbor or the environment. This does not mean that any individual is precluded from striking a good deal.

"Another difference between our government and yours is that each country, in our two worlds of Aquatus, has the same precious metal backing to all the varying types of currency. It is thereby virtually impossible for any country, or monetary establishment, to artificially manipulate inflations or depressions of economic markets by printing bogus currency. If there is a depression, we must rectify it as best we can. There can be no inflation, as precious metal by its very nature is limited.

"The one thing for certain in all nations of Trepleon and Spargus is that it is the citizens who hold the wealth, not government, nor government-controlled private institutions. Of course, as many of you from this country have realized, the precious metal backing of currency is a neglected benefit of the United States of America's constitution, and that precious metal transactions throughout your world are valued all the same."

A question-answer session ensued, during which tempers flared from time to time among the audience. However, many seemed to be mostly in agreement with what the little Aquatian had to say. After all, the Aquatus System had worked well for them for thousands of years. It was therefore most definitely tried and true.

At 2:00 p.m. exactly the small golden Aquatian held up her arms, indicating the conference had ended. She expressed her wishes that none be offended by Aquatus ideology, and, stepping down from the podium, took leave of the meeting.

In the Manor's kitchen waited Roxanne and Pooche, eagerly anticipating the excursion with Jayseeka up to the lake. The trek up to the lake did not turn out to be as pleasurable as Roxanne had expected. She noticed that the nearly perpetual smile of her small companion was scarcely apparent, and to Roxanne this was a clear indication of concern, or sadness.

The two best friends, with Pooche, made it up to the lake in a leisurely 50-minute hike. The discussion was mostly one-sided as Roxanne postulated about the ever-increasing hardships of Earth's wildlife, what might be their thoughts, and what survival techniques they might develop as humans continued to encroach upon their habitats.

Jayseeka listened attentively, speaking little, walking beside Pooche who wondered why he was not being ridden by Mistress Jayseeka, an activity he had enjoyed as much as she.

Upon reaching the lake, Jayseeka motioned for Roxanne to put down her berry bucket, and taking her by the hand, they walked out to the end of the pier and sat down. Roxanne removed her shoes and socks so as to dangle her feet in the water, and the three close friends sat silently upon the pier for about ten minutes. They looked out across the large expanse of calm water, disturbed from time to time by fish as they leaped in pursuit of agile orange and blue dragonflies and other insects near and upon the water's surface.

The sky was clear blue overhead, sprinkled sparingly with fluffy white clouds here and there. The temperature was mild, and birds were in full chorus as they sang of their properties to others of their feather. It was a delightfully beautiful day, disturbed only by the faint "put-put" sound of a helicopter somewhere in the distance.

"You need not concern yourself about the overcrowding and loss of animal habitat on your planet," spoke Jayseeka.

Roxanne looked curiously upon her little friend, puzzled by the remark.

The Aquatian had taken off her little backpack and was retrieving something from its interior.

Roxanne gazed with wonderment on the object Jayseeka now held before her, which seemed to necessitate the use of both of her delicate hands. She lowered the object slowly to the wood of the pier where it gloriously lay in all its mystical beauty. The magnificent amulet of 22-karat gold filigree was brightly polished, pleasantly reflecting a subtle rose hue, which caught the eye from time to time. The latticework of gold wove itself delicately but sturdily about a very thin shard of a stone. This, when angled toward the sun, shot forth a dazzling array of brilliant colors, shaming the finest diamond ever found and cut by human hand.

Roxanne resented the constant "put-put-hack-hack" of the distant helicopter spoiling the preciousness of the moment, when it suddenly became crystal clear in her mind that all was not well. Fear always brought tears to Roxanne's eyes, a childhood weakness she had not yet been able to overcome.

This moment was no exception, and in haste she stood up looking off to the west. There she spotted the first segment of the surrounding soldiers, now visible through the clearings between the trees as they rapidly approached the lake.

Jayseeka had now also risen to her feet, and was beginning to translucently take on the color of the lake's water. Bending down she lifted the amulet from the pier, placing it once more into the small backpack and handing it in turn to Roxanne.

It was a Roxanne of overwhelming dread and anxiety who stared at her small friend, eyes wide with fear and brimming with tears. "They are coming for you?" she hoarsely asked, all but choking on the words.

"Yes," calmly replied Jayseeka.

"Hide in the lake, and I will come back for you when it is safe!" pleaded Roxanne.

"There is no need," replied the little alien. "My mission on planet Earth has been accomplished and now I must leave."

"When will you return?" asked the girl with great sadness, hardly able to find the words.

The answer needed not to be spoken, as the immense sadness on the Aquatian's features told Roxanne that there would be no return to earth any time within the foreseeable future.

"I wish for you to do something for me, which may prove extremely difficult for you as time goes by," requested Jayseeka.

"Anything you ask, I will do," vowed the girl.

"It is very important that you always remember my mission to planet Earth to have been honorable. Whatever any may say about the Aquatus, our activity here was for the sake of humanity and your beautiful planet, and not for any personal gain on our behalf. We perceived Earth as a gem in the cosmos, worthy of saving.

"Do not lose my gift, as it will prove extremely important to you, as well as the rest of your species at some future time."

Roxanne glanced at the small but heavy backpack she held by its straps in her right hand.

"I love you deeply, my kind and good companion, and on Trepleon and Spargus your name, indeed your very visage, will be known to all for as long as our recorded history survives."

The soldiers, bristling with weaponry, had now surrounded the vast lake. A captain, his lieutenant, and two sergeants were preparing to move onto the pier, the captain announcing their intentions through a bullhorn.

"Will the two at the extremity of the pier accompany us back to the Manor? Please do not be frightened! We are here for your protection only. We have some very important questions to ask of Ambassador Jayseeka."

The soldiers hesitated at the halfway point on the pier, as there sat Pooche, eyeing them with cold malevolence.

Roxanne sat down in the lotus position on the pier, giving

her cherished small friend one last hug. "I'll love you always," she said.

Jayseeka took four steps backward, dropping off the pier into the lake, immediately disappearing into its depths

One of the Sergeants drew his pistol, just as Roxanne stood up from the pier.

"Come here, Pooche!" she commanded.

The huge dog growled wickedly then hurled several loud barks in the direction of the disconcerted solders before giving up his position. Then, apparently satisfied, he returned obediently to the side of his mistress.

The soldiers were now very excited as they radioed their contingency that the Aquatian was attempting to escape. The commander had brilliantly attempted to anticipate all eventualities, and within fifteen minutes two troop helicopters moved out on to the lake and dropped 33 war-ready frogmen at various locations.

Even a General Patton could not have anticipated what would happen next. A huge mound of water rose up near the center of the lake. The water of the lake began to rush towards the strange occurrence.

Suddenly the vast pile of water at the lake's center broke open, revealing the glistening black surface of the colossal *Mothership.*

The reverse action of the lake's displacement by the immense craft sent a foamy turbulent five foot wall of water racing towards the shoreline, scattering the confused troops in all directions as it pushed outward and into the surrounding fields.

It took twenty minutes for the chaos to subside, whereupon many of the frogmen originally dropped into the lake now found themselves on land. Wet, dismayed, but uninjured, the anxious troops began to reassemble themselves. None raised a weapon to fire upon the glistening titanic craft, now hanging motionlessly above the foaming, madly agitated waters of the lake. To do so would have been much like a mouse climbing the leg of a lioness with rape on its mind.

The spectacular vision hung steadfast and ominous above the angry lake for another five minutes before rising straight upwards, at ever increasing speeds, exiting the Earth's atmosphere at a velocity far beyond the ability of any earthly plane or missile to pursue.

The captain, his lieutenants, along with the ambivalently sad but happy young lady and her dog, walked slowly back towards Vincent Henry Manor.

## Chapter Twenty-Two

"A horse! a horse! my kingdom for a horse!"

Vincent Henry, Director William Faraday and Professor David Hauss met in the reception area of the White House.

The President had summoned them, and it was more than a polite formality that they attend the impromptu and urgently assembled meeting. Any and all persons who had had even minimal personal contact with the Trepleon Ambassador were placed under house arrest. They called it "being taken into protective custody" at two husky federal agents per individual. The seriousness of the situation was as serious as it gets.

Vincent Henry had just finished telling his friends what had happened at the 90-acre lake near the Manor four hours earlier. Faraday was not being told anything he didn't already know, as they were summoned into the conference hall.

To find all the authoritative rank and power of the United States of America silently eyeing their entry into the hall was further evidence that the trio was up the proverbial creek. Not only were they up the creek, but that their boat had sunk and they were in a foul-smelling situation up to their necks.

The President had on the table before him three very fat files, a variety of computer software diskettes and videocassettes, all neatly stacked and segregated. David,

Vincent and Bill where shown to their seats. They had been thoroughly searched at the entry area, and though there were no others seated between them and the President, they were not close enough to touch him.

All three guests in disfavor did not bother with the polite formality of a handshake; the guards would not have permitted it anyway. A combination of fear, malice and foreboding hung in the air of the room like 98 percent humidity.

"Well, ladies and gentlemen," began the President, addressing the assembly, "it has become very apparent that we have lost a war we didn't even know had been joined!"

The statement brought murmurs and low key discussion among the dignitaries, as they began to compare the information from the various sources to which they were privy.

"Gentlemen, please! Lets get all our ducks in a row before we begin any strategic discussions."

"How the hell could we lose a war not knowing we were in it? If we have been threatened, how long do we have before direct confrontation might occur?" asked a chief of staff.

"It seems that the conflict which one would expect under normal war circumstances may not occur at all. As the tally currently stands, Aquatus two casualties, Humanity 6.8 billion! More plainly put, the total extinction of our species within a single century. However, there exists the very real probability that the Aquatus may begin to harvest us as a food source, which will certainly hasten our demise."

Half the hall had now risen from their chairs, as panic and chaos began to replace logic and authority.

Indignantly slamming his gavel repeatedly upon the table, and shouting at the top of his voice, the President was once again able to gain control of the room. Then heatedly, he informed the assembly, "Another disruption of this delegated body such as that, and I will dismiss the disrupters and have them placed under house arrest. We cannot accomplish a single goddamned thing unless we calmly and rationally work together. Please, ladies and gentlemen! The future of humanity is at stake!"

Other than for some heavy breathing by several of the more weighty individuals in the room, silence and order again prevailed. All standing once more seated themselves, focusing their attention to the front of the hall and on the flush-faced man who was their leader. Gingerly the President patted beads of perspiration from his forehead and upper lip with a large white handkerchief.

"Time is of the essence, ladies and gentlemen," spoke the President. "We must work out some type of guidance procedure. I am praying that we can think of some way to prevent the extinction of humankind. I'm sure that these three gentlemen seated closest to me are going to provide us with a great deal of information regarding this eventuality."

There was no mistaking the glitter in the President's eyes, as he looked directly and individually into the eyes of the now infamous three.

"I'm first going to review with you the information which I have before me, and I advise all of you to diligently take notes. However, please broach no questions until I have finished. Then, in orderly fashion, we shall consider all suggestions as how to best proceed with the dilemma before us."

Evilly eyeing Director Faraday, the President pulled one of the large folders on the table closer for better access and began to shuffle through its copious contents.

Looking up from the documentation before him, the Chief Executive declared, "I've got a better idea."

He motioned to the ranking individual of the three CIA agents who had returned from South America with the well-documented evidence.

"Sir! Enlighten us regarding your team's mission to locate and retrieve the lost Lazarus Machine in South America, and please--include the details." directed the Chief Executive.

The well mannered, obviously adept combatant walked forward from his location at the rear of the seated assembly. He sat down at the table, to the far right of the President where he had easy access to one of the microphones.

The clear speaking, intelligent young man began his narration, aided by numerous photos, recordings and medical reports. The President had slid them to him across the large table.

"We entered the country posing as tourists, and within two days we had our suspect, El Presidente Piolet, under close observation," began the agent. "We had been tipped that he had perhaps stolen one of the Aquatus medical apparatuses, with the intention of clandestinely selling the invaluable instrument later to the highest bidder.

"Amazingly enough, it was on the morning of the third day that he would unwittingly lead us to its location. I know many of you will find this report hard to believe as I myself, in moments of weakness, think that perhaps I may awaken from the nightmare. To my misfortune, and soon to yours, we will find the evidence to be conclusive," added the astute agent gloomily.

He then began in earnest his report.

"Following Piolet and two of his bodyguards far off the beaten path and into the jungle, we were led to a cave which we later discovered had been designated as Piolet's clandestine base of operation. We were quite concerned that only two of his men accompanied him, as we had been advised to locate four, this being the number of guards he usually had with him. We had followed them cautiously up a coastal road, then inland, more by smell than sound, as we were not sure if Piolet may have had informants posted along the road.

"We arrived at a distance, just in time, to observe their entry into some well-concealed caverns. My two men then scouted the area of the sizable hill, which contained the caverns, as well as the military storage building at its top. I kept discreet surveillance near the entry of the cave.

"It took my men two hours and thirty-five minutes to wrap-up their investigation of the area, whereupon they returned to regroup with me at an observation point in the area of the cave entrance. Piolet and his men had not yet emerged. We had no reason to suspect that their exit from the cave might be from any other location, as we could discover no other openings where this might be possible. We had the location of their vehicle under scrutiny as well.

"Our game-plan was to wait for Piolet and his men to emerge from the cave and leave the area. Thereafter we would have the opportunity to further scout the area, as well as the interior of the cave, at our leisure. We continued to wait for another hour, during which time the hurricane, now in full force in our location, was beginning to push over many of the larger trees. One of these almost struck our vehicle, knocking agent Fred Bergman to the ground with its branches as it fell.

"Fred was shaken up, but fortunately uninjured. After nearly being crushed several more times by other falling trees in our area, we were obliged to change our plans and enter the shelter of the cave before Piolet and his men departed the area.

"We were fully equipped with night-vision equipment. This equipment only necessitates a single minute laser beam from one of our weapons to give us near-daylight type of vision within the cave. We made our way easily through the cavern's corridors, encountering no obstacles. Our electronic detection devices found no alarm or surveillance monitors in the floors, walls or ceilings.

"We moved in search of Piolet and his men, well assured that we could conceal ourselves within the large and extensive caverns, locating them first, without them being aware we had done so. We planned to wait for them to make their exit, after which we would continue with our original plans to search the area in hopes of locating and retrieving the stolen medical equipment. This most certainly seemed a likely place for it to have been hidden.

"Hopefully none here will consider the decision to enter the cave, prior to the exit of Piolet and his men, foolhardy. The storm that raged about us at the time was the absolute worst any of us had ever been in. We were in far more danger outside the cave than within, even with the possibility of discovery by Piolet and his men.

"It was strangely quiet within the corridors of the cave. We gradually pushed on in hopes of hearing voices. The cave widened pregnantly at intervals and at one point we came to an area where several smaller passageways became apparent, leading off into various other caverns. There was light in one of the passageways. We could faintly hear and smell a small gas-driven electric generator, somewhere in the far recesses of the caverns.

"We concealed ourselves beneath a rocky ledge and waited for the better part of another hour, hearing no voices. We could hear, ever so faintly, the wind from the storm outside. We considered this strange, as we knew we were deep within the interior of the hill.

"Another hour passed and I then decided that we should sneak a peek into the lighted area of the caverns. As quietly as possible, Fred and I eased along the wall with this intent. Eventually we crawled on our bellies to the entry area of the lighted passageway, Fred on one side and myself on the other. So as not to attract attention with rapid movement, I slowly eased a slight peek into the lighted area.

"I had located Piolet! His *head,* that is. It had been neatly severed with just enough of the neck remaining to keep it in an upright position on the floor of the cave. There were four other heads as well, which turned out to be those of his guards. Off to the right were five nude torsos, and to the left of this was a stack of severed arms and another of legs. Piolet and his men had been quartered and neatly stacked like cordwood.

"I thought I had gone mad as I motioned Fred to have a look into the lighted area. Just as he did so, I heard a gasp from Bill, the third agent in our party. By this time he had also crept up and taken a look into the lighted area. I was just about to make a decision about what to do, when Bill, unfolding from his crouched position, rushed into the lighted chamber.

"By the time Fred and I could gain our footing, we heard the rapid whispering of Bill's silenced weapon, as he unloaded his clip into targets within the chamber. When Fred and I entered the area, it was over. On the floor, close to the rest of the horror, writhed two stark, silver... *things,* each having two large sapphire blue eyes, two leg-like appendages, and four arm-like tentacles each.

"Bill said they had been black in color, before they saw him, and each had one of the dead men's severed arms, which they were holding close to their stomach areas. Before Bill's rounds began to enter the bodies of these ghastly things, he said he heard voices within his head asking him to 'please stop!" He was strangely compelled to do so, but in the horror of it all, his reflexes had become as automatic as his weaponry.

"Deftly inserting another clip into his weapon, he emptied this also into the now shattered bodies of the creatures, which continued to writhe and spill profuse quantities of whitish blood upon the floor of the cavern. With the advent of Bill's second clip, the two small horrors on the floor ceased to writhe, they were done.

"With great urgency, we then quickly surveyed the interior of the cave, hopeful beyond hope that we would find no more of the hideous little beasts within the area. After an hour or so of searching, we did not.

"We took numerous photos of the grisly butchery and all other aspects of the cave. We noted that whoever or whatever had slaughtered the men must have had access to some type of strong laser device. The heads and appendages of Piolet and his men were all neatly severed, and the tissues in the severed areas had been cauterized.

"We found the Lazarus Machine in a folded position just below a large rock stairway which led upwards to the surface of the hill. In this same location we found five stainless steel containers, which looked as though they might hold eight quarts of liquid each.

"The sound of the storm was still raging outside the caverns, now resounding down the stairway, as we examined the contents of the containers--blood! We later determined the blood to have been from Piolet and his men as, except for minor traces, the only type of blood on the floor of the cavern had come from the things Bill had wasted.

"Cautiously we made our way up the rock staircase. It opened out at the top of the hill where the storage building once stood, having now been removed by the fury of the storm. The worst part of the storm had passed, though the rain was still heavy.

"Fred and I took a quick look around the top of the hill and were entering the stairway once more, when Fred grabbed my shoulder and pointed upwards. At first I thought it was a large dark cloud hanging forty or so feet above us, but it wasn't moving. It was obviously some type of craft. As we looked upward we then heard a faint high-pitched whine which we determined to be coming from the thing hanging solidly in the storm above us. It was absolutely time to go.

"With maximum haste we were getting the hell out of that chamber of horrors. Fred and Bill carried the folded Aquatus medical instrument, which we found to be amazingly light in weight for its size, all three segments together weighing no more than sixty or so pounds.

"Becoming more rational, as I was almost becoming numbed to the danger we were experiencing, I retrieved one of the dead men's jackets from the pile of their clothing near their appendageless torsos. Wrapping one of the dead creatures up in the jacket--it only weighed about forty pounds--I threw it over my shoulder. Somehow I felt it would be of substantial government and/or scientific interest.

"On our way through the lighted area of the caverns, we heard a baby crying somewhere in the recesses of the cave. Fading into a darkened area, we put down our loads, leaving Fred to oversee the equipment. Bill and I began to search the darkened area using our night-vision equipment.

"We found a man, his wife, and newborn child, who thought that they were well hidden. The child was now quietly nursing at its mother's breast. Of course we could see them very plainly, and I, being fluent in Spanish asked them to come along with us. Conscientiously, I explained that we would not harm them and wished only to ask them some questions about what had gone on within the cave.

"Though they looked to be in good physical condition, their eyes radiated fear and confusion. Nevertheless, they came along with us, never resisting or trying to escape. As it would turn out, they knew a lot. Immediately upon our exit from the nightmare of the caverns, we retrieved our radio equipment from where it had been hidden prior to our entry.

"A naval destroyer, supposedly on random maneuvers thirty miles off shore, was actually there for our evacuation. They rushed us a helicopter after our radioed emergency. In a short while the copter arrived and equipment, Señor Blanco, his wife and child, the Lazarus Machine, the dead creature Bill had wasted, and ourselves were all lifted from the jungle within an hour. Damned good storm flying by the navy pilot, though every minute seemed like an hour to us.

"Whatever the thing was that we had observed from the top of the hill above the caves, it was still there when we lifted out. We postulated that more of the nasty little fiends, like the dead one we had with us, might still be inside it. We suspected them to be bad news when not taken by surprise, a presumption later verified by Juan and Gemma.

"We and the helicopter's navigator took several pictures of the unusual phenomenon as it hung above the hill, upon our rapid departure from the area. The storm had lifted enough for it to be clearly visible, but strangely the destroyer at only thirty miles out to sea could not pick it up on radar.

"Aboard ship the medical crew wasted no time in placing the corpse of the dead creature in quarantine, performing a careful autopsy and freezing all the pieces upon its completion. You will find the medical reports of the findings within that other folder before you, sir," said the agent, looking and nodding in the direction of the President before continuing his report.

"They must have been passed through the Aquatus medical apparatus at some time during their ordeal in the cave, as Juan and Gemma seemed to be in excellent health. They ate any and all food we brought them for a solid hour and a half aboard the Destroyer. Probably they would have eaten more, had they not been nearly falling out of their chairs from the exhaustion of their ordeal within the cave.

"We put them to bed with distended stomachs and Gemma's child nursing furiously at her breast. They, and we, were awakened six hours later for further debriefing, as the destroyer steamed full speed ahead towards Locust Point Maryland. What had happened to us in the cave was strange enough, but the story Juan and Gemma told us later, plus the evidence from the alien autopsy, served to make the ordeal that much stranger.

"We now know that the damned things wasted in the cave were Aquatus. Ladies and gentlemen," exclaimed the agent, as he looked out upon his spellbound audience, "the tape, photos and medical evidence are definitive.

"Señor Juan Blanco and his wife Gemma explained that they had been kidnapped by Piolet and his henchmen and brought to the cave over three weeks earlier. They had been told that they had broken the law by refusing to be treated in a special medical device.

"In their three week imprisonment within the cave, they had been fed only corn tortillas and water. Gemma had been raped repeatedly by two of Piolet's men, even though she was seven months pregnant, while her husband had been tortured repeatedly with extensive cruelty.

"When Piolet and his other two men arrived, she and her husband had been brought out into the lighted area of the cave, now more dead than alive. They then learned the intent of Piolet. He would kill them and pass their dead bodies through the stolen medical apparatus to see if it would bring them back to life. Should the macabre experiment succeed, they were to be killed again and again, being passed through the device to determine how many times it would resurrect them, only to be murdered in the end, one way or another.

"The girl claims her water had broken from convulsions within her stomach, brought on by the sheer stress and terror of learning their fate at hands of her Presidente. She was then led away towards the medical device in total despair. She and her husband had given up all hope.

"Now the story gets kind of tricky; the girl's husband claims that his wife passed out, falling to the floor while being roughly pushed towards the then upright and operational medical apparatus. Piolet himself dragged her by the hair to the front of the machine.

"Two of his men then picked her up and threw her haphazardly, like so much garbage, upon the extruding shelf that would carry her through the device. Then Piolet, to Juan's horror, unholstered his pistol, placing it to the stomach of the unconscious girl. What happened next, Juan swears before the Sacred Virgin Mary to be the truth.

"Tied and shackled, standing helplessly to the side, Juan watched the now closely-grouped men as they anticipated the murder of his wife and unborn child by Piolet. Juan prayed to his God that it would be quick.

"Suddenly, two black creatures about the size of medium dogs hurtled themselves out of the shadows of the cave, landing upon the backs of two of the men and wrapping belt-like things quickly about their heads. We deduced later that it was one or more of the four each tentacles they possessed. Then, without a moment wasted, they leapt from the first two men directly into the face and chest areas of the other two, holding on for several seconds, like two huge black spiders.

"The last two of Piolet's men had been able to unholster their weapons, but were unable to use them in the instant allotted. They in turn dropped like lead, joining their violently convulsing comrades, projectile vomiting, relentlessly slamming their own heads onto the floor of the cave.

"Piolet turned from the equipment and his damnable intent, face ashen with stark, incredulous fear. Spasmodically gripping his pistol, adrenaline and terror usurped the moment. His abject fear as well became an enemy, as he uncontrollably and ineffectively emptied his pistol into the ceiling and far areas of the cave. He had been unable to take aim at the horrific demons before him. Finally bringing his pistol in line with the hellish targets, Piolet could only pull impotently on its trigger, making hopeless clicking sounds.

"One of his fiendish tormentors simply reached upwards, grabbing his hand, pistol and all, with one of its tentacles. Then leisurely, almost as if in slow motion, the little beast pulled itself up and into the chest and face of the insanely screaming Piolet. The now inhuman screeching resounded off the walls and down the halls of the extensive caverns, seemingly with ever-greater intensity.

"The horrific little monster was most apparently taking its time in the performance of its atrocious deed. In the end Piolet was inflicted with the same grand mal seizures as his men--flopping about on the floor of the cave like a fish out of water, losing control of his bodily functions, convulsively and persistently hammering his own brains into jelly upon the cold stone floor of the cave.

"The only other thing Juan could remember concerning the attack of the creatures on Piolet and his men was the sizzling, snapping sounds that took place each time the creatures came into contact with the men, leaving a pungent, acrid smell hanging in the dampness of the cave. Our presumption of what could have caused the violent involuntary physical activity of the men, the acrid smell, and the scarlet welts upon their severed heads was an extremely intense electrical charge, a defense/attack mechanism much like that of an Amazonian electric eel, though obviously of even greater intensity.

"This presumption was later verified as correct by one of the medical examiners doing the autopsy on the alien we had delivered. It seems that the good doctor was knocked up against the wall by a passive electrical charge, still present within the body of the creature, as he cut into the tissues.

"Juan said that towards the end of his diabolical ordeal with the creatures, he was suddenly overcome with extreme weariness. He remembers nothing else regarding the creatures or the men, except that he lost consciousness as he stared with dread into the glistening eyes of one of the hideous beasts. It had glanced darkly upward at him from among the dead and dying on the floor of the cave.

"Juan's wife, Gemma, filled us in with further details, claiming she had awakened off to the side of the medical apparatus totally nude, against the wall of the cave, lying on her own clothing. Her newborn baby was sprawling across her stomach. Though strangely unable to move, she said she felt no fear and only mild concern for her child. A small, black, many armed, bizarre creature sitting beside her reached over with one of its appendages, touching the back of her baby. The infant immediately jolted to life and began to cry as loud as its newly found little voice would allow.

"The girl said she felt strangely well and safe in her location against the wall of the cave. However, as if in a dream, she found scarcely enough strength to enfold the child in her arms. Eventually she was able to accomplish this task, and her child immediately stopped crying, and after a bit went to sleep.

"Seemingly wide awake, those still unable to move, the girl said she watched, more with fascination than concern, as the creature that had been beside her walked over and began to assist the other of its kind as it unbound and undressed her husband. Upon completion of this chore, one of the creatures moved away from her husband and touched the strange, brilliantly lighted apparatus, which now seemed lower to the floor than before.

"A shelf extended from its interior, upon which, with amazing strength and agility for their small sizes, they lifted her still unconscious husband. He in turn disappeared into the interior of the machine.

"Gemma thinks she either passed out, or went to sleep, later waking up beside her husband, lying partly on and partly covered by some clothing. Her child was beside her, wrapped in a shirt. Gemma discovered this more through feel than vision, as they were now in a different, darkened locality of the caverns.

"The new mother then became fully aware of a commotion in another area of the cave, probably when we made our surprising entry into the lighted chamber. Waking up her husband, she took up the child, and they fled further into the darkness of the caverns. Later the baby began to cry, and the rest you all know.

"That's a wrap-up for me, gentlemen, except to say that in my estimation concerning the findings, and vaguely substantiated by the other classified medical personnel with whom I have spoken, the creatures we encountered may well have the ability of clairvoyance, as well as the capacity to telepathically manipulate thought patterns. However, my men and myself are reasonably sure that, if they possess this ability, it is limited by distance and/or substantial wall thickness; or else they obviously would have known of our presence in the cave.

"I would also hazard a guess that the things actually enjoy ultimate competition, as they attacked Piolet and his men using no other weaponry excepting their own physical capacities-- against substantial odds, I might add. The methods used to drain their victims' blood and dissect them into more easily transportable sections indicate their ability to develop and use other than physical weapons.

"In keeping with the medical evidence we have uncovered, the creatures were obviously of Trepleonian origin. Had there been others in the craft above the caverns, they most obviously would have monitored our approach. Probably the density of the storm and numerous trees in the area must have somehow obscured their orbital satellites as well."

Though the agents from the State Department had done an excellent job on their mission into South America, and the report given by their ranking member was exemplary and well documented, there was no applause as he left the side of the President. The dissertation served only to cement into the minds of the assembly what had previously only been speculation.

"Now I'm going to give some highlights of the rest of the material I have before me," spoke the Chief Executive, "and then we will discuss the subject further as each of you gives your individual views and suggestions about how to deal with this devastating situation.

"There can be little doubt that the creatures found in the cave were Aquatus, having all the same capacities as the Trepleon Ambassador Jayseeka. Unless we hear differently in the immediate future, we are assuming the worst.

"The one autopsied by the medical examiners had four

arm-like appendages, no demarcation of its torso above the upper--oh hell, let's call them what they are --'tentacles,' and the top of its head. It has the same type of eyes, and the weight is minimally different from the Aquatus we all thought we knew, 'Jayseeka.'

"The weight differs by approximately four pounds, due to the additional set of tentacles on the corpse we examined. There was a breathing hole in the back of its head, no nose in the front part of its body; and its gills are obvious. Its mouth is a beak-like orifice in the front-center of its body, near its stomach, covered by tissue flaps when not in use.

"The body contained little fat, was strongly muscular and had no bone tissue as do mammals. It supports itself on land by using an interior biological hydraulics system. It is obviously an agile swimmer capable of flattening its body-- its whole body, brain tissue included. Then with tentacles at its side, propelling itself through the water with an undulant motion much like, but more effectively than could a dolphin. The traces of red blood spilt when Bill slaughtered the two in the cavern would turn out to be human blood, from their stomachs; the white creamy substance was their own.

"As was reported by our State Department agents, it can change color depending on emotion, or the need for protective coloration, by the use of 'chromatophores' throughout its body. These chromatophores are also present in the many, almost hair-like tubules that cover the back of the creatures, from beneath its 'blowhole' in the back of its head, to just below its first set of upper appendages.

"By analyzing the stomach contents of the goddamned Aquatus corpse, we discovered human tissues and blood, making it most obvious that they relish eating human flesh. Another indication of this heinous preference is that after they had killed Piolet and his men in a most disgusting manner, they prepared them for transit like slaughtered hogs, blood included.

"Of course there are other curiosities in these folders I have before me, significant things left out of the picture six years ago.

"Little did we suspect that the only Aquatian that humans were ever intended to see--Jayseeka, Ambassador from Trepleon--had been altered with incredibly artful surgery. We have been beguiled with the image of a sweet, graciously innocent young girl child, which now appears most obviously to be a demonic creature in disguise.

"There are those within this room who well knew that the goddamned sneaky Aquatus were not only telepathic, but that they could also utilize this exceptional ability for mind control. The three persons who knew this are sitting closest to me in this very room. As I speak they are formulating answers in their minds and we will hear those answers soon."

Acid was in the voice of the Chief of State. If ever a group of three could be tried and hung for treason, there was little doubt as to Faraday, Hauss and Henry being topmost on the list.

The President then stood up and explained, "Although it will be difficult to sleep, concerning the gravity and urgency of the situation, all of us are going to need clear heads, unhindered by fatigue, if we are to be the least successful in our endeavors."

It was now 2:00 a.m., and nightclothes had been prepared and arrangements made for all to spend the night at the Mansion. Each of the assembly was furnished with toothbrush, shaving utensils, soap and towels. Their clothing would be cleaned, pressed and returned while they slept.

Brunch would be served at 10:00 a.m. and after this, they would continue with the pressing, depressing dilemma.

Professor Hauss, Vincent Henry, and Director Faraday were the first to leave the conference room, escorted by no less than six federal agents.

## Chapter Twenty-Three

---

Victorious,
The army kills not the enemy's young and old,
Destroys not the crops,
Seizes not those who retire without a fight.
Those taken prisoners are not those who surrender.
Asylum seekers are not abused.
The common people are not punished.

*(Earth: Wisdom of Hsun Tzu 273 B.C.)*
*(Entered into the Aquatus Archives 270 B.C.)*

---

The brunch had been well prepared. All consumed more than usual. They all knew that it could be many hours before they would eat again. Although the food would normally have satisfied even the most discriminating of tastes, its palatability went largely unnoticed. Heavy was the perplexity of the continuing conference, as it weighed upon the minds of the heads of state.

"Director Faraday, why were concerned others and I not informed as to the telepathic abilities of the Aquatus?" asked the Chief Executive. The reconvened meeting began with their leader cutting sharply into the meat of the matter.

The Director started to rise slowly to his feet.

"Don't bother to stand; just remain seated and answer the question!"

In an obviously morose manner, Faraday sank back into his chair.

"Sir, it was pretty much common knowledge that the Aquatus, at least Jayseeka, are telepathic," began Faraday. "However, how were any of us to know that they could, or would, use this ability as a powerful mind-manipulating mechanism, when one considers that the procedure is totally subliminal?  She had taken you in as well, sir, and many of the others now present at this meeting.

"If you will recall, most all of us did have a long and in-depth hearing right here at the White House, wherein she laid out her supposed mission. All of us were apprehensive in the beginning; but at the end of it we were totally delighted with the prospects and concepts, with the vast medical and technological wealth that was awaiting us simply for the taking.

"In retrospect I can remember times when I had wanted to ask questions of the Trepleonian Ambassador, but when in the same room with her, I couldn't for the life of me remember what they were.  I couldn't even be sure I had had a question to ask.  At best, on my most lucid of days when feeling that I needed further information, trying to remember in Jayseeka's presence was like trying to remember a twenty year old phone number; it would simply not come into my conscious mind.

"Curiously, I would give it up after postulating that the question had probably not been of great importance anyway. Often, in some pocket of my clothing there would be notes, and since I was unable to decipher their meaning they were simply discarded as if in a dream.  I convinced myself that it was just the pressure of my job.

"Of course, the questions that would further the mission of the Aquatus upon our planet were always ready to be blurted out, like verbal diarrhea.

"Given the facts now available to us, we can also suppose that many of these questions were subliminally suggested, a technique to brainwash us further and to guide possible human suspicions away from the hidden Aquatus intent. I can see the ploy clearly now, sir, and it seems very strange to me now that others and I could not have seen it sooner.

The Chief Executive looked at Faraday, then back to the stacks of information before him. He then shook his head slowly with the realization that once in the presence of the seemingly benevolent and solicitous alien, there was not a human chance to ever find out what they had been up against, until it was far too late to do anything about it.

"Mr. President," spoke up the Secretary of the Interior, "could you enlighten us further about the pending possibility of the end of humankind on Earth?"

This was a dreaded question that had to be asked, though most had heard it through the grapevine. It had something to do with the apparently time delayed, but now ever-increasing sterility of all who had passed through the Aquatus medical instruments. All eyes were riveted on the man with the explanation at the front of the room.

"It was a catch-22 situation," began the President. "As we all know now, it was the Aquatus intention, from the very beginning, to get every man, woman, and child to pass through their damnable apparatuses. We were all led to believe in the beginning that it was only the sick, maimed, and elderly who would receive the benefits.

"We were hoodwinked into a supposed benevolent escalation from then on. For once the sick, maimed and elderly reentered society, not only as happy, youthful, healthy individuals, but intellectually enhanced, and longer lived, everybody wanted to partake of the Aquatus Fountain of Youth. I would venture to guess that there is not a soul in this room, and few others throughout the world, who did not jump at the opportunity when it was offered.

"Under the guise of ridding humanity of the diseases that had plagued us from antiquity, who could doubt the proven performance of the Lazarus Machines?   Benefits proven beyond our most audacious dreams.

"All the world's leaders were obligated to partake, not just out of vanity, but also to be better able to compete intellectually with other leaders throughout the world.

"Once the benefits became glowingly apparent, nations virtually conspired, in all ways possible, to gain access to the devices for their citizens.  Never would humankind suspect that the bait had always been theirs for the taking.

"Many were motivated out of benevolence, but most were stimulated by the inevitably greater productivity of their labor-fueled investments.   It was a pigeon-drop rip-off of monumental proportions.  We, being all too human, always in search of the free lunch, jumped for it.  Now we know; in these final days, our parachutes were made of lead.

"Sterilization is their method of conquest, for in this way they inherit a planet unspoiled by a nuclear defense.

"Had we known from the beginning of the Aquatus ploy, we probably would have given nuclear defense a try, but it's far too late for this now.  All our nuclear devices, and others throughout the world, are totally disabled.  All radioactive elements on planet Earth are now approaching, or soon will be, useless lead.

"As it turned out, the 'anti-pollution Aquatus instrumentation' taken abroad to other countries, clandestinely disguised as altruistic devices for the neutralization of nuclear waste, was nothing more than a pollution cleanup scam.  The delivery routes taken by these 'anti-pollution devices' were often redirected in transit, passing through various countries, neutralizing not only atomic waste but nuclear stockpiles as well. Military personnel in charge of the cleanup hadn't been aware that the goddamned things had been continuously operational, even while in transit. Our own military aided in our own defeat, for Christ's sake!

"Any fissionable materials within a thousand surface miles of the instruments, and deep within the earth as well, have been or will soon be rendered inert through some type of enhanced atomic decay process.

"Countries which our intelligence sources didn't even know had nuclear weapons, until they became useless, that is, are hot.

"Now all the rotten S.O.B.s who shouldn't have had the goddamned things to begin with are claiming it was our intention from the beginning to disarm them for purposes of easy conquest, plotting together with the Aquatus.

"Nuclear energy for the generation of electricity was never missed, as everyone had converted to the pollution-free inexpensive use of hydrogen more than two years ago, aided by Aquatus technology of course. Medical applications for atomic materials had gone unused, as we are now all so goddamned healthy, and somehow the radioactive elements used in medical research went unaffected. We had clues, but not enough to make a case. Wanting to believe in the benevolence of the Aquatus intent, we trapped ourselves."

"Mr. President, are you saying that the human population of Earth will come to an end upon the demise of its current human inhabitants?" asked the Secretary of Health and Education, thinking that the Chief Executive might have gone too far afield from outlining the primary concern.

"I have had men working on this day and night for the last two weeks. We had begun receiving reports from various fertility clinics, they and the Bone Doctors being about the only ones working these days. The spreaders of old wives' tales recently have had absolutely no success when it came to advising and assisting their patients in methods of fertility. In vitro fertilization, having been only marginally successful down through the years, within the last four months is having a zero success rate throughout the world.

"Now this is with patients who have motile sperm or apparently receptive ova. Fertility shots, which cause multiple ovulation in the female, have failed to bring about a single pregnancy in the last three months. Human fertilization will simply not take place despite the best medical efforts. But, oh brother. Are those fertility doctors booked solid!

"At first we believed the low birth rates to be attributable to greater intelligence enhanced by the Lazarus Machines. Young people were going back to college, making careers for themselves, knowing how to better safeguard themselves against unwanted pregnancies. Perhaps we thought it was just the simple realization of the god-awful amount of work and expense in rearing and caring for children. These assumptions have clearly turned out not to be the case.

"Ladies and gentlemen, we have currently compiled evidence from around the world, from those in the top areas of their professions. It is estimated that the worlds' human population fertility has dropped off to as little as two percent. Even those few secluded populations of peoples in remote areas and others who refused the Aquatus medical services because of religious convictions are in the same non-fertile percentile as the rest of us.

"It is suspected that birth control biotics have been placed in their water supplies, or that they were exposed to anti-fertility radiation generated by the Aquatus while they slept or huddled from the storms. In these areas the animal life has become largely infertile as well.

"Therefore, folks," solemnly explained their Chief Executive, "by the time most of the current human inhabitants of planet Earth, somewhere around seven billion souls, meet their ultimate demise, there will be only about 140 million left. Giving the most obvious possibility that these 140 million souls will also be only two percent fertile as well, when this remainder will have lived out their lives, there will be but 2,800,000 to take their place, then 56,000, then 1,120 etc.

"Our scientists have informed us that the structure of our DNA has been altered.

"Now, when given the Aquatus life span of 620 years Earth time, most of them will still be alive to usurp our planet in their near future, unless they decide at some point to harvest us as a food source, that is. They just might keep a few of our species about, rejuvenate within them the ability to procreate, hence providing themselves with an on-going food supply. What has become obvious, and I do not mean this in the cultural sense, is that to them we are of good taste."

Despondency enveloped the room like doom; the gravity of the situation had become vividly apparent.

"As if things are not brutal enough," continued the President, as he wiped the beads of perspiration from his upper lip with a now neatly folded handkerchief, "I will brief you about other problems with which we are now confronted. Most probably, sooner than later, these things will also aid and abet the Aquatus in their objectives.

"There are numerous coalitions now being formed in this country, and in other countries around the world, demanding that government leaders be required to take annual polygraph tests in order to remain in office. Goddamned lie detector tests, mind you. How the hell are we supposed to function under that kind of scrutiny? They want mandatory eight-year limitations on the terms of our elected government officials as well.

"There are numerous reports of people bursting into flame! Spontaneous combustion of people is an occurrence once thought to be very rare, or simply exaggerated reports of people who had accidentally set themselves on fire. This has happened frequently with prisoners in our penal institutions. In their beds, sitting in the mess hall, in front of the guards, many in front of parole boards as they were being reviewed prior to release.

"Strangely enough, most of the victims, upward to 55 percent, had criminal records, although never imprisoned. They were living normal lives, with apparently normal jobs and some with families. We can only postulate what this means; perhaps it is the Aquatus way of telling us, 'You humans had better meet our demands, or this could happen to any of you!'

"Another strange happening, along these same lines, were a number of lab technicians and geneticists who had been making great scientific strides with various cloning techniques. The whole mother-loving lab went up in that one. Upon police and federal investigation, it seems that normal animal experiments had gone along just fine.

"Also, over the last seven years they had used the technology on numerous occasions to clone human tissues. Though the cloning of a whole human is a process recently outlawed throughout the world, up until a year ago these scientists had been dramatically successful in human cloning procedures. They had made numerous inroads into the possibilities of humans being able to grow their own organ transplants.

"This may have been a procedure we could have used to help reverse the effects of the human sterilization by the Aquatus, had the research been allowed to continue. Unfortunately, the lab and all its research records were reduced to ashes by burning people, literally human torches, as they ran wildly about trying desperately to put out the consuming flames that enveloped them.

"Only six out of forty people survived to bear witness to the grisly occurrence. Four had been hired to feed the various animals the scientists were cloning, and two were gardeners. None of these were directly involved in the cloning experiments, but gave unwavering testimony as to what had happened. They claimed that the flames had been so hot, and all devouring, that the victims couldn't even be put out with fire extinguishers!

"The religious coalitions! Jesus Louise! They are totally up in arms, saying that the Aquatus are the spawn of the Devil, and are blaming us for the diminishing attendance in their churches and temples. They are claiming that we, the ones they voted into office for guidance and protection, have conspired with the Aliens to brainwash their flocks.

"One of our more notorious southern religious leaders had me on the phone just yesterday claiming that 'he may have thumped the Bible from time to time in his ministry,' but that the dog-damned Aquatus were out to thump the universe, and that I was helping them to accomplish their evil task."

Clenching his teeth the President muttered, using only his lips, "Just wait until they finally get a load of the rest of the story."

The President had stopped in his discourse to his colleagues, as if to get a second wind. It was quiet in the room as all waited as if entranced for more bad news. Though the room was cool, the President blotted beads of perspiration once more from his upper lip. He then gazed intently at Faraday, who returned the gaze with a forlorn, pale, and vacant stare.

The Chief Executive was about to drop his eyes from those of his director to the documents on the table before him, when Faraday clenched his teeth, bursting the cyanide capsule he had carried in his cheek. Convulsing and gasping, Faraday entered the finality of his life.

The episode with Faraday served to add to the gloom of the situation. Two federal agents had quickly removed him from the room in a futile attempt to get him medical attention.

Despair was thick in the room as tears of sadness streamed down the cheeks of many, including his two closest friends David Hauss and Vincent Henry. Most present had known Faraday for the truly good and honorable man that he had been, caught up in a situation that had simply been beyond human control.

These were the worst of times; they were in the grip of a power from which there could be no salvation, and it posed itself to hurtle the whole of humanity into the endless dark of extinction.

No one would see the tears of their Chief Executive, as he adjourned the meeting for thirty minutes so all could regain their composure. Asking to be left alone during the interlude, he went to the large picture window. Looking outwards he saw nothing but the pane of glass before him. The Chief Executive contemplated, then fought the morbid desire for suicide, as it grew malignant within him.

He knew what Faraday had gone through, and knew intuitively that his personal friend whom he had deeply respected was dead the moment they fished the burst capsule from his mouth. Oh hell, sure Faraday had used a little blackmail to achieve what he felt in his heart to be a benevolent objective, but this was the nature of politics.

He stood by the window, still and quiet for twenty minutes, considering the loss of a genuinely good man, his own failure to serve and protect, and the bleak future of the now tragic human condition.

At the close of this interim the participants were now in the process of reseating themselves. One of the mansion's security staff perplexedly asked to speak to the President. This request was at first denied, but upon learning the gravity of the request, she was ushered immediately over to the front of the assembly.

The message was delivered in haste, whereupon the President, without explanation, instantly followed her and the other two of his security personnel from the room. Within fifteen minutes the President reentered the room followed by two hefty security officers. Quickly but carefully, they rolled a large screen television up to the front of the assembly.

Then, as the instrument was situated and activated, the image of the enemy appeared before the aghast audience. As the President raised his arms, the startled humans lapsed into silence. Previously they had gazed upon the Aquatian with gratitude and admiration, emotions now replaced with trepidation and hatred. Immobile, as if frozen in their seats, eyes riveted with fear upon their cannibalistic conqueror, in dread did they await the knowledge of their fate.

"It was with deep sorrow that we learned of Director Faraday's suicide. He was a heroic man to whom humanity owes a great debt," spoke the alien.

"What right?! What god-damned justification could you and your kind possibly have in making a statement such as that?" inquired the Secretary of Defense, rising to his feet so abruptly that his chair fell over behind him.

The spontaneity of the question, to which all longed for an answer, was quietly allowed. The man who had broached it stood silently awaiting the alien's response.

All in the room became aware that the forthcoming conversation would not be one-sided; special receptors and transmitters, at some point, had been installed in the large televising apparatus; the aliens had prepared for all eventualities.

"Had we Aquatus not taken a hand in human evolution upon your planet, 85 percent of your species would have died from the most horrible of viral diseases within the next hundred years. This would have occurred after the irreversible pollution of your fresh watersheds, atmosphere and oceans. The result? Numerous toxin-related cancerous and mutative illnesses to Earth's humans and the pitifully few of its other remaining animal species.

"Unfortunately and beyond apology, you, the most dominant life force upon this planet, were not able to wisely rule your destiny. Therein lay the inevitable demise of this most precious and beautiful planet.

"Bill Faraday aided us Aquatus, albeit inadvertently, in the saving of Earth. Had we Aquatus been unable to meet with success in the manner in which we did, our next plan would simply have been to hasten human exit from the planet by the introduction of an engineered sterility virus, dependent primarily upon human hosts, into fresh water supplies throughout the world. This was our only alternative, had the benevolent approach failed. We were committed.

"Unfortunately, such a drastic approach would have cleansed many other life forms from the Earth. Undoubtedly all chimpanzee species, as they are your closest relatives on the evolutionary scale, retaining 98 percent of your genes, and a goodly portion of many other beautiful creatures such as monkeys, lemurs, and other primates. Our only desire was to be effective; cruelty is not our way.

"Bill Faraday, along with Professor David Hauss and Mr. Vincent Henry, all good and honorable men, would probably have aided us in our mission, regardless, even if they had known from the beginning all the facts. However, the total knowledge of the Aquatus objective by any human could possibly have ended the mission in disaster, a chance we Aquatus could not have wisely taken. We apologize for that."

"What is all this equivocal bullshit about honorable intent, saving the planet, and Aquatus benevolence? Is it not true that you have clandestinely subjugated our species, rendered us incapable of procreation, and plan occupancy of our planet in the near future? What god-given right do you have to make such a decision? What god-given right do the Aquatus have to carry out such an odious vendetta on ourselves and this planet?" interjected the heatedly disturbed President.

"God-given right?" repeated the Aquatian. "It appears that perhaps you are laboring under the mythical concept that God has given you and your species dominion over the earth, regardless of your indiscretions towards its resources or each other."

Somewhere in space beyond the rings of Saturn the huge, now bright silver Aquatus mothership hung like a diamond in the cold empty blackness. Within this gem of the heavens was a Being with four times the intellectual capacity of the most intelligent human. She contemplated the perhaps-futile possibility of endowing these humans, a species she had grown to love and cherish, with a gift of logic. Her only fear was that they might not be evolved enough to understand. She would try.

"Are there any in this conference who ever asked the question, why are humans predominantly right-handed creatures? This is an attribute that no other animal on earth possesses. Of course there are a minority of left-handed humans who can perform just as well with their left appendage, as do their right-appendage-favoring brothers and sisters, but when this preference becomes stabilized, the human animal will persist in this preference in the vast majority of its manipulations. Why is this the rule?

"A clear choice is made at far too young an age for it to be attributed to the teaching by parents. Clearly this activity is instinctive, albeit an open-ended instinct which can be improved upon with learning and practice, but an instinct nevertheless. Why is this so? Why do young humans, in the vast majority of cases, when dinner is served, eat first the meat on their plates, leaving behind the vegetables?

"How is it that the vast majority of the young intuitively know how to lie, cheat, steal, be selfish and cruel with one another? It most certainly requires a parent or others to teach them fairness and kindness, and hopefully channel antisocial impulses into socially acceptable modes of behavior. Of course most parents naively blame other children and adults for teaching their child how to be bad, but from our observations this is clearly not the case.

"I will try to explain as best I can the true nature of your species, in the hope that you will eventually evolve to understand, for in the understanding of my explanations lies your salvation.

"Humans are the cruelest of animals upon the face of planet Earth, and yet this concept, due to your massive egos, is the most difficult for you humans to realize.

"There is an equally divided camp as to humankind's greatest antecedent invention. Some say it was the wheel while others insist that it was fire. However, of this you may be most certain. As unique and important as these two aspects of human achievement were throughout the ages, it was neither. The very greatest achievements of the human condition upon the face of your planet was the ability to kill at a distance, and the development of a society to utilize this concept to its greatest potential.

"You have failed to heed the evidence of your own fossil records. Numerous are the clues unearthed by your most brilliant anthropologists and archeologists. But when they procured the evidence, together with the skulls and bones of the upright Australopithecines, you denied them as your ancestors. Later, with evidence all-conclusive, humanity grudgingly admitted that these ancestral creatures of the dawn might have used tools.

"It was simply too difficult for humankind to admit that the club, obviously used by human pre-dawn upright ancestors with a brain half the size of current human endowment, was indeed a weapon. A weapon utilized in a right-handed manner against baboons, vicious animals of a most formidable strength and dagger-like teeth.

"The evidence clearly indicated that not only in self-defense did your ancestors bludgeon, maim and murder, but that they were predatory, utilizing these creatures as a food source. Food supplies were hard to come by in those times, but then, as has been evident down through the ages, humans survived the hard times, while numerous others became extinct.

"Humans are omnivorous much like your often maligned cousin the chimpanzee who has been known to hunt in social groups as well, I might add, meaning that you can subsist on vegetation as well as meat, preferably a combination of the two. Your species is very unlike the constantly eating vegetarians of your planet.

"At the dawn of humankind it was the weapon that made the day. A club with which to bludgeon or well-aimed projectiles from a social group provided an awesome defense. Precious meat could be more easily obtained. Such a windfall it was. For with a belly full of meat, condensed energy if you will, there was ample time to travel further, following the game, plotting your next kill.

"Many of your species have become vegetarians out of choice, and wise as this may be, it is an unintentional wisdom. Hormones and toxins contaminate much of the meat you now consume, pollution caused by yourselves, not normally occurring in nature. These substances, prevalent in domestic herbivores, have been placed there by your species with the intent to enhance bulking of muscle tissues. Hence, the animals gain more weight per quantity of vegetation consumed.

"Domestic herbivores, and their wild companions as well, are constantly consuming large quantities of human-made toxins in vegetation and water. This extensive consumption results in the condensation of these toxins into the animal tissues. Thereafter humans and other top carnivores ingest the bulk of these toxic substances, which accumulate most massively within their tissues. Hence the dire consequences which have, and will again if left unchecked, result in emotional illnesses, cancerous illnesses and numerous other health problems within your species.

"The survival fallacy of the vegetarian diet is found in the realization that outside current society, forming a gathering society of human vegetarian individuals, it is most likely that strictly vegetarian humans would soon perish. They could not survive the hard times without resorting to the consumption of meat.

"There are those who shun meat for benevolent, rather than health reasons, not wishing to harm living creatures. However, animal products such as milk, cheese or eggs should be eaten from time to time, to retain good health. Hopefully they are free of toxins. Also I will add that rare is the case wherein the vegetarian is more intelligent then the predator. I can assure you that there is no shame in being the Hawk rather than the Rabbit, or the Lion rather than the Zebra. You simply are what you are, and this you must also learn to accept.

"Your ancestors may well have been in a Garden of Eden, in those Miocene times, when they lived in the trees, consuming primarily insects and vegetation. However, upon your descent from this aerial abode, out of necessity or adventure, it was the weapon that carried the day. Without the sharp implement in your hand, replacing the daggers you lacked in your mouth, without the club in your hand to replace the claws you lacked in your hands and feet, you were and would have continued to be an easy catch for even the slowest of ground-dwelling predators.

"Before the weapon, your ancestors of the dawn must have died hideous deaths from predation. From starvation they must have died in piles during those hardest of times. But with the advent of weaponry, and its social use, humankind never looked back in its passion for the implements by which it had inherited the earth. There has never been a Dark Age upon the earth for weapons.

"Oh, yes! The proportionately numerous antelope humerus and jawbones found with the fossilized remains of human ancestry were indeed tools in the art of killing. The humerus bones were used as clubs and the jawbones, with razor-sharp teeth still intact, were used to butcher the beasts upon which they fed. So prolific were your ancestors in their slaughter through preferential digit and appendage use, that the genetic endowment of the opposable thumb, so as to best grasp a weapon, and right-handedness, became embedded in human genetic codes and was passed on to future generations up to the present.

"Humanity has bludgeoned, thrown, and shot its way to supremacy over all others of Earth's life forms. Now, in your hour of power, a time in your evolution wherein humanity can bring about the extinction of even the most savage of beasts, you miss the hunt. You miss even the possibility of being hunted.  You create monsters, evil aliens, huge, impossibly mutated insects, and humans turned vampires that drink blood.  Many are the humans who consider this frightening, as it satisfies an innate need to experience fear. Do you think that the meat in your markets simply drops from the sky?  Humanity the world over, with relish, naively consumes whole carcasses of animals, millions of tons of animal flesh daily.  It seems that the vast majority of your populations are completely unaware of the fear, pain and suffering of these animals which go into making meat for human consumption possible.

"'Scare me, I love it!' say your theater buffs. 'If there is no shooting, killing, raping, or pillaging, I will not buy the ticket to go see it!'  Mostly it is simply the vivid imagination of someone transferred to film, feeding upon carnal human desires.  Carefully analyze humor, and there will you soon find what caused the laughter--in most cases none other than the sad misfortune of another.

"Look not to the other animals of your planet for the most vicious among them, look to yourselves.  For within yourselves will you find the most cruel and vicious of beasts.

"You have asked what God-given right we Aquatus have to make the decisions we did regarding your planet.  Well now, we Aquatus presume the same right as you yourselves have presumed regarding the other animals upon your planet, and each other as well--the right of supremacy.  Do we need any other?

"We could have lasered your populations for the sport of it thousands of years ago when we first found your planet, much as your ancestors did when you murdered into near extinction with your rifles the great herds of buffalo which once inhabited your wild grasslands fewer than a hundred and fifty years ago.  Skinning them for only their hides, sometimes extracting the tongue as a delicacy, you left the rest to rot.

"This proved to be a double bonus of massive cruelty well calculated, as the European immigrants by design starved the native peoples of the Great Plains into submission as well. The buffalo had been their chief food supply. The cruel quasi-justification at that time was that the imported customs and religion of the immigrants were not the same as those of the natives. Those original inhabitants of the North American Continent were prejudged not human, therefore deserving of their fate against greater weapon superiority.

"Rare was the treaty thereafter made with these peoples that was not broken. Even today, great pressure is brought upon these Native Americans regarding their reservations.

"However, the Aquatus evolution upon Trepleon was much like your own, and we, not unlike yourselves, have been as cruel to each other as we were to the less intelligent life forms upon our own planet. The moral difference between us now is that we Aquatus know what we are. Humankind has refused to accept the evil within themselves. In ignorance, your masses are led into ever-deepening degrees of cruelty.

"Falsity does not become truth simply because an intelligent creature wishes it to become so.

"We Aquatus have indulged ourselves and are not innocent of foolish wishful thinking in our attempt to form utopian governments early on in our own evolution.

"The survival capacity of any intelligent social species depends upon the correct analytical steps regarding their beliefs. You as well as we Aquatus must continually review our social framework in the light of the most current evidence regarding our biological and genetic composition. Coddling a false belief in the pursuit of an unattainable goal, often as not, can only end in unhappiness or, worse, disaster.

"Upon your planet, over two hundred years ago, lived a unique individual who was brilliant in deluding others by professing beliefs which most of your species, for the sake of ego enhancement, wanted to hear. His name was Jean Jacques Rousseau. Unfortunately and most regrettably, he had not your current investigations into the truer aspects of animal behavior to draw upon.

"Rousseau professed that humankind was essentially born good, later to be corrupted by the influence of society. We Aquatus have fallen into this beguiling trap from time to time down through the ages. We, as well as you, wished to believe that we were fallen angels, corrupted by those among whom we had fallen, believing that if we could just get it politically right, we would once more achieve our heavenly grace, even though we may inhabit a physical form.

"The survival of us Aquatus, and humankind as well, depends upon coming to grips with the reality that it was, and is, the predisposition for violence and subjugation of others, within ourselves, which must be channeled into socially acceptable behavior. Therein can we realize that we are a mixture of both base and benevolent potential. The predisposition for good and evil is cemented into our genetic codes and there they must stay, for we cannot evolve intellectually without them.

"Let not the desire for ego enhancement lead you down the dark path to extinction.

"That Jean Jacques Rousseau was a genuine intellectual is a given. That he spoke against the tyranny of the times is indeed commendable. That he passionately professed a natural goodness in humankind was only a half-truth, but in full truth was lamentable. Future generations would be led to believe that limitless perfection, within the human condition, could be had by the removal of private property, and the subjugation of the individual to a supreme central government.

"The glaring truth on your world can be found in the butchery of millions of innocents by Joseph Stalin in the Union of Soviet Socialist Republics. The almost two million who lost their lives in the Socialist Republic of Cambodia during Pol Pot's reign. The millions upon millions who paid the final price for property ownership in the Socialist Republics of China, as well as the thousands in Vietnam, as those countries turned upon their own people. The obvious truth is simply that no totally socialist government can exist without tyranny, and even with tyranny with which to oppress its peoples, it soon proves productively ineffectual.

"The end result of this naive cruelty was even more massive hardships for their masses and the concentration of what little luxury which was left into the selfish hands of their totalitarian leaders. One can only imagine the abject despondency of those many humans who awoke one day to find that they had traded the pan for the fire; they had been governed poorly to begin with.

"What we Aquatus observed as a tragic occurrence during Earth's post World War II era was when the United States of America went into Vietnam in an attempt to control what it felt to be a potential threat against its people. It is most unfortunate that the leaders of your great country had so little faith in the integral strength of their own government. Rueful indeed that they would feel threatened by other governments built upon the shaky foundations that only socialism could provide.

"We Aquatus beseech humanity to put aside the romantic assumption that all are born naturally happy and good, and that should you fail to remain so, it is the fault of society. Humans could never have gained dominion over planet Earth had it not been for society.

"Do not discontinue to search for noble means to make it better, but please do it in the light of your current scientific evidence.

"The more numerous your populations become, the greater becomes the environmental stress. Hence, greater becomes the evil towards each other, human life becoming cheap not unlike any commodity that becomes abundant. Of course the other living creatures with whom you share the planet would have been the innocent recipients of the toxic filth you would have continued to pump into your atmosphere and waters, had we not intervened.

"Fortunately for you, we Aquatus have come to realize that humans have as great a capacity for benevolence as you do for cruelty. Most of your savagery stems from ignorance rather than intent. We have great hopes that you will take the gifts which we have bestowed upon you to enhance your benevolence. May humanity evolve to understand the darker aspects of its genetic makeup.

"We have saved you from killing your planet, and now you can learn its secrets."

About as happy as a man who had been told he didn't need surgery for his hemorrhoids, the Chief of State rose from his chair to confront his not yet vindicated mentor.

"If you are still insistent that the Aquatus intent regarding Earth is benevolent, could you explain the horrible, well-documented occurrence our agents experienced when they went in search of your missing medical equipment?"

The characteristic coy smile that all had previously known as Jayseeka's trademark had not once appeared upon her features during the exchange. The pint-sized conqueror was still sternly intent, commanding the nearly paralyzed attention of her human audience.

"It is regrettable to us that we would lose two of the most heroic of our staff in the incidents that took place within that cave. I can assure you that they meant no harm to your agents or the two poor peasants that had been cruelly tortured by Piolet and his guards. We do not regret in the least the dispatching of Piolet and his henchmen. If you have the documentation of which you speak, then you know them as the truly evil entities which they were."

The President stiffened as he shot a glance at the image on the screen before him. "What of the dismembering of those men and the human tissues found in the stomach of one of your staff?" he asked. The words came out in an unusually higher pitch; extreme was his anxiety.

"Strange that humans, the animals that have eaten all other animals, including snails and themselves from time to time, would consider it so horrifying that another species might find humans to be appetizing. I suppose that none of you were aware of the culinary humor that proliferated in the Asian news media when the advent of my friend Xenophonzia, the giant squid, became known to them?

"Hopefully you can shake off your reproach regarding the knowledge that we find humans, when properly prepared, to be as tasty to us as you find pork to be unto yourselves. Of course we eat raw flesh from time to time, much in the same way your species consumes sushi or steak tartare.

"We do not find your agents to have acted inappropriately, regarding the two of my staff who were killed in the cave. Your men could not have known they were in no danger. However we would appreciate the cremation of the remains of our colleague and the sprinkling of the ashes into one of your great oceans. She would have wanted this as she so loved your planet, severing all family ties in the study of it."

"Do the Aquatus intend to utilize us as a food source at some future date?" asked the Secretary of Defense.

"Absolutely not," responded the Aquatian. "The only reason I can fathom for my staff's preparation of Piolet and his men for consumption is that they were totally useless for any benevolent purpose. My staff wished not to waste their only redeeming value."

"What of the blood in the canisters which were found?" asked the President.

"Blood makes excellent bouillon, as you may inquire of any chef. Humans procure it from their many supermarkets in the form of small cubes, which they use to flavor stews or make soups. This is blood that has been dried and seasoned, of course. Generally it is of bovine or poultry origin. However in South America a fine sausage is made with pig's blood-- 'chorizo,' I believe they call it."

"You Aquatus, with intent and malice, have sterilized the vast majority of the human species. What was that all about?" asked the President.

"Human populations have risen at an alarming rate upon the face of your planet, so much so that nuclear and biological warfare, or viral plagues on the grandest scale yet imagined by yourselves, were soon to become inevitable. It is unfortunate for humankind that you often ignore the warnings of the more enlightened of your men and women of science.

"When it came to the breakthroughs in ecology, you virtually ignored the studies which proved conclusively that in dense animal populations it is seldom the lack of food that wipes out the numbers, but plagues or stress. Perhaps it is because many humans are vested in numerous business and real estate ventures and have tied those futures to an ever-expanding population base.

"By negligently desecrating the environment with burgeoning numbers, humanity nearly wiped out the ancient rain-forests of your planet. Unwittingly you have uncovered numerous ancient viruses. These tiny, most ancient inheritors of life upon your planet had posed themselves, ready to painfully and cruelly obliterate your entire species. It was only a matter of time that a 'hot' virus, which we ourselves would have been unable to stop, would have moved through your dense numbers with the ease of a flu virus.

"Most humans would have died cruel, painful deaths, while the remaining of your species would have been deformed, crippled or mutated in the most pitiful manner, unimagined in your darkest nightmares.

"We hope we are not too late in our decision. Your pollution of the environment, to the best of our calculations, is not irreversible, but within another seventy years of unrestricted population growth your environment would have been devastated. Of course, that would have been the case, had viral or nuclear holocaust not stolen the day."

The Trepleonian Ambassador then informed Earth as to the outcome of the human sterilization process, to which it had been subjected. She knew this to be uppermost in their minds, aside from being considered as a food source that is.

"When all of Earth's contemporary human populations have lived out their unusually long and healthy lives, due to the benefits they acquired from having journeyed through our medical devices, their procreative potential will be only approximately three percent. What this means is that Earth's human population numbers will have dropped, overall, to approximately two hundred and ten million people.

"These robustly healthy and industrious numbers of human populations will be a little less than half of what it was in the year 1350 AD, after Europe and Asia had been decimated once more by an epidemic known as the Bubonic Plague or The Black Death.

"These three percent of Earth's remaining human inhabitants will revert to previous reproductive capabilities. We Aquatus sincerely hope that at this future golden time you will have come to realize that all your current concerns --acquisition of territory, pollution, security, and the survival of your beautiful planet's flora and fauna--could easily have been resolved, had humankind put more effort into various satisfactory means of birth control research, rather than amassing atomic arsenals upon your planet.

"The Aquatus activities on Earth were and are intentional; however, it is not out of malice that we have intervened, but more out of compassion."

"The disarmament of our nuclear capability--did you also find this to be necessary?" inquired the Secretary of Defense.

"Rest assured that it would have been of little use to you against our overwhelming technology. We merely took that from you much in the same way as a parent would remove a loaded gun from the hands of an eight year old child."

All finally saw the faintest of smiles now play upon the beautifully formed lips of the alien.

"Nuclear capability was a danger only unto yourselves and your planet."

"What about the spontaneous combustion of prisoners, and others outside our prisons, in their homes and places of work? Do you also acknowledge this as Aquatus benevolence?" inquired the Secretary of the Interior.

"Upon the passage of most of your species through our medical devices, we were able to diagnose the vast difference between mental illness and incarnate evil. Our medical equipment, in constant contact with, and routed into our most sophisticated computers aboard our mothership could peer into the most hidden crevices of the human mind.

"Those men and women who combusted at our discretion were either currently involved in or soon would be active in the cruelest of mayhem and torture. Much of it would have gone unchecked, owing to the enhanced intelligence bequeathed to these evil ones by our medical apparatuses. Had we allowed these enhanced evil ones to live, it would have been a cruel injustice to the innocent.

"The infamous Piolet and his henchmen were scheduled to incinerate within the week, had he not met his demise at the discretion of the two of my staff.

"By the way, we always knew where our medical device was, and we were in the process of recovering it when my staff encountered Piolet and his henchmen. Most unfortunately, they were encountered in turn by your agents."

"And the incineration of the Institute of Genetics and Cloning? Did that transpire at the discretion of the Aquatus as well?"

The physique of the Aquatian suddenly began to take on a silvery aspect, as the faint smile that had recently appeared upon her exemplary lips suddenly vanished. It was replaced with a look of great sadness.

Jayseeka's voice conveyed the greatest of sorrow when, after a full minute of silence before regaining her composure, she answered, "Your scientists at I.G.C. were brilliant in their field, but they worked as if their hearts had been made of stone. The human embryos that they had successfully cloned were subjected to the most heinous of experiments in order to observe the effects of various toxic chemicals and drugs upon them.

"Many of these innocent, yet-to-be-born children had been placed in body temperature saline solution in glass containers. Therein they could be observed fighting their futile battles against the poisons introduced by the scientists into their small glass prisons. On numerous occasions these little ones were kept alive within the cylinders, for as long as seven months. All the while, nutrients, laced with various contaminants, were fed to them through their still-intact placentas.

"Finally, these 'Dr. Mengeles,' with their curiosity satisfied, and fearing discovery by others, simply cut off the nutrients. By doing so, they were able to observe the effects of starvation on their most tragic and pathetically sick little experiments.

"That a group of this many humans could rationally believe that human-cloned tissues were somehow inhuman amazed even us Aquatus. With heartfelt sadness did we observed the darker side of humanity when empowered by moral ignorance."

The ashen faces of even the toughest men in the room were tinged with green as they imagined the experiments done by the men and women at I.G.C. All looked to their Chief Executive for a denial; it was not forthcoming. They then knew by his silence that what the Aquatian had spoken, had sadly been the truth.

Adding to the information, Jayseeka informed her now more enlightened audience, "Upon the demise of all those who have received the benefits of our medical devices, those of your species remaining will find that their third generation of offspring will possess tissues capable of being cloned. We Aquatus sincerely hope that your scientists in those days will be of a greater moral stature.

"Another aspect of humans rejuvenated in our medical devices may not sit well with many of your religious community. It seems that many of them are of the belief that at some future date their deity will return to earth, and that the dead of their particular religious conviction will rise up from their graves. We find this a very unlikely event; nevertheless the methods of preserving these dead individuals in air-tight non-biodegradable containers, and the use of toxic materials such as the poisonous formaldehyde in the embalming process, are no longer options. The only method advised in the disposition of the deceased is that they be cremated or simply placed in some type of a biodegradable container and placed into the earth or dropped into the ocean. Any other method will result in spontaneous combustion or explosions.

"Let the wisdom of the words, 'From dust thou cometh, to dust thou shalt return,' suffice. This is truly the most desirable reality of all living creatures, that they should recycle their nutrients back into the environments from which their physical bodies came."

"Have all of your species now left Earth? If so, when will you return?" asked the now subdued Chief Executive.

"We are currently in orbit around a planet in your solar system known to you as Saturn. From here we intend to return to our home world; our mission to Earth is completed. Should we return to your planet in the future, it will be in much in the same way as it was previously, and it is highly unlikely that humans will be aware of our visitations. Yes, we will continue to do close-up studies of the condition of Earth's flora and fauna."

"Your physical appearance is totally unlike the two of your staff we encountered in South America. Why is this so?"

"My second-in-command and I of 'Mission Earth' were altered by cosmetic surgery so as to facilitate human cooperation with our objectives. We apologize for the deception. We consented to our 'disfigurement' for your sakes, as we knew our normal appearance would be upsetting to you, and we wished for your transition to transpire as smoothly as possible.

"It may come as a surprise to you that we have developed a strong bond of affection with your species, love, if you will, much like that which many humans develop toward dissimilar life forms upon your planet, and which they in turn develop towards yourselves."

The human-Aquatus dialogue continued for another hour, until Jayseeka ended the proceedings by wishing all of humanity the best in their pursuit of happiness. Her final words of wisdom were, "For wherein lies the purpose of any objective, save it bring some measure of joy in its pursuit, or in its achievement?"

Smiling, she waved her golden arm in farewell, her radiant image fading from the screen.

The fully recorded and documented discourse between the Aquatus and humans had also been observed first-hand by other nations' leaders. They had watched spellbound the dialogue that had taken place in Washington, D.C.

The Aquatus had indeed planned for all eventualities, as all other of the world's leaders had been, unbeknownst to the assembly in the White House, tuned in from the beginning. All nations could interpret the dialogue in any manner they chose, as it had been beamed to them in their own language with English subtitles.

Many would have liked to have been present at the meeting to ask their own particular questions. However there would be absolutely no disputing the questions asked, nor the answers given by the Ambassador from Trepleon on that historic day. No secrets, no suppositions--the interpretation of the dialogue would be left up to the discretion of all humanity, regardless of race, creed or culture.

## Chapter Twenty-Four

Of small perfect stature, gracious image of Gold,
From a faraway world came She.
Across cold empty space, at incredible pace,
Bearing gifts for chimerical Humanity.
Why did she do it?  Why would she try?
Why would she care about us?
She could have ended our sojourn on this Planet,
In the short time twixt dawn and the dusk.
With astounding compassion! With astonishing kindness!
Our Emancipation her primary desire,
Altruistic denouement; Earth reaps the blessings,
Safe from disease, and the fire!

*(Song of Jayseeka:*
*Composed in the year 12 A.J. by Roxanne Henry.)*

Roxanne Henry was in her 90th year of life when she wrote her memoirs, after nearly 65 years of refusing to do so. She had not wanted others to respond to her in any way other than they would normally have responded to any student of an enlightened teacher.

The alien Jayseeka and her teachings had been a profound occurrence in the life of Roxanne Henry.  Aside from a love affair or two, she would devote her remaining years in the study of the Aquatus religion, their government, and the ongoing results of their mission to Earth.

So dedicated was Roxanne in these endeavors that in the writing of her memoirs she fixed historical events as "A.J." signifying "After Jayseeka" or "E.T.J." indicating "Earlier Than Jayseeka." She was quite surprised when the entirety of her fellow travelers, in the various meditation retreats throughout the world, also utilized this method of time calculation.

These centers of higher education had even improved upon the previous traditional calendars by creating one that divided the year into 12 months of 30 days each, inclusive of another space of time called "Fifth-space." It was determined that "Fifth space" would consist of five additional days, each augmented to include an additional one hour, ten minutes and 2.4 seconds, hence compensating in a more exact manner for the true solar year. "Fifth Space" later became the most devout of times for students of the Aquatus theosophy. That special time of the year was spent in intense meditation, special meals, study, and a most congenial togetherness between the many Sister-Brotherhoods that had grown out of the theology.

The Aquatus had left behind a message of clarity regarding their beliefs, but had left no ultimatums, though there were those who insisted down through the years that the inhabitants of Trepleon were continuously looking on. Also, they professed that if humankind did not meet with Aquatus moral standards, they would most surely return with a vengeance, looking upon humans in this future time strictly as a food source. But then, this was the same type of controlling mentality that had so often used other theologies in the past to move the masses, and had absolutely nothing to do with what the Aquatus intended or believed.

Sixty-five years had passed, and humanity had been successful in terraforming and colonizing various valleys of the planet Mars and productively mining its rare elements.

Soon these materials would be used to build interstellar spacecraft. Sixty-five years earlier, few were the visionaries to see these goals as realistic, not to mention productive, but then a mere 108 years prior to that, few were those who envisioned humans in flight.

Humanity was now perched upon the brink of interstellar travel, and though they had not yet built an engine as sophisticated as the Aquatus space-drives, the engines they had built could propel a ship at more than three times the speed of light. Humankind was diligently working towards, and would soon arrive at, a time when the crafts propelled by these mighty engines would hold together under the stress generated at these fantastic speeds.

The latest calculations as to Earth's human population decrease indicated that the Aquatus had been exactly correct as to numbers. Also indicated was that the children born to those who had passed through the "Lazarus machines" had suffered no genetic defects. In fact they seemed to be, percentage-wise, of far better health and intelligence than those children born in pre-Aquatus times.

Population statistics were carefully tallied, and strangely enough it became apparent that the dense pre-Aquatus populations were more out of error than design. Those who wished not to be burdened with children now had numerous drug-free methods by which to avoid unwanted pregnancies, and few were the families with more than two children. The miserable poor that lived in pre-Aquatus times, who had had numerous children in hopes that some would live to support them in their old age, no longer existed.

Calculations were checked and rechecked with increasingly more sophisticated medical and computer development. Results clearly indicated that the few offspring of those who had taken advantage of the Aquatus medical devices, would consistently prove to be just as, if not more, fertile than their pre-Aquatus predecessors.

Humankind's greatest heritage was no longer the material things for which many wars had been fought. In these latter times nations would be esteemed by the number of healthy, happy and intelligent children with which they had been blessed.

Real estate had been a bad investment for more than 30 years and would continue to be so for quite a long time to come. Every family had a house, and all but a very few lived in extravagant comfort. More than 75 percent of all farmland had begun to return to its natural state; fence lines were either torn down or rotted away. The buffalo, bears, and wolf packs were proliferating, along with other wildlife that had inhabited these expansive areas prior to the advent of dense human populations, and what had been called Manifest Destiny.

Northern and southern rain forests were now completely free from human intervention, and were rapidly healing themselves, returning once more to their original pristine states.

A small portion of the remaining original inhabitants of northern America had actually gone back to what they had determined as their "ancestors' society." They became hunters and gatherers six months out of the year, returning to populated areas the remaining six months for medical needs and educational materials for their children.

There were standing agreements between Nations that the world populations would never exceed 900 million, and all agreed that this was a practicality that had previously eluded humankind. As time went productively by, it was considered an almost immoral act for any family to have more than three children. Two children were plenty, if the children were to receive the necessary attention and education they deserved and required.

The vast majority of now healthy, happy humans eventually would be well educated in some type of specialty trade or profession. With the invention of various memory and creativity enhancement methods, learning became a pleasure for all, rather than a chore. Upon entering the workplace, it was rare that even the most unskilled laborer worked more than a five-hour day; there was simply no need to do so. More time with family and friends and the pursuit of personal interests became the rule.

Humankind was being catapulted into the security of self that had heretofore been for the most part elusive. It would not be communistically oriented societies that would win the hearts of humanity, but societies wherein if one worked to obtain a goal, be it wealth, private property or whatever, that item of his or her endeavor would become that individual's personal possession. If persons decided to share their property with others, then that was their choice, and not that of the government under which they lived.

No more would it be in the better interest of any government to tax under the guise of benevolence and then spend the money on Pork Barrel projects; there would only be specific taxes for specific purposes. Only those persons upon whom a tax was levied were allowed to vote on its passage into law, and these persons could also annul a tax if they so voted.

The politics of government finally fell to those who acted from patriotic motives. There was absolutely no reason to pursue political positions for ego enhancement, power quest, or wealth as many control freaks had done in the past. All holders of government jobs were obliged to take polygraph tests at least once a year, honorable intent and excellent mental health being top priorities. Juries were randomly computer-selected from the populations at large to judge the moral character of their leaders.

All governments which practiced despotism and subjugation soon found themselves without a people to govern. Their unhappy inhabitants gradually slipped away to build new lives in just about any other country of their choice. Everyone knew that if they chose relocation to a new country, they would be both joyously received and dutifully assisted in their endeavors. Nations vied in all ways save warfare to gain skilled inhabitants; fair and honorable government was a given.

Orphanages had ceased to exist, and although children were doted upon, none were overindulged. Parents were obliged to earn the respect of their children. Soon they realized that the respect of children towards their elders was not automatic, nor was it a God-given right. "Do as I say and not as I do" was no longer an option. Many were the aunt, uncle, or grandparent waiting in the wings to accept the upbringing of any child. Parents would consider in depth their reflection in the eyes of their children.

Contemporary psychiatrists had long realized that children who were respectful towards parents and adults had only minor problems in school and interacted well with their peers. One could honestly say that children had an innate need to be respectful to parents and other adults; they simply got along well with each other when the home front was secure.

There were certain basic educational requirements that all children were required to master for grade school, high school and college. However, once each year, for a three-week period of time, all students attended what were known as Exploratory Development Classes, or "E.D.C." Locations for this exploratory research were held in areas of natural beauty, generally in mountain retreats.

In these classes, which only comprised four hours each day for four days of the week, the children underwent investigation as to what it was in the realm of knowledge that they found to be of the most interest. It finally had become apparent that children, who would eventually enter the work place as adults, accomplished best those pursuits that intrigued them most, regardless of what their parents thought. Children without stress laid on them were allowed to choose their own calling, and if they felt later that they had made an incorrect choice, they would simply return to school to learn a new profession.

In the well-funded E.D.C. retreats, should any child show more interest in one specialty than another, be it music, math, life science, art or whatever, they would be granted any and all assistance that would lead to the greatest development of expertise in that field. The potential for greatness of any country had always lain in the minds of its youth.

Within the mind of any human there will always be at least one area in which she or he may excel, one area whereby his or her family and/or country will be most enriched. No individual was ever forced to work, but if they chose not to be a productive individual, it was best that they have a friend or relative to support them. Long gone were the days of easy government dole, and only productive individuals who had a job, a house, or some other type of property were permitted to vote.

Psychology was finally on its way to becoming a real science. Great strides had come with the understanding that a human, rather than just being a blank slate at birth, later to become only the accumulation of the social imprint to which it was subjected, was actually an instinctive animal--perhaps "open-endedly instinctive," but instinctive nevertheless.

The profundity of the words of Charles Dickens, "It was the best of times, it was the worst of times," had been realized by many during the past wars upon the planet Earth. A most vivid example would be the English people during Earth's World War II.

England had been at war with Germany long enough to develop an intense hatred and fear of their adversary--fear of espionage, fear of being pounded with the infamous V-2 rockets, and constant fear of invasion. With the whole of England, family and loved ones in constant danger, most assuredly these days of enmity were The Worst Of Times.

From the onset of the believable possibility of invasion, the English people sacrificed for one another, working tirelessly and unceasingly together as if a single unit, for the good of the nation. They behaved the same even to strangers, comforting one another in that most frightening environment. But there, in those times of terror, would awaken the instinct of amity, creating the deepest of respects, friendships, and loves, more profound than any occurring during years of peace.

The amity instinct pervaded even the most self-serving of individuals and these were undoubtedly The Best Of Times. Upon closer investigation into and understanding of this latent amity-enmity instinct, it was easier to understand the reasons why many individuals became so engrossed in various social sports. Unconsciously perhaps, but most assuredly, it was a sublimation of the need for warfare and identity, as they projected themselves into their favorite player and team.

Humankind became aware that if you took away the violence, guns, blood, and depiction of cruelty from the theater, and asked what remains? The answer would be "a movie that not many wish to see." No good person, no bad guy or girl, no hero to project themselves into? The majority of humankind would rather stay home and eat. Due care not to erase the latent amity-enmity instinct from the human genetic code had been taken by the Aquatus. Mankind needed it desperately; to remove it from their genes would be to remove motivation as well. The removal of motivation would have brought about the dwindling away of humanity, as it headed down the self-imposed road to extinction as the animal that just didn't give a damn.

The instinctive need to search for emotional stimulation, as opposed to boredom, was also found to be an integral aspect of an emotionally happier, healthier, human psyche. Humankind, through research, would prove to be territorial creatures and would continue to be so in the future. Personal property, which strengthened identity, would prove to be an innate need. The failure of past collective societies to prosper, or be held together under any but the most tyrannical of governments, was a very good indication of the evil inherent within them. Oh yes, those socialistic idealistic societies had been attempted with the most benevolent of intentions.

Religious communities could often prosper under collective conditions, as they had a central benevolent theology that held them together which all as individuals could accept. But never did tyranny or threats of eternal damnation enforce the rules. All individuals within these groups had the choice of accepting these rules, or they were free to leave the community, choosing another more to their liking.

Charitable benevolence had become the prerogative of religious communities, never again to become the business of governments.

Nearly all but the most emotionally disturbed could find that aspect within themselves which would make them unique among their fellow humans. The need for self-identity could be fulfilled in a socially acceptable manner. Few would suffer from anonymity as in the past.

The old analogy that "leaders are made and not born" would prove to be a fallacy. The reality was that nonleadership types of individuals could learn leadership, but that leaders were indeed "born" and could increase their predisposition for leadership through education. Humankind could at last live within the security of knowledgeable leaders. The anxiety of the past created by unskilled leaders, which had often led humankind down dark paths of despair, became a rarity.

**********

To be eulogized by others, or the enhancement of her ego through titles or wealth, had never been of any importance to Roxanne Henry. The ignorance regarding her personal, though otherworldly friend, Jayseeka, and the message of compassion she had brought to Earth, however, was. For this reason only she would deliver to humanity her personal understanding of the world-shaking events which happened in that most profound phase of her life more than 65 years earlier. Roxanne would publish her memoirs of these events and the manner in which she perceived their aftermath.

Roxanne had borne a son in the 29th year of her life, and she had often looked upon him with a tinge of sadness. She knew that the blessings of her passage through the Lazarus Machine would in all possibility extend her life beyond his. Her son's pleadings were the final encouragement for Roxanne to decide to publish.

Centers for the purpose of meditation and the study of the religious and moral beliefs of the Aquatus had become established by The World Continuity of Compassion, a strictly non-profit charitable organization. The well-defined bylaws of the association, abbreviated T.W.C.C., adamantly proclaimed the adherence to all governing laws of the state or country in which they were located. Should the laws of the land be prohibitive regarding their activities, they would simply move from that area, reestablishing themselves under more favorable circumstances.

Exodus from any country simply because of religion, providing the beliefs did not injure the believers, others, or the environment, was not desired by any nation in these latter times. Labor shortages abounded throughout the world.

T.W.C.C. refused any government assistance or intervention in their affairs. Their self-contained sanctuaries were open to all interested or in need.

On the first day of her 90th year, Roxanne Henry prepared her writings about what she felt to have been the intent of the Aquatus and their visitation to planet Earth. She had done this on many previous occasions; however, this time it would be recorded for posterity, later to be published. Her lectures at the various T.W.C.C. centers, along with other essays by her, were released under the title, "Aquatus?   None Need Fear."

The Center of the Priceless Gem had originally been the Vincent Henry Estate, and had been the first institution set up by T.W.C.C. The monks and nuns of the institution later wrote precise exacting records from recordings of what the Aquatus had taught. These teachings, together with Roxanne Henry's many lectures and memoirs were transcribed onto thin sheets of gold. These sacred inscriptions in turn were made available for all to view within all the T.W.C.C. centers.

Additionally, duplicated documents were in later years translated into the language of the land and buried with reverence, deep within the concrete foundations of the many new institutions as they were built. Upon the silver sheets were transcribed the constitutional laws, very similar to those of the United States constitution, which governed the two worlds of the Aquatus.

Upon the gold sheets were transcribed their religious

beliefs.  This practice was initiated because of the Aquatus philosophy in which they believed: "Laws passed by governments were only the shells of morality, but a truly good person, open-minded and open-hearted, was the seed." Was it not true that if all men and women were good, there would be no need for law?  The Aquatus had inferred on many occasions that it was only by recognizing the dual nature of good and evil within the human condition, indeed within the individual, that true morality could be found.  Therefore they deemed the pursuit of benevolence and the understanding of the self to be the most valuable of endeavors.

Roxanne Henry had become a very private person, having given her entire inheritance to T.W.C.C.  Most of her time she spent in the study of the social activities of various winged and furry creatures throughout the world, coupled with extended periods of meditation in search of The Unthinkable.

The honor of Roxanne's presence in the assembly was known only by the senior abbot.  Had it been common knowledge she would be speaking to the assembly, the institution would not have been able to accommodate the crowds that would have flocked to see and hear her.  Her presence at any of the institutions was a rare occurrence.

It was 6:00 a.m. on a Saturday.  After an hour of quiet meditation, Roxanne Henry ascended the platform in preparation to deliver her understanding of the Aquatus visitation to Earth.  The sixty-three delighted monks and nuns contemplated their good fortune.

Roxanne arranged her robes, seating herself with quiet comfort upon the cushion in the chair of discourse.  She prepared for her delivery to the assembly.  She smiled radiantly into the audience, totally secure within her person.  All who looked upon her would proclaim the obvious: she was one who had ascended beyond the common thoughts and cares of the mundane world.

"Let it suffice that the growth of a child, from a single cell upon its conception, to become an organism comprised of trillions of cells upon its birth nine months later, upon a planet within one of the countless galaxies in the cosmos, is an event miraculous and fully beyond our complete understanding. I was not a virgin upon giving birth to my son, as has been rumored."

Muffled laughter could be heard from various locations throughout the assembly.

From his seat in the back of the meditation hall, her son glanced upwards to his mother with a foolish grin on his face, then back to the recording device which he was operating.

"From beginningless time there has been but a single Entity from which all things have derived, be they Great or Small, Infamous or Sublime, Empty or Full, Hot or Cold, Visible or Unseen, Solid or Soft, Known or Unknown. For matters of simplicity we may label it the Ultimate Principle. However, this is for convenience only, as this essence of all things, this Totality, is immeasurable and beyond the capacity of any mind to define; therefore, any label used will suffice. No mistake can be made, whatever It is called.

"We, indeed all things, are derived from this Ultimate Source. Within us it dwells, and we are never apart from it.

"Is this Ultimate Principle aware of each starling that falls? Indeed it is. For It is that very creature, and all others as well. Omnipresent, you cannot escape It, for It will be with you throughout beginningless/endless time.

"Are you loved by the Ultimate? Let it suffice to say that you have always been, and always will be loved. All living things are cherished by the Ultimate with a compassion immensely beyond the experience of any living creature to know, for It is indeed That from which all compassion has arisen.

"Those of a religious nature will, often as not, adopt the religious views of their parents or the societies of peoples from which they sprang. Though many of these beliefs are preposterous beyond reason, they fear to relinquish them. These individuals fear becoming outcasts from the fellowship they came to know in their formative years. Many are those who fear being cast into torment for eternity. This foolishness their theologies proclaim to the believers in their doctrines.

"Let me ask you this. Wherein do the souls now dwell of the many millions of humans that existed upon the earth prior to the advent of any formalized religion? Perhaps it is because of a failure to perceive that the beliefs of numerous individuals can be incorrect. For instance, at one time most of humankind believed the world to be flat, and that the sun traveled around the Earth.

"Is it not distressful that many humans have suffered immense cruelties, even death, because of their beliefs? No living creature has a monopoly on morality, though many are the myths to which morality has been attributed, and indeed many do contain truth.

"In the folklore of the Eskimos is found a most fascinating myth wherein the great herds of caribou were once dying out. The Eskimo people of that long ago time were starving in their cold and distant habitat. The wise tribal elders went to inquire of the most spiritual of all their people, Medicine Woman, who listened with great compassion to what the Elders had to say.

"Medicine Woman was quick to realize that the world was in need of a great knife with which to carve the sick and the weak from the few herds of remaining caribou. Only then could the caribou grow in strength and numbers, and diligently find food to last them through the hard, cold winters. Once this was done, her people would not starve.

"The next day Medicine Woman went to the great frozen ocean, and with stick and rock she struck a hole in the ice. After she had rested from her labor, she reached into the hole and pulled forth a male wolf. After further contemplation, she reached in once more and pulled forth a female wolf.

"The Elders watched with amazement the miracle wrought by Medicine Woman. But many became frightened that soon all the people would starve, as the wolves ran off in the direction of the few remaining caribou. It was obvious that the wolves and their offspring would need to eat.

"Nevertheless, soon the caribou herds once more began to flourish, and all praised the wisdom of Medicine Woman, singing songs of her down through the ages.

"It was only within the more recent year of 40 E.T.J. that ecologists noticed that the caribou herds in our great northern expanse were becoming dangerously few in number. It was almost as if the caribou had suddenly taken it upon themselves to die out over a short period of time. Only then, after careful investigation, did we discover that the sparseness of caribou in these areas could be directly correlated with the predation of humans, not upon the caribou, but upon the wolves in those areas for their pelts. Without a sufficient population of wolves to weed out the sick in the herds the sicknesses were more readily spread to the others.

"Now then, in light of what we now know regarding the natural predation of wolves and their relationship to caribou," said Roxanne smilingly, "let me ask you this: Did Medicine Woman bring into existence, in that long ago time, two wolves from a hole in the ice?

"Let us freely investigate the secrets of life and the cosmos, unencumbered by myths from which some believe morality derived. Let us not forget that within many myths both morality and truth can be found.

"Allow us to explore the beliefs of the past, in light of what we now know of life and the present, open-minded and open-hearted to all those who would participate. Let us strive to go forward with the understanding that a myth, like 'a rose is a rose,' is none other than a myth. Permit us to be fully aware that although a myth may well be a vehicle whereby morality can be handed down from generation to generation, it can also be a method of handing down cruelties and obstructions within the human condition.

"Allow us to move forward in search of truth, whatever that conclusive truth may be. May we have the clear realization that a myth, no matter how sublime it may sound, no matter how numerous, or how kind may be those who would believe it, must and will always be none other than a myth.

"Therefore, let it be clearly understood that Jayseeka of Trepleon believed that the spiritual essence of all living creatures, ourselves included, would eventually return to that original Pristine Source from which they had derived. Her wish was only that we should understand the theosophy of the Aquatus in hopes that we might attain this divine goal within our current lifetimes. Jayseeka was convinced that it was indeed possible for any of our species to do so, also claiming that many of our species down through the ages had achieved this ultimate goal.

"The Aquatian Jayseeka was aware that there would be many who would consider the Aquatus theology mythical. Nevertheless, she encouraged us to explore our inner selves, through intense meditation and contemplation. By so doing she sincerely hoped that we would all become aware that she had indeed spoken, to the best of her understanding, the truth.

"Jayseeka also indicated that many of the more intelligent species they had encountered throughout the cosmos had come to similar conclusions. She also believed that their continued survival had been dependent upon these beliefs.

"Never did Jayseeka threaten humanity with hell or damnation should any of us not understand or believe what she had to teach. Compassionately, she only wished for us to understand so as to hasten our journey through the cosmos. Her claim was that all creatures, great and small, are spiritual travelers in space and time and that all will eventually come to realize their original nature.

"Also she suggested that we be kind and compassionate at every opportunity, as indeed an act of virtue would be repaid with virtue, whereas evil would be repaid with evil. Evil is a hindrance upon our celestial paths. Furthermore, no human or any other living creature or deity would or could permanently intervene on behalf of the one who would incur an evil debt. Nor would any who had done good not be rewarded eventually, in this life or the next.

"Therefore, 'Do good,' she said, 'for this will smooth and make straight the path upon which all will eventually develop the skills with which to hasten our return to that most immaculate origin.'

"Jayseeka often encouraged me in my studies, claiming, 'The hard path only looks easy,' and that upon the realization of that Ultimate Principle it would not be a knowing, as there is no living mind empowered with the ability to truly know 'It.' A tacit realization only could be gained, wherein one would become as if awake within a dream. Once this understanding is realized, it would be indescribable and far beyond any earthly joys or pleasures.

"I encourage each and every one of you to be diligent in your quest; remain steadfast upon the 'path.' You cannot go wrong."

Roxanne filled many of those assembled before her with incredulity that day, continuing, "Of this all of you may be assured: it is not by thinking that one obtains this magnificent spiritual goal. When in meditation one should be in a comfortable quiet location and endeavor to vacate their thinking, going within themselves to a greater depth than thought. Nor does it depend upon a superior intellect to obtain It; however, the desire must be genuine.

"Should you be victorious in obtaining this most sublime realization, your greatest desire will be that all should have it. You may become a beacon unto them, pointing the way best followed to the achievement of it; however, you will be unable to give It to them as a gift. This most subtile and tacit awareness, beyond ability to explain, can only be achieved by the union of meditation, modesty, and purity of heart within them. They must accomplish the task on their own."

Roxanne gazed with compassion upon the congregation. "Do not let the past events of your lives obstruct you in your most spiritual of quests. Intense meditation will cause you to become aware of how best to rectify the harm you have unwittingly or knowingly caused others.

"In the exploration of your own biological makeup, you can become aware of many things. The waves of energy we know as light transmit color and images received by the eye. Thereafter, these colors and images travel upon a network of nerves to the tissues within the brain. Here they are separated and analyzed by the brain's neurological network. Therein do we become aware of those things that transpire outside the self.

"However true this may be, I wish to give you this to ponder: *What is that within yourselves which looks out upon the world, moreover into the cosmos?*"

TO ORDER A COPY OF THIS BOOK
SEND $26.95 + $3.00 FOR POSTAGE & HANDLING
(SALES TAX WHERE APPLICABLE)

TO

AREA 51 PUBLICATIONS
P.O. BOX 44138
LAS VEGAS, NEVADA 89116

SEND CHECK OR MONEY ORDER
(NO CASH OR CODs)

PRICES AND NUMBERS
SUBJECT TO CHANGE WITHOUT NOTICE

VALID IN U.S. ONLY

ALL ORDERS SUBJECT TO AVAILABILITY

FOR ANY FURTHER INFORMATION
OR
FOR ORDERS OF QUANTITY

PLEASE CALL 1-702-641-0970

FAX: 1-702-641-6605

OR

SEE OUR WEB SITE AT WWW.AREA51PUB.COM